THE HARVARD WIFE

BUSISEKILE KHUMALO

SELF-PUBLISHED WORK
OF BUSISEKILE KHUMALO

nicolkhumalo@gmail.com

ISBN 978-0-620-77709-4

All the character in this book have no existence outside the imagination of the author, and have no relation whatsoever to anyone bearing the same name or names. They are not even distantly inspired by any individual known or unknown to the author, and all the incidents are pure invention.

Cover Design By Nkastoworks Africa

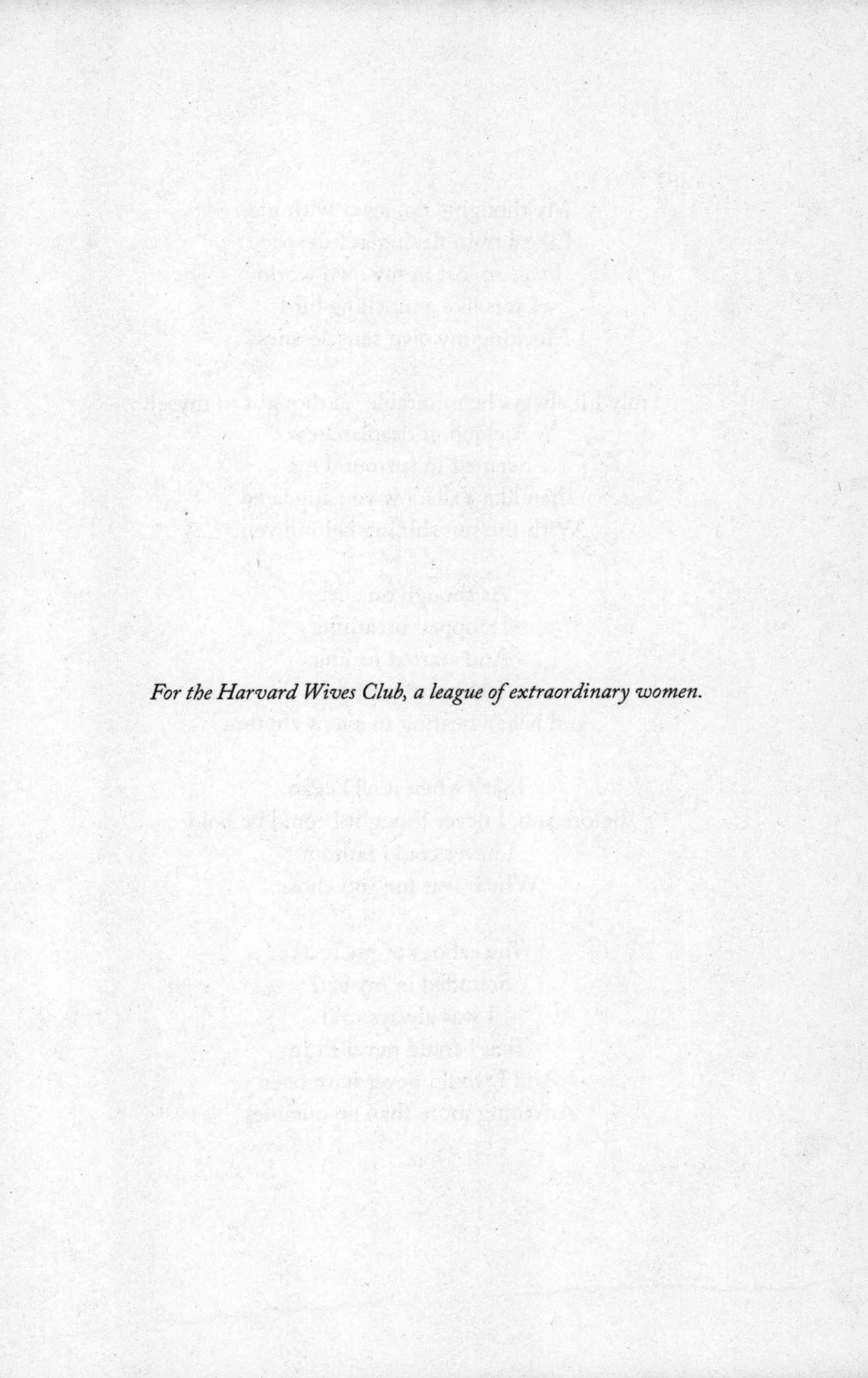

For the Harvard Wives Club, a league of extraordinary women.

My thoughts ran away with me
Like a train fleeing at full speed
I was so lost in my own world
I was like a mocking bird
Mocking my own senselessness

"Truly I'll always be miserable ", l thought to myself
A cloud of desolateness
Seemed to surround me
Then like a shadow you appeared
With the sun shining behind you.

As though on cue...
l stopped breathing
And started feeling.
My heart stuttered
And began beating to a new rhythm

That's when it all began
Before you, I never thought l could be bold
I never could fathom
Why it was me you chose

The echoes of my fears
Sounded in my ears.
I was always told
That l could never fit in
And I would never have been
Anything more than an outsider.

But when your eyes fell upon mine
My mind cleared
And I wanted to be nearer to you
Like a fool, I couldn't look away
I was magnetized too
Hopelessly betrayed by my own heart

From that moment
The fear disappeared
And nothing else mattered.
It was just me and you against the world.

CHAPTER ONE

Fireworks sounded all through Johannesburg, mocking and taunting her pain.. She could hear the sound of celebration even from high up in their master bedroom. All it served to do was make her even more miserable. Tears welled up in her big brown eyes and she forbade them to fall but the bloody traitorous tears fell regardless. Where had they gone wrong? What could she have done better? Why her? Why now? Why again? Had she really become this woman? The questions darted through her mind unanswered. One wayward tear splashed onto the glimmering rhinestone of her engagement ring sliding effortlessly past the simple gold band which was her wedding ring. Logically she knew that crying wouldn't solve anything that the tears would only cause her another migraine, somehow that seemed to open the floodgates even wider.

Rapid knocking broke through her misery, still the tears fell uncontrollably.

"Mpumi open this door right now."

Still she rocked herself slowly tears coursing through her face collecting a debris of mascara forming streaks across her foundation tipping over the stubborn set of her full lips, paying no heed to the urgency in the crisp notes at the door. The commanding voice at the door took on a chillingly angry note as it continued, "People are beginning to wonder what has become of their hostess and I for one am not going to be made a fool. Now stop this nonsense before I break down this door."
"Go away."

There was no trace of tears or sorrow in her voice, it sounded hollow and lifeless to her ears.
"I'm not going to tolerate this bout of self-pity from you, as the minister's wife you have to act accordingly. If you are not down in ten minutes there will be hell to pay. Do I make myself clear?" Perfectly she thought, she was in no mood to play happy hostess but she had no choice, again logic settled on her like an old unwanted gauntlet. She felt more than heard his footsteps fade away. She looked around at the bedroom they seldom used, this was their 'Public house' where they usually hosted events or for hosting dignitaries. She wanted to be back in her own room but duty called and she wearily got off the carpeted floor. In the bathroom after washing her face she could barely recognize the puffy reflection that stared back at her, the reflection seemed crushed and pathetic. Resolutely she set about restoring the damage of the aftermath of the storm that still raged within her. At least for now the floodgates seemed to have receded leaving her devoid of any emotion.

Thin arms enveloped her in a bear hug the moment she finished her descent down the stairway threatening to open the floodgates she had painstakingly built up only moments ago. She hugged back her daughter with equal force drawing some strength from her comfort. "Mama are you alright? You look so pale." The concern in Oyama's voice clogged her throat, the only response she could summon was to kiss her reassuringly.

"Your mother is fine, but I suspect she might be coming down with a bug of some sort." Nompumelelo shot Daniel a thunderous look, hating her husband for answering on her behalf wishing she could wipe off his pretentious devoted husband look. Daniel responded with an icy warning in his eyes yet his voice dripped of love and concern, "Feeling better my love?" Well two can play at this game she thought, grimacing inwardly as she noticed for the first time that they had a captive audience.

"No darling you are right, I think I might be coming down with a stomach bug. I'm going to call it a night." Wrong answer, Daniel's eyes flashed at her but she was past caring. She felt her husband's glare drilling holes in her back. Oyama feeling the tension between her parents took her mother's hand, "I'm coming with you mama" her chin thrust in a stubborn angle that her mother and father knew all too well. Conceding defeat Daniel escorted the willful women in his life out of the ballroom, Mpumi only stopped along the way to plant kisses on her mother's cheeks and her best friend's lips. Outside in the icy early morning some fireworks were still flashing randomly in the bright clear sky illuminating the otherwise starless sky. Daniel stood stoically next to his family while they waited for the driver to bring the car around. He wished he knew what was going on behind his wife's luminous brown eyes but a wall of indifference shut him out and his daughter's worried gaze kept darting from his wife to him made him feel like a jerk. "Mpumi…" he began to question why she looked so haggard, real concern finally niggling at his consciousness but then the car slid to a halt in front of them.

Ignoring the plea in Daniel's voice, Mpumi stepped into the cushy backseat of the car and stared the opposite direction shutting out the concern she felt from her husband. It was too little too late. Oyama slid into the seat next to her mother and as the car slid out of the driveway a comfortable silence settled over them. After passing a few miles Oyama broke the silence, "Did he hurt you again mama?" Mpumi's heart twisted painfully, she hated how her daughter who had only just stepped into teenage hood had to bear the role of being her constant comfort. She took her daughter's hand and kissed her palm and lied glibly, "No baby I just wasn't feeling up to the party so soon after…you know but it's nothing you should worry yourself about." Mention of her mother's recent miscarriage assuaged some of Oyama's curiosity but she still needed convincing so Mpumi rushed on to change the painful topic avoiding her daughter's intuitive gaze. "Are you ready for your retreat trip tomorrow?" Oyama's eyes lit up at the mention of her school trip, "I'm so excited mama, I haven't been to Capetown since our last family trip there and that's been ages ago."

"I know Yaya and Capetown is so pretty you get to go to the table mountain we never got time to go there. Have you packed everything? Last time when you went to Durban you forgot your toothbrush and all your panties" Mpumi teased her daughter's forgetfulness, Oyama was a very bright girl and loving to a fault but her mind was always preoccupied with one flight of fancy after another and she was always forgetting. Mpumi's mother always reprimanded Mpumi that she babied Oyama too much instead of treating her like the teenager that she was. "I forgot them because you were at a business conference and only aunt Nomusa was there to help me pack." Her best friend, and Oyama's godmother was an IT whizz but hopeless at packing, Mpumi smiled "What would you two do without me." Oyama snuggled on her mother's lap like a baby, half-lying on the car seat. She hadn't snuggled up to Mpumi in a long
time and Mpumi welcomed the almost cuddle. "We are hopeless without you mama, I will miss you."
"All of five minutes then you and your girls will be tearing up Kapa and you will forget about your boring
old mother." Oyama's voice carried a smile, "Ryan will also be there."

"Ryan as in your crush Ryan the goofy basketball hunk?"
"Maaa..." Oyama got off her mother's lap and Nompumelelo laughed.
"Come on sweetie your face takes that dreamy look when you talk of Ryan." Oyama snuggled back and sighed wistfully "I do like Ryan but he never seems to notice me he treats me like one of his homeboys."
"Maybe it's because you act like one of his homeboys."
"I don't know how to act differently I've never liked a boy before and when I'm around him my tongue says the most stupid things like your basketball looks cute I mean who says that mom." Mpumi laughed at the self-indignation in Oyama's voice and she caressed her kinky hair kissing her forehead, "It's normal Yaya when I first met your father I was tongue tied too, I came from a very strict family and dating was strictly forbidden my first taste of freedom was at university so you can imagine I wasn't as polished as the other girls and I would stammer whenever he talked to me." No matter how many times Oyama had heard this story it was hard to reconcile the sophisticated and poised woman that her mother had become with the stammering naïve young woman she had been when she first met her father. All too suddenly the door opened and they noticed that the car had come to a halt in front of their home. Oyama got off Mpumi's lap and was helped out of the car by the driver, "Thank you Tom, happy New Year" Oyama gave the rather startled driver a brief hug and was rewarded with a wide grin. The driver also helped Mpumi out of the car. Arm in arm chatting happily mother and daughter stepped into the mansion, Mpumi's inner turmoil abated in the meantime. After hugging and kissing mother and daughter headed to their rooms to retire for the night.

"Now remember to take as many pictures as possible and email them to me, ok? I charged the camera battery as well as the spare battery," Mpumi hugged her daughter fiercely and kissed her on the lips.
"Yes mom I will and you have to take care of yourself till I get back."
"Don't worry about me I'm fine, have a great time it's your last trip before you start prepping for matric."

"I know, I know even though my matric exams are ages away," Oyama grumbled looking towards the school bus where her friends were already waiting for her.

"Fine I get the message off you go young lady love you" Mpumi settled for a last kiss and after a muttered "love you too mama" Oyama rushed to join her friends and they got on the bus laughing and screaming joyfully. As the bus pulled away the kids threw kisses at their parents leaving behind a lonely silence. Mpumi walked slowly back to her car where Nomusa was waiting for her. Sadly her thoughts turned to her husband. He hadn't been there at the breakfast table. Their housekeeper had relayed the message that Daniel had gone out to look over some tenders which were meant to be given to people to mark the New Year. He hadn't bothered to say goodbye to their daughter and Mpumi suspected he had forgotten that her trip was today. Even though Oyama was hurt she tried to shield her pain from her mother and had been perky as they went through her luggage. They had picked up Nomusa on their way to the school and godmother and goddaughter had been chatting and laughing while Mpumi drove. She had given the staff the day off and was lucky that Nomusa was available to talk to. "Back to earth

Mpumi," Nomusa gently broke into her thoughts, "where have you gone to boo you seem miles away." Mpumi smiled wanly at her best friend, she and Nomusa had been best friends since they were in diapers and she regarded the former as the only sister she had. "I'm right here girl, just wondering if Yaya forgot anything."

"Liar." Nomusa could easily read her friend and knew that something was up.

"Let's go to that cozy coffee shop down Kelvin Drive and you can tell me what the hell has been going on with you lately." Mpumi sighed knowing she couldn't shake off Nomusa as easily as she had shaken off Oyama, "Fine but you are paying."

The duo managed to find their favorite spot out on the patio of their getaway coffee shop. The sun danced beautifully across their tiny haven,

warm but not intrusive. Nomusa looked at her best friend who had stuck around through all her bad relationships and her almost run-in with the altar. She saw a beautiful woman whose age at a glance was undiscernible but Nomusa knew it to be 38. She had flawless ebony skin, warm chocolate eyes speckled with gold highlights giving her face an exotic look. Her natural kinky hair was long, curly and at times unruly but currently was tamed in a turquoise shellhairpin which matched her stiletto pumps managing to transform her casual denim and loose top into an alluring feminine look. Though her unmade-up baby face was almost angelic her voluptuous Xhosa body was undeniably all woman with curves in all the right places unlike the skinny trend that most of their peers fought to obtain. Nomusa noticed how drawn Mpumi looked and she put a hand over her tense fingers. "Pum-pum what's eating you up?" The use of her childhood nickname coaxed a smile from Mpumi and she sighed inwardly, Nomusa was like a dog with a bone and she wouldn't let up till Mpumi came clean. Taking out a folded manila envelope from her purse, Mpumi quietly handed it over to her best friend. She looked at her friend as she poured through the glossy contents, Nomusa's sharp intake of breath mirrored her own shock at the private investigator's findings. The seconds trickled past as Nomusa looked through the damning evidence of her friend's turmoil and she could only imagine the blow these pictures dealt on Nompumelelo. "How long have you had these?" Mpumi couldn't quite meet Nomusa's eyes afraid of the sympathy she might find there, how pathetic she must seem. "How
long Mpumi," Nomusa demanded insistently. "Since yesterday I met with the investigator just before
the charity ball."

"I thought after last time you terminated the investigator's services, you said you and Daniel were on the mend that he agreed to go to marriage counselling and that he swore he would never cheat on you again." The concern in her friend's voice threatened to burst open the floodgates again and Mpumi struggled to bring her emotions in check, "I know what I said, I lied ok, I was tired of looking so pathetic in your eyes and I hoped that he would change but he didn't it got to a point where we started sleeping in separate bedrooms then then.." this was the extremely difficult part,"...then I fell pregnant and he seemed remorseful he acted the part of a devoted husband when I found out it was all an act the same way he lures in his constituents, I freaked out so much I lost my baby." Nomusa paled, "God, Mpumi why didn't you say something?" Bitterly, Mpumi stared unseeingly at the scenic view, "because I'm a mess Nono, I didn't want to become that woman who is always crying about her cheating husband. How I longed for that perfect life and I was tired of the pity that I saw in your eyes each time. I'm a fraud such a fraud." Nomusa took her hands comfortingly and let her continue to rant. "You know stupidly I thought I could fix him, fix us but I was wrong. I even bought tickets for a romantic getaway for us since Oyama will be away at camp. I hoped that maybe when it's just the two of us he would remember why he married me in the first place." A painful silence settled over them shrouding them like a dark cloud in the sunny café and their coffees turned cold unnoticed. Nomusa felt a deep rage over that pretentious prick, Daniel could slither away from a lot of things and worm himself into people's good grace but he had never been able to fool her. She and Mpumi had gone to different colleges and she hadn't been there to warn her friend against Daniel and when they had been introduced it had been too late Mpumi had been infatuated and had thought that Nomusa's pleadings had been unfounded and once her best friend and lover got to know each other Nomusa would love Daniel. Nomusa knew that Mpumi could be pigheaded when she wanted to be and loyal to a fault and that if she were ever to leave Daniel it would have to come from her not anyone else even her lifelong best friend. After a while Mpumi continued in a dull voice pointing at the pictures, "But this, this is too much even for me, there is only so much I can take. I'm only human after all."

"Have you confronted him yet?"

CHAPTER
ONE

"No, I couldn't bring myself to ask him yesterday, I don't think I have any fight left in me I feel so empty." Alarm bells flashed through Nomusa's whole body, yes Mpumi had been through more than most in her life but somehow her friend always persevered with quiet dignity underneath that sweet and at times fun-loving exterior was a layer of steel. And now looking at her sagging shoulders and the taut lines on her face, Nomusa had never seen her friend who was more like a sister, look so defeated and it scared her. She playfully lifted Mpumi's chin up and held it up between her hands schooling her expression into a playful one, "You said something about a romantic getaway, where were you planning to take him?" The response was indignant, "I'm not taking him anywhere anymore I'm going to cancel
the whole thing."

"Who said anything about taking Daniel with you? I haven't been on holiday for so long especially an expensive one and we never go together anymore. So what say you my lady, you and me out there sipping margaritas in the Caribbean and checking out all those surfers?" Nomusa was relieved to be rewarded by a real smile, "Sorry to disappoint you but you and I, my friend are not going to Bahamas or Hawaii or anywhere that even requires our passports to be stamped." Nomusa feigned comical
disappointment "So where are we going?"

"It sounds corny but it's an eleven day romantic safari by the Ultimate Africa Safaris called Wild at
heart."

"Sounds erotic, I bet we are going to meet so many yummy men."
"On a honeymoon safari? I doubt that very much, the single men we are likely to meet there are either
jilted or psycho."

"There you go being all realistic on me, that kind of negative aura should not be coming with us on this trip. I can feel it in my bones I'm going to find my prince charming." Mpumi smiled at her friend's excitement and wished wholeheartedly that she found what she desired Nomusa deserved to be swept

off her feet by a decent guy who wouldn't string her along. As for herself, she had had enough heartache to last her a lifetime, romance was off the cards for her and she said as much to Nomusa adding, "All I hope is that this trip will serve as a retreat of some kind and help me figure out the mess that is my life." Nomusa sobered at the abject misery that Mpumi had sunk back into and while she cradled her hands, vowed silently that she would look out for this woman who had given her so much. To distract Mpumi, she asked, "When are we leaving for the trip?" The trip was to commence the very next day, Nomusa suggested some last minute shopping hoping some retail therapy at her beastly husband's expense would help lift her friend from her funk. It was agreed that after shopping the ladies would pick up some of Nomusa's stuff and spend the night at Mpumi's house before their departure.

That is where they found Daniel waiting for them seemingly calmly in the leather recliner of their plush lounge. The interior décor had been done by one of the Top Billing designers. Though the earth colors were meant to warm the place up and present a cozy setting, the obvious costly antiques and portraits of Nelson Mandela, Steve Biko and Daniel's great-uncle Walter Sisulu gave the lounge and the rest of the mansion a stately and expensive presence. Nomusa could understand why her friend was smitten with the man lounging on the cream recliner, with his legs stretched out he seemed like a panther ready to spring on its prey. Daniel was classically handsome, with no scratch or scar or any common disfigurement that mere mortals usually have, yet underneath that porcelain perfection and calm exterior there was an edge, a hunger for power and an obvious ambition that made him an enigma. Nomusa knew that he was capable of turning his charm on

and off like a state-of-the-art air conditioner with his whip lash wit, a master puppeteer who loved nothing more than pulling the strings and staying
on top of every situation. Sardonically he inclined his head at her, "Nomusa."
"Daniel." There was no love lost between those two, Mpumi sighed inwardly and asked Nomusa to give them a moment. After an aggressive stare down Nomusa took their purchases upstairs and Mpumi remained standing on one end of the room. "Aren't you going to sit down and have a civil conversation with your husband?" Daniel queried softly, to avoid a confrontation Mpumi took the sofa opposite him
and waited for him to continue. "Where have you been all day? I've been calling you since morning you
didn't pick up any of my calls."

"My phone was on silent, I went to drop off Oyama for her trip then spent the afternoon with her
godmother."

"That trip was today? Why didn't you remind me and why do you still hang around with that woman you
know she is beneath you and…"
"Leave it Daniel, Nomusa is my friend not yours I will not allow you to talk about my only friend in that manner." A silence ensued, Daniel was trying to gauge his wife's mood and he failed. She had become a master at tucking away her thoughts and feelings behind an impeccable elegance. Daniel remembered a time when he could read all her emotions and thoughts, she had always been refreshingly an open book with a big heart. When the troubles in their marriage had begun she had withdrawn from him bit by bit and now Daniel honestly feared she had withdrawn from him completely. But his pride wouldn't allow him to show how much he needed her to go back to trusting and loving him. Frustrated he paced the floor and she stared at him, waiting for him to continue. She wasn't quite prepared for what came next, "Why do you

always have to fight me? How many times do I have to try to make things right between us but you always have to go and make a scene?" She was incredulous and speechless at her husband's self-righteousness but he wasn't done yet with his reprimand, "You always have to make me look like the bad guy in front of your family and friends like your little show yesterday in front of my constituents. You forget your place woman, you are my wife and your place is beside me smiling and supporting my career. But no you always have to prance around with your single friend knowing that I forbade you to be with her."
"Are you done?" Mpumi didn't wait for him to answer and picked up her purse and made to exit the room, he blocked her exit. "And where do you think you are going? I'm trying to carry a civil conversation with you."

"I'm going to pack upstairs, Nomusa and I are going on a safari tomorrow."
"That won't be possible, you have to plan for the Save the Children banquet we are hosting next week and I forbid you to go anywhere with that woman."
"I wasn't asking for permission Daniel."
"What is the matter with you? The last two days you have been acting like a woman possessed with God knows what, defying me at every chance you get, making me look like a fool in front of my constituents." Daniel angrily grabbed her arm his nails digging painfully into the soft flesh just above her elbow, she tried twisting away but he only dug deeper. Both of them had been so caught up in their fight they hadn't noticed Nomusa come back into the room and they were startled by her voice, "Lay your hands on her one more time Daniel and I will make it my life's mission to bury your political life." "Butt out of this you witch, she is my wife and you will not tell me how to handle her." The tension in the air was palpable and one could slice through it with a Swiss blade, Nomusa advanced threateningly towards Daniel and something in her eyes convinced him to let go of Mpumi's arm

in disgust. Pointing a finger menacingly at Nomusa, "I want you out of my house and you," he turned to his wife, "if you go with her never come back and you will never see my daughter again." A chill went up and down Mpumi's spine yet a stubborn streak settled over her and she tilted her chin up, "We will be out of your hair come morning, now if you will excuse us, we have some packing to do." Leaving a stunned husband behind she took Nomusa's hand and they headed upstairs. Up in the guest room that Oyama and Mpumi had fondly nicknamed Nomusa's room, Mpumi sunk gratefully onto the armchair that was beside the huge four poster bed. The designer had aligned a European medieval décor in the bedrooms with deep sunk baths and silk quilts. Nomusa watched her friend shiver from the aftermath of the first active defiance against her husband with a mixture of awe and respect. But she was also worried about the side of Daniel she had never seen before and she had to know, "Has he ever hurt you before?" Mpumi's only response was to rock herself much similarly to the night of the ball. Nomusa took both her hands into hers, Mpumi's hands were icy cold, and stared into her troubled eyes, "You can tell me Mpumi, has he ever hurt you before tonight?" Nompumelelo shrugged her friend's concern aside and walked over to take her phone saying over her shoulder, "I don't want to talk about him anymore." There were numerous missed calls on her phone most from Daniel and her mother, sighing inwardly and knowing she was probably going to regret it she called her mother back. MaNtuli picked her call after the third ring, and she sounded peeved at her only child,

"Nompumelelo where have you been all day, umkhwenyana has been looking for you we were all
worried"

"Hello mother, I'm fine I had gone out with Nomusa."

"You are a married woman Nompumelelo, you have to be with your husband. And what is this I hear…" Alarm bells started off in Mpumi's mind, Daniel had gotten to her mother before her as he always did.

"…you are taking Nomusa on a safari against your husband's wishes."
"Yes Ma, we are going on an eleven day trip just to get away from thin gs." "That's the problem with you modern women always running away from your problems, instead of sitting down and fixing your marriage you are off trotting the world with your single friend. I have set up a meeting with Reverend Mphahlele for a marriage counselling session and umkhwenyana has gracefully agreed to attend to help you come to your senses."
"I'm not going to marriage counselling Ma I already told you and Daniel, I'm going on a safari with
Nomusa. I paid a ridiculously large amount on this trip and it's non-ref undable."
"Then why don't you take your husband with you? That man has been nothing but patient with you all
these years."

"You mean through all the miscarriages and his cheating? He's my husband Ma he is supposed to be
patient and stand by me but no he was out there with every other women." "I am your mother and I would be letting you down if I didn't tell you that every marriage has its setbacks and that men cheat my child that's our reality you won't find a man who doesn't." "No Ma you are my mother your duty is to look out for me, make sure I don't get hurt and hold me when I am hurt like during my last miscarriage when he sent his secretary to send me a condolence card and flowers. But all you do is stand up and make excuses for him, so forgive me but I have to pack and get away from all of you, if you are so concerned about umkhwenyana wakho, you can come and check up on him." Frustrated, Mpumi hung up tears threatening to spill again, Nomusa saw the tears and felt pain for this woman who was always in other people's corner but who had no one in her own corner. Knowing the only thing that would cheer her up, Nomusa suggested, "I'm sure that Oyama has settled in now why don't

we set up a skype call with her?" as she had predicted, Mpumi smiled and went to take her laptop from her room across the hallway. Oyama was laughing when she answered the call her big
eyes bright with laughter, "Hey pumpkin did you travel well?
" "I did mama, the bus took us to the airport and the flight went off without a hitch." Nomusa pitched in, "Who sat next to you on the plane kiddo" Oyama actually blushed, "No one aunty…Mama you won't
believe how gorgeous Cape Town is and the camp we are in is totally to die for." "I believe you sweetie and we have a surprise for you too, your aunt and I are coming to Cape Town tomorrow." The teenager's scream of joy was contagious and the older women smiled, Mpumi continued, "It's the first lag of our safari, we are taking a trip. The first four days will be in Cape Town and if you want I will come up and see you at camp."

"Are you kidding of course I want you to come I will be mad if you don't, we have a hockey match in two
days hope you will be there."
"I will be there honey, I promise."
"Aunt Nomusa?" Nomusa shrugged her shoulders elegantly, "I'm not promising anything kiddo I hope to catch myself a man in the Cape Town waters." Amid laughter, Mpumi demanded for pictures and Oyama emailed them to her and when they signed off Mpumi felt a weight lifted off her shoulders.
Nomusa was certain that Oyama was the only teenage girl she knew who was so into her mother. Starring at the happy carefree picture of Oyama, love welled up in her heart and that love gave her the courage to keep packing.

The next morning there was no sign of Daniel. The housekeeper reported that he had left for a conference a few moments before they came down for breakfast. Relief and regret niggled at the back of

Mpumi's mind, whatever differences she and her husband had she still held on to the notion that somehow he would change back into the tall lanky young man she had fallen for at varsity. It helped having Nomusa with her because Nomusa kept up a flowing chatter of office gossip and had her laughing along at her outrageous stories. The Uber that was taking them to the airport arrived and they packed their cases and after some last minute instructions to the housekeeper, Mpumi got in next to Nomusa. As the car pulled out of the driveway Mpumi looked back at her house, without Oyama she wasn't particularly attached to the huge mansion and felt nothing at leaving it behind. Mistakenly Nomusa saw her look back and thought she had misgivings about their trip, holding her hand she promised solemnly that the trip would be one they would never forget. Neither of them could have foreseen just how much this safari would alter the course of their lives.

CHAPTER TWO

While Nomusa flirted shamelessly with the guy seated across them, Mpumi drifted in and out of a restless sleep. Mercifully the flight was short and uneventful and soon the plane was taxying into the airport. They found their escort easily enough and their bags were cleared, packed into their ride and made their way to the Twelve Apostles Hotel. Mpumi was preoccupied on their way to the airport, she did not revel in the beauty of Cape Town as she usually did and she kept on dwindling her rings. She remembered how she got engaged, it had taken place on their way to the airport. Nompumelelo had graduated on top of her class had won three book prizes and a scholarship to study her masters in Harvard. She and Daniel had been dating for a year, when he graduated second in their class his uncle had taken notice of him and wanted to take him under his political wing. Their futures seemed miles apart and though Daniel had been supportive Mpumi had expected him to break things off with her. On the bus ride to the airport, none of their families had owned a car back then and they could not afford a taxi, only Daniel accompanied her. He had gently taken her hand in his and looked her in the eye, "Promise me you will come back to me." Mpumi had been mesmerized by the way he earnestly looked into her soul and she had promised. "I know I don't have much now, I couldn't even buy you a ring but I promise when you come back I will send my uncles to pay lobola to your family and you will be my wife." Those words had carried her through that period of her MBA, she had had her doubts but Daniel had kept his word and she had felt she owed him her hand in marriage. Mpumi felt a light shake on her arm, it was Nomusa telling her they had arrived at their hotel.

The hotel was gorgeous as Oyama would say, the building was set against a mountainous background with lush vegetation which begged to be explored. There was a serenity to its seclusion and oneness with nature that was immediately soothing. The foyer was an even more pleasant setting, the high ceiling made it spacious and welcoming the chandelier and fresh flowers in antique vases gave the hotel an intimate and rustic feel. There weren't a lot of people in the foyer when they arrived and Mpumi was relieved to be away from the hubbub of Johannesburg and was doubly glad that Nomusa took over the checking in and chatting with the bubbly receptionist. Naturally Mpumi was a friendly person but the strain of the past few days was taking its toll on her and all she wanted was a warm bath and to dive into their renowned Spa. Their luggage was carried for them to their room by a chatty bellboy who was excited to let them know that their room was next to the presidential suite and he launched on to tell them of the famous people who had resided in said presidential suite. He let on that the chairperson of the hotel chain that owned this very hotel was currently residing at the presidential suite. Mpumi was happy to get into their room and to see the back of the chatty bellboy. Nomusa let out a whoop of joy, "Pum-pum look at our room, its perfect I probably couldn't afford a room of this nature on my paycheck." Mpumi agreed wholeheartedly with her, the room was perfect the high ceiling and the floral wallpaper gave the room classical elegance. The four poster bed screamed poignant romance with minimalistic throw pillows it held promises of perfect bliss. There was also a cozy sofa in the room as well as a walk in closet which Nomusa inspected with glee. Mpumi took off her shoes and curled her toes into the plush carpet feeling some of the tension seep away from her ankles. "So what are we going to do today? The tour only officially begins tomorrow. I was thinking of a massage at the spa and a walk to the beach just to get a feel of this place and maybe watch a movie in the private cinema at night." Nomusa squirmed uncomfortably at her friend's suggestion, "ummmh yeah that sounds nice"

"But?"

"It's nothing just that Amo had asked if he could come pick me up for dinner tonight." Nomusa was actually blushing and Mpumi's curiosity got the better of her.

"Amo?"

"Amogalang. The guy I was talking to on the plane but its fine I will call him and cancel."

"By talking you mean the guy you were heavily flirting with on the plane and no don't cancel, remember you swore you will find prince charming on this trip I don't want to stand in the way of true love."

"I can hear your sarcasm, he will understand right now you need me here."

"I'm fine, I don't need a babysitter and since you are going on a date you might as well join me for a massage and facial maybe squeeze in some waxing."

"Nompumelelo Ndinisa-Sisulu your mind is filthy, on a first date wouldn't that be too forward." Mpumi laughed and she could sense uncertainty beneath her friend's indignation and she assured her, "It wouldn't hurt to be prepared either way if nothing happens he won't be any the wiser." Reluctantly Nomusa agreed to go on the date she felt as if she was abandoning her friend in her hour of need but Mpumi was adamant and Nomusa had to concede defeat.

The trip to the spa was a novelty and the ladies came out glowing and relaxed and headed back to their room. While Nomusa took a shower, Mpumi waddled in the bath feeling safe in the cocoon of the scented bath only leaving it to help Nomusa pick up an outfit for her date. "Where is he taking you?" Nomusa had no inkling as to how their date would fare so it was agreed on a casual chic look of a simple A-line dress with a plunging neckline and wedge pumps which could easily fit into any location without being overdressed or under dressed, Mpumi borrowed her a silver necklace and clutch to complete the look. Both ladies were satisfied with the look when there was a knock on the door, Amo had come to whisk his date away. Mpumi approved of him instantly, he was soft-spoken with an apparent Ubuntu, charming yet humble and she could see why Nomusa was so taken by him. When the couple left Mpumi felt deeply lonely and so she called Oyama to confirm where their hockey match was being held. Her daughter was happy and bubbly as usual and that lifted Mpumi's spirits considerably, the match was in the University of Cape Town which was a relief as that was close to the hotel. At ease, Mpumi changed into a skimpy swim suit which was really a bikini held together by thin straps which Nomusa had persuaded her to buy claiming that it was made for her body. She knew she was past her youth and felt that having gone through pregnancies her body had changed a lot. In a bout of selfconsciousness she donned an oversized linen shirt on top of the swimsuit which almost reached

her knees and a pair of flip-flops and let herself out of the room. She was so focused on going to explore that she forgot her keycard and her phone inside their room.

In a lighter mood, Mpumi smiled at the receptionist as she exited the hotel and walked down the trek that seemed to lead to the beach. There were mountain terrains all around the hotel and Mpumi marveled at nature's grandeur. The grass felt cool as it brushed her ankles and she found herself humming, she didn't mind being alone. She remembered what a loner she had been in university. All her life her only friend had been Nomusa, their parents had been close and they had been closer. When they separated in tertiary instead of making new friends Mpumi had stuck it out alone. Her shabby but clean appearance had made her stand out. Mpumi's father had died when she was in High School. Just thinking about her father made her so sad. He had always been her pillar. She had inherited his love for books and his intelligence and they would argue about Shakespeare, world politics often shutting her mother out. While her mother had wanted her to learn about sewing and cooking, Mpumi had been out being taught to ride a bicycle by her father. She smiled remembering how patient he had always been with her. He had owned a book shop and also helped people to type their CVs and made a comfortable living for his family. When he died suddenly of a heart attack, Mpumi's world had come crumbling down. His relatives had swooped down like vultures grabbing any assert they could lay their grubby hands on leaving MaNtuli and her daughter in abject misery and near poverty. The only thing they had not managed to rob them off was the school fees trust that Muziwoxolo Ndinisa had set up for his daughter and that had been Mpumi's lifeline. MaNtuli had been resentful that her husband even in death had somehow managed to exclude her and chosen his daughter's welfare, their mother-daughter relationship suffered further. While Mpumi continued her education MaNtuli had to become a domestic worker to put a roof over their heads. While the clothes MaNtuli bought for her were minimalistic they seemed shabby in comparison with other girls at tertiary and Mpumi found herself alone most of the time and used to her own company until Daniel had taken notice of her. Realizing that her thoughts were darkening her mood, Mpumi pulled herself from reminiscing and fully focused on her surroundings. She was now at the beach, it wasn't a huge beach just a small private stretch of sand and blue water. Looking around Mpumi thought she was alone, the beach seemed deserted so she was comfortable taking off her shirt. She ran into the water, it was freezing yet refreshing at the same time. She took confident laps even staying underneath water for a while enjoying the sensation of water flowing over her body. After some time she grew tired of swimming and went to lie down on the beach. It was so peaceful, Mpumi felt serenity creeping over her and she drifted off to a peaceful slumber.

Mpumi was woken up by a sharp sting on her calf and she felt the pain shoot through her whole leg. "Ouch!" she cried out and looked around for what had bitten her and she couldn't find anything amiss. She tried standing up but the pain shot through her leg again and she crumbled back to the ground. Panicking she started shouting, "Help! Somebody help me!" Desperation gripped her, she was certain the beach was deserted. She had to try to stop the poison or venom or whatever was injected into her blood by the sting from spreading. She tore her shirt frantically and tied the area on top of the sting tightly as well as underneath it. The skin there was already shiny and swollen, Mpumi started shivering uncontrollably yet she felt suffocated by the heat. Sweat beaded her lips and dripped down her back and she let out a silent prayer. She could die out here all alone. She saw her father walking towards her and she stretched out her hands to him, "Tata help me, please help me." She knew she had begun hallucinating and she felt convulsions and she tried holding onto consciousness but the darkness was winning. She kept thinking of Oyama, her daughter couldn't lose her mother, Oyama needed her. Her last conscious thought was of Oyama waiting for her and the hockey match and she slipped into oblivion.

Mpumi felt the heaviness of her head, her mouth felt dry like she had swallowed a whole handful of sand and she tried to open her eyes but they were heavy. Finally she managed to open her eyes and had to blink before she could get accustomed to the brightness in the room. She was in a hotel room but this one was different from the one she and Nomusa were sharing. This room was even more spacious than theirs and was all in white, she was lying in white Egyptian sheets and the bed was so soft. She tried moving her leg but it felt heavy. In fact there was a solid form pining her down. However, the solid form was also warm and from the smooth and callous texture she hazarded that the solid form was a human. She tried remembering what had happened. Then she remembered the sting and her convulsions. Maybe she had died and gone to heaven. She tried moving her head but it was still too heavy. She closed her eyes and chided herself, breathe Mpumi and stop panicking she reprimanded herself. She opened her eyes again and was able to shift her head slightly whoever was sleeping behind her was cradling her like a precious baby. Mpumi had to admit the sensation was heavenly and she was finding it calming. The person had a woody musky scent that tickled her sense of smell, she could feel her nipples hardening from the scent. Gosh she had been without sex for so long that she was now getting aroused by a mere scent. Whoever was holding her must have sensed her movement because their hold on her tightened slightly but was still gentle. "You are awake finally, I became so worried and so was the doctor," the solid form also had a deep baritone. Mpumi tried responding but her voice came out a croak. She felt the bed give way and the form left her side. In a way she couldn't explain, she felt alone and unsafe when the arms which were holding her left her side. She still couldn't lift her head and she felt the solid form lifting her head and bring a glass to her mouth and gently tilt the glass. She drank the water greedily and almost choked, "Easy easy, take small sips your throat must be constricted." The baritone again, funny for such a solid presence the baritone sounded extremely gentle and patient it reminded her of her father and a tear slid out of the corner of her eye. She drank the water more slowly until the glass was finished. "Thank you," she croaked out her voice was still dry. She tried sitting up but she was too weak. The solid form lifted her up from behind propping pillows behind her and making her sit up even fluffing her pillows. She looked down at herself she was wearing someone's pajama

top, but it was so big it reached down her hips. There was no sign of her bath suit, she wondered who had undressed her and put her in this top. Judging from the musky scent the pajama top probably belonged to solid form. It was time to face her savior, he was crouching in front of her his chest broad and bare, and wearing the bottom of the pajama she had on. She stared at his eyes and felt a cold hand on her spine. No it couldn't be him maybe
they were just similar. But those eyes! He had the same exact piercing blue eyes which had the color which was in between the sky and the ocean. It was like staring at a ghost from her past. The creepy part was that he was also staring at her as if he couldn't believe his eyes. "Lelo?" Oh God she groaned inwardly. This wasn't happening, but she immediately knew it was him. He was the only person who had ever called her Lelo and it seemed as if that had been in another lifetime. The coward in her wanted her to act as if she didn't know or remember him but that would be wrong, he probably saved her life just now. Drawing a deep breath she nodded slightly and said, "Yes Jarred it's me. But how did you find me?"

"I found you passed out by the beach last night. It seemed you had been out of it for a while. You were smart to tie your calf like that the poison hadn't spread throughout your body."

"What bit me?"

"We are not sure but the doctor thought it's probably a scorpion and if the poison had reached your heart…" Mpumi felt a chill and he must have seen her shiver because he pulled the duvet cover around her. "Wait you are saying you found me yesterday? What time is it?"

"It's a little after nine."

"Crap, I have to go I have to be at my daughter's hockey match at ten."

"Lelo you can't go anywhere in your condition. You could barely move your head a moment ago."

"I'm better now and I will be fine after a shower. I just have to get to my room."

"Which room are you in?"

"I don't remember the number where is my keycard the number was on it."

"There was nothing next to you when I picked you up just your flip flops" "My phone?"

"Nothing Lelo just you in a pretty bad space." Mpumi felt herself panicking again and Jarred sensed that and he quickly made a suggestion, she could shower in his room and he would go and buy her something to wear and he would take her to Oyama's match. Mpumi was reluctant to impose on him more than she had already. But she admitted to herself she was still weak and sore from where the doctor had sucked out the poison and she still felt dizzy and a little nausea. It was a relief that he would be with her. She had so many questions and he probably had more but they could wait, Oyama always came first. Conceding to his plan, he made the bath for her and helped her to the bath, she was nervous about letting him undress her. "Come on Lelo I have seen you naked before I won't look." Mpumi blushed but she had no choice and she was grateful for his gentleness. As promised he left to go and get her something to wear. Wow things were moving so unexpectedly, Mpumi had never thought she would see Jarred again in this lifetime. She had met him in Harvard and she had more or less ran away from him when she left. Life really did move in mysterious ways. She bathed quickly careful not to injure herself even more. From the movements in the adjourning room she could hear that Jarred had come back and she was curious to see his purchases. Mpumi tied a huge fluffy hotel towel around
herself because the robe smelt too much of Jarred all wooden masculinity. He had bought her a beautiful white summer dress with a wide skirt and a synched waist with a gold belt and gold Greek-style sandals which she had to tie all the way to just beneath her calves. The underwear he had bought for her made her shy, it was sexy yet comfortable panties and bra set, how he had guessed her exact cup size

she didn't want to know. He even bought her a wide brimmed hat and big sunglasses. Surprisingly the clothes fit her to perfection, "How did you know my size?" He grinned at her and just winked at her and she was reminded of the cheeky fresh faced near man she had known all those years ago. Feeling a pull in her heart she looked away from him and told him they had to go. He looked at her like he knew exactly what was going through her mind but he let her be and led her out of the room holding her like a fragile flower. He was driving a Jeep, Mpumi settled gratefully into the front seat. After a few moments of silence she had to ask, "So did you know it was me last night?" He kept his gaze on the road ahead and answered after a heartbeat, "Not at first, you have changed from the waif of a girl I used to know."

"Oh you mean I've grown fat."

"No I mean there is more of you to hold." Mpumi blushed he was looking at her with so much intensity even though it was just for a moment. He noticed her blush and continued, "Actually I saw you when you were checking in yesterday and you were so quiet while your partner kept talking."

"Partner? Oh you mean Nomusa she's my best friend, wait did you think we were gay?"

"I was busy kicking myself for having the hots for the sexy lesbian, every man's worst nightmare." Mpumi found herself laughing, she couldn't help it, Jarred had always had an outrageous sense of humor and she knew he and Nomusa would get along.

Oyama was surprised to see her mother with a guy she didn't know but after the initial awkwardness, when Oyama asked Jarred if he was married and he looked at Mpumi while responding, "I came close to marrying this one lady but she left me." Oyama nodded understandingly while Mpumi looked away uncomfortably. After that initial hurdle they hit it off. Jarred had played hockey in his heydays and they were now chatting with Oyama as if they had known each other their whole lives. Mpumi was content to just sit back and watch them bond, she was still weak but was feeling much better. Jarred had offered to take them to lunch and after talking to Oyama's teacher they had all trooped into Jarred's Jeep and had gone to a cozy little Italian place that Mpumi had never heard about. While they ate Jarred kept them in stitches with his outrageous stories and he had them hanging onto his every word. They called Nomusa on Oyama's phone and she had sounded frantic. "Mpumi where have you been? I've been looking for you, I almost opened a missing person file but the police said you had to be missing for 32 hours."

"I got bitten yesterday and someone helped me out."

"So you slept at her room? I swear when I came in this morning and found your keycard and phone I thought someone abducted you."

"Whoa so you slept out?"

"That's not the point, I was scared and they came to take us on the tour."

"Where are you now?"

"Desmond Tutu's church I don't even know why they included it on the tour, I mean can you handle friend." Mpumi had to laugh, Nomusa was so over the top she was saying it loudly probably even in front of Desmond Tutu himself, they agreed to meet at Kirstenbosch Botanical Gardens as Nomusa also wanted to see her goddaughter. Mpumi was willing to get an Uber to go and meet Nomusa but Jarred was having none of it and Oyama seemed attached to him already they were walking around holding hands both of them eating caramel fudge ice cream. Mpumi was outvoted and shut out and she watched in awe as her daughter fell under Jarred's spell. Nomusa rushed over to fuss over Mpumi and Oyama was the one now introducing Jarred. Oyama had lacked fatherly attention most of her life and Jarred's attention, him listening to her every story was making her shine brighter than she usually did. Nomusa raised an eyebrow and Mpumi had to explain that Jarred found her near to death and he had looked out for her. Nomusa was not fully appeased by this explanation and Mpumi knew she was going to be drilled when they got back to the hotel. The penguins at Boulder's Beach were a hit with Oyama and she claimed that she wanted to be a Marine vet, Mpumi and Nomusa exchanged looks Oyama had changed professions more times than King Mswati took another wife. The tour ended on a perfect note with the picnic lunch and it was time to send Oyama back to camp, she seemed reluctant to leave Jarred and he promised her that they would meet again.

"So who is Mr. Hunk who can't keep his eyes off you?" They were back in their room, after spending the night in Jarred's room, theirs had lost the perfection she had felt when they first arrived. Mpumi ignored Nomusa's question and took off her hat and glasses sinking into the couch. She was still a bit weak from last night's ordeal. "I need water" Nomusa handed her water remembering that her friend had almost died the previous day. She also handed Mpumi her phone and she went through it. There were ten missed calls from Nomusa two from Oyama and a message from an unknown number, it simply said, "You are still the most beautiful woman in this world. Dinner?" Mpumi smiled, she had no idea how Jarred had gotten her number.

"Did he call?"

"He texted he wants us to have dinner."

"Huh? Daniel wants to have dinner with you?" Mpumi blushed when she realized that Nomusa had been asking about her husband. Now Nomusa's curiosity was really piqued and she came to sit next to Mpumi waiting for her to open up. She sensed that Jarred was more than just her friend's savior and she wasn't letting this one slide. So she sat and waited for Mpumi to open up but she wasn't ready for what her friend said next. "Jarred is the first man I ever slept with, back when I was in Harvard."

CHAPTER THREE

"Harvard was a scary experience. I was young alone in a foreign land and I really stuck out. I remember the stares and the whispers in the corridors and me thinking they are probably wondering what this black monkey is doing here. You have to understand I was the one of two females doing my MBA and the only black in my class and a foreigner to boot. The people who actually did come up to me wanted to know which village I came from in Africa, one actually thought South Africa was a village in the South of Africa, none of them could pronounce my name. Most of the lecturers ignored me, I was depressed I was ready to quit and come back home. Then along came Jarred a drug like nothing I had ever known. I was in the cafeteria sitting alone as usual and he came and sat in front of me, I stopped eating and stared at him, he stared back. "God you are so beautiful." Those were the first words out of his mouth, I was taken aback by his random compliment all I could do was stare. "I'm Jarred by the way you can call me Red." You should have seen him Nono, he had his hair long and tied in a ponytail and he was skinny like he didn't eat much all features in his face were sharp, the most remarkable thing about him was his eyes and when he looked at me it was like he was piercing my soul. He also couldn't pronounce my name even Mpumi so he said he would call me Lelo because I was so exotic. He sat with me every day after that. At first I was awkward around him but he was good at putting me at ease till I began opening up to him. I ended up opening up to him about things I was even scared to think out loud and he always listened. I told him I was promised to be married back home and his response was, "I'm in love with you Lelo and I have a feeling I'm going to love you for eternity." I was committed to Daniel and I let him down every chance I got but he was persistent. In him I found a best friend which was weird because you know I don't open up to people. We did everything together from studying to shopping and sightseeing. I soon learnt that Jarred was from one of those elite families and he was considered a catch. Consequently I became more ostracized than I had been before I started hanging out with him, the ladies there loathed me and the guys kept their distance. In a month I felt like I had known him my whole life. Coming from the movies one day he just drew me into him arms and he kissed me. I had been dating Daniel for a year so I knew kissing by then but it didn't prepare me for the onslaught of Jarred's lips. He didn't just kiss me he bared my soul there was so much depth so many emotions in one kiss. There was no getting back from that kiss. He was surprised when I told him I was still a virgin but in a typical Jarred fashion he said, "You know it's gotta go at some point." For all his jokes he still made me feel like a queen he went out of his way to make me happy. I had never felt so at peace with myself before and excited, you never knew what to expect with him. He could be so gentle like the first time we made love, he was patient and he put my

Comfort and pleasure first, he could be so passionate as well and possessive. He made me know that I was his world and it was scary too to have someone love you so fully. We fought as hard as we loved and our arguments ended as quickly as they started. I felt guilty about

Daniel but somehow when Jarred was there he totally eclipsed him. We spent most of our breaks, holidays at his brother's house, the brother was a great guy. Time seemed to fly and we got serious, he asked me to marry him I told him I was confused. He took me to his home and introduced me to his mother. She hated me on sight. I could never be good enough for her son, I was too unrefined, too black, too shabby and too brainy. She made it obvious that I was unwanted there. In hindsight I guess she worked so hard to tear us apart and well in the end she won, I left Harvard in tears running from Jarred and he had no idea why or where I was going and to me that was the end of our romance." Nomusa had been sitting mesmerized throughout Mpumi's narration and there were tears in both their eyes when she finished. Nomusa suspected that her friend had always carried a torch for Jarred even when she was married to Daniel and whatever it is that had broken them up must have been huge. Nomusa had felt the change in her friend when she had come back from Harvard but hadn't known what was behind it, she had always assumed that Mpumi had only ever loved Daniel. Their room was now dark and they had barely noticed. Nomusa turned on the lights and asked, "Now what are you going to do?"

"I don't know love, I never thought I would ever see him again."

"He deserves answers Mpumi." Mpumi sighed, even though Jarred hadn't asked anything yet, she knew he would. "It all happened a lifetime away, I've changed so has he, and maybe we should just let bygones be bygones. I'm married now I can't get into anything with Jarred now."

"Do you still love him?" Mpumi blew out a breath and stared down for a minute when she looked up her eyes were full of tears and so much anguish but when she spoke her voice didn't break, "I never stopped loving him, I just learnt to live without him." Nomusa drew her into a hug and she sobbed her heart out for that young couple who hadn't stood a chance, she cried for what could have been and she cried for what she wished could be. Nomusa let her cry, quietly soothing her back, this hadn't been part of their holiday retreat plans but

Nomusa felt that it was necessary.

The light streaming in through a space in the curtains woke Mpumi up from a deep sleep. She and Nomusa had slept late last night, they had gone to the private cinema in the hotel and had watched an old romantic movie while stuffing themselves with frozen yoghurt. Apart from a slight brain freeze they had a great time, Mpumi had ignored Jarred's invitation to dinner. Nomusa was still fast asleep, that one loved her sleep and Mpumi let her be. They had also talked about Nomusa's date with Amo, he had taken her to some jazzy spot where there were poem recitals. It had been a unique night and yes Mpumi had been right the waxing had come in pretty handy. No wonder the poor thing was sleeping like the dead, she probably didn't get much sleep. 5.30am the clock flashed at her, if she made it in time she could catch the last moments of the sunrise. Wrapping an oversized robe over her Sleeping Beauty pajamas, a mother's day gift from Oyama, she left the room quietly making it a point to take her keycard. There was no one around as she slipped out of the hotel, this time she took another route and sat on a boulder staring out at the ocean. The sunrise was spectacular, it was reflected on the water and it was so perfect she took out her phone and took pictures. She didn't hear him coming, she only felt him wrap his arms around her from behind and she could smell his woodymusky scent. She tried resisting but he held her steadily, "Come now Lelo don't spoil our sunrise moment, we haven't had one of these in over a decade." She sighed and settled into his arms, watching the sunrise, sunset and stars had been their thing when they had been an item and he always had her wrapped in his arms. Somehow this felt different, Jarred was no longer a skinny starved looking young man, it seemed like he was working out a lot. His now broad shoulders and stocky arms were solid and she found herself laying her head on his chest and they watched the sunrise in silence. After a while, he turned her around and stared at her. She felt selfconscious, her face was unwashed and bare of any make up, and luckily she had very clear skin, one of the perks of being dark-skinned. "You stood me up last night."

"I didn't agree to have dinner with you, in fact I ignored you."

"Nc nc nc such attitude to someone who saved your life in this very beach. But since I'm such a benevolent savior I will allow you to redeem yourself. Let's have breakfast."

"Ok let me go and shower and change out of my pajamas."

"No, I'm not letting you run away again, we are having breakfast right now it's already set up." He grabbed her hand and was leading her to the other side of the beach. Curiosity got the better of her and she followed him with a bemused expression on her face. And right there next to the sea there was a table set next to a boulder, there were two white chairs, a blue table cloth, two picnic baskets, and a blue vase with fresh daffodils. While she was still admiring his ingenuity, he pulled out a chair for her and she sat down feeling pampered. "You didn't have to go to so much trouble." "Are you kidding me, I know this was the only way to get you to eat with me." He was already taking out food from the basket, ham, croissants, toast, strawberry jam, fresh apricots, bacon and orange juice, a meal fit for a small army. Mpumi was on a diet and she saw all her effort go flying out of the window, "Jarred you do know that all of these carbs are going straight to my hips, you want me to look like a hippo." He frowned angrily as if she had said something disgusting, "Why do you have to keep putting yourself down? So what if you are fat you are so sexy, more so now as a woman than when you were younger." Mpumi was short of words and she let him pile up her plate, the sparks between them often led to small fires. As quickly as he had become intense he changed back to his easygoing self, "Your daughter is a delight, and she stole my heart." Like any proud parent Mpumi preened at the compliment, "She's the one constant joy in my life, she's writing her matric at the end of the year but she isn't taking it seriously." He frowned slightly, "Isn't she a bit young to be matriculating?"

"Actually she is turning 15 in December. Oyama is what they call a gifted child. Once when she was two I left her in my study to get her a snack, when I came back I noticed that the study was too quiet. I was expecting the worst, imagine my surprise when I found her reading my David Copperfield. There was so much intensity in her little face. They made her skip grades but I made sure they didn't put her too far ahead." Jarred seemed suitably impressed by this story and said as much to her. "She looks nothing like you though." Mpumi smiled other people would probably notice that and say nothing at least to her face but Jarred wasn't most people, he was Jarred. She took a gulp of her juice and he asked, "What about our child?" Mpumi choked on her juice and he had to get up and rub her back while she coughed and spluttered. When her coughing fit lapsed she looked at him and he seemed nonplussed waiting patiently for her response, she could only say "She told you." "Yes she did, she told me that when you left you were carrying my child." Suddenly she lost all appetite and she pushed her plate away and stood up, she sat on the boulder knees to her chest and began rocking. Jarred followed her every move with his eyes then he went to stand beside her but made no move to comfort her, he wanted answers. He had wanted answers ever since he had come back home with his brother only to be told by his mother that his Lelo had left him with no explanation not even a bloody letter and just like that she vanished from his life. He had only gotten some explanation when his mother died a few years back leaving him with a letter apologizing for chasing Mpumi away especially when she had been carrying his child and she pleaded with him to find that child. Mpumi started speaking in such a low voice he had to bend to hear what she was saying. "I didn't know I was pregnant, I only found out when I fainted while shopping with your mother. When the doctor told me I was pregnant she had been so kind and she told me that she hadn't wanted it to come this far. I didn't know what she was talking about. She said you had sent her to break up with me since you were marrying your fiancé and if I didn't believe her I should call you and ask you. You never picked up any of my calls, I kept calling and calling and I started panicking. She wanted to take me to a doctor who would do an abortion, I refused so she gave me money for my flight back home and made me promise that I wouldn't try to contact you again."The letter had more or less said the same things and his mother had even told him that she had offered Mpumi more money to take care of the baby but she had refused and only accepted the flight money. He let her continue, "I came back home alone pregnant and scared. I told Daniel I couldn't marry him anymore that I was pregnant, I was prepared to raise the baby alone but he stuck by me. Then one night I woke up and there was a sharp pain on my abdomen I couldn't move my lower body. My nightdress was sticky and wet I screamed and my mother came rushing into the room when she switched on the lights there was blood everywhere. I think she knew immediately what had happened but I was frantic I wanted them to save my baby. We went to the hospital but it was too late I had miscarried my baby and the doctors didn't know what brought on the miscarriage." She looked at him and he saw the anguish in the depths of her eyes, "You wanted to know about our child, our child died in my womb." He felt a stabbing pain in his heart and he lashed out at her, "Did our child die in your womb or did you kill our child?"The slap was instant and left an imprint on his cheek while he was still reeling she got off the boulder and ran off towards the hotel. He didn't run after her, he grabbed a glass full of juice and smashed it on the boulder. He mourned their unborn baby and he cried deep, heart-wrenching sobs there beside the sea, Jarred cried for what could have been.

Mpumi ran all the way to the hotel and she was relieved that Nomusa was still asleep, she didn't have the energy to tell her what had just taken place. She felt emotionally drained, of all her miscarriages her first one was the one she had moaned the most, she had been devastated. But it was all in the past and though it was a fresh wound for Jarred she had lived with it for close to sixteen years now. She shrugged out of her pajamas and went to run water in the bath, she poured all the hotel bath oils and she sunk gratefully into the water and she wallowed in the bath. Nomusa came to stand by the bathroom door while she stretched herself. "What time is

It? Why did you wake up in the middle of the night?" Mpumi smiled, her friend loved her sleep, "I'm not sure I went out to look at the sunrise, then uhm I went for a jog." Nomusa was still too fuzzy from sleep to notice that her friend was hiding something from her, she went to take a shower while Mpumi finished her bath. Both ladies decided to skip the buffet breakfast and had fruit then they were on their way to take a cable ride up the Table Mountain, Nomusa was chatting about their childhood keeping Mpumi distracted. Every time they came to Cape Town it was the same, they got homesick and they reminisced about their childhood. The cable ride was over shortly and Amo had joined them to go to the wine testing. Amo was easy to talk to and he included Mpumi in their conversation so she didn't feel too much of a third wheel. The wine was heavenly and Mpumi downed glass after glass. Daniel hated her drinking, the model 'Minister's Wife' wasn't some sloppy alcohol loving bimbo in his words so she rarely drank. But this was Kapa and what happened in Kapa stayed in Kapa she was having more fun than she had had in a long time. She saw Nomusa staring behind her shoulder and when she looked around there he was carrying a 1941 bottle of Inglenook Cabernet Sauvignon and that goofy smile of his. He offered the bottle to her and she heard Amo gulp, "Truce?" She couldn't really say no to a ridiculously expensive bottle of wine so she pulled a chair out for him. After a momentary tension broken by Nomusa's chirpy, "Open the damn wine Mpumi!" the drinking spree continued. They were laughing so hard, Mpumi felt sad when the wine tasting session came to an end. She tried standing up but she felt woozy so she sat down, Amo and Nomusa wanted to take her back to the hotel before proceeding with their plans but Jarred insisted that he would take her, they could go. He pulled her up and casually put his arm around her waist, to any onlooker they seemed like a touchy-feely couple but in actual fact he was guiding her towards his Jeep. She smiled lamely up at him and kept giggling when he caught her smiling, she couldn't remember the last time she had been so sloshed. He got her into the Jeep without incident and started the car. On their way back, his phone rang and he smiled when he checked the caller ID then he answered, "Baby…" "Yes baby I miss you too, no I can't come back yet my work isn't done this side….no you can't come this side we talked about this…… I promise to be back before Valentine's Day… Of course I haven't forgotten…Anything for my baby……Ok I've got to go now, take care I love you…Always and to infinity." Mpumi sat through the whole conversation and she felt a cold hand go up and down her spine seeping away her drunken happiness. Oh God this can't be happening! She thought desperately. She remembered their morning almost date, she had almost become the dreaded other woman. Because she knew in her heart of hearts if Jarred had made a move on her that morning before all that soul searching talk she would have given herself to him fully no questions asked. That's how desperately horny she was for him. And he had the nerve to take the call in front of her! It stung, she felt embarrassment and anger stirring up in her, he thought so little of her. She feigned sleep so that she wouldn't look at him, she couldn't face him. He must have known she was faking because she heard his low sexy chuckle and that infuriated her even more. The nerve of this man! She continued feigning sleep all the way to the hotel. When he came over her side of the door and tried to help her out she hissed in a low voice, "Let go of me, I can manage quite well on my own." He raised his hands up in mock surrender and she tried to walk straight away from him as fast as she could but she was still drunk and he caught up with her easily enough and got into the elevator. It must have moved only one floor up when he jammed it and he forced her to look at him by tilting her chin up. "Why are you mad at me? What did I do this time?" she refused to answer him and she stared him straight in the eye. "Are you jealous Lelo?" She looked away and he took that as a yes, "But why would you be jealous you are the one married and with a daughter." She looked at him again with murder in her eyes, "At least I told you upfront. When were you going to tell me about your wife? Before or after you seduced me?"

"Whoa hold on no one has seduced anyone here or do you want me to seduce you?"
"That's not the point Jarred I deserved to know!"
"You so sexy when you are mad, my little fire spitting vixen. Even more so when you are jealous." While he was talking he started rubbing her chin and the back of her neck, she could feel the tingling sensation all the way to her toes. She opened her mouth to utter another biting retort and before she knew it she had her back pressed against the elevator wall, one leg arched around him and he was feasting on her lips like there was no tomorrow, she wanted to slap him but her traitorous body was yielding to his touch and responding to his kiss stroke for stroke. She heard a moan from a voice that oddly sounded like her own, she moved to be closer to him feeling like their clothes were standing in her way. Somehow he had pushed her panties to one side and was rubbing her clit aggressively, every movement was like a lick of flames and she purred at this torture. She felt his manhood throbbing and pushing against her stomach even through his pants and all she wanted was to take his pants off and hold the throbbing shaft in her hands. As if he could read her mind he let her go slight and let down his pant to his knees and without warning he pushed into her pressing her against the cold glass wall. She wasn't accustomed to his size anymore but when he started grinding into her she felt the flames almost consuming her. The suddenness and urgency of her orgasm surprised her but seemed to spur him on, she had to wrap her legs around him to stop herself from falling. While she was still floating from the throes of her first come he kept ramming into her and she felt the build up for a second one she held on for dear life trying to hold it in but her body betrayed her again. This time they came together so explosively she could feel his seed shooting into her body and she dug her nails deeply into his back but he seemed oblivious to everything. Even when they had both finished getting their fulfilment he still cradled her against the wall. She caught a sight of them on the opposite wall, him with his pants half-way down still attached to her and her with the skirt of her dress open,

her legs twined around him and her eyes still puffy from her orgasm. This was insanity! What had gotten into her to have sex in an elevator with another woman's husband? Without any protection at that. Reality began to sink in, they were in a public elevator probably with CCTV footage, if anyone leaked this out to the press, it would be the end of her and she had a daughter to protect. Scrambling down from him she tried to put down her dress and right her panties. He took his time dressing up then he unjammed the lift and they were soon in her floor. She opened the door and wanted to quickly shut him out but he was bigger and quicker than her, he was soon in their room and he made himself comfortable on their couch picking some grapes from the stand next to the couch. She folded her arms on her chest and stood looking at him, he was acting like nothing had just happened when they committed adultery in a freaking elevator just moments ago. "Aren't you going to say something about what just happened?"

"That was the best bloody making out session I have ever had in my life and I'm not going to diminish it with words." Making out session? She gave up on him and sat sullenly at the edge of

the bed, he had just touched her soul and he called it a making out session wow, but why did it have to hurt so much. "She's not my wife you know," when she looked at him blankly he rectified, "on the phone that wasn't my wife." Oh so now she should feel better because he had cheated with her on his girlfriend, she kept her silence and let him talk. "It's Joseph's daughter Lola." Joseph was the brother they sometimes went to visit when they were still in Harvard. She felt a little relieved, but she still had cheated on her husband. Running away from that train of thought she asked, "How is Joe?"

"He's dead. Car crash. Both him and his wife. Lola only has me now." He said it so calmly but she knew how deeply it must have hurt him and still hurt him, he and his brother had been very close. She went to sit next to him on the couch and rested her head on his shoulder, he rubbed her arm comfortingly but it was he who need the touch more. "She's lucky to have you." He didn't respond just continued cradling her and they sat side by side quietly for a while. "Does he make you happy?" Mpumi contemplated the question and after a while she said, "He's a good provider, he protects us from everything." She looked into his eyes and they compelled her to go on, "He's also a controlling serial cheat and he is abusive at times." A sharp intake of breath was his only reaction. "Does he hit you?" She looked away suddenly ashamed. He forced her to look at him, "No he's very careful not to assault me, he manhandles me sometimes." When she saw his anger she rushed on in her husband's defense, "But he hasn't in a long time, the last time was when I was threatening to leave him so he…he threw me on the bed and said he would show me who wore the pants in this marriage. He… he ripped my clothes apart like I was some slave I kept telling him no Daniel stop…but he was too strong." She hadn't meant to blurt that out. She had never told anyone of this incident which had left her with her last pregnancy. She still remembered her screams and the look on his face, he had turned into a savage beast, he had forced her thighs open and when she continued struggling he had smacked her hard on the ribs and she had felt the air leaving her lungs. Then she stopped struggling and cowered tears streaming down her face till he stopped and got off her. There had been murder in his eyes and she had been so scared, he grabbed her arms and came close to her face, "You are not going anywhere, I'm not done with you." Mpumi hadn't realized that she had become lost in her thoughts and that she was shivering till she felt Jarred touch her arm and she jumped fear stamped all over her face. "Hey, hey, it's me Lelo. Look at me darling, you're ok, he won't hurt you again, I promise. You're safe now, come here." She resisted going into his arms but he held on anywhere, funny she couldn't cry anymore but she was shivering uncontrollably. He held her till the shivering stopped and still he held her stroking her hair in much the same way she comforted Oyama. She was grateful for his comfort.

"The CCTV footage from the elevator…"

"Don't worry I'll take care of it Lelo, no one will ever know." His word was enough, she trusted him.

CHAPTER

THREE

Nomusa came in late, way after Jarred had reluctantly left but Mpumi had wanted to be alone so he left. Nomusa was in high spirits and she dished all the details of her date with Amo punctuated by gushing "wuuuuu chomma!" her happiness was contagious and Mpumi was also smiling along with her. She would have talked all night but Mpumi insisted on sleep, the next morning they were travelling to Sabi Sands. Just as she was snuggling in her blankets a text came in from Jarred.

"I'm sorry."

"For?" she texted back. He responded, ***"For calling what we had earlier a bloody make-out session. It just shook me to the core. It was explosive. Didn't mean for it to happen in the elevator. Had planned out a whole night of seduction. Sorry I lost control. You deserve better."*** She smiled Jarred was so comfortable talking about sex, in fact he was the first person who had ever talked to her openly about sex. She texted back ***"It was explosive for me too"*** and added a smiley face. She had forgotten that being with Jarred was like being on a rollacoster, she had gone from bitch-slapping him to getting drunk with him, getting insanely jealous which had led to the explosive sex, then she had poured out her secrets to him and now here she was blushing over his texts. She wasn't as comfortable talking about sex, it must be a black person thing. Her mother had never talked to her about sex, all she had been told was that she should save herself for her husband. And on her wedding night the aunts had told her that she must never deny a man his cookie jar else he would stray. No one had ever told her what to expect, even Daniel never talked about sex whether he enjoyed it with her or not. She had wanted Oyama's experience to be different so when her daughter had turned 13 she had done her research, even compiled a placard, and had sat Oyama down to give her 'The Talk'. Oyama had surprised her by stating after she had just got started that she had googled all about sex. So Mpumi had put her research aside and had held her daughter's hands, "What you might not have found on the internet is that sex is a sacred act between two people. And the first time is scary and painful so you need to have it with someone who cares about you, who will be gentle and who will appreciate the gift you are bestowing him. You should be comfortable in your sexuality and don't settle for anything less. Now no mother wants to acknowledge that her baby will ever have sex, but when you do baby promise me I won't have to see it on the internet." Oyama had been grossed out by even the thought of it, she was still in her 'boys are gross stage' that was before Ryan had turned into a dreamy-eyed hunk. Just thinking about the incident made Mpumi smile and she took out her phone from under her pillow and texted Oyama, "I love you nunu kamaa wakhe." Oyama was probably asleep by then so she put her phone back under her pillow and drifted to sleep.

CHAPTER FOUR

Mpumi was woken up by her phone buzzing insistently under her pillow. It was still dark outside, she groaned. If it was Jarred, he was going to know her skanky side, but maybe something had happened to Oyama. She took the phone from under her pillow and checked the caller ID. Whoa there was no way in hell she was taking Phindiwe's call. She was going to let it go to voicemail. "Why aren't you picking that call?" Nomusa groaned and snatched the phone from her, but when she saw who it was she put the phone on silent. Phindiwe was Daniel's elder sister. She was the career aunty type who lived to micromanage her brother's marriage. She had never been married herself, had seven children with different fathers but she would always tell you were to get off when it came to treating your husband. They had nicknamed her Rabheka, she had the same loud hoarse voice as Rebecca Malope only there was nothing musical about Phindiwe's voice. She had left a voice message. "Hee wena mfazi ndini we Harvard (you little Harvard wife). You think your two little degrees are going to keep your man happy?"

It's three actually but they continued listening to the message, "That's the problem with you educated women, your husbands always come second. You are out there in God knows where, while your husband suffers alone. This is not what we paid lobola for. You are a wife start acting like one what example are you setting for my brother's daughter mxm mindless heifer. You can't even give him another child but you can spend his money on holidays with your floozy friend. I bet wherever you are, you are busy spreading those fat thighs, safari my foot. When you come back you will know me nxaaa." Her voice was even louder on the phone, Mpumi rolled her eyes, she should get married first then come and tell her what married women should do. All her seven children were supported by Daniel so she always thought Mpumi was wasting money that should rightfully go to raising her brats, never mind that Mpumi earned a six-figure salary herself. She was like that demanding baby-mama always calling to say the boys needed this and that, forget that Daniel wasn't her children's father. After deleting the message they started packing, they wouldn't let meddlesome Rabheka spoil their trip.

They were on the first class coach on their flight to Mpumalanga with those fancy little nuts and champagne, Nomusa settled in to enjoy how the other half live. First class wasn't bad for two Khayelitsha homegirls. She looked over at Mpumi, she was reclining on the flight chair a glass of Mojito on one hand, while thumbing the pages of a novel called Hlomu or some such thing, Nomusa had never been a reader. Something had changed about Mpumi in the past two days, she was smiling as she read and even laughing at whatever outrageous thing was in that novel. Even after that dreadful call in the morning she had gone to bath singing, *"Even though I have fat thighs, flabby arms a potbelly still gives good lovin"*, in the shower. And she had even been dancing to Meghan Trainor's "All about the Bass", when she was waiting for Nomusa to finish dressing. Nomusa hated to admit it but the bitch had moves. Nomusa remembered the first time she had seen Mpumi dance, it had been their Matric dance and everyone had been mindblown. Mpumi had always had her nose behind a book, the serious scholar who knew more than their Sangweni High teachers, so she wasn't even a teacher's pet. The other children thought she was a snob, her only friend was Nomusa and even Nomusa struggled to get her out of her books. One of the boys, Mbulelo was his name, made them drink alcohol. Mpumi went wild. She was even puffing on some weed and getting high. Next thing Brenda Fassie's Weekend Special had come on and she started dancing the 90s version of a twerk. If Nomusa had not been there she would never have believed it, stuck up Mpumi was a freak when she let go. Mpumi hadn't let go in years but the previous day Nomusa had seen her let go and that side of Mpumi was always fun. It must be the work of the blue-eyed god but Mpumi was tight lipped about what happened when he brought her back to the hotel after the wine tasting. She had changed. She didn't look defeated anymore. She had that spring on her step and that sway to her hips. Blueeyed god must stay, Nomusa decided as the plane taxied its landing. After a short chopper ride, they finally arrived at Sabi Sands. How can one even begin to describe Sabi Sands? It had a majestic feel to it that could not be crafted by man. There was a stillness that you could just slice with a knife. The trees. The birds. The grass. Even the air was perfect. Mpumi had her camera out and she was taking pictures. Nomusa's squeals were even louder when they got to the Lion Sands Ivory lodge. It comprised of six spacious and far apart private villas. Their villa was a modern building with a round and thatched roof. The walls were cream, a tiered bedroom with a huge bed with white linen and black throw pillows, the windows were three quarters of the room it was like sleeping outside. Between the lounge and the bedroom there was a heated rim flow plunge pool, how awesome is that, Nomusa was already uploading pictures on Instagram and Snapchat, eat your heart out bitches. Their whole villa overlooked the Sabi River and Kruger National Park, Nomusa had died and gone to heaven. She just felt it in her bones that this had been the original Garden of Eden. After unpacking Mpumi wanted them to explore on a foot safari, Nomusa would rather have wallowed in the plunge pool but her bully of a friend was having none of it.

Nomusa looked like a teenager in those tiny shorts, Mpumi thought and she laughed within at the way their guide was trying to look everywhere except Nomusa's thighs. Oblivious to the poor man's plight Nomusa kept asking questions about every animal they came across. Mpumi was content to let her friend talk while she continued taking pictures. Photography was her

Second passion after children, one director at her company had seen some of the pictures she had taken and urged her to become a professional photographer. She had been flattered but hadn't taken the compliment to heart. She had a knack of capturing things in mid-action, the gazelle as it galloped to join its herd, the eagle in mid-flight, she had a keen eye and she loved the click click sound of the camera. Jarred hadn't called or texted her today and for some weird reason that bothered her. Snap out of it, she chided herself, he didn't owe her any calls or texts but still it stung. She had thought they had something going but she had to come to terms with that it was just a holiday fling, she was after all the married mother of a teenager. Nomusa was still talking off the ear of the guide and Mpumi took another shot of the African sky. She had no idea why Aristotle had thought this to be a dark and cursed continent, when it was so obvious that God had taken his time in creating this place, no money could buy such majesty. But why hadn't he called! That guy was seriously messing with her head, she shrugged thoughts of him furiously to a small box in her mind and shut the lid tightly. Just as she was enjoying nature, Nomusa decided to leave the guide in peace and turn to her. "So?" Mpumi had a feeling she wasn't going to love this conversation, "So ntoni?" she hadn't meant to snap like that but Nomusa wasn't easily deterred.

"So what's happening between you and the blue-eyed Adonis?" Sigh.

CHAPTER
FOUR

"Nothing is happening, we talked a lot yesterday"
"And I must look like an idiot to you, ooh wow is that a blush?"
"I'm too dark skinned to blush idiot."
"You are detracting, what happened?"
"Fine, if you must know, we shagged in the elevator."
"Whaaaaaaaaaaat?" The shock on Nomusa's face was comical and Mpumi felt smug. She ignored Nomusa and went back to taking snaps. Nomusa was having none of that and she grabbed her camera, Mpumi sighed. "It wasn't planned it just happened, one moment we were having a heated argument the next moment he had my back against the wall and my knickers around my ankles."
"Mpumi that is so dirty and so unlike you, I love it! I just knew something had happened. I mean you were singing in the shower. Shaking that thing I just knew it."
"Don't get too excited it's just a fling. I'm still married, remember?" The way Nomusa brushed off her marriage wasn't even funny, "If you were happy in your marriage you wouldn't have slept with Adonis and Daniel would be with you on this Safari, the Universe is telling you something." Mpumi laughed Nomusa had no morals whatsoever and had few scruples. "Sorry to disappoint the Universe but I needed to blow off steam and I committed adultery, it was a fling and that's all it was. Now let it go and let's enjoy the beautiful safari." Nomusa did not agree but Mpumi had had enough and she wanted to continue taking her pictures.

Mpumi just kept calmly dropping bombs on her and Nomusa was left reeling. They were back in their villa and Mpumi had promptly undressed and gotten into the pool. She wasn't going to talk about Jarred anymore. Contrary to what most people had thought, Mpumi had always been the daring one and Nomusa had followed her. This one time she had talked Nomusa into climbing over their neighbor's gate. The owner of the house had been a motherly lady whom they had all called mother, she had a huge iNgobamakhosi tree (hard pear tree), it had berry like fruits which turned from coral pink to bright red when ripe. Usually the woman would allow them to climb the tree and feast on the fruit. But the woman's mother had passed away and she had gone to Kimberly for the burial. Two weeks had seemed like eternity to the children and Mpumi had come up with the brilliant idea that they should jump the gate 'mother' would understand. The others hadn't been totally convinced but Mpumi was hardcore and she was quickly over the gate and she dared them to follow. By the time they had all jumped the gate she was already on top of the tree stuffing her little face with the berries. She was careful to spit out the hard, woody centre, they joined her. Being children they forgot they were perpetuating a crime and they were shouting and screaming on top of the tree and that was how Mpumi's mother had found them. She had called them to follow her and stupidly they had followed. That woman's hand was wicked, she had thrashed the naughtiness out of them and their little behinds had suffered. Nomusa felt that the daring side in Mpumi was showing itself, it had been dominant for too long. With Daniel, Mpumi was the perfect wife, the perfect hostess who probably never went down on her husband. This American brought out the reckless Mpumi, all that sex in the elevator was freak on another level. Nomusa knew that Mpumi would feel guilty but she thought that guilt would be misplaced, Daniel had done nothing to inspire Mpumi's loyalty. Amogalang was calling her, Nomusa felt warmth on her face, that Tswana boy was driving her mad. For the first time in her life, Nomusa was falling head over heels-teenage dream-talk on the phone all night-kind of love. But she was also scared. She didn't really have a record of happy relationships. Being single at her age she got prayers from her mother and her father saying she needed a cleansing. She wasn't going to bank much into this thing she had going with Amo, she would just enjoy the moment.

Two days in the wilderness passed so fast, they went on safaris took so many pictures and even rode on the back of an elephant. There was still no communication from Jarred and Daniel hadn't contacted her too.

CHAPTER

FOUR

At first she had been furious with Jarred then she had begun panicking. What if he had left her like she had left him all those years ago? She couldn't blame him if he had. She tried calling him but his number was unavailable, then she got worried maybe he had been involved in a high jacking. Get it together Mpumi, she chided herself, she was acting like a love-struck teenager. Speaking of love-struck teenager, Mpumi had never seen Nomusa so deeply in love. She talked to all hours of the night on her phone with Amo. They texted like teenagers, that idiot was even blushing at those texts. She was happy for her. Nomusa deserved a decent guy who was crazy about her. Funny when they were younger, Nomusa had never had any trouble snagging guys. She had been the lighter skinned prettier friend. She was also bubbly and easy to talk to. Mpumi had made a small fortune from guys who wanted her to hook them up with her bestie. An insensitive aunt had raised the issue during Mpumi's lobola negotiations, "We always assumed that we would be negotiating lobola for your

pretty friend and that you would die an old maid alone with your books." Nx! Mpumi hadn't wanted to go back home and to give those people anything more than they already looted from them at her father's funeral. But Daniel had insisted that they had to have a proper traditional wedding. The aunt hadn't known of course that Nomusa had almost been married two months prior to Mpumi's lobola negotiations. The man had been a Zulu, Nhlaloenhle Ndaba, he had swept her off her feet and proposed. It was on the day of the wedding, Nomusa had looked so beautiful and so in love walking down the aisle. Mpumi of course was her best girl she had been holding her veil. It was when the priest was asking if there were any objections to that union that all hell had broken loose. A very pregnant woman had stood up with a small child on her hips and holding a not much older one by hand. The groom had looked like a deer caught by the headlights of an oncoming car. The woman was the bitter wife of Nhlalo, after the screeching and tugging match which was broken up by elders she then told them who she was. Her husband worked in Joburg while she had stayed KwaMlalazi looking after his children and his sickly mother. He had started coming less and less home, she heard about the upcoming nuptials from a gossiping relative. She had packed her children to come and see for herself. She couldn't believe that her husband was living it up while she struggled to feed his family. The stupid fool had claimed that he loved them both and wanted Nomusa to be his second wife. Nomusa had been devastated and humiliated in front of all her family and friends. Mpumi had helped her pick up the pieces but she suspected that from that day onwards Nomusa had shied away from any guy who even smelt of commitment. She had jumped from one playboy to another. Mpumi had a feeling that Amo was different and Nomusa was in denial. Since Nomusa was mooning over her phone, she probably wouldn't agree to go explore and meet more animals. Mpumi decided she had to do something about her hair. Her mother had taught her how to plait it and she could plait herself. She sat in front of the mirror and took up her combs and clips. It was hard opening lines, her hair was coarse and crowded, and so when she opened one line if she didn't clip the hair quickly the line would disappear. She decided to plait cornrows just four rows would do the trick. Nomusa came to take a sit on the chair behind her and watched her, she didn't even offer to help. But Mpumi had a feeling she was about to say something stupid. "You have millions to your name, not to mention that your husband is the freaking Minister, but you are too stingy to even go to a proper saloon." Where would she find a saloon in the middle of Kruger National Park? Thankfully Mpumi had a comb on her mouth but she let her eyes glare her response. "I mean a Brazilian weave wouldn't hurt either, you didn't even grow up in the rural areas but your arse screams farm girl." Ok she was much more fun when her nose had been stuck behind her phone. Ping! Pheeew Mpumi had been saved by a text, Nomusa went back to her love world.

It was their last night at the Ivory Sands and Mpumi had fallen in love with the place. There had a dumbwaiter system which was no doubt ideal for those famous married men who wanted to spoil their mistresses to a safari. This was probably an ideal place for Daniel to take one of his floozies but thinking about it didn't hurt her anymore. There was a note left by the dumbwaiter and a single rose addressed to her and the note simply said, 'Meet me at the Kingston Treehouse'. Mpumi felt excited, she was sure it was Jarred, then she remembered that he hadn't called her or texted her since they had left Cape Town. Nomusa was wrapped up in her phone so Mpumi slid out of their room unnoticed and made her way to the treehouse. It wasn't a traditional treehouse, it wasn't even on a tree. It was made of glass with a thatched roof, it was suspended on wooden beams and there were lamps on the ramp leading to the treehouse. The lamps cast a beautiful glow on the whole place. There he was standing just inside the doorway. He was so tall and solid. His face in the lamplight made her catch her breath, she understood why Nomusa had nicknamed him Adonis. He was chiseled perfection. Mpumi had to remind herself firmly that she was angry at him. So she stood in front of him legs slightly apart and her arms folded and a no-nonsense look on her face. "You look like a goddess with those plaits on your head." The man thought he was God's gift to women, the epitome of charm. "They are cornrows," she snapped at him, "and all goddesses were Greek there wasn't a black goddess."

"Are you sure? I think I read about a black goddess once. She was the hottest. Actually Sir Godfrey Higgins asserted that all the gods and goddesses of Greece were black."

"I don't care if there was, you can't just go AWOL then come back thinking you can charm your way into my panties." He was amused by her outburst and that made her angrier. "I just love how your mind always runs to that dirty place. Missed me much?" Arrogant fool! She walked past him and went to stand at the railing looking up at the clear night sky. He stood behind her prisoning her by placing each hand on the railing next to hers, his chin was resting on her cornrows. "Have you ever noticed how perfectly we fit?" she had noticed but she didn't feel like talking to him. He sighed, he knew how she got when she was giving him the cold shoulder. "I'm sorry I didn't contact you." He was going to have to do better than that and he knew it. She wanted an explanation even if she didn't ask for one. "Lola had pneumonia so I had to drop everything and go back to her."

"Is she better now?" the concern was immediate.

"She is fine, the doctor thought a change of climate would do her a world of good so I came back with her."

"Oh." She wanted to know where she was. He could read her easily, "She is in my villa, fast asleep. The journey was tiring to her." She had finally relaxed in his arms, he was partly forgiven. "I missed you Lelo, since I came across you I'm alive again. Every moment apart from you was hell" ok he was overselling himself now but his words warmed her heart, she felt the exact same. "I missed you too."

"Hallelujah I thought you were going to stomp out of here with your delicious cookie." She had forgotten that naturally he was an idiot. He turned her around to face him and then he was kissing her. Tiny butterfly kisses all over her face then he dipped to her neck. The kisses were getting more heated as they moved to her cleavage. He buried his face in her bust and she was squirming from the electricity he was generating with his kisses. "I want to get drunk on you. I want to feast on your body," he was talking against her skin sending tingles all over her body. This must be the seduction he had promised her. It was torture, she wanted him inside her but he was in no rush. He led her inside the treehouse. It was like being outside in the wilderness and she was shivering from need. "Please." He knew what she wanted but he was determined to take his sweet time with her. He laid her gently on the cushions which were laid out on the

floor. He was taking off her top. She felt self-conscious, this was different from the elevator. He had last seen her body when she had a flat tummy and now her stomach was slightly rounded and it had stretch marks. She put her hand over his to stop him but he brushed her hand away. "Let me see how beautiful you are." She looked deeply into his eyes and she saw that he meant it, she relaxed and let him continue.

CHAPTER
FOUR

The way he was staring at her made her hot with longing. "You're beautiful..." kiss, "Breathtaking..." kiss, "Perfect..." kiss "Voluptuous..." the longest kiss. With each kiss he was sliding down closer and closer to her cookie jar. She felt him slide the zip on her jeans open and he slid them down slowly yet so easily like he was peeling her open. This seduction thing was killing her softly. She wanted him. He knew she wanted him. But he wanted to explore all of her. Jehovah! He was sucking on her labia. He was really taking his time licking and sucking so thoroughly she felt her insides quiver. He remembered all her weak points, his stub of a beard was brushing against the insides of her thighs. She tried closing her legs when she couldn't take it anymore but he held them apart and he drank from her cookie jar. She felt the orgasm coming and she tried to move aside but he kept sucking and teasing until she couldn't hold back anymore. She came in his mouth, shuddering and groaning. He didn't stop sucking till the last of her orgasm shivers stopped. Then he looked her straight in the eye. His eyes had changed to a stormy grey and she knew he wanted her. To hell with this, she wasn't going to be subjected to this torture anymore. She shoved him on the cushions and ripped off his clothes with an urgency he found exciting if the bulging in his underwear was any testimony. She removed that too and his manhood was pulsing and ready as steel for her. She didn't have the time for pleasantries so she straddled him and his groans said he loved her aggression. She was in control now. She rode him increasing her tempo and he was grunting like an animal. He was grabbing her arse like it was his lifeline and his breathing was much nosier. He was closing his eyes but she wanted him looking at her, seeing him tortured as much as he had tortured her. But he wasn't taking it lying down. The next moment she was lying on her back, her legs on his shoulders and he was pumping into her. He came in three strokes and she came with him. She had never had an orgasm that long in her life and it left her shaking. He was cradling her on his chest and she was trying to catch her breath. His heartbeat was also erratic. Talk about working out. He kissed the top of her head. It was a long time before she could talk, "You never told me what you were doing in Cape Town." He laughed that low sexy laugh only Jarred could pull off. "Not quite the raving review I was hoping for." He drew her even closer to him, "I was there on business. I want to expand the hotel chain and I had to come personally to see the deal through."

"Wait so you are the chairperson of the Twelve Apostle chain?"

"How did you know?"

"A nosy bell-boy. Don't ask. So what's the deal you want to see through?"

"Building another Twelve Apostle hotel, maybe in Durban this time."

"That could take years…"

"Actually I'm going to be done in three months." He said it with such arrogant confidence, Mpumi cringed. This was a new side of Jarred she didn't know, a ruthless side she wasn't sure she liked. She had known him before he had taken over the reins of the family business. Joe was always going to be in charge so Jarred had been the easy going charmer that he had been since he had saved her life in Cape Town. Getting a tender to open a hotel as huge or upmarket as the Twelve Apostles usually took a lot of negotiating through red-tape but there was nothing like the stamp of Foreign Investor to cut through that red-tape. Apartheid and slavery had never ended they had gone to private school and come back in the form of Capitalism. If it had been a black Nigerian it would have taken years but as a white investor it didn't matter even if you were from the mafia family the tender would be yours. It must be nice being a foreign investor, Mpumi thought scathingly. "Why?" he asked, oops she had thought out loud. "All you have to say is jump and all we ask is how high." She said.

"Surely you can't blame me for your own system?" They were getting into a fight, Jarred noted that not wanting to cork block himself he changed tact. "Business talk is tedious, and I need a huge favor from you." Her silence meant he should go on, "I will be tied up in meetings for the next four days so I won't have time to look after Lola. Can you please look after her?"

CHAPTER
FOUR

"But she doesn't even know me! And we are going to Mozambique for the last lag of our safari." "I've already arranged for her to go with you." The arrogant certainty in his voice!

"Without even asking me first, really Jarred?" Whenever she said his name in that particular tone it never ended well, "Look I know it was presumptuous of me Lelo but I can't leave her alone or entrust her on a stranger. I really need you on this one babe." His forehead was pressed against hers and he was looking at her with sad puppy eyes, "Please?" She sighed, he knew how to tick all her boxes. He was already kissing his way down her body.

"You're not playing fair here. You are not going to bribe me with sex..." her voice was already taking on a hoarse fiber. He looked at her with a mischievous glint in his eye and she knew she had lost to him. He kissed the sensitive area just behind her ear and she was moaning, "Yeeeeees."

"Thanks babe I knew I could count on you," he grinned wickedly. She hadn't been agreeing to anything, he had tricked her and she didn't care she wanted him. So she kissed him and shut him up. He was the one groaning as she lengthened the kiss. He was her weakness and he knew it.

CHAPTER FIVE

"Tell me again why we are stuck being babysitters on ***my*** dream vacation?" Mpumi rolled her eyes, she wasn't going to hear the end of this. They were waiting for Jarred and Lola to come so that they would be on their way. Nomusa had been whining ever since she told her that Lola would be joining them. Never mind that Mpumi had paid for the whole trip, the drama queen here would just have to be strong. "He must be more amazing in the sack than I thought." Mpumi wasn't going to dignify that comment with any response. She knew Nomusa was fishing but she wasn't in the mood to kiss and tell. She was nervous. Besides Oyama she didn't really have much experience when it came to teenagers. When Oyama's friends were sleeping over she generally avoided them. Yes she loved Oyama to destruction but she wasn't a very maternal person or an outgoing one at that. She had overheard some junior staff calling her an uptight snob and she owned up to it. Yes she was ruthless when it came to negotiating multi-billion dollar contracts, she could stare down any man or woman for that matter. But she was shit scared of a teenage girl. So what happened if Lola didn't like her and they had to spend the next four days together? She felt like a new makoti trying to impress in-laws on the first meeting. Only she already had in-laws and they hated her. They called her The Harvard wife because according to them she acted like she was too good for their family because she had an Ivy League degree. There was a knock on the door. Pheeew it was time to go. Mpumi picked up her case and went to open the door. He had that mischievous glean to his eye and even when he was greeting Nomusa he kept his eyes on her. She was blushing so she turned her focus to Lola. The girl was not at all what Mpumi had expected. "You're so beautiful." She hadn't meant to say that out loud but the girl took her breath away. Lola dimpled at her compliment, "And you are the woman in the picture." Picture? Mpumi turned a puzzled look to Jarred who was suddenly avoiding her eye. The girl went on, "The picture daddy keeps in his wallet. Show her daddy." Was that a blush she spotted on his cheeks? Mpumi was intrigued so was Nomusa and they all waited for him to produce the picture. Looking uncomfortable, Jarred took out his wallet and handed Mpumi the picture. Nomusa was also all eyes. The picture had been taken at the beach it was a face portrait she had been laughing at something and she seemed so pretty and carefree. She had had braids on, it had been summer vacation and they had been tearing the beach up. She hadn't known that such a picture existed. Jarred snatched the picture from her and put it back in his wallet. He still wouldn't meet her eye and that wasn't like him at all. "It's time for you ladies to go, I have back to back meetings," he said kissing Lola on the forehead, "and you young lady behave for your mother here, ok?" While Mpumi was still shocked by what he had just said he kissed her smack on the lips and just like that he was gone leaving an awkward silence behind. Nomusa's eyes said she had a lot of questions and Mpumi was glad that Lola was there with them. The flight to Mozambique was just an hour from there and they would take a short chopper ride to Benguerra Island.

On their flight, Mpumi couldn't help looking at Lola. She had expected a blue-eyed blonde girl but Lola was far from that. She was a Latino with long curly honey brown hair, strangely her eyes were a sparkling green almost emerald in color. She had the longest lashes and they framed her big cat eyes. She had dimples and full pink lips which formed a perfect pout. Though her body was still that of a teenage girl you could just tell that she was going to have a killer body with a perfect Kardashian butt. She caught Mpumi looking at her and she smiled, her smile was easy and warm. She wasn't bubbly and loud like Oyama but she was also easy to love in her own down to earth way. "You must look like your mother because you look nothing like your father." The dimples again, "Daddy Jarred says so, I never knew her or my father. They were involved in a car accident while my mother was pregnant with me. My father died on the spot but my mother held on even though she was in a coma. They took me out through C-section. Daddy said she held on till she heard my first cry then she let go. I was premature I had to stay in the hospital for two months." Mpumi was shocked, Jarred had told her about the accident but she had assumed it had happened recently. That meant that Jarred had raised this girl from birth. Knowing him he had been with her even in the intensive care unit. Her heart went out to him, it couldn't have been easy after losing his brother. Then having to step in and father the girl while taking over the family company. "How old are you Lola?"

"I'm turning 15 on October the 15th" Wow, she was almost the same age as Oyama. "I have a daughter about your age her name is Oyama."

"Daddy told me about her, he said she is a beautiful Frankenstein." Mpumi couldn't help but smile that sounded like something Jarred would say. "I think the two of you will get along just fine." Mpumi was loving talking to this soft-spoken girl. Nomusa wasn't butting into their conversation but Mpumi knew she was filing away comments for later. "I can't wait to meet her, besides daddy there really haven't been a lot of people in my life. I struggle to make friends." Mpumi felt they had that in common, "What about your grandmother?"

she asked. Lola shrugged her elegant shoulders, "Mima never liked me much. She said it was a pity I looked nothing like her son. I also think she hated my name. I was named after you, you know." Why hadn't Mpumi figured it out? Lelo. Lola. Nomusa had that look on her face like she was hearing local umgosi, she was finding all this fascinating. Mpumi was grateful for her silence, she loved her friend but Nomusa suffered from Foot in Mouth disease. She had a talent of saying the most outrageous things. "Yeah she never liked me too, pumpkin." Lola looked tired and Mpumi remembered that she was in recovery from pneumonia. She reached over and reclined her seat till the girl was sleeping comfortably. She took a small wrap and covered her with it. "Do you need to take any medication?"

"I already took it." She yawned and her voice sounded sleepy, Mpumi let her rest only brushing her lips on Lola's forehead. Nomusa had that look on her face that said she was thinking really hard and Mpumi ignored her. ***"Why did you tell her I'm her mother?"*** she texted Jarred. "Because you are going to be her mother." Response. He was really frustrating at times. ***"I'm married to someone else Jarred, you shouldn't confuse a child like that."*** She had to remind him. ***"In a meeting now, talk later."*** Coward. Another text came in, ***"I love you Lelo."*** She was just going to ignore him.

"Chomma you are in too deep." Mpumi sighed she knew that but hearing Nomusa say it made her worry more. They had arrived at Benguerra Island Lodge, Lola had still been groggy so she was sleeping and Nomusa had taken the chance to pounce at her. Mpumi had had to upgrade their room to the family villa because they just couldn't share a single bed anymore. That had been done quickly and discreetly and they had settled Lola in then taken off to talk. They were walking on the beach, there were palm trees along the beach and it was breath taking. Mpumi wasn't paying much attention to the scenic view she was worried about what Nomusa had pointed out. "I know you thought this was a holiday fling but blue-eyed Adonis isn't on the same page with you. To think he kept your picture all these years, in his wallet chomma no less. And to name his daughter after you! It's like something from the script of a telenovela you know those ones on Telemundo." Only this wasn't some cheesy sitcom, it was her life. It had been easier thinking that she was the only one who still carried a torch for him and that he was only acting on the passion that was between them. Knowing that he had loved her over the years too changed everything, it made her heart break. Nomusa was comfortable to do all the talking, "And that child of his is too beautiful, she looks like a doll with those witch eyes. And that figure, she even has a butt!" According to Nomusa all white women had no butts either they were totally flat or they had butt implants. "She isn't totally white Nono, she is also half-Latino."

"So Donald Trump is going to be deporting her soon, is that why she is here? She's been deported?" Sigh.

"No, she is Latino not a Mexican immigrant. She's an American citizen, she could be of Spanish descent or Latin or Greek. And she is here because her doctor said she needs to breath in a different climate"

"Well she looks like a Mexican to me. And that hair! I could ask her to cut it then I have it custom made into my own Brazilian wig." That Foot in Mouth disease was out in full force. "But seriously Mpumi, what are you going to do? Adonis loves you and you love him but then there's Daniel and Oyama. It's a true Romeo and Juliet story." Nomusa had to start reading these books if she was hell-bent on making comparisons. But she had a point, Mpumi had found herself in a love triangle. On the one hand though Daniel had hurt her deeply, she did care about him and their family. On the other she had come to realize and accept that Jarred was the love of her life and being with him felt like the right thing. If only it were so simple. Nothing was ever easy for her. "I don't know Nono, I don't know."

"I like Jarred," Big surprise there, Mpumi rolled her eyes. "No hear me out Mpumi. I like him because of who you become when you are with him. You smile a lot. You laugh. You drink wine and you are like a carefree young woman. I haven't heard you once complain about carbs or your diet. You should see yourself you are literally shining from within. Now you know me and Daniel don't get along. I think he's your safe bet, even though he cheats it doesn't shatter you as it would if it was Jarred cheating. Daniel is the sensible choice, you have a family together it's logical that you keep your family together. But Jarred is risky because he's the one person who has the power to hurt you. You should have seen yourself when he didn't call or text, you were a wreck, you went from worrying to angry to scared." Mpumi sighed it didn't help much when Nomusa was making sense and being very observant. Jarred was a risk she was scared to take. Nomusa was also right, Jarred alone had the power to crush her. There was something allconsuming about their love. "Let's go back, Lelo might wake up and think we have deserted her."

They found Lola still fast asleep. She only woke up around midday complaining of hunger. That was a sign of recovery. After bathing and eating she joined them on the beach bed just outside their villa. She was looking around like she couldn't believe her eyes. "This is like a little piece of paradise. It's not exactly how I pictured Africa."

"How did you picture Africa?" Nomusa asked. Lola suddenly looked embarrassed, "I don't know but I watched The Good Lie." Mpumi and Nomusa laughed, this kid was cute. "That movie was unfortunate, it does show a side of Africa but not the whole picture and I think they exaggerated for effect."-Mpumi

"What she means is that The Good Lie is a lie, we are not some uncivilized people who don't know how to turn on a light switch."-Nomusa

"I also didn't understand why the other guy was wearing the Just Do It t-shirt he was given at the refugee camp when they were kids when he was now a doctor"-Lola. Nomusa seemed to love this comment and just like that Lola had been accepted by Nomusa.

"What do you do for a living?"-Lola

CHAPTER
FIVE

"I design websites at an IT company in Parktown."-Nomusa

"And I am the Company Secretary of an Investment group in Randburg. I also lecture Corporate Law part-time at Wits University."-Mpumi

"But daddy said you studied for your MBA with him."-Lola seemed puzzled.

"Yes I did. But the Company Secretary isn't really anyone's secretary in the traditional sense. I am also a shareholder. I notify board members of incoming board meetings. Help in the drafting of the yearly budget. I largely deal with the legal issues in the group among other things."Mpumi Lola nodded her understanding. The kid seemed fascinated by Mpumi's cornrows, "Who did your hair?" Nomusa was smirking and Mpumi ignored her, "I did." Lola also wanted her hair to be plaited so Mpumi fetched her combs and started plaiting her. She had only ever plaited her own her and Oyama's hair, Lola's hair was softer and silky but it tangled easily. "Before I went to saloons my dad used to do my hair." Mpumi was surprised she couldn't imagine Jarred combing this unruly mass of hair. "But surely you had some female or another around from time to time?" Mpumi was fishing, she couldn't explain why she wanted to know and why a picture of another woman playing mother with Jarred's daughter made her feel so jealous. "No actually, mostly it's just been me and daddy. Mima didn't come around much and he never introduced me to any of his girlfriends. I never had a governess."That somehow made Mpumi feel warm inside, gosh she needed to get a grip. At least Nomusa was engrossed in her phone, she would have made some snide remark.

Their days at the beach flew as fast as those days when everything is perfect and you don't want it to end. Mpumi and Lola went snorkeling, Nomusa was not stepping anywhere near the ocean where there might be sharks lurking around. But she did agree to go horseback riding on the beach the pictures just blew up her Instagram. Mpumi had a gift when it came to taking pictures. Suddenly people who hadn't been talking to her in ages where talking to her, "Girl is that you?" that seemed to be the question on their minds. It was amazing what one could achieve with filter these days. Mpumi thought she was too old for these social media platforms but Mpumi had always been stuck up. Amo had also been bugging her about social media, why was she on snap chat, why were most of her followers male, why did she post pictures of herself in a bikini like she would wear a maxi dress to the beach. That Lola girl was adorable and she had shown her how to take selfies that were the 'bomb'. Now that Tswana man was all up in her business acting like he owned her. He wanted to know what she was doing at every point of the day. If she didn't text him back quickly enough he became whiny and insecure. Why were men so sensitive and clingy nowadays? They acted like it was them who had the hormones and menstruation. She wasn't used to a man who paid her that much attention. Most of the guys she dated forgot about her until when they wanted to fuck her. Why couldn't he be like most men, he was too interested in her web designs, in her family life, he wanted pictures of where she was, video calls and voice calls. He wanted to be her profile picture as she was his. If there was any such thing he loved her too much. Nomusa felt too loved and she was panicking, she kept waiting for the other shoe to drop. Jarred's Mexican girl seemed interested in web designs and Nomusa could just feel Mpumi's mind locking that information away. Her friend had fallen in love with that green-eyed girl and Nomusa was dreading the end of their safari. Mpumi was glowing. There was no better word to describe her. She was eating chocolate cake on their picnics and swallowing it down with wine. Nomusa always wondered why Mpumi had weight issues. True she wasn't tiny but she wasn't exactly a big girl either. She was curvy, attractively so. Like at that moment Mpumi was in a skimpy peach bikini, her curves were on fire and instead of darkening her it became her. She hadn't wanted to buy it but Nomusa had insisted. The cornrows Nomusa had been laughing at made her look ten years younger and she was laughing as she was having a water fight with Lola. Nomusa watched them from the comfort of the beach bed. African air was doing a world of good to Lola her skin had a golden glow to it and those plaits made her look like a doll. She still couldn't understand how the child had such a perfect butt. The two of them were cute out there in the ocean, Nomusa decided to take pictures of them without them knowing. Ping! ***"When am I seeing you again?"*** Ping! ***"I miss you so much, I want to be with you every day."*** Ping! ***"Are you ignoring me?"*** Ping! ***"Are you mad at me baby?"*** Ping! ***"Baby buwa lena tlhee."*** Sigh, now she couldn't even enjoy sleeping on the beach in peace. She wasn't going to respond to any of his messages, Amo just had to give her some air to breathe. She had just put the phone down when it started ringing. It was him. She put it on silent and let it go to voicemail. "I love Africa!" the Mexican was shouting at the ocean, shame man let her get mugged at Bree Taxi rank or hustled at Hilbrow she would be screaming a different tune.

Too soon it was their last night in Mozambique. Mpumi had loved every minute of it. She went to check on Lola when she came from her bath. The little angel was resting peacefully her long lashes resting on her chin. Funny even when she was sleeping the dimples were there. Mpumi had expected her to be a spoilt brat but though Lola clearly had Jarred under her little finger, she was well-mannered and kind. She also loved the water and the camera just loved her. Mpumi tiptoed out of Lola's room to her own. Oyama would be home the next morning and Mpumi would only be home in the evening. Daniel would just have to deal with buying her school things, she was after all his daughter. Funny how eleven breath-taking days could change one's outlook. She hadn't opened a single email since she had been on holiday. Whatever crisis was there at work she was sure they would survive it without her. Mpumi still had problems but she was calm now. She didn't feel like bursting into tears every time she thought of Daniel and his silence didn't even bother her. She wasn't looking forward to going back to reality. After switching off the lights Mpumi took off her night gown and settled under covers. She was glad she didn't have to share the bed with Nomusa. She always ended up squashed on one side of the bed while Nomusa terrorized the rest of the bed. It was peaceful here, she would bring Oyama here next holidays. She felt someone slide into the bed and cover her mouth with a hand. God! She couldn't be abducted now! Then she could smell his woody-musky scent and she relaxed in his arms. He turned her around and kissed her deeply. When he finally let her come up for air, she punched him lightly on the chest. "Don't ever scare me like that again!" he flashed his teeth at her in the darkness, "I see I was deeply missed by my beautiful muse."

"You aren't even an artist…No Jarred we can't have sex in here they will hear us. Come on lets go outside." He moved reluctantly from sucking her breast and quickly rushed her outside and laid her down on the beach bed. "How did you even get…?" He shut her up with a kiss old school style. She only got to talk when he was satiated. "We really should stop doing this."

"Why? You don't enjoy making love to me mi amour?" Mpumi laughed, his French impression was really bad. "I do enjoy it but we have to stop jumping on each other the moment we are left alone. Like two mature adults."

"I can't promise that. You are too irresistible. Especially here under the stars. Your eyes are shining." How is it that he said the corniest shit with such sincerity and it spoke to her soul? Never in her wildest dreams had she ever thought she would be making love on a beach bed out in the open where anyone could just walk across them. If only her mother could see her now. He shifted and sat up facing her. She could feel that he had suddenly become serious. "Lelo you have to leave him." Here we go, she sighed.

"I can't just leave him Jarred, he's my husband I promised to stick by him till death do us part. We have a daughter."

"Dammit Lelo, the man raped you for Christ sake!"

"He is my husband he can sleep with me whenever and however he wants."

"Stop defending him. You of all people know the law, marital rape is..."

"Whose law? The Roman-Dutch law? My culture states that a woman should never deprive her husband his conjugal rights he is entitled to this vagina. So don't tell me what the law say."

"I don't give a flying fuck what your culture says. He..."

"Wow. There it is finally. Now listen to me Jarred, just because you have been fucking me all of five minutes doesn't give you the right to bully me culturally. Daniel is my husband and this is my life so butt the fuck out of it!" They were both shouting now, he ran a hand through his hair, the way he did every time he got frustrated. He looked like he was holding back the urge to shake her. "No Lelo, you listen to me and don't interrupt me. I don't care what your culture or what the law say. He hurt you. And I will never forgive myself for not being there to protect you. I should have come after you but I let my stupid pride get in the way. Now you are stuck in a marriage where your husband has treated you in the most degrading manner. He violated you and yet you are still defending him. How do you think that makes me feel? Should I wave you goodbye to suffer more pain? Tell me what do you expect me to do when you are ripping my heart into shreds!" his voice was raw with emotion and when he got to the last syllable it cracked. Mpumi couldn't stand his pain, she drew him into her embrace. At first he was cold and unreceptive. She rubbed his back then he finally broke down. He was crying. This man who loved her so dearly was crying and it was her fault. She held him and they cried together. She held him till his tears had dried. Sometime during their fight they had stood up. Now she led him back to the beach bed and they lay there cuddling. "We just had a naked screaming match on the beach. We can tick that off our bucket list." She was talking softly now almost in a whisper. The beginning of a smile touched his lips. He was still feeling low. "I know it doesn't make sense to you Jarred but I need to go back to him. I need to face him and work out things my way. God knows I want to stay with you here in the beach making love, running around, fighting with you. But I need to do this." She was pleading with him to understand and he looked her straight in the eye. "I've waited for you for sixteen years Lelo and I can wait for you a little longer. Please don't make me wait forever." There wasn't any anger in his voice or pain, his voice only held promise. Then why did she feel as if someone had stabbed her straight in the heart?

Nomusa had been surprised to wake up and find blue-eyed Adonis in their midst but she had learnt not to ask. Something was going on with those two. They were very clingy today yet Mpumi couldn't look him in the eye. Lola was plying her dad about all the adventures they had and he laughed and smiled but he didn't seem like his ordinary self. Again Nomusa wasn't going to ask. She had problems of her own. Amogalang wanted her to move to Cape Town. Now he was sulking because she had refused flatly to do so. She had a career! It might not be as lucrative as his but she was not about to become that woman who let her dreams go to sit and hold her man's hand. If he wanted to be so close to her, he should move to Jozi. But he was hearing none of that. Men! Zizinja shame, it was always their way or the high way. She was a grown arse woman if he didn't like it he could go to hell for all she cared. But there lay her problem. She cared. A lot. He treated her like a Tswana queen ought to be treated. Even Instagram wasn't cheering her up today. They were going on a last picnic but the vibe up in that place you would swear it was the last supper. Jarred held the picnic basket in one hand and he had his other hand wrapped around Mpumi. Those two should seriously get a room and they seemed to be forgetting that she and Lola were with them. Lola fell in step with her and Nomusa was surprised how easy it was to talk to her. She had a maturity which Oyama lacked. Both of them were spoiled brats but Lola was street smart where Oyama was book smart. The picnic was in some remote island and Nomusa had a feeling that they should have just let the lovebirds come out here alone. Thankfully they didn't stay there long. They had to go back and pack. Their flight was at 4pm. When they were saying their goodbyes Jarred held Mpumi for the longest time like he didn't want to let her go. There were tears in Mpumi's eyes even when she was kissing Lola goodbye. Nomusa looked away. It felt like she was watching a break-up, the sad type where there was no anger just tears. She had known their parting was going to be painful but this felt like a funeral of a favorite aunt. They were taking separate flights. Mpumi and Nomusa were headed to Joburg while Jarred and Lola were going to Cape Town. On their flight Mpumi wasn't even reading a book this time and she turned down the hostess's offer of wine. Nomusa knew she didn't want to talk about what had gone down between her and Jarred. Nomusa was fine with that, she wanted to talk about the Amo situation, Mpumi was the most independent career oriented woman she knew, surely she would understand. Mpumi listened as she told her what Amo wanted and what she wanted. Mpumi had that you won't like what I'm about to tell you but I'm going to tell you anywhere look on her face. "You can easily apply for another job in Cape Town, you would actually be closer to your family. But you can't expect him to uproot his whole Haulage truck business to Joburg. He has a client base and employees to consider."

"But I'm in line for a promotion at my current company! Relocating will set back my career. What if I don't find a job there?"

"With your qualifications and experience you will easily find another job maybe one that even pays better. What's your real reason for not wanting to move to Cape Town?"

"I can't just up and leave because a man likes me now, what happens when he jilts me all the way there in Cape Town and you are in Joburg? You and Oyama are the closest family I have."

"That's still not completely it I can just tell. Talk to me Nomusa."

"There's also the thing about him not having even a Matric certificate. You know men are easily intimidated by women who are smarter than them. What if he feels threatened and it doesn't work out?" Mpumi sighed in a way that Nomusa was accustomed to. It meant that she was about to get deep. "First of all just because you have a degree and he doesn't, it doesn't mean you are smarter than him. Secondly as long as you respect and love him he will never have to feel intimidated or threatened by you. Nono not every guy is out there to jilt you. Amogalang is not Nhlalo. He is not a phuthu eating Zulu. That Tswana guy loves you. I know you love your career but is that enough? I know you put the gloss on single life but is it what you really want? You are turning thirty nine this year and I know you act like you don't like them, but I know you want children. Now you have found a decent guy who is crazy about you that he wants you with him all the time. I'm not promising that he won't hurt you or that it will always be smooth but you owe it to yourself to see where this goes. I know you are scared, making a commitment with a person especially one who could potentially break your heart is scary. But right now you need to stop running. That man won't be waiting for you forever." Nomusa sighed, she hated it when Mpumi was right. She took her hand and kissed it, "Thank you chomma. I think you should take your own advice with Jarred." Mpumi didn't acknowledge her advice, she looked out the window like she was fighting back tears. It was going to be a long flight.

CHAPTER SIX

Oyama had come back in the morning. There was still no sign of Mpumi. Daniel didn't know what to make of his wife's behavior anymore. When he had made her an ultimatum and she had calmly walked out, he had been floored. Yes she was stubborn and independent but his wife had never openly defied him before. The house had been empty without Mpumi and Oyama. He had had to cancel the Save the Children event. He had expected her to call and apologize for walking out on him. But there had been no call and no text. In politics one had to know their opponent's strategy and that was how Daniel had always stayed ahead of his competition. But this wasn't politics. This was his marriage. And he had no idea what Mpumi's strategy was. Something must have happened before the New Year's Ball Gala. Something so bad that Mpumi had locked herself in their bedroom. He had tried going back to the events of that day, tried to think of what he could have said or done wrong. He had come to a blank. Women should just be made with a how to handle manual, that would make our lives so much easier black Jezus. He was the first to admit that he wasn't the world's greatest husband. But dammit he was trying his darn best. Why couldn't she appreciate that? Mpumi was so fixated on his mistakes. He wasn't proud of sleeping with those other women. They meant nothing to him why couldn't she see that? He was a man. Yes he was weak however he loved his wife and respected her, he always made sure he covered his tracks. And he always came home to her. But that wasn't enough for her, she had to go digging and throwing a fit when she found something she didn't like. She had wanted them to go to see a marriage counsellor or a therapist. That shit was for white people, if they had problems she should talk to him. God knows he had tried talking to her but she shut him out. Now their daughter needed stuff for school and she was out there prancing around with that loud mouth friend of hers acting like a single woman. Oyama was looking at him like he should know what to do. Mpumi always took care of these things what was he supposed to do. Sigh. He might as well go buy the stuff. "Where is your list of school things?" The girl looked frightened of him, "I don't know Tata, and mama always keeps the list." He wasn't about to call Mpumi and ask for her help, he would rather look through her stuff. Mpumi's study was simplistic and organized like its owner. There wasn't a pen out of place and the papers were organized in alphabetical order. There were those little stickers she put around the house, reminders, duties, motivational quotes and to-do lists. She even organized his underwear and ties for each suit. He missed his wife but he didn't know what to do to make things right. The miscarriages hadn't made things any easier. He felt guilty that he saw her in pain yet there was nothing he could do. Daniel wasn't a very demonstrative person, he didn't know how to comfort her. There was a picture of their wedding day on her desk. She had been looking up at him with such a big smile. There was another one of him holding Oyama, it had been taken in front of their first house in Mondeo. She had been so excited when they bought that house. Those had been simple times. Happy times. But Daniel had always felt like he came second to her. Like he was her rebound guy and that hurt. Oyama was standing at the door staring at him. He realized that he was still holding their wedding photo and he put it down. "Mama e-mailed me the list Tata." His little girl was grown up, around him she was a bit reserved but with Mpumi she was bubbly and childish. Mpumi had always been pressuring him to spend more time with her. He couldn't make up for the missed hockey tournaments or ballet rehearsals and those swimming galas. But he could be here for her today. "Grab your things Oyama, we're going shopping."

Daniel had taken out his latest baby for a joyride. It was a Lamborghini Gallardo LP560-4 it was part of the Lamborghini Exclusive Series and he was smitten. It felt great to be behind the wheel and feel the car purr softly as he drove out of his gate. He hated being chauffer driven but it was more practical as often times he had to be briefed just before he made a speech or he had to go through what he had written. There was also the occasional car sex, fortunately once he shut the panel his driver could see or hear nothing. Not that his wife would ever agree to have car sex, she was the uptight kind so he got kinky with other women. He loved the finer things in life, like the R250 000 Gucci watch he had on his wrist. Daniel had never really been a sports kind of guy but he watched sports to get something to talk about with other men besides politics. He did love cars especially the sleek and powerful sports cars. Mpumi hadn't been too impressed when he had come home in the red Lamborghini, she said he was a Minister not a flashy football player. She didn't understand his need to get the best and latest of everything. To say that growing up money had been tight in his family was an understatement. His father had come from a powerful family but they disowned him the moment he had chosen his mother to be his wife. His mother had been a Shangaan from Maputo and the family had expected a Xhosa wife who would be advantageous to their political lives so they washed their hands on Daniel's family. His father hadn't been used to the low income lifestyle so he had turned to alcohol. He had been a raging alcoholic who had spent every weekly wage on the white beer that he bought illegally. To this day Daniel hated alcohol and he never touched it. His mother had been the hardworking type, so she had had to take on two to three jobs to keep their family afloat. The raising of them had been left to his older sister Phindiwe. She had always pushed him more than the other children, she spurred him to do his schoolwork. She always said he was their ticket out of that life. Her efforts had paid off when his uncle had taken him under his wing when he had graduated from university with a law degree and another degree in Political Science. Thankfully back then tertiary education had been free, they were actually paid to go to university. He had sent money home to get them out of that hell-hole in Alexander. Remembering the dingy shack they had called home for so many years still gave him nightmares. But Phindiwe had made it all bearable, yes she was a bully but she had made him into the man he was. So even when she called demanding this and that for those bastard nephews of his, he never complained. He gave her everything and anything she wanted. The ride was too quiet, Oyama kept looking at him as if he was going to bite. "What do you think of my new ride?" he asked to break the awkward silence. "It's impressive Tata. I can't make up my mind on a favorite between the Hurican and the Aventador." Daniel was pleasantly surprised. The child knew her Lamborghinis, she was definitely his daughter. He had thought she had inherited nothing from him. Oyama looked like her. Her mannerisms were mostly from Mpumi and she was the booky type always with her nose behind a book. He was happy that she had taken something from him, "I can't wait for the Super Trofeo Asia Series Season to start. My PA got me two tickets, would you like to go with your old man Oyama?" The look on her face! She looked so happy her whole face lit up. Then she seemed to remember something and her face fell. "What's the matter?"

"It's just that I don't want to be too excited then when something comes up Tata like it always does I'm going to be disappointed." He really had messed up as a father. He had been so focused on not being a man like his father that he had ended up neglecting his child like his father had neglected them. He had worked hard to put Oyama in the school she was in and to make sure she had all she could ever need financially. In the process he had deprived her of a father-daughter relationship. He held her hand and she looked at his hand over hers in surprise. "I promise we will go together this time nana. You're going to have a date with your father. I promise." This was one promise he intended to keep. She looked him in the eyes looking for assurance and she seemed to believe him. Then she relaxed and her face became animated again. She began asking him questions about cars. Her knowledge was deeper than he would expect for a fourteen year old. He had to lie here and there so he wouldn't lose face in front of his daughter. She hung to his every word. Daniel was glad he had taken the time to come and shop with her. Father and daughter were finally bonding.

Daniel wasn't a fan of shopping. If Mpumi had been with them she would have wanted to go store by store comparing prices and quality. She was careful about money. You could just see the wheels turning in her head calculating every cost. He had been surprised that she had even gone on a safari and when he looked at their financial records it hadn't come from his bank account or their joint account. She must have paid for it from her own account. He appreciated that she knew the value of money, she had forced him into almost all his investments and though he hated to admit it they had turned out to be very lucrative investments. She was controlling but he trusted her with his money. Oyama didn't seem to be too keen on shopping either. To make both their lives easier Daniel asked for the manager in the very first store they entered into. The man magically appeared as if he had been lingering quite close to them. To this man he was a Minister and the manager seemed hell bent to impress him. He handed over the list to the manager, "Please get us everything on that list. Make sure everything is from the top brands. I want only the best of everything."

The man scurried along to do his bidding. There seemed to be a host of shop workers at their attendance. One showed Daniel where to sit while the others fussed over Oyama. Luckily their school uniforms were sold exclusively at their school. So they only had to buy school shoes and Alice bands and other ridiculous things on that list. Daniel sat back and watched his daughter being fitted for shoes. One sales rep was busy taking down notes on Oyama's favorite colors and one seemed to be trying to gauge if parsley went well with her complexion. Daniel could just feel Oyama's irritation from where he sat. Mpumi had done a good job raising his daughter. Although she babied her a lot, she had taught her to say please and thank you. She wasn't too self-absorbed. In record time the things on the list had been packed and he had produced his black card. He asked for the things to be delivered to their house and they left the shop. The things power gave to one. Next they had to go to Oyama's stylist for her hair and manicure. These BEE children of theirs. But Daniel was happy that she seemed so happy.

They were now at the stylist, Daniel had expected a woman but it was a man. He didn't want any man touching his precious princess. Then he noticed that the stylist was gay so he relaxed. Oyama wanted a weave but that wasn't what was on her list. She was supposed to plait braids. Feeling benevolent and wanting to get back at Mpumi he told the stylist to use the best weave they had. He sat down to wait for her. He had never gone with a woman to do her hair, it took up too much of his valuable time but taking Oyama felt right. He had a lot of time to kill and nothing to do. All the magazines there were fashion magazines. People kept giving him judgmental looks and he felt like explaining that Oyama was his daughter not his mistress. He remembered the day he had first met Nompumelelo Ndinisa as she had introduced herself to him. The one word which had fully described her was regal. Even in her shabby clothes with no make-up, Mpumi had held herself as if she were the Queen of England. She wasn't very welcoming and had an invisible sign written Keep Out. He had been intrigued. Mpumi wasn't like most

of the girls who kept the clothes they came with from home locked in their suitcases while they paraded around in clothes bought for them by their sugar daddies. They now called them Blessers but the concept was the same. And those college girls were easily persuaded to open their legs. In one of his not so proud moments Daniel had also dated a college girl. She saw the car and he took her to a costly bar by her standards but which was a tiny drop which barely
left a dent on his bank account. Within two days he had slept with her, when he thought about it now it actually made him sad. One day that could be his Oyama. But Mpumi had been that girl that you just knew you wouldn't mess around with. The kind of girl you introduced to your family. The girl you kissed and held hands with while you secretly nursed your blue balls or fucked a whore on the side. Daniel had been tempted to take her virginity many a time but something about her made him hold back. Then she had gone to Harvard. When she came back sobbing that she couldn't marry him anymore because a white asshole had gotten her pregnant, he felt disillusioned. She didn't want to talk about him so he had deduced that the white pig had done a hit and run stint on his girl. He had never felt a bigger fool. He had respected her wish to wait till marriage and yet she had opened her legs to the first white guy who had shown her any slight interest. The Mpumi he had put on a pedestal, his Mpumi didn't exist, she was just like every other girl. He had been hurt. A male ego doesn't heal from that. Its one thing for your girl to cheat but for her to lose her virginity to the other guy and come back carrying his brat was devastating. There was no way he could pass off the bastard as his. That had been his dilemma, Mpumi had betrayed him in the worst possible way but he loved her still. Then his problem had disappeared and he got to hold her while she cried and she finally gave herself to him. In the throes of his passion, while he was grunting and huffing on top of her, he had heard her call out the pig's name. He had pretended that he hadn't heard her. Oyama was done with her hair and nails. She twirled around for her dad to see. Mpumi had been right to forbid the weaves, it made her look older and mature.

The damage was already done. All he could say was, "You look beautiful my princess." Firmly refusing the stylist's offer to give him a haircut on the house, Daniel led Oyama out of the saloon. Not wanting their quality time to come to an end, Daniel suggested they go for lunch at the family favorite restaurant Mimo's.

Daniel had settled for Buffalo wings in barbeque sauce with fries while Oyama had chosen Chicken mayo pizza. He had to order more wings because his daughter kept eating his portion as well. Daniel couldn't remember the last time she had been so comfortable around him. Guess it was true that a girl always looked up to her father as her model of an ideal man. But Daniel knew that the number of women sexually abused by their fathers kept rising. No wonder so many women hated men. How could you begin to love any man when your ideal man was an incestuous rapist? Daniel had done a lot of things he wasn't proud about but the thing he could never forgive himself for was when he had forced himself on Mpumi. She had wanted to leave him and he had panicked, if she ever left him he would probably kill himself. She had looked at him with that frightened look that he had seen on his mother countless times when his father had come home drunk and beat her at the slightest provocation. He had always felt helpless, he couldn't protect her. But then one day the old man fell on his way home from the beerhall, he hit his head on a rock and he died. His body had been found the next day by a vendor who had come back from stocking his products. Daniel hadn't felt sorry that his father was dead. When he had seen that look on Mpumi's face he had wanted to wrap himself around her and say, "I'm sorry I will protect you." But how could he protect her from his own demons. Since that incident he hadn't been able to bring himself to touch her again. He couldn't trust himself. They slept in separate bedrooms now. "Tata what's wrong?" She must have seen the self-loathing on his face. "Nothing my princess, let's go and grab some ice-cream before going home." Leaving a couple of notes on the table, he took her hand and they left. He shouldn't be thinking of the past when he was with her. He lay awake being tormented by his demons every day. Now being with Oyama made him want to make amends with his wife. He would apologize, beg if he had to and probably take her to Dubai or anywhere she wanted to go. He had a lot to make up for. He wanted to be a better husband and a better father moving forward. Today he would focus on his daughter. She was talking of her camp. "It was so much fun Tata wish you had been there. Mama came to see my hockey tournament." She had? Daniel had no idea where Mpumi's safari was and he was ashamed to admit that. "When was that Oyama?"

"The day after she left home. She came with her friend Jarred. He knows a lot about hockey. I liked him Tata, he took us out to lunch. Then we met up with aunt Nomusa. I was sad when I had to go back to camp."

Daniel didn't hear a single word she said after Jarred. What the hell? So not only was Mpumi cheating on him with the pig who had abandoned her when she was pregnant, she was blatantly going on trips with him under his very nose. No wonder she hadn't paid from their accounts probably that pig was funding the whole shagging spree. Eleven days, she had been gone eleven freaking days! But to bring him to meet his daughter? Daniel was seeing red. Oyama looked worried like she sensed she had said something she shouldn't have which had annoyed her father. Daniel had to calm himself down so that he wouldn't ruin his perfect day with his daughter. They would have their ice-cream. He would deal with her whore mother later.

Oyama had seemed content and Daniel had felt proud of himself maybe he didn't totally suck as a father. She had gone upstairs to prepare for her first day back at school and probably an early night. She had hugged him and kissed him before leaving him. That had made him feel warm inside. He loved his little girl. The moment she left he had headed to the lounge and switched off the lights and sat there waiting for his whoring wife in the dark. Mpumi had crossed the line and for the first time in his life Daniel needed a drink. A stiff one. Maybe it would numb his rage. Buried deep in the rage was hurt as well. How could Mpumi do this to him? He had given her everything he had. Had trusted her with his daughter, his money. She was probably scheming to take his money with that no good boyfriend of hers. So all these years he had felt like shit for cheating on her while she had calmly been seeing that pig behind his back. Well it ended today. He wouldn't be played the fool anymore. He heard the key turning on the door, he looked at his phone it was 8.15pm. She switched on the light in the living room and she was surprised to find him sitting there in the dark. He noticed that she had changed. She was wearing a bloody jumpsuit, it was loose and short made of that material which normally made sarongs. Her curves were on display, must have been for her boyfriend's benefit. Her hair was done farm girl style and it made her look ten years younger. She had that glow of a woman who had been deeply fucked and was satiated. "Daniel what are you doing sitting in the darkness?" Her calmness fueled his rage. "How was your trip Mpumi?"

"It was… fine. We need to talk Daniel."

"Oh did you have fun?"

"Yes it was fun. I need to talk to you."

"About what? About how you were busy fucking that pig Jarred?" she looked shocked and scared and she began walking backwards. No bitch you don't get to slither away so easily, I haven't even started with you, he thought grimly. "Talk to me Mpumi I'm listening." He was blocking her exit.

"I can't talk to you when you are like this." Her voice was shaking ever so slightly.

"When I'm like what? Do you expect me to be serenading you right now? Applauding you for best whore award?"

"It's not like that…"

"What is it like Nompumelelo? Was he good? Did he fuck you till you were trembling in his arms? Did he screw you till your knees were weak? What is it about this guy that you can't keep your panties on when he's around? Does his penis have something that mine lacks? Did you call my name when he was about to orgasm or is that treatment only specially for me?"

"Daniel please…"

"Please what Mpumi?"

"Please don't be like this. Hear me out."

"You want me to hear more lies Mpumi. You said you were done with that man when you came here carrying his bastard piglet. I forgave you Mpumi. You were promised to me yet you gave your virginity to another man. I forgave you. Damaged goods that you were I still married you. I gave you my name, I gave you my heart, I gave you my child, and I gave you my home. I gave you everything Mpumi. That wasn't enough for you, I was never good enough even when I gave you my all. And this is the thanks I get?!"

"Daniel you're hurting me!" He let go of her arms instantly and pointed her to the couch. She sat down at the edge of the couch but she looked shit-scared. Good. He went to the hidden compartment next to the couch she was sitting on and took out a gun. She looked like she was staring at death but there were no tears. He put the gun next to her and sat on the coffee table facing her. Both his legs were locking her in, she had nowhere to go, she couldn't flee. He looked her straight in the eye. "You wanted to talk to me Nompumelelo. Talk." She was a tough girl. She drew in a deep breath and started talking. She said she hadn't known she would meet Jarred in Cape Town. It had been a chance meeting he had saved her when she was bitten by a scorpion. And dancing unicorns also existed. He must look like a fool to her. It was too much of a coincidence to be true. She said meeting Jarred like that had made her realize that their marriage was a farce. Just like that, one chance meeting and eleven days of fucking she decided that sixteen years of marriage were a farce. They couldn't keep hurting each other like that, she wanted out of their marriage. "Jonga I am not an imbecile. You expect me to believe that you were drawing unicorns down there in Cape Town? I can smell that white pig all over you. So you think I'm going to let you walk away in the sunset with your pretty boy. This isn't a bloody Mills and Boon woman."

"Daniel I know that she's pregnant." She said it so calmly. Who? She was trying to trick him now. "Who is pregnant?" Mpumi took out a manila envelope from her handbag and handed it to him. It was him and Candice. He had his arm draped around her and he was kissing her. She was evidently pregnant. She was seven months along now. How had she gotten hold of these pictures? He remembered that day the pictures were taken just a day before the Ball. He looked at his wife, she still looked scared. "So you are having me followed now Mpumi? What are these for? You want to blackmail me?" She took a deep breath, "No Daniel. At first when I saw those pictures it felt like my whole world had come crushing down. I had booked that Safari to go with you to try to fix our marriage, to fix us. Then the private detective gave me those pictures. I just needed to get away. I've realized that neither of us can fix each other. We aren't broken Daniel, we are just not meant for each other. We've tried to force things but we keep hurting each other and now we have gone back to the people we have been hurting each other with. How do you think I felt when I saw her pregnant? I failed to give you a child Daniel but she does it so easily." There were tears sliding silently down her face. Daniel felt a panic attack starting and he had to control himself. He had to hurt her as badly as she was hurting him. "So that's it? He comes back into the picture and just like that you are leaving me for him. I killed that pig's baby in your womb so that you would never go back to him." He felt a weight lift off his shoulders when he blurted that out, one good hurt deserved another. She looked as if he had shot her straight in the heart. One moment she looked wounded then the next she had rage and murder in her eyes. She picked up the gun and she was pointing it at him. He wasn't scared, she had already killed parts of him she might as well finish the job. "What do you mean you killed my child?" her voice was eerily calm. "I put a pill in your juice which induced you to have a miscarriage. It was untraceable in your system." If he was dying he might as well come clean. "You selfish bastard!" she was screaming now but the gun was still steadily aimed at his brain. "I told you I could raise that child on my own. I wanted to break off the marriage. What did my baby ever do to you? But no you had to make me your wife you were probably gloating. And you know what the worst part is? You made me raise yours and Candice's child! You made me raise your child, I have loved your child all these years. I raised her like my own flesh and blood. Yet you knew, you knew you killed the one being who had meant so much to me before he even came into this world." Daniel let her rant and somewhere during the rant his anger had melted and he felt shame. He had been selfish in letting Mpumi raise Oyama when he had killed her child. But he had been fueled by a thirst for revenge. She wasn't shouting anymore but she was still talking, "The only reason I have stayed in this marriage is that child. Her father is a monster but I stayed for her. I could kill you right now but death is too kind for you. I'm leaving and I'm taking Oyama with me."

"You are not taking my child with you Mpumi, she is mine not yours."

"I have a birth certificate that says I am her mother. You had it all planned out. You bribed a nurse and used my ID to take her birth certificate. There is no way in hell you can ever tell anyone that she isn't my daughter without implicating yourself. You took the birth certificate not me. Now move out of my way." He tried to reach out to her but her glare froze his hand in mid-air. The hatred in her eyes made him coil, he loved her and now he had made her hate him. She was wrong, he was a broken man. He let her walk away the gun still in her hands. If she had left it he would have blown his brains out. He was his father's son.

CHAPTER SEVEN

Oyama had known she had made a mistake the minute the name Jarred had left her lips. Her father's face became contorted into an ugly expression. She hadn't understood why, her mother had a lot of male friends and associates and her father had never seemed to mind. She hadn't thought he was the jealous type. But then he had smiled and bought her ice cream and she thought she must have imagined that expression. She hadn't seen this side of her father in a long time. He was being so cool and she couldn't wait to go with him on their promised date. She had finished packing and prepping for the first day of school. It was the first time that she was doing this on her own without her mother. She took care not to forget anything so that her mom would be impressed. She also packed the necklace she had bought for Ryan. She just had to get the nerve to talk to him. He had sat next to her on the plane. He was chilled for a jock and
he was also funny. She had been laughing at his jokes. He also had a tattoo. Bad Boy vibes! He was seventeen but because she had skipped

grades they were in the same class. She waited for her mom to come, she had so much to tell her. She had seen pictures of them on aunt Nomusa's Instagram and Snap Chat, they were so lit Oyama was jealous. She also wanted to ask her about the girl who had been cozy with them in some of the pictures. They hadn't talked much after she saw them at her hockey match. She had only called her to ask for the list. Oyama heard voices from downstairs. Good, mama was home. She went out to go and throw herself at her mother. But when she got to the stairs she could hear her father's raised voice, it sounded menacing. She could see them when she got to the bottom of the stairs. Her father was shaking her mother and talking to her, Oyama couldn't hear what they were saying. What was she going to do? All the servants didn't stay in the house they stayed at the servants' cottages around the estate. Oyama contemplated going to take her phone upstairs so she could call 911 but what if he hurt her before the police could come. Oyama was panicking. Then he let go of Mpumi's shoulders and was pointing her to the couch. Oyama sneaked closer to the doorway. OMG! Her father was taking out a gun! There was a gun in their house! He put it next to her mother. She still couldn't hear exactly what was being said. But she could see her mother's face from where she was partly hidden. Mama looked frightened but she was trying to seem calm to her dad. What was happening? Would her parents kill each other? Oyama was scared to get into the room in case it would make her father shoot her mother. Her father was cursing a lot something about a pig but she couldn't hear her mother's responses. Whoa! Her mother was picking up the gun and pointing it at her father! This was really bad. Oyama didn't want to see anymore but she stood fixated by the scene unfolding before her very eyes. Then her mother was screaming, "You selfish bastard! I told you I could raise that child on my own. I wanted to break off the marriage. What did my baby ever do to you? But no you had to make me your wife you were probably gloating. And you know what the worst part is? You made me raise yours and Candice's child! You made me raise your child, I have loved your child all these years. I raised her like my own flesh and blood. Yet you knew, you knew you killed the one being who had meant so much to me before he even came into this world." What?! Who was Candice? Was the child mama talking about her? No! NO!!! This couldn't be happening. So her whole life was a lie? Her mother wasn't really her mother. Oyama couldn't believe what she had just heard. Her mother or the woman she believed to be her mother had stopped screaming, Oyama couldn't hear what she was saying anymore. She had heard enough, she had to get out of there. She was half way up the staircase when Mpumi came out and saw her. "Yaya!" she called out to her but Oyama couldn't look at her. Her whole world had come crushing down. Her whole life was a lie! Mpumi was coming towards her concern and worry written on her face. Oyama ran all the way up the stairs and stepped into the bathroom. She locked the door. She heard Mpumi's footsteps come thudding after her and she heard her trying to open the door. Tears were streaming down her face. Her mother, her best friend wasn't even her mother. Had she been stolen from her birth mother? And her father had killed Mpumi's child? What kind of monsters had raised her? That woman was staying with her father because of her. It felt like Oyama didn't know herself or her mother anymore. "Oyama sweetheart please open the door. Let me explain baby." Her moth… Mpumi was pleading with her. Oyama couldn't breathe. The pain was suffocating her. She opened the medicine cabinet and took out all the pill bottles and emptied them. Mpumi's pleas on the door where becoming more urgent and more desperate. Oyama ignored her and stuffed all the pills into her mouth. She heard Mpumi shout "Daniel! Daniel!" She was running back down the stairs. Why weren't these pills working? Oyama knew her father would break down the bathroom door and they would pump out the pills. She didn't want to live anymore. Maybe if she died Mpumi would be free to leave her father. She searched through the medicine cabinet again. She found her father's Gillette razor blade. Oyama was scared of blood but she wanted out of this lie that was her life. She looked for the veins, she didn't know which ones she had to slit. The first slit was excruciating.

But Oyama couldn't stop. She kept deepening the cut. She had to cut the right wrist as well. Her blood was warm and sticky. The right wrist was harder to slit. She heard pounding on the door. Her father's deep voice commanding her to open the door. She heard the bang sound of the gun as she finished cutting the last wrist. She felt weak. She slid down the bathroom floor. The blood was gushing out now. It was all over the floor. She had made such a mess. Her parents came crushing into the bathroom. Her eyes flew to Mpumi's face. There was so much sorrow in her eyes. Why was she so sad? Oyama was giving her back her freedom. The pills were kicking in. She felt like she was floating on a cloud. She saw her mother hugging and kissing her on her first prize giving day. Her father teaching her how to ride her first bicycle. But that was all a lie. "Oyama don't close your eyes. Stay with me baby please." She heard the voice, it sounded far like it was coming from a tunnel. She couldn't feel the pain anymore. Death felt so welcoming. She let the darkness envelope her.

It felt like she was waking up from a deep sleep. Her throat felt dry and patchy like she hadn't drank any water in years. She first opened one eye, the lights were too bright. She quickly closed her eye and the darkness felt comforting. She couldn't make out where she was but she felt the beep beep sound of machines. There was something sticking on her arm and it was painful but she didn't have the strength to remove it. She heard a door opening and closing. "Has she woken up yet?" That loud raspy voice could only belong to her aunt Phindiwe. That voice could wake the dead from the grave. But she kept her eyes tightly shut. She loved her aunt but she didn't want to see the judgment in her face. Why hadn't she died? She had felt certain she was dying. Her aunt was certain that spirits had taken hold of her and that these white people medicine wouldn't help her. She knew a traditional healer who could do the cleansing. She seemed to blame Mpumi for what had happened to her niece. Fortunately she didn't stay long. There was silence again.

CHAPTER
SEVEN

"Mpumi I'm sorry…"

"Not now Daniel, not when my child is still fighting for her life. You don't get to be sorry." She had never heard her mother's voice so cold before. So it hadn't been a nightmare. It was real. Oyama was still very weak she was drifting away again. She felt someone holding her hand and that woke her up, she was careful not to open her eyes or make any movement. It was gog' MaNtuli, she was praying softly. When she was done she started talking to Oyama like she could sense that she was awake. "She can't live without you Oyama. I know to you she has always been your mother. But to me she will always be my baby. I lost her once when she had her first miscarriage, she didn't want to live. I felt that I had lost her for good. Then you came. From the moment she held you in her arms, you became her reason to live. Right now I feel that I'm losing her again. She doesn't eat, or bath all she wants to do is to sit here and wait for you to wake up.

She feels all this is her fault. Please don't take away my baby's reason to live. I had to force her to go and bath. She hasn't eaten in three days. Please don't let me lose my child. I know it's hard, you have many questions but you should never question that she loves you. She has been a better mother to you than I ever was to her. We need you nana." Those words pained her so much. She hadn't asked for any of this. Maybe if she slept again this time she wouldn't wake up. She heard aunt Nomusa's voice in her sleep. "Blue-eyed Adonis has been asking about her. He wants to come and see her."

"That won't be possible Nono. Daniel would have a fit. Now I need to put all my energy on my daughter. I can't deal with their drama. I just can't." Who were they talking about? Oyama still felt weak and tired all she wanted to do was sleep. The next time when she woke up, she opened her eyes and lifted her head slightly. There was only Mpumi in the room, this must be her hospital room. Mpumi was slumped over her chair, her head resting on Oyama's hospital bed. There were tear stains on her face and there were exhaustion lines etched on her face. Oyama's heart went out to this woman who had raised her. Oyama had never lacked any maternal affection. Why hadn't God made this woman her real mother? She had questions about her real mother. What was she like? Did she look like her? Why had she left her? Why hadn't she wanted her? Where was she now? Instinctively she knew that asking Mpumi these questions would hurt her. She had gone through enough hurt because of her. But Oyama needed to know. Maybe tomorrow she would have the courage to wake up and face them. She slept again. She heard her father's voice breaking into her sleep-fogged mind, "Candice wants to see her Mpumi…"

"She lost that right when she gave her up at birth."

"Mpumi please she has to see her daughter!"

"Oh so now she's her daughter? Where was she when Oyama had to have her appendix removed when she was only three months old? Why didn't she have to see her when she fractured her ankle at crèche? Where was she when she had chicken pox and I spent sleepless nights nursing her? Now she knows that she is her daughter. Don't insult me Daniel. I might not have given birth to Oyama but she is mine. She is my baby. So your Candice can go straight to hell or whatever hole you dug for her that she's been living in." Ok maybe right that moment wasn't the right time to 'wake up', she had never heard her mother sound so distant. Her mother was all warmth and hugs not this bitter woman she was hearing.

When Oyama finally opened her eyes, the first person she saw was her mother. Yes she had finally resolved that Mpumi was her mother even though she hadn't given birth to her. Her mother looked like hell. She had no make-up, she still had those cornrows but they weren't cute anymore. She was wearing some ugly dress that could only have been picked by gog' MaNtuli. Her mother who was the epitome of style and elegance looked like a hobo woman. "Mama." Her voice was a croak but Mpumi heard her and she was hugging her, laughing and crying at the same time. She smelt of tears and sweat, there was no hint

of that expensive perfume which
was her signature scent. "Ouch!" she was hugging her too tight. She had been there for a week now, she was told, and she had spent three days in the Intensive care unit. "Yaya, my baby you're ok. Its ok baby, everything will be ok. I promise." Oyama had expected recrimination but her mother seemed so happy that she was alive. "Sorry. Mama." Speaking was still a struggle, "Shhhhhh its ok baby, I'm not mad. I was just worried about you. Don't worry about anything. It's ok." It wasn't ok but hearing her mother saying it was going to be ok, she felt better. Her father was also there but he couldn't look her in the eye. Were those tears in his eyes? Oyama wasn't sure how she felt about him. She was glad that he didn't move to embrace her. That would have been awkward. Her mother was fussing over her, making her sit upright, fluffing her pillows and giving her water to drink. There was a drip attached to her arm and it was hooked to a bag of blood. Her wrists were bandaged. Her stomach felt empty like someone had removed her intestines. Her father went out of the room. He must have gone to call her family because moments later they all came pilling in. She was kissed and fussed over till she grew tired. None of them asked her why she did it but she could see the question in their eyes. They were treating her like she was glass. They were a rowdy bunch all her cousins were also there. The nurse came in and shooed everyone out. The nurse reminded her of Nanny McPhee. She had a stern unsmiling face, even aunt Phindiwe reacted to her commands at once. Only her parents remained. There was an awkward silence, she waited for them to speak. "Oyama we are sorry you had to find out the way you found out. And we are sorry you had to witness our fight." Oh so he was talking to her now. She didn't know what to say so she remained silent. "Oyama I know that you were overwhelmed but hurting yourself doesn't solve anything. You could have died and that would have hurt your mother and me."

"Just like it hurt her when you killed her baby?" Oyama saw her father blanche, his face turned an unhealthy shade of grey. "Yaya don't talk to your father like that. You shouldn't concern yourself about that it's in the past. I have you and that's all that matters. Promise me you will never try to kill yourself again" She sighed, she would never forgive her father. To kill an innocent child? What he said next probably made Mpumi regret backing him up, "Oyama your birth mother wants to come and see you" She had thought about her birth mother a lot when she woke up and when she heard her parents arguing about her. She might not know the circumstances but one thing was clear. That woman had abandoned her. If Oyama hadn't found out the way she had, she would probably have never known about her. And she didn't want to hurt her mother who had been there all along, holding her hand, loving her. Oyama looked him straight in the eye and said, "I only have one mother and she is sitting next to me."

She had changed. She could just feel it. Her mother had shielded her a lot from reality and now it was time to grow up. Now she noticed a lot of things around her. When she looked in the mirror she noticed that she looked nothing like her mother or even her father. She had a heart-shaped face with big black eyes and a naturally pouting mouth. She also had a classically high forehead and she was light in complexion. Why is it she had never noticed something so glaringly obvious. She must look like her, that woman that gave birth to her. She hated her reflection in the mirror. She took the mirror off the wall and threw it at the opposite wall. It broke into a thousand pieces and she felt better. The nurses came rushing in and when they saw the mirror they called the doctor and he had to sedate her. That was another thing that had changed about her. When
she wasn't feeling empty she felt a deep rage. Mostly it was directed at that woman but also at God. Why had He given her the wrong mother? They took her to therapy. The doctor there asked her many stupid questions. She had a high IQ, yes she was traumatized and in the early stages of depression, she knew that. She didn't need him asking her questions about her childhood. She was still a child. He was a Boer, tall and bulky like most of them. He had that clinically inserted smile

always pasted on his face. He must be thinking that this little monkey belonged in a straightjacket with all the other monkeys. Oh yeah she had dark thoughts like that now. She had always had positive thoughts of rainbows and cupid's arrow but this shit was her reality now. Her father avoided coming to see her when she was awake so sometimes she pretended that she was sleeping and he would tiptoe into her room and kiss her cheeks. She tried hard not to cringe. He seemed to cry a lot these days. Maybe the Boer doctor needed to look at the big monkey as well. Her mother worried about her, she could just see it. She still refused to leave her bedside, she only bathed when gog' MaNtuli or aunt Nomusa were there. Only aunt Nomusa still treated her the same. She probably didn't know that Oyama wasn't Mpumi's real daughter. But did that mean that she was a fake? She had begun asking herself philosophical questions like that. "You mustn't tell anyone that Mpumi isn't your biological mother," her father had pleaded with her. He was probably worried about how a scandal of that magnitude would harm his precious career. She wanted to blog about it just to get back at him but that would also hurt her mother and Oyama couldn't do that to her. So what was the point of going to therapy when she couldn't say the thing that was at the root of her depression? They had taken off the bandages on her wrists. She had jagged scars on her wrists and they would always be there. Always remind her of who she really was. Sometimes if she closed her eyes really tight and wished really hard, she almost believed that she was her mother's daughter. She no longer wept. Tears had deserted her. Her school friends came to see her but she felt detached from them. They brought her schoolwork and she buried herself in that, trying hard to shut everyone out. Ryan also came to see her, he was just a boy she noticed now. Maybe she would give him her virginity just for fun. What was the point of holding onto her innocence when she didn't have any left? The Boer doctor did help her find alternative ways to let out her frustration and anger. She was into kickboxing now. It helped. Maybe sex would help too. She didn't want drugs that would make her even more pathetic. The days stretched while she was in hospital. The nurses there gave her looks. To them she was probably just another self-entitled rich spoilt brat craving attention. Don't judge me, focus on your miserable lives changing other people's poop, she wanted to scream at them. She didn't talk much now. She only spoke in single syllables. She couldn't remember how to smile.

She had been in that bloody hospital for a month now and she was feeling restless. Her mother took her out to the hospital gardens. They sat on the benches and her mother looked at the trees as if they would help her decide on what she was about to say. "Oyama I know you have many questions and I am going to try to answer them as honestly as I can." She kept quiet for a moment also looking at those trees. The question that had been burning her the most was, "Why did you do it? Why did you agree to raise me?" her mother was quiet for so long she didn't think she was going to answer her. "No one ever prepares you for losing a child. When I
left Harvard I thought Jarred didn't love me anymore so I took all the love I had for him and transferred it to his baby. It hadn't even started kicking yet but I would talk to it every day. I would rub my belly and marvel at the life growing in me. Then when I woke up to blood on my sheets I told myself there was no God. How could He give me so much joy then snatch it from me while I slept? I was married to your father by then traditionally. Then one day they, him, your aunt Phindiwe and my mother, they called me to the sitting room. Then Phindiwe came in with you wrapped in a baby blanket. They told me that your father had gotten a girl pregnant but she was too young and she had to go to school, they begged me to take care of you. To raise you like my own. My first instinct was to refuse. How could they be so cruel and insensitive I had just lost my precious baby. How could they expect me to raise another woman's baby? But my mother firmly placed you in my arms. Then I looked at you. You were so perfect, with your tiny fingers that you were suckling in your perfect little mouth. I saw my baby in you like his spirit

had gone into your body I can't explain it. But I bonded with you that moment. God had given back what he stole from me." Oyama had thought she had no more tears but as she looked at her mother talking she felt them slide down her cheeks. Maybe this woman really loved her like her own child. "Is my birthday even on the 6th of December?"

"Yes apparently your father had stolen my ID and he registered Candice under my name so your baby card was issued to me as your mother with the actual date and the actual hospital."

"Who named me?"

"I did, you gave me the strength to lean on God when I thought He had turned His back on me." Oyama had never known her mother to be such a religious person. But the way she was talking was beautiful. "Did you ever meet my birth mother?" This was the difficult part, "Only once. I gave her money to go and study abroad."

"How much?"

"Oyama please…."

"You said you would answer my questions truthfully. How much did you give her?"

"I gave her R30 000, it was all she asked for to go and study."

"I think she could have at least asked for R50 000. I was probably worth that much don't you think?"

"You are looking at this the wrong way. She didn't sell you to me. She was 16 still a child and she had gotten pregnant for a married man. She wanted her child to have a better life. One that she couldn't give to you. So she gave me the most precious gift. She gave me a second chance at life and motherhood." They were both openly crying now. But she still had more questions, "Do you ever regret taking me?"

"Never! Oyama you are the best thing that has ever happened to me. You were my lifeline. I don't think if you were my biological child I would love you more than I already do." They were talking woman to woman, heart to heart and it was better than the month of therapy she had undergone. But she could feel that her mother still had something to tell her so she waited for her to talk. "I'm divorcing you father. I know

I've always treated you like a child. But now you
know everything. You have to decide for yourself. Do you want to stay with me? If you don't want to because I'm not your mother, I will understand I won't be mad. I will only fight for sole custody if it's what you want." Oyama had thought this was only difficult on her. But she felt that her mother thought she wouldn't see her in the same light or love her the same. She also need assurance. Seeing her mother so vulnerable made her love her even more and her wounds were beginning to heal. There were still scars but the healing process had begun. "I want to stay with you. I hate my father."

"Oyama he might have done some terrible things but he is still your father. Hating him only hurts you. Forgive him so that you can fully heal." She loved her mother but that was the one thing she couldn't find in her heart to do. "Do you want to see her? You must be curious about her." Oyama knew who her mother was talking about. "When I look in the mirror mama I see her, I know I look like her. But I'm not ready to see her yet."

"Its fine baby, when you are ready just let me know I will arrange a meeting." Oyama was grateful to this woman, for so many things but mostly she was grateful for her being there at all times. She was glad she was her mother and that she was in her corner.

CHAPTER EIGHT

Mpumi felt numb. That was the only word she could use to describe the hollow feeling within her. The last month had been hell. Memories from the safari were a distant memory. She hadn't laughed in a whole month. She had had many miscarriages so she had thought she knew everything about losing a child. Through each miscarriage she had felt a little part of her die and she had felt empty. She had been wrong, holding your child on the bathroom floor trying to stop the flow of blood from her wrists while waiting for the ambulance was the absolute worst feeling. That was hell, she never wished that feeling on her worst enemy. The doctors had managed to bring her back to life but her bubbly, forgetful, ever laughing dose of sunshine died that day on that bathroom floor. Now she had to look after this angry sullen teenager. Oyama was a ticking time bomb, they had to tiptoe around her. She didn't know how to get through her child anymore, Oyama shut everyone out. Daniel wasn't the same man. He was always apologizing, she didn't hate him anymore. She just felt sorry for him.

He was suffering the brunt of Oyama's wrath and Mpumi couldn't bring herself to help him out. He had dug his own grave. She had gotten rid of the gun, Oyama hadn't been the only suicidal one. But Daniel wasn't her problem anymore. Oyama was getting discharged after six weeks in the hospital. Mpumi hadn't left the hospital in those six weeks. Daniel must have told her employers what was happening, they had come to see Oyama. They had said Mpumi could stay with her as long as it took. She hadn't really cared because that was what she was going to do even if they had fired her. She felt tired. In fact she had been feeling the fatigue for a couple of days. Her mother had been saying she looked sick but she had ignored her. Was she supposed to look like a pop star when she had almost lost her child? She was going to see Oyama's doctor for him to process the discharge. She hadn't spoken to Jarred since they had left Mozambique. Things had been too hectic and he respected that she wanted to sort out things on her own. She missed him. She wiped the tear from the corner of her eye. Being with him had brought so much destruction to her family but she wouldn't regret those magical days. She couldn't. He seemed to keep tabs on her via Nomusa. Mpumi was glad that Nomusa was dragging her feet on the move to Cape Town. Nomusa and her mother had kept her afloat. Nomusa had even looked for an apartment for them. The apartment was at The Residency in Sandton close to Oyama's school thankfully. There was no way she was going back to that house. And until their divorce was final and their combined asserts were sorted out, she didn't want to move into any of their properties. The doctor had another patient in his office so she waited for him in his foyer. She had to do something about her hair but it was the least of her worries. Oyama flatly refused to repeat grade 11, she was hell bent on writing her Matric that year. She wondered how Lola was doing, her pneumonia was probably over by then. Had Jarred sent her back to America? She had been tempted so many times to call him. She must have dialed his number a thousand times but she had chickened out. It would complicate matters even further. She had had no idea that Daniel hated him that much. The look in his eyes when he had been confronting her about Jarred had been scary. He looked like a deranged man possessed with a thirst for revenge. She was scared of what Daniel would do to Jarred if they ever meet. Yes physically Jarred was taller and muscular but Daniel was like a man possessed nowadays. He blamed Jarred for the mess he had brought on himself. Her stomach felt queasy. She couldn't remember the last time she had a meal. That would explain why she was feeling so dizzy and so lightheaded. She had to get some food. She would try the hospital canteen the food there wasn't half bad. She stood up to go to the canteen. The room suddenly seemed to be moving on an axis, she tried to hold on to something but the darkness shrouded over her.

She woke up in a hospital bed. She wondered what had happened, Mpumi wasn't a fainter. The strain of the past month had finally caught up with her. The doctor was looking at her with concern. He reminded her of her father, he was the fatherly type. "Mrs. Sisulu you have to look after yourself better. When was the last time you had a decent meal? And decent sleep?"

"I don't remember," she mumbled. He didn't seem very impressed by her response. "I think the strain from having your daughter here has finally caught up with you. But I would love to have an ultrasound on you. I already sent your blood samples to the labs. Your blood pressure was exceedingly high. I want to be sure that it's not a virus or something else." It was probably fatigue but she let him check her anywhere. He seemed to harrumph to himself a lot as he applied the blue jelly on her belly. It felt so cold she shivered. Then he was moving that machine over her stomach while looking at the screen. She hadn't had an ultrasound since her last pregnancy. Wait, was that…? The doctor seemed to go back to that little dot and zoomed in. "Well at least now I know it's not a deadly virus. Congratulations Mrs. Sisulu you are going to be a new mother again." No! How had this happened? When? Then she remembered that in all the time she made love to Jarred they hadn't used any protection. But she was on birth control. This would only make things even more complicated. How could she be so irresponsible? The doctor seemed oblivious to her inner turmoil he kept going on with the ultrasound. He seemed puzzled by something, he kept going back over the same spot. Mpumi became worried. Was there something wrong with her baby? The doctor was pointing at a spot on the screen, "You see this? It's not supposed to be there. I think there is a tear in your placenta."

"What does that mean for my baby, doctor?"

"I think I need to call your husband before I tell you."

"No! Please don't call him. Please. Tell me what's wrong with my baby." The doctor was surprised by her reaction but he made no comment about it. "What it means is that the fetus as it grows is going to be oxygen deprived because of this tear. That could lead to still birth or miscarriage." God, why was nothing ever easy for her. "What can you do for my baby, doctor?"

"I could perform an emergency operation to cover up the tear. But the chances of success are 50-50. It's a high risk procedure."

"But without it my baby will definitely die?"

"Unfortunately yes."

"How soon can you perform the procedure?"

"I would need your medical history from your gynecologist, but I could perform as early as tomorrow evening. It is a costly operation I must warn you." The cost of the operation was the least of her worries. She was booked to be in the operation theatre the next night at eight pm. After supplying her gynecologist's information and signing the necessary documents, she left the doctor's office with Oyama's discharge papers. Daniel must never know about this pregnancy. She still cringed when she remembered what he had done to the first one. There was no doubt as to the paternity of this child. The doctor had said she shouldn't eat anything six hours before the operation but he had sternly told her to eat something now. Now she had a baby to worry about. She went to the canteen first. Oyama was being discharged the very next morning. She felt the panic mounting. She couldn't do this on her own. He picked up her call on the second ring. All she could say between her sobs was, "I need you. I can't do this on my own. I need you." All he wanted to know was where she was then the phone call was ended abruptly. Mpumi had to get herself together, Oyama shouldn't see her like this. Nor Daniel for that matter.

Mpumi was feeling pensive. Daniel was hearing none of them moving out, he was clearly in denial about the state of their marriage. He kept whining that they should work hard to keep the family together that he was willing to change. It was too late for that she felt sorry for him. But there was no way that she was going to stay with him especially now. She had to protect this child from him. She asked him to come outside the private room with her. "Jonga Daniel, this isn't about you neither is it about me. That girl in there is still emotionally fragile. Going back to that place and being around you could make her have a setback. We will talk about us when the time is right but right now you have to give her some space. You will come and see her when things cool down. I won't keep you from your child I promise." He didn't seem fully convinced but he agreed nonetheless. Pheeew. Now she needed to organize someone to look after Oyama when they got home. A stranger wouldn't do. And her mother would probably report her every movement to Daniel. She would ask Nomusa, she wouldn't say no and at least she wasn't walking on eggshells around Oyama like the rest of them. She felt exhausted and sleepy. But she couldn't let it show. At least morning sickness hadn't kicked in yet. Daniel would know immediately that this child wasn't his. The doctor came to sign Oyama's release forms. Mpumi gave a silent prayer that he wouldn't congratulate Daniel. Thankfully the doctor didn't talk about her situation he merely focused on Oyama. Jarred had come to the hospital last night. He had looked disheveled. He was wearing a suit like he had just come from a meeting. He said he had boarded the first plane out of Cape

Town, the jet had been used by his lawyer. He thought she called him because something had happened to Oyama. She had found him at the reception barking at the receptionist because they wouldn't allow him to go through. He clearly wasn't family. She had taken him out to the park much to the relief of the frayed receptionist. "Did something happen to Oyama?" She had drawn a deep breath, "No Oyama is fine she's being discharged to go home in the morning."

"But you called me crying I thought something bad had happened."

"Something did happen but it's both good and bad." He had looked at her with confusion and that look that said explain why exactly you dragged me all the way from Cape Town. "I collapsed earlier today…relax I'm fine now. The doctor did some check-ups. And… well I'm pregnant." The look of wonder in his face was priceless, he had embraced her for the longest time. Then he sobered, "But you said it's good and bad. Is it Daniel's baby?"

"No! I wouldn't have called you if it was." He looked like he wanted to believe her but he was wondering how she could be so certain. "I haven't slept with Daniel since my last pregnancy, when he… you know." He seemed relieved to hear that, "Then what's the bad part Lelo?" She
took another deep breath. That had been harder to say than she had imagined, "The doctor also found that there is a tear in my placenta. He has to perform an emergency procedure tomorrow night to close it otherwise our baby will die." He had looked at her for the longest time, "There is something you aren't telling me babe. Level with me." Sigh, he could always see right through her, "It's a high risk procedure with a 50-50 chance of success."

"Does that mean it will be putting your life at risk?"

"Yeah, sort-of. The doctor really didn't say."

"Then you aren't doing it. Yes I want nothing more in this world than our very own child but it's not worth risking your life for. We will find an alternative together."

CHAPTER
EIGHT

"I have to do this Jarred. Nothing you say will change my mind. All I need is for you to do is to stand by me. I can't do this without you by my side, holding my hand." He knew her well enough to know that she wouldn't back down. "I won't leave your side." He had slept at a hotel last night, it had been hard letting him go. She was ashamed by how much she depended on him. He hadn't come with any bags, he had just left in the middle of a meeting. Lola had come with him, she was also at the hotel. It was finally time to take her baby home. Daniel left them reluctantly, he seemed so dejected. Oyama was silent on the journey to their apartment. The weave she had on made her look older and there was just an air about her which said keep out. Mpumi was too worried about the coming procedure to try to draw her into any conversation. They found Nomusa at the apartment. She was in the process of getting tenants for her house, her furniture had been put in storage waiting for her move. So she would be staying with them till she moved. The apartment was a bachelor suite with two bedrooms, open-plan lounge and dining room with a separate kitchen and bathroom. It had come furnished with upscale modern furniture including built-in cupboards with Quartz counter tops in pastel and grey colors. It was chic but it was also warm and cozy. The best part was that it was safe and secure which was important with all the journalists who had been tailing them. Oyama promptly went into one of the bedrooms, Mpumi was really worried about her. She wanted to go after her but Nomusa held her back, "Give her some space, she will come to you when she feels like it." This was so hard but Nomusa was right, she couldn't baby her anymore. "I have to leave her with you tonight Nono."

"Wow you not even divorced yet you already getting your freak on." There was no hope for Nomusa, well she was going to be Amogalang's problem now. "I have to go to the hospital." She was instantly concerned. "I'm fine don't look so panicked. Well I'm pregnant."

"Daniel's?"

"No, thank God. It's Jarred's baby. But I have to go get a simple procedure to prevent anything happening to the baby." Mpumi had to downplay the procedure, she needed Nomusa to be calm because if she panicked Oyama would tell that something was up. Nomusa seemed to believe her which was a relief, she was tired. "I'm going to take a nap please wake me up at around 4pm."

He texted her at six o'clock on the dot, ***"I'm downstairs babe."*** She was ready and she was also starving. But she couldn't eat until after the procedure. She had already said her goodbyes to Nomusa and Oyama, the latter hadn't seemed interested to know where she was going. She just prayed that her daughter would come back to her eventually. She let herself out of the apartment she just hoped that she came back to it alive. He had rented a Cadillac, he always had taste in everything. He was dressed more casually in jeans that molded his muscles and a plain white t-shirt with a black blazer, he kissed her knuckles and held her hand even as he was driving. She needed his strength so she leaned on him. "Who did you leave Lola with?"

"She's alone. She's fine don't worry about her."

"Jarred! You can't leave a teenage girl alone."

"There is security outside our hotel room." By security he meant a bodyguard, she relaxed slightly. They arrived at the hospital and she checked in. They changed her into hospital scrubs and Jarred didn't budge from her side. When the doctor came and saw him cradling her hand, he looked taken aback but he had the good taste not to question. She wasn't proud of herself either. But she needed him here, there was no one else she could go through this with. He explained the procedure to them with Jarred interrupting now and then to question him. Mpumi trusted the doctor, it felt like her father was with her. Hopefully he would protect her and his grandchild. They were administering anesthetics on her. She wouldn't feel anything and if everything went well the procedure should take three hours. The last thing she saw was Jarred looking at her like he would never see her again, he kept repeating "I love you Lelo." Like it was a mantra of some sort. She loved him too but she was getting foggy she couldn't tell him but he knew.

She woke up and she found him sleeping next to her. There were worry lines on his forehead even in his sleep. He hadn't let go of her hand. She had been in this hospital for so long it felt like a second home. It was now morning, except for slight cramps she felt as if the procedure hadn't happened. "Good you're awake, the procedure went perfectly Mrs. Sisulu." The doctor was smiling, she was relieved. Jarred woke up and he seemed embarrassed that he had been sleeping on the job. "You will have a little bleeding that's to be expected but if it persists please come back. I have already scheduled your review date. You gyne should be able to take over from here." Mpumi felt an unexplainable panic rising. "Dr Babalwa please can you be my doctor till I give birth?" He seemed surprised by her request, "But I'm not a gynecologist Mrs. Sisulu." Jarred was pissed by the reference to her marital status she could just see it in his eyes. This was awkward on all of them.

"Please call me Nompumelelo. I know that but something in my gut tells me only you can deliver my baby safely." The doctor seemed to consider her request, "Although this is highly irregular not to mention the burden you are putting on my shoulders, I will do it. Your pregnancy is still a high risk one, I will have to monitor it closely. I will have my assistant email you your scheduled appointments." After the doctor left Jarred was very quiet, like he was brooding over something. "Hey you. What's on that big brain of yours?"

"Are you sure you want this doctor to monitor you? He said it himself he's not a gyne. I can get DC's best specialists flown here to monitor you." Mpumi couldn't explain it but call it woman's intuition, something told her to stick with this doctor. "I'm hundred percent certain. I'm going to be fine and our baby too."

"Okay, you're the boss my lady but you only have to say the words and I will have the specialists at your doorstep." He was so cute at times and thoughtful. Must be the hormones which were making her extra aware of him. She was horny. "Come here baby-daddy." He was smiling that dare-devil smile of his. His embrace and kiss were so gentle like he was afraid he would break her. He smelt divine. How she had missed him! She wanted more of him, she started kissing his neck right there on the hospital bed but he stopped her. "No sexual intercourse after the procedure till after the first trimester has passed. That's when the baby will be out of danger. Doctor's orders." What?!

"When did the doctor tell you this?"

"Soon after your procedure. I told him I'm the baby's father. He looked like he wanted to punch me." Somebody shoot her now. How was she supposed to last that long when she wanted him so much. He looked like he was having as hard a time with this as she was. Good. She had been discharged so she took her sorry arse off the hospital bed and got dressed. She took her sweet time dressing in front of him. The look on his face though was heartbreaking. He looked like a puppy who couldn't remember where he buried his bone. But Mpumi could see it clearly from the bulge in his pants. They had to wait till he cooled down before they could leave the hospital. It was going to be a long six weeks.

She kept waking up at night to check if there was any blood on the sheets. There wasn't. She breathed a bit easier. They had passed the critical twenty-four hours without any incident, small mercies. She knew she and the baby weren't out of the woods yet but she was relieved that they had survived the procedure. You have to be strong for mommy my little fighter, she spoke silently to the baby. Oyama was sharing the bed with her. She had thrown the covers away from her body just as she had when she was a child. Mpumi pulled the covers around her and placed a kiss on her high forehead. She had finally checked her e-mails that afternoon, there had been a reminder from her gyne that she had to come and renew her birth control. That explained why she had fallen pregnant. There were also a bunch of emails from journalists wanting an exclusive interview over her daughter's near-death scare, people had

no more shame. She had promised Jarred that she would help him find a school for Lola. She was good friends with the Principal at Oyama's school and she would be able to help them out. She had sent the principal a message and had gotten Lola an interview for the coming week. Jarred would now be based in Jozi throughout the duration of her pregnancy. That made her feel safe. There was a message alert.
"Are you alright?" She checked the time it was just after one am, what was he doing up? ***"I'm fine so is the baby. Go to sleep."***

"I can't. Have a raging boner that you started." This fool! Mpumi had to cover her mouth as she giggled, she didn't want Oyama to wake up.

"Stay Strong."

"You're mean babe."

"What did I do? Doctor's orders."

"I wish I was sleeping next to you right now." Mpumi sighed she wished that too but she had to sort out her life first. ***"You will be. Just be patient. Goodnight or good morning I'm tired."*** She waited for his response. He texted back, ***"I love you Lelo."*** If only her life was simple, she would be sleeping with the love of her life right now. He was very proprietary he usually slept with his hand over her cookie jar the whole night no matter which position she slept in. She had to get her horny-self to sleep, she couldn't even masturbate with Oyama sleeping with her. Mpumi had mastered the craft of masturbation. Perks of having a wandering husband. When he was always away on 'business trips' or when he felt too tired or he wasn't in the mood, she had had to fend for her sexual needs. She had even bought a dildo, it made her orgasm more than Daniel did. She had never understood how men could simply deprive you of sex and you had to deal with it but when the shoe was on the other foot they would read you the Riot Act. She hadn't masturbated much since Jarred had hurtled back into her life. Now that was a man who knew how to put her sexual needs first. Now they couldn't have sex for the next two months! She turned a couple of times before she fell into a deep sex-deprived sleep.

CHAPTER NINE

Amogalang was driving her crazy. He was growing impatient but there was no way Nomusa was leaving Mpumi when she obviously needed her. He couldn't understand that Mpumi wasn't just her best friend, she was her sister. Even more of a sister than that slutty sister of hers who only called when her children needed something. Nomusa had tried unsuccessfully to get her sister to go back to school but the little minx was having none of that. Her argument was that at 22 she was far too old to go back and spend the next 5 years behind a desk only to be an unemployed graduate. All Noswazi was now was a 22 unemployed single mother who was currently holed up with a 36 year old married man who wanted nothing to do with her children while she looked after his kids who also had different mothers. So the burden fell on Nomusa and the government to raise her three brats. To her family Nomusa was an ATM. She was the only one who had a successful career and she didn't have any dependents so they leeched off her. That was another reason she was delaying the move to Cape Town. She wasn't looking forward to the unexpected family visits where they would raid her wardrobe and her cupboards. "Hai mntase those boots are nice maan can I have them? And that dress would just fit perfectly with the boots, and that brown handbag." She could just hear her young sister's excited voice. And the way they were excited about her move to Cape Town was making her shudder. She loved her family but they were too much. Mpumi is the one who always looked out for her and being so far from her would be difficult. Mpumi looked like hell, that tummy of hers was beginning to show which was still a bit early. She had lost weight instead of gaining and she needed a hair intervention, Nomusa didn't want her scaring off umlungu bae. She had hooked up with umlungu bae on Facebook and they had exchanged numbers, then she had gone all FBI on all his Facebook pictures. When all she came up with where pictures of him and his Mexican child, Nomusa had gone third degree and Google searched him. Apart from numerous sleazy bimbos who hung on his arm on functions, he didn't seem to be attached to any other female. She had been impressed when his name came up in the Forbes top 40 rich people in America. Amachankura! Mpumi surely knew how to haul in the biggest catch. Today was Oyama's first day back to school after her hospital stay. The problem with kids these days is that they idealized death, she thought wanly. Growing up in Khayelitsha they had been surrounded by death and it wasn't pretty. Seeing someone being burnt beyond recognition or being stoned to death for being a mpimpi or for stealing was horrific. The only time you saw someone hanging from a tree with crap in their pants was when someone hung them there. You never attempted suicide because you knew if you failed your mother would give you an arse whooping so bad death would seem like a holiday. Instead of sending that girl to therapy they should have given her such a whooping that every time she saw a razor blade she would bury it. Nomusa had volunteered to drop her off on her way to work. She was working off her two months' notice. Mpumi had been right she had found a job in Cape Town with a bigger salary, it even had health and housing benefits. She started work there

next month and she was looking forward to it. When she finished her coffee she looked at her watch that kid was going to make them both late. She went to get her from their bedroom. She found Oyama in front of her laptop looking at
stories of herself on the Internet. "SISULU PRINCESS ATTEMPTS SUICIDE" was the caption of one story. Some had gone so far as to say she had died. There was a picture of her in the hospital bed, one of the hospital stuff must have taken it and leaked it to the media. Knowing Daniel he would deal with whoever had done that thoroughly. This pity party of Oyama's had to come to an end. "Get your bag kid we're getting late."
"I'm not going." Spoken like a true sullen teen. Well Nomusa was having none of that, she noticed that Oyama kept rubbing the scars on her wrists. She took out her blazer and made her wear it then held her by the shoulders, "Look kiddo I can't begin to imagine what it is you are going through. But that's real life for you. You think I want to go to work where the men leer at me and grab my butt as I pass? No I don't but I go anyways and when they grab my butt I kick them in the balls." Was that a smile? Nomusa knew she had to get through to her god daughter. "People are always going to say mean things about you lala but that's because they hate their own lives. You could have died but you didn't so now you have to snap out of it. Life goes on. Now go out there and if any of them are mean to you kick them straight in the balls." She was relieved to see Oyama take her school bag and follow her to the lounge. She hoped the kid didn't take her literally, Mpumi would kill her. Mpumi was sleeping in, this pregnancy was making her cranky and she was always tired. But Nomusa was going to knock off early and drag her pregnant butt to the saloon. She couldn't stare at that overgrown farm hairdo another day, she would lose her sanity.

When Nomusa came back to their apartment she found Mpumi still in bed. She had to drag her out of the blankets into the shower and out of the house. She was such a grouch lately. Her hairstylist looked as if he was going to have a stroke when he saw the state of Mpumi's hair. He had always been such a diva! Nomusa also forced her to do her nails, but Mpumi drew the line at fake eyelashes. Waxing followed as well as a facial. When she was satisfied with the makeover she led Mpumi to the Mall of Africa. Nomusa believed in only two forms of therapy, retail and alcohol since the latter was off the cards, retail therapy would have to do for now. Nomusa wanted to know how white meat tasted in the sack and if Jarred was a better lover than Daniel but she had to get that one drunk before she loosened her tight lips. When she was sober she was such a prude! It only took three glasses of wine to get Mpumi ratchet and the things she squealed when she was drunk, SMH, Nomusa should start recording her. Mpumi had to get some maternity wear anyway she looked like she was squeezing that baby bump in that halter top and maybe they would also buy one or two cute baby clothes. Nomusa knew that being so far away she would miss out on the tiny tot's life. Her very own colored niece, yes she wanted it to be a girl. But the way Mpumi was becoming so ugly it was probably a boy nx! Thinking about baby clothes and babies just made her so broody. Imagine little yellow Amogalangs running around with those bedroom eyes, chubby cheeks and killer smiles! Nomusa had never been the broody type she found children especially babies annoying and demanding too much of her attention. "So what are we doing at the mall Nono?" She already looked better with the new hairdo, Nomusa had forced her to get a Peruvian weave. She was too rich to be walking around in overgrown cornrows. "We're going to buy you some maternity wear and

maybe some cute clothes for my coming niece or nephew." Mpumi paled so much Nomusa had to get her to sit down. She was shivering and sweating, Nomusa became scared. And then? Had she said something wrong? Maybe it was hormones making her act so weird. She gave her some mineral water which had been in her bag. After a while some color came back to Mpumi's cheeks. "What's wrong?"

CHAPTER

NINE

"It's just hearing you talk about baby clothes. I can't Nono. What if the baby dies in my womb like the rest of them? I am 38 years old and I have never worn maternity wear. I wake up every night to check my sheets for blood and when I go to pee I'm scared to look at the tissue when I wipe. I have nightmares of waking up at the hospital and when they hand me my baby wrapped in a baby blanket but when I look at my baby there is no child just baby blankets!" She was now crying and talking loudly, people were beginning to stare at them. Nomusa had had no idea that the miscarriages had left such a traumatic impact on Mpumi. She had always seemed to move on quickly from each miscarriage. Nomusa tried calming her down till her sobs stopped and the tears receded. A stupid fool had once said on Twitter it's better to cry in a mansion than in a shack. Pain was pain. Mpumi's pain was cutting right through Nomusa. "Mpumi look at me, you can't let the past haunt you. You have mourned those babies sweetie now you have to let them go. You have to believe that you are going to hold this baby. You have to marvel at its growth, enjoy every change that's happening in your body. Because you will hold this baby I promise you and you will have sleepless nights when it cries and it's always pooping. Take this child as your new lease in life, no more tears only moving on." Nomusa knew she was promising something she had no control over. She let out a silent prayer, please Lord you have taken so much from her please give her this one thing. At least she was quiet now and calmer. They had to fix her make-up at the mall toilets. Nomusa insisted that they should still buy the baby clothes as a sign of hope. Mpumi's face when she was touching those little clothes was heartbreaking. She wanted to feel every fabric and smell everything. Nomusa wasn't an emotional person but even she felt teary just watching her. She was going to miss this dear soul. They bought some groceries as well and headed home.

The way she walked into their apartment as if she owned it. Nx! Her nose was in the air like she was Miss Universe. In another

life she had been pretty but having seven children with different men had taken its toll on her. That weave and that lipstick where not age appropriate for her. She was one of those Joburg old women who never wanted to act their age. One of those old birds had harassed Nomusa for calling her 'gogo' in a taxi back when she was still new to Jozi. Nomusa had learnt her lesson. This one who had just barged into their apartment was headed in the same direction. She was somebody's grandmother for crying out loud. Why was she so loud though? "How the mighty have fallen! Heeee I had to see it with my own eyes to believe it. The Harvard wife living in such a low class apartment! Bawo!" Only Phindiwe would call a Sandton luxury apartment, with rates which could buy more than 20 of her fake-arse shiny Brazilian weaves, a low class apartment. Nomusa had never been a fan of Phindiwe that woman was just a mean bully. She hated how Mpumi always treated her with respect even when the woman pushed her around. She was lucky Nomusa wasn't her makoti, she would have dealt with her by now. Most bullies didn't know how to throw punches. Today she just might deal with her, Mpumi must have read her mind because she asked Nomusa to give them a moment alone. She went to the kitchen where she could hear everything. Even if she was in the bedroom she would have heard Rabheka but Mpumi was more soft-spoken. "So you left my brother to come and live in this pig-sty?"-Phindiwe
"I assume you didn't come all this way to insult me and where I stay."-Mpumi

"I always knew that for an educated woman you are stupid and your actions have proven me right." The nerve of that she-devil!

"Listen Phindiwe this is not your brother's property. Now before I bitch-slap you with a protection order tell me what it is you want in my apartment?" Yass tell her chomma!

"Can't I come to see my brother's child?" She hadn't even asked about her precious brother's daughter in all the ten minutes she had been there. Eye roll.

"Not in my house you can't. You will just have to wait for her to come to your brother. Now if that's all, please see yourself out." Nomusa was proud of the quiet control in her friend's voice. The old witch must have seen that today she wouldn't be able to walk all over Mpumi because she changed tact. "Makoti I know that things haven't been well between you and my brother but you are still family. Is this how you treat family now?" The sly fox!

"Phindiwe you still haven't said what brings you to my house." That woman's hormones were evil! Take that you old bat.

"I came to apologize." Say whaat? Now this Nomusa had not seen coming. Mpumi was probably giving her a doleful look because she went on hurriedly, "I want to apologize for mistreating you all these years. To be honest you are the best thing that has ever happened to my brother..." oh so now she saw that "...he loves you Mpumi. That's why when he came to me telling me you were pregnant for another man I knew I had to do something." Wait what was this old witch talking about now? Mpumi was silent throughout her apology if one could call it that. Phindiwe went on, "I am the one who gave him the pill that induced you to have a miscarriage. He didn't..." Tjo! Nomusa couldn't remember the last time she had heard such a loud clap. She rushed into the lounge to find the old bat holding her cheek and Mpumi with the look of murder in her eye. She was advancing towards Phindiwe who was cowering on one end of the sofa. How she had gotten there was a wonder to Nomusa. This reminded Nomusa of those catfights over men which broke out in sheebens in Khayelitsha. It was like a scene from Lokshin Biskop. Even though she wanted Phindiwe to get the whooping she deserved, she had to think of Mpumi's pregnancy so she came in between them. "It was the only way Nompumelelo, he couldn't claim that your white bastard was his." That old bat surely had a death wish, Nomusa had never seen Mpumi move so quickly, she wiggled past Nomusa and she was on top of Phindiwe and bitchslapping her with one hand while strangling her with the other. Things were really hectic. It took all of Nomusa's strength to get her off the old hag. "Get out! Get out of my apartment you witch before I kill you with my own bare

hands. May you and your brother rot in hell!" Mpumi was shaking with rage, she was breathing heavily and her weave was standing on ends. She had that crazy woman look in her eyes. Phindiwe didn't need to be told twice, she scuttled out of there
like she was being chased by the devil himself. Only when the door closed behind her did Nomusa let go of Mpumi. Wuuuuu shame, never mess with a pregnant woman! She sat there on the sofa staring at space. Nothing Nomusa said could get through to her so she left her there staring into space.

The weeks following the Rabheka saga things started slowly going back to normal or the new version of normal they were currently living. Oyama ignored them most of the time but at least now she talked to them during dinner. She didn't mention how the other children were treating her at school so Nomusa assumed it must be really bad. Teenage girls could be so ruthless and so shallow. Oh and when Mpumi told Oyama to have that weave removed they dropped her off at the saloon and when they came back she had white braids on. Not grey but snow white. Mpumi almost strangled her but Nomusa intervened. She reminded her of the time when she and Mpumi had slipped out of their homes on New Year's Eve to go and party when they were 15. Oyama was acting out like most teenagers Mpumi should just let her be. Then she had wanted a tattoo. The kid was also into rock music now, hardcore rock that made your ears buzz when she was playing it at maximum volume. There was never a dull moment in that apartment. Mpumi was also acting very shady these days. She was officially working from home now. So when they left her in the apartment in the morning she would be bathed and dressed working on her laptop. But when they came back she would be having a different outfit and the house would be spotless. Nomusa suspected she sneaked in blue-eyed Adonis the moment they turned the corner. She was acting very sneaky. Then there was her diet. Mpumi now lived on cereal. Other foods seemed to tick her off, Nomusa couldn't understand why it was called morning sickness when her friend was spending the whole night in the toilet. The weird part is that instead of adding milk to the cereal she used Ultramel, yes the yellow custard. She added it to Corn Flakes and to Muesli. Yuck! Last weekend when they had gone to the movies she had added Smarties and Jelly Beans to her popcorn. No wonder she was getting so big. Or to be more accurate her stomach was getting so big. Nomusa still thought they should get the dates re-checked because there was no way that tummy was not even three months yet. She was already showing and Nomusa didn't think it was normal. But then again she couldn't be too sure she had never had a child. They had thrown a farewell party for her at work. She had been pleasantly surprised, she hadn't thought they cared. Then there was Amogalang her yellow bone Tswana, she missed him like crazy but he got on her nerves easily. She had told him that he should tell all his whores that she was coming to town, she wouldn't tolerate any hussies all over her man. He liked it when she was being possessive. She had to buy herself a homecoming present. For a parting gift Mpumi had bought her Victoria's Secret lingerie, it was a red and black lacy number. It was so skimpy Nomusa had blushed when she saw herself in the mirror. It came complete with its own pair of wings. Just when you thought you knew your prude friend, Mpumi would go around and surprise you. Wait till her bedroom eyed man saw her in that getup, he would know what a freak meant.

It was during her last week in Jozi that they had another unexpected visitor. Nomusa had assumed the role of butler because it took ages for Mpumi to get off the sofa and Oyama was always locked in the bedroom with her rock music. The first thing Nomusa saw was the protruding belly, that woman could give birth in their lounge. It didn't take long for Nomusa to recognize who she was, that kind of stunning beauty was impossible to forget. Even when she looked as if each step cost her dearly, her face unmade-up and a bead of sweat on top of her pouting lip she was still beautiful. The heart-shaped face looked drained and the big black eyes were full of apprehension. The sole fact that she had reached their twelfth floor apartment without going into labour was a miracle on its own. If she hadn't been pregnant Nomusa would have shut the door in her face but that would be a sin in her current state. She let her into the apartment. Mpumi looked up from her laptop and she seemed like she had seen a ghost. But she recovered quickly and she sat upright removing her feet from the other sofa and closing her laptop. Their visitor sat perched on the sofa that Mpumi's feet had just vacated. Nomusa could just cut through the tension in the room with a butter knife. She braced herself to be the bouncer if these two highly hormonal women got into a catfight. "Nompumelelo."

"Candice." Wow the greetings were not very cordial but that's to be expected as one had been screwing the other's soon to be ex-husband. Nomusa kept looking from one woman to the other like that forward kid who would be listening in on adults' conversations. Mpumi was looking at her to continue but Candice seemed to have lost her nerve. "What can I help you with?" she didn't sound like she wanted to help the poor girl at all. Candice had to clear her throat a-couple of times before finally talking, "I want to see Oyama."

"Why now?" She said it so coldly. Tjo!

"I need to make things right with her before I give birth." The girl had spunk Nomusa gave her that.

"Oh so Oyama is the only one you have wronged Candice?" The eye Mpumi was giving the poor girl was glacial.

"No… I also wronged you I'm sorry." She was really humbling herself ngoku.

"What exactly are you sorry for? Screwing my husband and being pregnant with his child yet again. Or are you sorry that you screwed me over by taking my money claiming you needed to go to school while my husband made you his mistress?" Nomusa made a note never to cross Mpumi, she was ruthless and she didn't even raise her voice.

"I'm sorry for everything. I was wrong I shouldn't have done any of it. But I love Daniel." The things we choose to love. Sies! Wait till she discovered that he was screwing his PA and half the Cabinet wives and the female Cabinet members. She would just have to be strong. Mpumi was quiet for a long time as if she had fallen asleep but Nomusa could see that she was really struggling with herself. Pretty girl looked scared but she was standing her ground. "If you want me to grovel I will. Please I just need to talk to Oyama." She was really about to kneel in front of Mpumi. Nomusa hadn't expected to feel sorry for Candice but she did. Mpumi waved her up, "You don't need to kneel before me. I forgive you. I'm leaving Daniel." There was no hate or malice in Mpumi's voice she probably meant it. Nomusa would never have forgiven a slut who slept with her man continuously so easily. The girl seemed shocked by this revelation. Daniel probably hadn't notified her of his impending status change. Men!

"Oyama is in the second door to your right. If I go and talk to her first she won't agree to come out." Nomusa knew it took guts for Mpumi to say those words.

"Thank you." There were so many emotions underlying Candice's words, her eyes were tearing up. It must be the hormones, Nomusa was used to the random tears by now. She heaved herself slowly up, none of them offered to help her they just watched. Candice waddled painfully to Mpumi and Oyama's room and she knocked on the door. When there was no response she went in and closed the door. Nomusa wanted to go and see what was happening but Mpumi placed a restraining hand on her arm, "Give them some space Nono." Nomusa had no idea how her friend still remained so calm through all of this. There was no sound coming from the bedroom. At least it meant that Oyama wasn't throwing things at her birth mother. Candice must have stayed about ten minutes in that room and then she came out. She was crying openly, her tears were streaming down her face. Nomusa rushed over to her and made her sit down, Mpumi brought her tissues and water. She cried for a long time but no one made a move to comfort her. They didn't know how to. Finally when she was almost calm and the tears had almost dried up she drank the water and wiped her face. When she spoke it was in a low voice, "She hates me. My own daughter hates me." Nomusa had expected that, probably pretty girl had thought that Mpumi was the one keeping Oyama from her. They let her talk, "When I was talking to her she looked at me with so much hatred. She didn't even say a single word to me. I begged her and I apologized but she kept looking at me with hatred in her eyes. I tried to explain to her that I only wanted her to have a better life than I could give her. She hates me. She hates me so much and it hurts. Ouuuwww!" Ok it must really hurt because she was howling now. She was breathing heavily. Whaat! She had wet their sofa, Nomusa couldn't believe that girl. Mpumi cursed softly, "Her water just broke. Shit Nomusa call the ambulance." Oh God! This was not happening. Where was her phone? Nomusa was panicking she had never seen a woman in labour before. Candice was now moaning and wriggling and Mpumi was trying to make her sit more comfortably. Nomusa grabbed her phone and dialed the ambulance. Candice screamed. Nooo! She couldn't have her baby in their lounge. The ambulance was on its way. Mpumi seemed calmer than Nomusa, "I don't think we can wait for the ambulance, let's drive her to the hospital." Oyama had come out of the bedroom when Candice started screaming and she looked scared. Mpumi was giving out orders, "Oyama come and help Nomusa hold her. Grab a throw blanket from the bed and hand me those keys. Candice you have to breath and don't start pushing just yet." Trying to lift her up was a struggle, both Nomusa and Oyama were huffing and puffing. Mpumi was already opening the door for them and they left the apartment. The elevator took ages to come and Candice was writhing in pain. Mpumi kept breathing with her, Nomusa was as shit-scared as Oyama. Finally they were in the elevator. Candice let out another curdling scream. She was sweating profusely and Nomusa just hoped they didn't have to deliver this baby on their own. Mpumi drove like a demon while Nomusa was trying hard to hold Candice down. At least for now there seemed to be a lull in her pains. Oyama was wiping her brow with a wet cloth. So much for the mother-daughter reunion that Candice had been expecting. They must have gotten so many speeding tickets by the time they reached the hospital. It wasn't the hospital where Candice had registered so the nurse at the reception area

was giving them hell. Mpumi finally snapped and told her exactly were to get off even threatening mal-practice law suits if they didn't get Candice into the Delivery Room. Mpumi tried calling Daniel but his phone was on voicemail. It was Parliament season he was probably in Parliament at that moment. Or maybe he was busy flashing his red Lamborghini and designer clothes worth a million on the red carpet if it was the opening of SONA. "We can't leave her alone here like this. Nomusa stay with Oyama here while I go with her to the Delivery Room." She was rushing after the wheelchair Candice was in as she spoke. Nomusa was glad to finally put her butt down but the hospital chairs were uncomfortable. Oyama was oddly quiet and her face was as white as her braids then when Nomusa looked at her closely she noticed the tears. Nomusa held her god-daughter while she cried. "How can I hate her aunt Nomusa when she went through the same pain to bring me into this world?" Nomusa had no comeback for that or even any wise words of comfort so she just held her.

CHAPTER TEN

She held on to the toilet seat as wave after wave of nausea hit her and she threw up for what seemed like forever. She had told him repeatedly that she couldn't stomach the full breakfast he had made for her but the daddy-to-be was adamant. Now he was paying for it by holding back her weave and looking worried as she threw up her guts. Nomusa had finally gone to Cape Town and the apartment just wasn't the same without her. The last month with Oyama had really tried her patience and most of the time she had felt like strangling her but Nomusa had been the one who held her back. Nomusa had been the one who could get through to her and understand Oyama when Mpumi had almost given up. Nomusa had also been the one to teach Oyama how to cook, clean and do her own laundry. Mpumi had been ashamed that at almost 15 her baby didn't even know how to boil water. But that was because she had been waited on hand and foot by a fleet of servants all her life. Staying in a two-bedroomed apartment was a new experience to the kid. In her crazy way Nomusa had been the glue that had held them together and Mpumi already missed her. Finally she was done puking and he helped her stand up. She had never suffered from morning sickness this severe before. Jarred shame he looked green as well maybe next time he would listen to her when she said she couldn't stomach food. "Baby I have to go and grab a file I have to fax I think I forgot it at the hotel room." He placed a swift perk on her temple and just like that he was gone. Mpumi laughed softly he was such a coward. She got into the shower and let the water wash off the stench of puke from her. The past week had been a crazy one. Nomusa said she was strong for helping Candice but Mpumi didn't think she was strong, a part of her had thirsted for revenge but then she saw Oyama standing at the bedroom door looking scared and she had had no choice. In the delivery room during her lucid moments Candice had tried to explain that she had gone to school, beauty school but had only bumped into Daniel two years back when he had been accompanying an 'acquaintance' to her beauty salon. Mpumi hadn't been interested and she told her to save her strength for delivery. She had given birth to a healthy baby girl and when the nurses had cleaned her up Candice had wanted Mpumi to be the first to hold her. She was a tiny replica of Oyama, she reminded Mpumi of the first day she had held Oyama in her arms. Nomusa had been right at the mall, it was time for Mpumi to lay the past to rest and focus on her present and future. Jarred, Oyama, Lola and this baby growing inside her were her present and her future. She was happy these days. The best moment had been when Oyama had held her baby sister, there was so much love there, and Mpumi had taken pictures of them together. Oyama would thank her later. Then Phindiwe had come with Candice's bag, she couldn't look Mpumi in the eye. Apparently Phindiwe had been staying with Candice this whole time. The nerve of some people, Mpumi had been surprised that that woman who had come begging her to return to her brother was staying with his mistress. Mpumi was just glad she was getting out of that union. She had emailed and faxed Daniel the divorce papers she had already signed but he hadn't responded. It was going on a month now. If he wanted to play hard ball she was game, as far as she was concerned their marriage had ended the moment he had admitted that he had killed her baby. As Mpumi was drying herself she heard a knock at the door. Who could that be? She wondered because Oyama was at school and Jarred had his own key. They were moving out of this apartment soon. Jarred had insisted just the night before when she had called him at eleven pm to tell him that she was craving braaied meat. The poor man had to trek all the way from the other side of Jozi to look for the meat and when he finally came to her apartment two hours later she said the craving had vanished. To say he had been frustrated was an understatement. She could see the smoke literally coming out of his ears and nose. "That's it Lelo, I'm buying a house we are moving in together." When she had tried to protest he had looked at her with a withering stare and she had immediately shut the fuck up, "I can't be leaving my daughter alone in the middle of the night at a hotel and I worry every night that something might happen to you and I will be too late to do anything to help you." So they were moving that was final. With a robe tied firmly around her Mpumi went to open the door. Daniel walked into their apartment and made himself comfortable on the sofa. Mpumi's hand automatically moved to her belly. There was no way she could hide the bump from him now and he was already looking at it. She sat on the sofa across from him and waited for him to state the purpose for his visit. He was only carrying a brown envelope and as usual he was in a designer tailor made suit that fit him like a glove. "This pregnancy really suits you more than the rest. You're glowing Mpumi." That she hadn't expected him to say and she didn't know how to respond all she could muster was an awkward "Thank you," she wasn't going to tell him that it also gave her the most severe morning sickness. He didn't ask whose it was because he knew. After looking around the apartment he said out of the blue, "Phindiwe told me that you gave her a thrashing." Mpumi was still ashamed of that saga and she couldn't look him in the eye but when she did she saw that he was smiling broadly. That was unexpected. "No one has ever stood up to my sister before. Thank you for what you did for Candice…" he changed quickly from being playful to being very serious, he seemed to struggle with the words which was unlike Daniel, "…I don't think if I were in your shoes I would have helped her." Mpumi looked him straight in the eye but he kept shifting his gaze, "Oh so you would have expected me to let your child die just because you murdered my child in my womb?" He let out a long breath, "That is the one thing I regret more than anything I ever did in my life." She must have given him the yeah right expression because he quickly went on with even more conviction. "I'm serious Mpumi, I wish I could take it back or make things right. If only I could go back in time but I can't." She was still disbelieving, she remembered how he had been taunting her with the news when she came back from the safari. "Do you know why I couldn't look you in the eye after each of your seven miscarriages after that one?" He had been counting her miscarriages, Mpumi widened her eyes in surprise. "Because each time we lost a child I knew I was paying for the child I took from you. I was the reason you had all those miscarriages. I felt guilty for the pain I made you go through. I know you may not believe it but I have never loved any woman the way I love you. And if there is anything I can do to make up for all the hurt and neglect I've subjected you to please let me know. I'm really sorry Mpumi." At that moment Mpumi realized that karma did exist and what you do to people comes back to you with twice the force. Daniel hadn't really been punished for his sins but he had been punished by them. It really was a moving speech but it didn't move Mpumi one inch, she knew how Daniel could switch the charm on and off even when he seemed sincere. This man had put her through hell especially the last months. "Did you also feel guilty about raping me? The only thing you can do for me Daniel is to sign the divorce papers so that I can move on with my life and be happy." Yep she needed these hormones of hers to be checked Nomusa said she was turning into a grouchy ice Queen. He looked like she had slapped him across the face. He had the wounded look on his face but she stared him down with a withering look. He took some papers out of the brown envelope and put them on the coffee table and also took out a pen from his inner pocket. Mpumi held her breath as he signed across the dotted lines. Freedom was looming near. She hadn't thought it was going to be this easy to persuade him to sign the divorce papers. She had even devised a speech about how Mandela had divorced Winnie and later married a 'Kwerekwere' the unpleasant term used for other African foreigners but the same narrow-minded people still held him in high esteem. And also how Mugabe had an affair with his secretary while his wife was battling for her life and thirtysomething years later he and his side-chick were still ruling Zimbabwe. But hey she wasn't complaining, she wanted to be free from him. He took his sweet time signing but finally he was done. But she also had to make sure they were on the same page about one crucial thing, "I get full custody of Oyama Daniel and that's non-negotiable. If you try to pull any stunt and I mean any, I will drag your good name through the gutter." She stared him down, he let out a weary sigh. "Its fine, Oyama already hates me I only hope that she agrees to come and visit me." Mpumi wasn't about to console him or give him false expectation, Oyama was almost an adult she would make her own decisions. She changed the subject, "She said she loves you." He knew who she meant and he gave a dismissive shrug, "I could never marry her. She doesn't have the right pedigree or even come from a good family. And the moment people see us together they will put two and two together and our secret can never come out it would ruin my political career and she's not worth that." He said it so coldly with such disdain. That's the problem with dating a married man, he might promise you heaven on earth but some never even left their wives and even when they separated with the wives, he might never elevate you to the coveted wifey post. In Candice's place she had given him two beautiful daughters and she was still not good enough to be considered wife material and Phindiwe would probably be the first to kick her to the curb. But it was not Mpumi's problem, she had gotten what she wanted and Daniel's presence was now beginning to annoy her. He must have read her easily because he stood up and came to stand next to

her, "Goodbye Nompumelelo, I hope he makes you happy." He kissed her on the forehead and that was the gentlest he had ever been to her during their whole marriage. She was happy that this was how they left things, there was no love lost but there was no animosity either.
"He lives to make me happy Daniel."

After Daniel had left Mpumi sat staring at his signature on the divorce papers, she would give it to her lawyers to file for her at the High Court. 16 years of marriage where coming to an end and she felt alive for the first time in a long while. Now she was free to live her happily ever after! She stood up to go and place them in a safer place. Wait until she told... "Jarred!" He was standing quietly in the kitchen with the makings of a sandwich in front of him. Mpumi had thought he had gone back to his hotel room. There was a file on the small table on the passage, he must have found it and when he had come to make her a sandwich he must have seen that she was with Daniel. As she wondered how much of their conversation he had overheard she began to panic. Damn Daniel and his love for English she cursed him silently, if they had been speaking in Xhosa Jarred wouldn't have heard the whole thing. She had told him that Oyama wasn't her daughter but she hadn't told him that Daniel had slipped a pill in her juice which had caused her to miscarry Jarred's child. The look on his face said he had heard the whole conversation. She had never seen him so detached and icy cold. "What are you doing here I thought you had to pick something at your hotel room?" Mpumi's voice sounded rushed and breathless to her own ears, he just continued looking at her with that cold rage gleaming in his eyes. "So he killed my child and you never told me?" The words were softly spoken but they still made her shiver. "Baby please he only told me the night Oyama attempted suicide, I didn't know before then." She was pleading with him and when she attempted to step closer to him, he gave her the look and she put down her hand. "So you have known for over two months now and you kept it from me." If only he would shout and rant, his calmness was scaring her, she rubbed her belly in frustration. "I was scared of your reaction. When he told me I almost shot his brains out. It's done Jarred let's move on and live our lives."

"He killed my child Lelo and you are telling me to move on with my life. Do you fucken hear yourself when you are talking?" Jarred had never used that tone with her, ever, it was scathing. He let out an angry growl and the next instant the mayonnaise and bread and other ingredients were crashing into the floor. He walked past her and hit the hall on the passage hard. He was out of the apartment and she was left with a messy kitchen floor. "Ouch!" she cut her hand as she was trying to pick up the mayonnaise glass from the floor. Just when she was thinking she could start her life afresh this had to happen, she was beyond tears now. After cleaning up the kitchen, she tried calling Jarred his phone went unanswered. What if he had gone to kill Daniel? Mpumi was panicking and she really wished Nomusa was still around. She changed into a long flowing Greek-style dress and flip-flops and she rushed out of the apartment. She kept the doek on her head, she didn't have time to comb that blasted weave. Jarred wasn't there in his hotel room, neither was he at Daniel's house she checked and kept calling and he ignored her. She was beginning to worry. What if he had been involved in an accident driving in such a rage? It was getting late she had to pick up the kids from school, Jarred was the designated driver but today she had no choice. Oyama's uniform hadn't been that short when she left home in the morning, Mpumi would deal with her later. "Lola have you seen your dad? Or has he called you?" Mpumi regretted the question as soon as it left her mouth, the girl was immediately worried. "No did something happen to him?"

"No no, he was looking for a document he needed to fax so he thought maybe it had gotten misplaced in your schoolbag." The lies we tell our children, she sounded convincing to herself and Lola seemed to believe her. "And you have to sleepover tonight, he had to go somewhere, he should be back by tomorrow." Dear God please don't make a liar out of me, Mpumi prayed silently. Jarred couldn't be doing this to her, she was carrying his freaking child! Mpumi's worry was being replaced by anger. He was probably sulking somewhere and she was worrying herself sick. She couldn't afford to be unduly stressed. When they got to the apartment, the girls changed out of their uniforms and started working on supper. Mpumi was restless, she tried calling and there was still no answer. Lola and Oyama seemed to be getting along they were laughing as Lola taught Oyama some Cuban dishes. Lola's mother was from Cuba and Jarred had made sure she learnt Cuban Spanish, Cuban culture and Cuban cuisine. The spices would probably give Mpumi major heartburn but she let them cook. She kept expecting Jarred to walk through the door but he was nowhere to be seen. She ate the dinner and listened with half an ear to the girls' talk, she barely ate. This was not like Jarred at all. When he got mad they usually ended up having hot steamy sex not him storming out and ignoring her the whole day. The girls were picking up on her restlessness and they had become subdued as well, after dinner they cleaned up quickly and went into their bedroom. Mpumi had a bad feeling in the pit of her stomach, something was definitely wrong. When the clock struck midnight she had to drag herself to bed and hope that he would come back to her and his children. It seemed like she had just fallen asleep when her phone woke her up. It was him. She was fuming as she picked his call, "Where the fuck are you?" There was a silence on the other end of the line, "Ummm hello madam, do you know owner of this phone?" It was a Nigerian voice in what sounded like a loud place. Mpumi felt her heart sinking, this was the line most people used before they told you the worst news of your life. She had to calm her breath before she could say anything, "Yes, is he in any trouble?"

"I think its best you come down here right now madam. I will text you address." Mpumi was about to scream at the caller in frustration but he had already ended the phone call. She dragged herself out of bed and pulled the dress she had been wearing on and also grabbed a jacket and her car keys. The address she had been sent was of a nightclub owned by Nigerians and mostly frequented by Nigerians and those money-grubbing skanks. It was in Rivonia on Kelvin Drive at 90 degrees. She had heard about the place from some of her party loving workmates. As to what Jarred was doing there at two am, she couldn't understand. If he had died the man on the phone would have told her she tried to assure herself. Just the thought of Jarred in some nightclub lying there dead instantly made her eyes began to tear up, she had to wipe the tears from her eyes as she tore through the almost deserted streets. The staircase leading to the club was steep and she had to hold on to the railing. People were staring at her as she made her way up the staircase. They were probably wondering what the pregnant woman with the crazy eyes was doing in a nightclub at the early hours of the morning. She had to shout for the large bouncers at the door to hear what she was rumbling about. Normally she would have been intimidated by them, they were tall and buffed up but today she was almost insane with worry. They were very friendly to her though it must have been because of her pregnant state. One of the bouncers ushered her into the dimly lit room, there was some loud Naija songs blasting away and girls in skimpy clothing who seemed a bit older than Oyama were on the arms of some tall thug looking men. Mpumi tried locating Jarred but she couldn't see anything. She was being led into a back room which looked like an office at least this one was brightly lit. Jarred was lying on the floor and a huge man was kneeling next to him trying to hold him down. Mpumi rushed to where he was lying. His face was contorted in convulsions, his arms and legs were moving in a jerky movement and there was white froth on the corner of his mouth. He seemed to be conscious because his eyes widened when he recognized her and his convulsions worsened. "What did you give him?!" she screamed at the man kneeling next to him who seemed like the manager or owner of that joint. "Nothing madam, he had been sitted alone at

the corner nursing his whisky, he barely touched it and he sat there for hours not talking. Then one of the hostesses called me to say white Igwe had toppled over to floor. When I go there I found him like this.

I promise no one gave him anything." The man was sweating as he told her this, he desperately needed her to believe him, but how could she when Jarred seemed like he was having an overdose episode. "We run a clean establishment madam please believe me." Mpumi didn't have a time to listen to his excuses, she was cradling Jarred and he was still having seizures. Oddly his temperature felt normal even though his skin was clammy. She couldn't risk moving him then. "Call an Ambulance!" It seemed all she could do was shout and scream. "The ambulance will be here now now madam." How could he put her through this? He had been really angry but to take drugs? She felt disappointed in him and Jarred seemed like he wanted to say something but that only made him foam even more. "Hush baby, its ok I'm here now, you're going to be ok." She had said the same words to Oyama but right now she didn't believe them. The tears she had been holding back were flowing freely now.

She was once again back at the hospital. They should just give Mpumi her own set of keys, she thought wryly. This time she was pacing the corridor outside the emergency room, they had chucked her out of there because she continued to panic. This time there was no relative with her, she was three months pregnant with no mother offering endless coffee and no Nomusa to give her reassuring hugs. She only had the tall Nigerian manager who quietly watched her pacing up and down the corridor. He had insisted that he would come with her to the hospital and Mpumi was glad that he had. After what seemed like hours later Dr. Babalwa came out of the Emergency Room and beckoned her to follow him to his office. She sat pensively at the edge of the leather chair in his office and waited for him to give her some news. "Mrs. …Nompumelelo contrary to what I first assumed when the paramedics brought him in, your hus… the patient did not suffer from a drug overdose," the doctor said in his calm voice. Mpumi was even more bewildered, she had been there she had seen him convulsing. But she waited for the doctor to continue, "I'm still waiting for the results from the lab to prove me right but he's fully conscious now and he seems stable like the seizure never happened. He is however tired and sleeping. Until I get the results we won't know for certain what triggered the convulsions." Just hearing that he was better was making Mpumi breathe easier, she asked, "May I go see him now?"

"Yes just take care not to upset him until we are sure what we are dealing with." She had no intension of upsetting him, she just needed to see for herself that he was ok. She assured the manager that Jarred was fine and that the doctor suspected that he hadn't suffered from a drug overdose. Only then did he leave her to go back to his club and she went in search of her man. She found him sleeping, they had moved him from the emergency room to a single private room. He was sleeping so peacefully as if he hadn't just turned her whole world upside down. She smoothed a lock of hair from his forehead and kissed him gently careful not to wake him up. "Daddy is fine baby," she whispered to her stomach and gently rubbed it. She sat next to him and held his hand the way he had held hers. His hand was warm and limp, she kissed all his fingers prepared to watch over him till he woke up. She must have fallen asleep because she

was woken by a gentle nudge on her shoulder. It was the doctor, he called her outside. Jarred was still sleeping deeply. "The results are out ma'am." Why did he have to leave her in such suspense, she just wanted him to give her the verdict. "As I suspected, he came clean of any drugs and with little traces of alcohol. From your description I would hazard that he had a simple epileptic partial seizure and it's cryptogenic, I need a second opinion from a neurologist." Mpumi went from relief to slack disbelief, the doctor ushered her into a hospital seat. Jarred epileptic? He was so full of life always in control and seemed perfect to her. There had to be some mistake, she had known him for so long and he had never suffered from an epileptic seizure. Surely he would have told her that he was epileptic. Instinctively her hand reached for her stomach, what did all this mean for their baby? "You did not know that he was epileptic?" the doctor queried softly, he must think them a very weird couple to say the least. "No I had no idea, it's come as a shock to me." Mpumi was surprised by how calm her voice sounded. The doctor seemed puzzled, "So you mean he has never had any such episodes?" She would have told him he was epileptic if he had had such episodes. Mpumi struggled to not roll her eyes at the doctor.

"Not that I'm aware of, you will have to ask him when he wakes up." Her tone was a bit snappy to her own ears. The doctor cleared his throat suspiciously, "Ok then you can go and be with him, I will talk to him when he is awake." Mpumi went back to the room with a heavy heart, this man who said he loved her had kept something so important from her that could affect their child. Not that she would love him or the child any less but she had deserved to know. He had suffered alone in silence and helped her fight her battles. He was beautiful in sleep with a stub of beard shadowing his cheeks. His eyelashes were long and curly, they rested a bit on the upper part of his cheeks. She had kissed those soft pink lips of his many times, they were surprisingly full well for a white man anyway. His straight little nose twitched in his sleep. He was her perfection. She got a message alert on her phone, it was Oyama. ***"Mom where are you?"*** Oh crap! She had totally forgotten about the girls it was just after 7am, she couldn't tell them about Jarred's episode she instinctively knew he didn't want any of them to know. ***"At the hospital, had minor cramps. But I'm fine now, the baby is also fine."***

"Ok, we going to take an Uber to school."

"Did you get all your school things?"

"Yes."

"I'll see you after school love you." As she expected there wasn't a response to her last text, but she was relieved that they could take care of themselves now, her girls were all grown up. The tone must have woken him up, Jarred was stirring from his sleep. He kept his gaze fixed on her hand which was holding his like he couldn't look her in the eye. "I'm sorry you had to see that." His voice sounded subdued, she could feel his shame and his pain and she wanted to assure him that she loved him and he was perfect as he was. The doctor chose that moment to come into the room. “Good you’re up Mr. Levine. How are you feeling?” Jarred focused on the doctor,“I feel like I was hit by a train doc.” At least he still had his humor Mpumi thought.

“Have you ever had such an episode before yesterday?”-doctor

“Yes, as far as I remember the first was at my father’s funeral when I was a boy, back then they were more frequent then I was put on medication they stopped. That is until the death of my brother and his wife but that seizure was isolated. Yesterday was the most severe one.”-Jarred

“So you were diagnosed with epilepsy?”-doctor

“Not to my knowledge my mother got her doctor friend to give me medicine for my ummmh episodes.”-Jarred sounded embarrassed

“Is there anyone in your family who has ever suffered from epilepsy?”-doctor “No.”-Jarred

“Are you always conscious during the seizures?”-doctor

“Yes I can see and hear everything but I just lose control over my body.”-Jarred

“I see. When was your father’s funeral?”-doctor

“When I was fourteen.”-Jarred

“So before that you had never suffered from such episodes?”-doctor “No.”-Jarred

“Have you ever suffered from head trauma?”-doctor

“I did during the car wreck that claimed my father’s life.”-Jarred

“I see, I recommend that you see my friend whose practice specializes in neurology. Can I fax her these notes?” Jarred seemed to hesitate before mumbling “Yes”. Mpumi had sat quietly throughout this solemn exchange as Jarred responded and the doctor took down notes and her heart went out to her man. His father’s death was something they had never gotten into, she hadn’t known that he had been there in the car with his father when the car crushed. When the doctor left there was awkward silence. She had to ask him, “Why didn’t you tell me about the seizures?" Jarred was still not looking her in the eye, "I didn't want your pity." Mpumi was shocked by the bitterness in his voice, "Why would I pity you baby? You're the most perfect human being." This time he did look her in the eye as if he wanted re-assurance that she wasn't bluffing, he squeezed her hand gently. "When the seizures started my mother would lock me in my bedroom, she said she didn't want people to know that she had given birth to a freak." Mpumi felt rage well up for the poor traumatized boy who had needed his mother's love and medical help but had been shut away in his room while he convulsed alone. That woman had been heartless hopefully she was rolling in hell. As if he could read her mind he squeezed her hand again, "Don't look so sad my brother was always with me through each episode and he held me till the convulsions ended the way you cradled me last night." It was still a sad image to picture in her mind, they had unlimited funds he could have easily gotten the best medical attention. "Did you ever get hurt?" she asked him with tears in her voice. He pointed to a tiny scar on his forehead, "I fell and hit the corner of my bed once." She kissed the scar softly then kissed him on the lips. At first he was unresponsive then he held her tightly and kissed her savagely. She was probably going to get bruised lips but she wanted to share his pain. When he finally let her go, she cradled his face in her hands, "Promise me that you won't ever suffer alone or in silence again." He smiled and kissed her gently, "Yes mama bear, I promise. You scared the shit out of that huge man at the club. Did you see how profusely he was sweating?" She smiled and snuggled up to him on the hospital bed, her man was back and her joy was complete.

CHAPTER ELEVEN

Two great things had happened in the past two months. The first was that they had moved into their new home. The house was more of an estate than a mansion in Fernbrook. It was a beautiful Tuscan style single floor house with a very high ceiling. It was pale cream on the outside and the inside walls were white. But the floor tiles where a marine blue which shined and shimmered so that when you walked it felt like you were walking on the ocean's bed or walking on water. On one end the lounge had been sunk a bit lower than the other rooms and it was built just under the swimming pool. There was bullet-proof glass separating the lounge from the swimming pool it was like being in an Aquarium because you could see someone swimming in the pool and at night they could see the stars shining as reflected by the water. It was Mpumi's absolute favorite room. But it came second to the main bedroom which was furnished Haram style, they were cushions to sit on and the colors where festive and exotic. It was also sound-proofed. Wink. She had half-jokingly threatened Jarred that if he turned their bedroom into an actual Haram she would shoot his whore and him. When it came to him she didn't want to share even a single hair on his head. And the bed! The bed was pure heaven it felt like a waterbed but Jarred said it was an orthopedic bed, it was perfect for Mpumi's ever aching back. Each bedroom had an ensuite bathroom and walk-in closets, there were seven bedrooms in total excluding the room designated to be the nursery. The girls' bedrooms were side to side and Jarred had given them carte blanche on the paint color, style and décor of their rooms. Oyama's room was gothic rock and Lola's room had funky edge to it and Mpumi mostly kept away from their bedrooms. There was also 'Nomusa's room' which was in soft earth colors. There was a diamond chandelier in their dining room which was huge and they agreed that it would only be used for formal gatherings. Mpumi wasn't much of a cook but the black and silver kitchen had state of the art kitchenware it even had an electric blender, Jarred was the chef of the family. There was a music room which had a piano and a harp, very bourgeois and the kids practiced their instruments there. There was also a 'dance studio' it was a sound proofed room with a disco style sound system. At least now they didn't have to suffer through Oyama's rock music obsession. The indoor gym would help Mpumi lose her baby-fat and the Jacuzzi soothed her on the rough days when her whole body felt swollen. Jarred had thought of every tiny detail in buying the house. There was a walk-in pantry which he filled with all kinds of food. Mpumi loved working in the sun room which had a glass ceiling, she preferred it to her study-office. All in all there were eighteen rooms inside the house. There were no servant quarters in their new home, Jarred liked his privacy and the cleaning agency sent someone three times a week to clean and do the laundry, everything else they did for themselves. There was a mini hockey court where Jarred and Oyama had their one on one matches at times. Lola's horse stayed in the mini stables with another horse which Jarred sometimes rode with her around the grounds of the house. Mpumi did not want those horses anywhere close to her, at least Oyama was learning how to ride as well. Mpumi had flatly refused when Jarred had wanted dogs, their children would have to be their pets. There was also a jet-pad on their roof, Jarred had to be up and down across the world and he knew how to fly his own private jet. There was a beautiful garden as well which Mpumi was taking care of but only the minor stuff the heavy stuff was taken care of by the gardener who also came three times a week. This house even though it was over the top felt like home, it was sunny and warm and it showed all their personalities. It was just a portion of the three-story house she and Daniel had lived in mostly, but this house felt personal it had an intimacy to it maybe because it had been remodeled with the whole family in mind. Mpumi felt that they could make many happy memories in that house. She could see her future children running around it driving Oyama and Lola crazy. When Mpumi had video called Nomusa to walk her through their new home she had been screaming all the way down at Kappa. She wanted them to mail her set of keys. Mpumi had noticed that Nomusa seemed to have lost weight but she would wait to see her in person before she asked what was going on with her. Things had been hard after that episode with Jarred he had been awkward around her. He told her that he had blamed himself for the death of their first child because he thought he must have passed onto the child a 'strange' gene that had strangled the child in the womb. Trying to re-assure him Mpumi had booked a scan with Dr. Babalwa to see the child. Jarred had looked pensive as he held her hand while the good doctor had prepped her for the scan. They had seen a huge blot on the screen and the doctor had been frowning as he went over her belly. Mpumi tried hard not to panic, then the doctor had handed her the machine he had been using to listen to the child's heartbeat. Then she had heard the heartbeat it was strong and steady yet there seemed to be an echo. Puzzled Mpumi had given the machine to Jarred and he also didn't know what to make of it. They both looked at the doctor and that's when the second greatest thing happened. "Congratulations it seems you are having twins." Twins! Mpumi had looked at Jarred and seen the tears in his eyes, "But how…?" she had to ask the doctor.

"That's what I was trying to figure out because there is only one fetus showing but it is unusually big but the double heartbeat means that there are two of them and I think they are holding each other or the other one is hiding that sometimes happens with twins."

"Will they also be epileptic?" Jarred had asked the question so solemnly.

"I can't say for certain till they are born and further tests are done on them and when your tests come back as well." The doctor tried to re-assure him. Mpumi felt hurt and she asked the doctor to give them some time alone. "Come here," she patted a spot next to her on the bed. "Do you know the exact moment I fell in love with you?" He hadn't been expecting that question and he looked at her with a little frown. "It was on the day you taught me how to swim. I was so scared but you looked at me and said I should trust you. When I looked into your eyes I felt safe. Since my father's death I hadn't allowed myself to need or depend on anyone but I depended on you and I knew I could hold onto you and you wouldn't let me drown." There were tears in his eyes and he was blinking them away. "You're always on my case about me looking down on myself now I need you to do the same for yourself. Having epilepsy doesn't make me love you less or make you any less perfect to me. You were made exactly the way you are for me. We want healthy babies yes but if they have epilepsy they will still be perfect because they will be little pieces of me and you. Hopefully they will inherit your kindness and your love for life. And we will love them unconditionally." He was smiling more like his usual self and there was so much love in his voice, "And I hope they inherit your fire and your drive my feisty goddess." They cuddled with both their hands on her belly. They were going to survive whatever life threw at them, together. They stayed like that till there was a knock on the door it was the doctor. He told them that since it was already a complicated pregnancy having twins heightened the risk and she couldn't carry the babies' full term. They would wait for her to be six months along and she would give birth via C-section. She was already three months along.

CHAPTER

ELEVEN

It was a long weekend and Mpumi had to take the girls to her mother in Soweto. MaNtuli had only wanted Oyama but Mpumi had made it clear that they were a package deal, where Oyama went Lola also went. Her mother hadn't been too happy about that but both girls were going. As they stopped to buy groceries at the Spar on 90 degrees, Mpumi was reminded of her mad dash to the club upstairs. She wondered if she should go upstairs and look for the manager, she wanted to apologize for concluding that they had sold drugs to Jarred and also thank him for accompanying them to the hospital. He had been so helpful after the rude way she had shouted at him but she was too embarrassed to go to him and she had the girls with her they knew nothing about that night. So instead she turned her focus to her mission at hand. She had to be careful when buying groceries for her mother, MaNtuli was a proud woman. Daniel and Mpumi had offered countless times to buy her a new house in the lower density suburbs but she flatly refused. MaNtuli had bought that house in Soweto with her savings from her maid jobs when Mpumi had been accepted at the University of Johannesburg, she had packed up everything and moved there to be closer to her daughter. There had been nothing left for them in Cape Town, Mpumi's uncle had taken over their house in Khayelitsha. As Mpumi drove down the N1 she remembered that when MaNtuli had bought the house it had only been one room with an outside toilet but it had been home her mother had seen to that. Even though she had protested, Mpumi had helped MaNtuli set up a cleaning company where she employed mostly single mothers from Soweto and helped them get cleaning jobs for houses in Naturena, Kibler Park, Mondeor, Glenvista, Alberton and other areas around the South including companies as well. The business had flourished and having an MP for a son-in-law hadn't hurt either. Mpumi snuck money now and then into her mother's bank account but she was proud of how her mother trained and looked out for the women who worked for her. Mpumi turned at the intersection at the Protea Glen mall and made her way up to the

Shell garage in Extension 11. As
always Soweto was vibrant, there were people walking on the streets, groups sitted under trees, loud music blasting from some local 'spots' and the occasional horn of irritated taxi drivers. Mpumi had to be careful not to run over children who unexpectedly ran into the street, one child stood in the middle of the road and openly stared at her car. They passed a food stand and Mpumi felt a craving for ikota what her Model C daughter called a bunny-chow. She stopped the car and went to place her order, Oyama had turned her Model C nose up when Mpumi had told them that she wanted to buy ikota, Lola was more receptive so Mpumi placed an order for two and she asked for everything to be added and extra atchar on hers. The young man making their order was very chatty his name was Sphola and he was fascinated by her car, he said he was eighteen years old. At least he didn't look like he was into nyaope, in fact he looked very clean and boyishly handsome. Mpumi gave him a generous tip when he gave her the order. From the startled expression on his face she gathered that people never tipped him. Then Oyama came out of the car to check on her and Sphola looked as if he was struck by lightning he couldn't tear his gaze away from her daughter. Oyama wasn't even aware of the effect she had on the poor boy she didn't even glance his direction, Mpumi felt bad for him he looked like a love-struck puppy. Mpumi said her goodbyes to him but he just kept looking at Oyama, ok now he was beginning to creep her out, she quickly got in the car with Oyama. "Let's eat in the car MaNtuli will kill us if we go with this to her house," Mpumi told Lola as she handed her the food. Damn she had forgotten how good ikota tasted, you could only find the good ones in Soweto. Lola kept asking questions at the back and Oyama was pointing out places to her, Mpumi was relieved at their easy sister relationship, there were a lot of squabbles over clothes but there was also a lot of love and understanding. Those two were even learning to cover for each other she thought smiling because it reminded her of her and Nomusa at their age. Oyama had been accepting of her pregnancy although she had

been subdued at first she had been excited when they let them watch the scan video, both girls were already looking up names. As she turned to her mother's big black sliding gate Mpumi hoped MaNtuli would also be as accommodating because she hadn't told her of her pregnancy yet. MaNtuli opened the gate for them herself, she must have been waiting for them on the veranda. She had extended the house it was now a high-ceiling house, those that resembled mission hospitals and it was painted in a cheerful yellow and MaNtuli kept it in pristine mint condition. Not a stone or even a blade of grass was out of place. Even her tenants who stayed in the rooms behind the main house knew that their landlady tolerated no dirt in her yard. Mpumi parked her Range Rover and in a moment of weakness didn't want to leave the car, she opened the boot and the girls started unpacking groceries after hugging their gogo. MaNtuli after inspecting Lola seemed to accept her and hug her, Lola was just loveable. Mpumi finally gained the courage to get out from the car and suffer her mother's inspection and raised eyebrow. While the girls were unpacking in their room, the dreaded interrogation began. "Nompumelelo so you are living with the white boy now?" Mpumi wondered how her mother managed to sound so condescending while calmly sipping her tea, it must be an art and it reduced Mpumi to a stuttering child. "Yes maa."

"Mmmmmmh and what is this about a divorce that we had to read about in the newspapers?" Her mother should have been a drilling sergeant her intimidation tactics were on point, and she had a way of looking you down without even glancing at you for more than a second. Someone at the Clerk's office had leaked their divorce papers to the media and the story had made headlines. Mpumi had to clear her throat before responding, "Daniel and I decided our marriage wasn't working so we agreed to get a divorce."

"I see so you just woke up one morning made a cup of tea and you both said our marriage isn't working let's go to court. Yet I can see there is a baby on the way." Mpumi couldn't look her mother in the eye. "It's not Daniel's child." There was a prolonged silence and then all MaNtuli said calmly was, "I see." Mpumi felt shame well up and swallow her, she wished she could dig a hole and hide her head like an ostrich. She waited for her mother to continue speaking. "Do you have any idea of the shame you have brought on me? I see those books of yours have made you forget who and what you are. Umkhwenyana did not just sign papers and make you his wife, he paid lobolo for you and asked for you from your ancestors. You are not a Ndinisa anymore you are a Sisulu even when you die you will be buried among his people." There was quiet finality in MaNtuli's voice which brooked no argument. Wasn't she a devout Christian?

"But maa..."

"No buts, listen to me Nompumelelo. I raised you better than this and this is the second time you are bringing ihlazo shame onto me. And you are now openly living in sin what must I tell your uncles and your in-laws?" Mpumi felt like a child being reprimanded but she had to be strong.

"I don't care what you have to tell them maa there is no way I am going back to Daniel." Instead of sounding defiant her voice came out sounding hesitant and shaky. MaNtuli folded her arms on her chest and gave her the look. You know the look that only your mother can give you which makes you feel small no matter how old or big you actually are.

"Is that so? Very well I won't say anything to them." Mpumi felt uneasy by how chilled about this situation her mother seemed to be. But MaNtuli wasn't finished saying her piece, "Because you will tell them yourself in the family meeting next weekend." Mpumi felt the air leaving her lungs.

"What family meeting?"

"You think uqhawulo womshato (the separation a marriage) is something to be taken lightly? The Sisulu elders who were present at your lobolo negotiations have requested a family meeting and your uncles have agreed." Her mother sounded triumphant. Culture could be a bitch at times.

CHAPTER
ELEVEN

"I'm not going to any family meeting, it's over between me and Daniel we both signed the divorce papers." At least she sounded defiant there, her hormones were kicking in giving her wings. Her mother clapped once and there was a smirk in her voice, "This wasn't a request to one of your fancy ball functions, you are going to the meeting madam." Mpumi felt tears of anger welling up in her eyes, damn this pregnancy for making her so emotional. MaNtuli must have mistook the tears for pain because she immediately softened. "I am not the enemy here Nompumelelo, you have to understand that you are not just married to Daniel you are married to the whole family. You made your bed and now the family has to help you resolve this mess. It's not an ambush but more of a mediation, we have to leave in good relations with the Sisulus." Mpumi knew there was no arguing or fighting the inevitable. "Where will the meeting be held?" she asked quietly.

"Where it all began Nompumelelo."

Mpumi had been in a black funk after leaving her mother's house, a family meeting was no joke and the elders' verdict was binding. Forget her defiant stance with her mother she had to go to the meeting. Feeling frustrated she dialed his number, he answered on the fourth ring with a chirpy "My love." Mpumi's hands tightened on the steering wheel and she spoke through her teeth, "I am no longer your love Daniel."

"Oh sorry force of habit," he lied through his teeth, she didn't have patience for his games.

"What is it that you're trying to pull with the family meeting?"

"What family meeting?" he sounded genuinely puzzled.

"The family meeting your uncle requested with my family." She was barking in frustration, he swore softly.

"He did call me about the article on the newspaper and he was fuming he said he would fix the mess I had made. I'm sorry Mpumi I had no idea he would call a family meeting."

"How convenient for you," her voice dripped sarcasm.

"I mean it Mpumi don't worry about it, I know how to handle my uncle, I did promise you your freedom." She hung up on him, she was so frustrated. She felt hot all of a sudden even though the air conditioner was on she opened the windows. Why couldn't people or Nomusa's Universe just allow her to live in peace with the love of her life. She didn't trust Daniel one bit, he had proven how underhanded he could be to get what he wanted. She got home and found that Jarred had prepared lunch for her, it tasted like cardboard she had no appetite. She was still feeling hot so she took off her top and asked him to unfasten her bra. He could tell something was bothering her, he pulled her feet onto his lap and started massaging them gently. "Mmmmmmh yes that feels so good," she felt herself relax for the first time that day. He looked at her like he was trying to figure her out before asking, "Do you want to tell me what's gotten you crankier than usual?" Mpumi sighed they had agreed on no more secrets, so she told him about the upcoming family meeting that she wasn't looking forward to. He seemed to take the news worse than her, his face had a glum expression. He looked as if she would never come back to him after the meeting. "When are we ever going to be allowed to love each other in peace?" she had no response to that question. Mpumi understood his frustration she was also feeling frustrated but she wanted to cheer him up. "You know we have the house all to ourselves for three days and two nights and we are cleared to make love as loudly as we want," she batted her eyebrows seductively. Jarred was now in a black funk as well, he rubbed her belly but he seemed to be thinking deeply. Mpumi had to get him out of that funk and she had a few tricks up her sleeve. She looked him deeply in the eyes as she unbuckled his belt, he stilled and looked back at her suspiciously. The moment she put his manhood in her mouth and began sucking gently and heard his soft groans, she knew she had gotten his mind off dark thoughts or any coherent thought for the time-being.

CHAPTER
ELEVEN

They were lying in their bed the night before Mpumi was supposed to leave for the Eastern Cape with her mother and uncles. Her mother was sleeping in one of the guest bedrooms, they had been awkward tension during dinner only her mother managed to make people feel awkward around her. Jarred had insisted that Mpumi and her mother should fly in his private jet to Cape Town where Nomusa would pick them up in his Jeep and drive them to get her uncles and go to the meeting. He was not hearing a single word of his precious Lelo driving all the way to Transkei with his precious cargo. Mpumi was glad he asked Nomusa to drive them she would need Nomusa along for moral support and she needed someone in her corner. Her mother wanted her back with Daniel and her uncles just wanted to make sure they didn't have to return the lobolo which they had probably sold by then. Mpumi loved cuddling with Jarred, they were lying on their sides with her in front of him and he was cradling her baby bump. "Your mother looked like she was about to strangle me," Mpumi laughed at the attempted hurt in Jarred's voice, he would have to brace himself. He brushed his lips on her hair and suddenly his tone was serious, "I don't want you to go there Lelo, what if something happens to you and our babies…" She turned slightly and placed her finger on his mouth, "Nothing is going to happen to us and we are going to come back to you and we can start on a clean slate." His brow was furrowed in worry, "I can't lose you, not again Lelo I just couldn't live without you now." His body radiated so much warmth. She snuggled closer to him her naked butt brushing against his crotch, "I love you Jarred and you are the only man for me. If Daniel tries to pull any stunt I'm prepared to leave with you. We can start our life afresh in America." He was quiet and only his steady breathing betrayed that he hadn't fallen asleep.

"How come you haven't ever asked about my life after you left me?" he asked softly.

"Because nothing else matters except that we still found each other again," the answer came straight from her heart and then she remembered something and giggled. "Also because Nomusa already investigated and did a google search on you." Jarred laughed and his laugh was so warm and infectious, "Don't believe everything you read on the internet."

"Hmmmm but the camera never lies, I swear there was a new lady clinging on your arm at every event."

"Is that jealousy I dictate in your voice?" his voice held a teasing note.

"Of course, I should have been the one hanging on your arm granted I wouldn't have been arm candy but still you are mine." Something about him made her very territorial.

"None of them ever came close to you my Aphrodite, you have my heart and my soul in your soft hands. I get horny just by thinking of your hands." Everything made him horny! She wanted to stay in his arms like this forever and listen to his crazy talk and his deep husky voice.

"So how come you never looked for me?" That question had bugged Mpumi for the longest time.

"At first it was my stupid pride, I was hurt that you could just leave me with no word not even a note. And then when I read my mother's letter I was filled with shame I never should have doubted you and you thought I had abandoned you and my child. I wanted so many times to
look for you but I was ashamed I didn't know how I would face you and you would probably have moved on."

"I'm sorry that I just left without hearing what you had to say." There was regret in both their voices, they had wasted so much time and now everything was complicated. He sighed and drew her even deeper into his embrace. They were molded into one person and when he talked his words vibrated into her body. "It doesn't matter anymore, everything happened for a reason, we wouldn't have Oyama if you hadn't left. All that matters is now, we have each other and we mustn't let go no matter what. Now sleep you have a long journey tomorrow." He was so solid and wholesome, he made her fully alive. She held on to his hand even as she was beginning to fall asleep. She had no plans to ever let him go. But he was right the journey that lay ahead of her was long and it was going to be strenuous both physically and mentally. She had to brace herself for whatever Daniel had up his sleeve.

CHAPTER TWELVE

As the jet taxied onto the runway Mpumi felt a sense of relief. That had to have been the longest hour of her life with her mother judging her the whole flight. She couldn't wait to be rescued by Nomusa, if they didn't have to take her uncles they could have landed at Queenstown Airport. But at least they were driving with Nomusa, her mother had been disapproving of that arrangement but Mpumi didn't care. MaNtuli had already forced her to wear umbhaco the traditional wear for Xhosa married women, technically she was still a married woman but it wasn't exactly travel-wear. It was black and blue she had worn it to the last traditional wedding that she and Daniel had attended. To give her mother credit the outer material of her attire covered her baby bump and ingxowa the purse she was carrying was also perfect camouflage. Nomusa raised an eyebrow when she saw her before she hugged her, Mpumi rolled her eyes, "Don't even ask." They couldn't really sit and reminisce with her mother hovering at them disapprovingly, they went straight to Khayelitsha to get her uncles. Their

former home still had the hedge her father had planted and no gate, it was rundown now her uncle had built a shack with aluminum sheets and had painted it a glaring orange in the back of the two roomed house where he and his family stayed. In the house he had put up tenants and it looked like there were over twenty people staying there. There were children playing around the yard and some women were gossiping under a mango tree and they looked at them curiously. The paint was
peeling off on the house as well as the shack, clearly rent money didn't go to the maintenance and upkeep of the house. Mpumi cringed as she remembered how lovingly her father had overseen the building of that house and how her mother had spent hours applying red polish on the stoop and shining till it shone. Now the stoop was muddy and it seemed as if someone had used black floor polish on it but there were still streaks of red in it. There were still tiny shoe prints embedded on the stoop, Mpumi had walked over it before the concrete had fully set when she was a tiny girl and her mother had given her an arse-whooping. The yard had overgrown weeds, there was a rusty bicycle lying on the ground and there were chicken running around, the scrawny township type. The state of the house broke Mpumi's heart and it seemed to be even harder on her mother because she kept looking around the yard. The sooner they got out of there the better. Her aunt was also there, that one who had made the snide remark about Nomusa being married first because she was prettier and lighter than Mpumi. She had that selfrighteous I-knew-it-was-going-to-end-this-way look on her face, Mpumi didn't even know why she had come but as udadobawo her father's sister, she couldn't exactly leave her behind. The way her uncles were eying Jarred's Jeep made Mpumi cringe, she could just see their greedy minds turning. Her two uncles, her mother and aunt squeezed into the backseat while she sat in front with Nomusa. Mpumi put on music to drown out her aunt's meddlesome questions. She was being rude but she didn't care, these people who called themselves her family had only ever taken from her life. It was going to be a long day. At least the drive along the R27

was picturesque there were hills and small mountains and the slopes where a lush green even the sky seemed clear and beautiful so she spent most of it looking out of the window. Even Nomusa was a bit subdued not her normal crazy foot in mouth self. The road wound up the hill and as they passed eNgcobo centre Mpumi was reminded of the lady who had made her wedding day umbhaco, she had stayed eNgcobo. It had been snow white with beautiful black beadwork even a tiny bead veil was attached on her head gear, she wondered if the woman still worked in her small stall. Maybe she would pass by and check her on their return. Jarred kept texting her and that made her even more apprehensive. Daniel texted that they were already there eQutubeni and they were waiting for them, she didn't bother responding they would get there Daniel and his family could just stew a little. As they entered a somewhat rutted gravel road, Mpumi looked around the area. She and Daniel had walked down this road as the whole community had come out to see them, it was a tradition called ukucanda ibala in which the bride was welcomed into the community. It was beautiful, she wished she had brought her camera with her hands were itching to take pictures. The area had improved a lot maybe because it had attached some tourist destination status, the round huts had fresh paint and the fields seemed ready for harvesting. Nomusa didn't need any directions, she had come here with Mpumi on her wedding day and they had stayed for a week. As they drew closer to the Sisulu homestead, Mpumi grew more apprehensive. It was at the end of the winding gravel road, it was the biggest homestead with a main brick house with the rondavel huts around it. There was a huge water tank inside the yard and at the gate just next to a small hill there were graves. There was no smoke coming out of the kitchen because they had electricity, but Mpumi hadn't liked coming here she usually avoided coming by using work as an excuse. She only came for weddings and funerals. She could see Tat' Xhamela's white head sitting on the veranda of the main house he had some elders sitting with him drinking umqombothi as they drove into the homestead. This was it, Mpumi got out of the car to head into the trial, although it was a family meeting it felt like a trial.

They had been about to put their butts down after the greetings when Mpumi's mother instructed them to go and help in the preparation of food in the kitchen. They found Tat' Xhamela's senior wife MaNgidi and Phindiwe in the kitchen with most of the food ready. At least the other wives were away, they got on Mpumi's nerves. MaNgidi was a warm loving person with a smile and a kiss always ready for the next person, she had a big bosom and a big heart. Mpumi was happy to see her and when she enfolded her in her motherly embrace she felt the babies kick for the first time. MaNgidi must have felt them too but she made no comment, she only fussed over her and exclaimed on how beautiful she looked. Phindiwe looked like she had swallowed something sour but they all ignored her. Nomusa took warm water in a jug and a basin to go and wash their hands, it would be difficult for Mpumi to kneel and stand in front of each elder and wash their hands. Mpumi followed with the plates piled with istampa (samp) and meat with salads, instead of kneeling she curtsied as she handed out the food. Daniel followed her out as she went to get more food and when she wanted to walk past him he held her arm, "Mpumi wait, I know you think I set this whole thing up but I didn't. Please just let me do all the answering during the meeting," Mpumi looked at him, he had really lost his mind or he thought she had lost her mind, "Please trust me one last time maMlaba." He had only ever called her with her clan name when he was begging for something or when he was trying to soften her. Mpumi might live to regret it but she nodded once and continued on her mission to bring them all food. Fortunately it was taboo for the daughter-in-law to eat in the same room as her fatherin-law the role assumed by Tat' Xhamela so Mpumi, Nomusa, Phindiwe and MaNgidi were going to eat in the kitchen. Mpumi ignored Phindiwe's proffered plate of food and accepted food from MaNgidi she wasn't taking any chances with that witch, she might have placed some poison on her food. "MaMlaba we have missed you, where is Oyama?" MaNgidi was always soft-spoken.

"She had to go to school so I left her back in Johannesburg, she is writing her Matric this year."

"Hawu they grow up so fast, it seems like only yesterday she was running around this yard scared of a puppy." They all laughed at that story, Oyama had been three years old and the puppy had wanted to play but she had thought it wanted to attack her, instead of going back into the car she had run around the yard as fast as her short legs could carry her. "She still hates dogs to this day," Mpumi told MaNgidi when they had caught their breath after laughing.

"You should bring her here so that we hold the Intonjane ceremony for her." MaNgidi was referring to the coming of age ceremony held for girls as their initiation into womanhood.

"She turns fifteen in December I will bring her then." There was no specific age for the ceremony and Oyama had begun her menses the previous year but Mpumi knew how important the ceremony was in grooming young ladies. Hopefully Oyama wouldn't be too difficult and all Model C about the matter. They continued talking and MaNgidi kept telling them village stories which kept them shaking with laughter only Phindiwe was not participating, Mpumi had relaxed and she wasn't as tense as when they had arrived. After they collected the plates, MaNgidi said Mpumi should go in for the meeting they would do the dishes and clean up. Phindiwe wasn't happy at all she probably wanted to be there at the meeting but MaNgidi knew her and she kept her away purposely.

"*Ndinisa, Mzomba, Mlaba, mbhobho kabikwayo, Mzomba, Thuliswayo, Masibekela, wenowasibekela inkosi ngothuli, amazomba ayekhathana maseyebandla, kwasuka dludlu kwahlala unkalakatha, intuthwanencane ngokubhala amadoda, ibhejelibomvu labothul'swako* thank you for coming so that we resolve the children's issues." Tat' Xhamela's voice held quiet dignity as he addressed Mpumi's uncle with their clan names, iziduko. Mpumi was sitted on dried animal skin with her

head slightly bowed next to her mother, her friends in the Feminist movement back in Harvard would have a fit if they saw her submissive stance. Her uncles and Daniel's uncles were granting their appreciation then her elder uncle cleared his throat.
"Xhamela lina amaGcina, Helushe, Ncancashe, Magwebulikhula, Malambedlile, Nokwindla, Thyopho, Bahamba bepheth'isali, ihashe bakulifuman'emlungwini, izinto zabantu abazibi koko bayazigcini, bathi igusha ziziduli zentaba thank you for inviting us we hope to resolve this matter as peacefully as possible." Mpumi's obnoxious aunt was ululating as her brother also chanted their in-laws clan names now they could commence with the meeting. They waited for Tat' Xhamela to speak he was after all *intloko yemilowo*, the leader of Daniel's family. The elder took his sweet time, he was stroking his beard as he looked first at Daniel then at Mpumi and the he returned his gaze to Daniel. "I am very disappointed in you my children. First our grandchild almost died and did anyone inform us? No, you took her to the white man's hospital and spent almost two months there. We had to read about it in the newspaper. If she had died would you have buried her alone? Or did you think we were planning to finish her off?" there was no denying the authority in his voice and it made Mpumi squirm, she kept her eyes fixed on a spot in the floor.

"We apologize for not informing you it was my fault I overlooked the matter, our heads were just everywhere but it's not an excuse please forgive us." There was deference in Daniel's voice.

"We hear you. Make sure it is the first and last time that such a thing happens. Now we also heard from the newspapers that the two of you are divorcing. Is this true?" Tat' Xhamela sounded angry.

"Yes sir." Daniel was still doing all the answering.

"MaMlaba?" Tat' Xhamela directed his gaze to Mpumi.

"Yes Tata it's true." Mpumi kept her gaze fixed on the floor, the other elders were uttering sounds of disapproval, and Mpumi had never felt smaller in her life.

"And who did you tell that you had problems in your

marriage?" Both Daniel and Mpumi remained silent, Tat' Xhamela continued addressing Mpumi's uncle, "Mzomba did they come to you with any problems?"

"Not at all Ncancashe, as far as we know our daughter is happy in her marriage," Mpumi felt irritated by this bold faced lie, her uncles had never asked her if she was happy or not in her marriage they had taken the lobolo cattle and disappeared from her life.

"Now tell us what has been happening that has made you file for divorce." Mpumi held her breath hoping that Daniel wouldn't mess up. She stole a glance in his direction shame he was even sweating a little.

"Everything is my fault I take full responsibility for the demise of our marriage. Nompumelelo has been a good wife to me for the last sixteen years but I neglected her when she needed me the most. I did not stand by her when she had miscarriages to make it worse I had a wandering eye and even though she caught me many times she stood by me like the good wife that she is. I even impregnated one of my mistresses and when she found out we had a fight and our daughter overheard the fight that's why she decided she wanted to take her own life. I am ashamed that I have brought so much grief to my wife and our daughter so when she asked to be free I gave her the freedom from our marriage." Mpumi hadn't expected Daniel to take the full blame for their divorce and he sounded sincere like he really regretted his actions. She felt tears slip down her face, bloody hormones! She could feel Tat' Xhamela's eyes on her bowed head.

"Is what he saying true makoti?" well it wasn't the gospel truth but when Mpumi looked at Daniel he nodded re-assuringly at her.

"Yes Tata he is telling the truth." She affirmed quietly.

"I see but why didn't you come to me my child, all these years all this has been going on and you suffered in silence." There was empathy in Tat' Xhamela's voice that Mpumi hadn't expected.

"He apologized and I forgave him each time he promised he would change and I believed him. But when it hurt our daughter I realized we couldn't go on hurting each other."-Mpumi

"But he seems remorseful surely he will change now, you have to give your family one last chance my brother's daughter," Mpumi's forward aunt interjected. Mpumi gave her a cold glare.

"I don't know aunt maybe the next time we will hold another meeting will be at my daughter's burial. This marriage nearly broke me but I won't allow it to destroy my child." Mpumi hadn't meant for her voice to be so hostile but her aunt infuriated her. Tat' Xhamela cleared his voice cutting through the tension, "We hear you my child but are both of you sure the dissolution of your marriage is the only solution left?"

"I agree with my wife we can't continue hurting each other and hurting our child in the process. Oyama's suicide attempt was the last straw." Mpumi was grateful for Daniel keeping his word. There was silence for a short while before Tat' Xhamela talked again, "MaMlaba do you remember the name I gave you when we accepted you into this family?" That was so random, as per culture after giving the family gifts on her wedding day to show that they accepted her into the family she had been given a new name. "Yes Tata you gave me the name Buyiswa."

"I gave you that name because you brought us back our son and you brought our family together. You have loved and respected us as your family and we will not hold you back. But you must know that you will always be a Sisulu. You are welcome here anytime it is still your home, I give you my blessing to live your life as you see fit and may you find happiness." He probably wouldn't be so gracious if he knew that she was carrying another man's twins but Mpumi was grateful for his kind words.

"Thank you Tata." There was so much emotion in those words, Mpumi meant each word.

"What about their child? In our culture the child remains with her father's family." Mpumi wished she could strangle her aunt, the woman lived to make Mpumi's life miserable.

"We agreed that it's best for our daughter to stay with her

mother we don't want her to harm herself further." Daniel had come to her rescue and Mpumi gave him a grateful look.

"Then that's that. Even though you hadn't involved the family I am glad that you resolved this matter reasonably between the two of you. We just pray that maMlaba you will not make our child a stranger." Mpumi's aunt didn't seem too happy but there was nothing she could do Tat' Xhamela's word was binding. Mpumi hadn't expected the meeting to take this route. "And since the husband is at fault, the bride-wealth is forfeited." Mpumi's uncle seemed pleased with himself. The greed of these people! He had probably been having heart palpitations wondering where he would get the one head of cattle to return the Sisulus signifying the termination of marriage if Mpumi had been the one found at fault. Mpumi was tempted to spit out her affair just to wipe that smug look off her uncles' faces but she didn't want Daniel to lose face. When Mpumi mentioned that they were leaving since the meeting was over Tat' Xhamela would hear none of it. "There is plenty of room here for you to sleep we wouldn't send you on your way this late, you will leave in the morning." There was no coming out of that without sounding churlish, so they were spending the night.

Jarred wasn't impressed when Mpumi told him that they were sleeping over, it was as if she and Daniel would be sharing a room. He was sulking so he simply texted her goodnight at 8pm, Mpumi let him be she was just glad she was spending the night with Nomusa. After the meeting she had asked Daniel why he had taken the blame for everything. She had been curious it wasn't at all what she had expected from him, he had been quiet for a while and she had thought he wasn't going to say anything. "The look you gave me the day I told you that I gave you that pill was full of hate and that really killed me because all I have ever wanted to do is love you and Oyama but now both of you hate me. And I wouldn't be able to live with myself knowing that I had brought you even more pain. And that day at your apartment you had a glow that you never had when you were with me. I love you Mpumi I probably always will and I finally gained the courage to let you go and let you be happy because I know that he makes you happy." Mpumi had been deeply touched and she had hugged him, she would probably always care about him too. After updating Nomusa about the meeting and how her aunt had tried to sabotage her, Mpumi turned to Nomusa and really studied her. Nomusa had lost weight and she seemed preoccupied. "What's happening with you Nono you don't look happy." Nomusa sighed and avoided Mpumi's inquisitive gaze, "It's Amogalang I don't think we are going to work out." Mpumi was shocked, she hadn't thought things would sour so quickly between Amo and Nomusa. "Start from the beginning what's wrong?"

"Everything Mpumi. Amo is too… he's too critical." Nomusa sounded dejected

"What do you mean when you say he's too critical?"

"Nothing I ever do is good enough for him, I could boil water and he would say I boiled it at the wrong temperature. He criticizes me at every chance he gets. How I dress, my eating habits, the food I cook, the way I drive, my friends, my job everything Mpumi and its so frustrating." Mpumi was surprised the man had seemed to worship the ground that Nomusa walked on. "You know what the worst part is Mpumi? When he calls me names, he says I'm stupid Mpumi, he said I embarrass him he is even afraid to go with me in public. He says I'm too forward and I need to grow up and start acting my age. And the sad part is that I end up believing him." Mpumi was hurt, no one should be made to feel inadequate by the person who claims to love them. She hugged Nomusa close and rubbed her back, "Hush you're not stupid Nono, you are the smartest friend I have."

"That doesn't count I'm your only friend!" Nomusa wailed.

"What I mean is that you hold your own, in your family you're the only one who got to college at work your peers respect you, you always put others first. You're loyal and you don't pretend to be something that you are not. You speak your mind and you don't let anyone walk over you. If he can't see that then he is the problem babe not you." At least the tears had receded, Nomusa never cried and when she did it was scary.

"But I love him Mpumi and besides the name calling and the criticism he treats me better than any man ever has."

"How can he be treating you better when you're so unhappy you're even losing weight?!"

"You don't understand, you've had a man since tertiary and even now you divorcing him you already have another man who would give you the world if he could. I'm 39 Mpumi and I have never been married, I've never even been pregnant. Most men are either intimidated by my independence or think I can be their meal ticket." Mpumi hated seeing her friend like this, Nomusa was the most amazing human being she knew.

"Have you tried talking to him about how his words make you feel Nono?"

"I have but he always brushes me off he says he would be joking and because he loves me he has to be honest with me if I'm flopping." Mpumi sighed in frustration, words hurt more than physical strikes. Amogalang's words were leaving Nomusa unsure of herself they were eroding at her confidence in herself as a woman.

"So what are you going to do?"

"I don't know but I know that I'm not leaving him." Mpumi hated the finality in her friend's voice.

"Then you have to do things that remind you how great you are, because you were great before him and you can't lose yourself because of him." Nomusa looked confused so Mpumi continued, "You have to develop a thick skin to his criticism let it pass over your head and keep being you, he will have to love you for the vibrant, loud, dirty-mouthed, fun-loving queen that you are."

"For a moment there I thought you were going to say the fun-loving bitch that I am but you were always such a prude." LOL Mpumi was glad to see that the spark was returning to her friend's eyes.

She would have to have a talk with Amogalang next time their paths crossed. No one should ever dim the sparkle from Nomusa she always gave Mpumi life.

Jarred had personally came down to Cape Town to fetch Mpumi. They had said their goodbyes to the Xhamelas in the morning and then had been on their way. Mpumi had wanted them to pass eNgcobo where the seamstress had her stall and she had gotten the lady's details. Her aunt had refused to be dropped off with her uncles at Khayelitsha where they had found her so they had to take her to the bus station to board the bus to Kimberly and of course Mpumi had to pay for her bus fare. MaNtuli had said she wanted to take the chance to also visit her family in Cape Town so she had to be dropped off as well. Mpumi was anxious to get back to Jozi and her family and all these drop-offs were driving her crazy. Jarred hadn't even texted her good morning so she assumed he was still sulking only to find him waiting for her at the airport. She ran to him pregnancy and umbhaco be damned she had missed her man. He had swung her off her feet easily and twirled her around, he only put her down when she threatened to puke. "What are you doing here? And the girls?" she asked breathlessly.

"I couldn't trust those Chosa men with my beautiful goddess, when you couldn't leave last night I thought they were holding you captive." Nomusa laughed at his pronunciation of Xhosa, Jarred could be so silly at times.

"So you came all the way to Kappa leaving my children all alone."

"They are not babies anymore a few hours alone won't kill them." He brushed off her concern and let her go long enough to hug Nomusa warmly. He insisted that he would take them out to lunch first before they flew back home. He took them to the Italian place he had taken her and Oyama to it seemed like it was ages ago. Mpumi watched as Jarred and Nomusa talked easily and laughed, these two crazy people kept her afloat. The meal was divine and Mpumi ate enough for three and no one made any remark on it. Jarred was loaning his Jeep to Nomusa since he only used it when he was in Cape Town which wasn't often any more. The excitement in Nomusa's face was priceless, if she had liked Jarred before now she would love him till he died. Nomusa drove them back to the airport and waved them off. Jarred drew her into his arms the moment they were seated in the jet, the hostess who had been walking in with wine and juice put the beverages down and left them alone. He kissed her like he hadn't seen her in ten years, "Don't ever leave me like that again."

"It was only two days baby," Mpumi protested he was behaving like a big baby now.

"It felt like two decades that bed was big and lonely without you." He was cute when he was pouting, she planted another slow kiss on his lips, "I missed you too my blue-eyed Adonis." His smile was precious and it drew her in. Mpumi couldn't remember the last time she had ever been this happy. She rested her head on his chest and felt his steady heartbeat, when he brushed her belly the twins kicked. "Did you feel that Lelo?" the wonder in his voice warmed her heart. She didn't have the heart to tell him that the babies had already kicked for MaNgidi so she let him believe that they were kicking for the first time. "They are happy that you are here." He kept brushing her tummy and then he lowered his head to talk to them, "Daddy won't let you go ever again, I love you." Mpumi felt happy tears fill her eyes, this was their second lease at having a family and she knew he would be with her every step of the way.

"You look beautiful in that dress, you should always dress like this." He could just forget it there was no way she was wearing umbhaco again for a long time. She felt hot and flustered in it, she couldn't wait to get home and remove it then listen to what Oyama and Lola had been up to the whole weekend.

CHAPTER THIRTEEN

Mpumi was in the operating theatre and she had to change into hospital scrubs. It was chilly in June but she felt hot nonetheless. She was very worried about the operation but they would only let her stay till he was under anesthetics and then she would have to leave till the operation was done. Dr. Babalwa's neurologist friend who insisted they call her Lucy, had concluded through EEG testing that Jarred's epilepsy emanated from the head trauma he had gotten from the car crash that had claimed his father's life. She said that whenever Jarred went through a traumatic experience like the death of his brother, the sudden surge of electrical activity in the brain caused an overload which in turn triggered temporary disturbance in the messaging systems between brain cells. That was the reason why Jarred could see and hear everything during his seizures but he had no control over the movement of his body. The neurologist had first prescribed medicine and a VNS (vagus nerve stimulation) but when she continued monitoring Jarred's brain cells she had discussed with them that the underlying brain

condition causing the seizures was correctable through surgery but it would be their choice. Just the words brain surgery were scary but Jarred said it was a chance he was willing to take. He didn't want the seizures to harm his family, he was scared of driving with them in the car in case he had a seizure. Mpumi knew that he hated the feeling of not being in total control of his body and although she had only witnessed one seizure she didn't
want him to suffer either. But what if the surgery wasn't successful? She had tried pushing that question to the back of her mind, she couldn't have found Jarred again just to lose him like this. Yes she hadn't been to church in years and she rarely prayed but God couldn't do that to her. How was she going to raise four children on her own? Mpumi was a realist she had to try to brace herself for any possibility but even the thought of Jarred dead made her cry. He hated seeing her cry so she would go into the bathroom and get into the shower and cry her eyes out. What made it worse was that Jarred had flown his lawyers in to amend his will and include Mpumi, Oyama and the twins, it was as if he was putting his affairs in order. They had told the girls of his epilepsy and both girls had taken the news badly, Lola had been teary and Oyama had locked herself in the music room. Mpumi worried about Oyama, she didn't show much emotion anymore. Nomusa said she worried too much she should stay positive. At least the girls were not around. Mpumi had forced Oyama to go with her father on the promised date to some car show in Asia. Oyama had wanted to go to Cape Town to her aunt Nomusa. So they had compromised, Oyama had gone to the car show and then she and Lola had then proceeded to Cape Town for the holidays. Daniel had expected to get her for the whole holidays but he had a lot of patching up to do before his daughter warmed up to him. He had said as much himself after their trip, Oyama had totally iced him out. Their divorce would be final in two weeks. Daniel had insisted on paying her alimony, she didn't need it but he felt as if he owed it to her and Nomusa told her not to be silly and just take the money she had earned it raising his daughter and sitting

through all his infidelities. All these thoughts were a ploy to distract herself from how scared she was of losing Jarred. Mpumi was exhausted with worry but she tried hard not to let it show as she took Jarred's hand. He seemed so healthy, he was a work-out freak and Mpumi just couldn't understand how he was the one going through surgery while other people smoked like chimney pipes and drank everyday like it was their last day and they didn't have to have surgeries. He was smiling re-assuringly at her yet she was the one who was supposed to be comforting him. She let him hold her belly and brush his fingers on it as if he was silently communicating with their babies. She remembered when she had been the one lying on the hospital gulley and he had been holding her hand. There was a lump lodged in her throat when they put the mask on his face, she had to let him know how she felt in case he didn't ever wake up. "I love you Jarred and you have made me so happy I can't wait for us to make new memories with our babies. I can't raise them on my own they need you and I need you. So please fight to come back to us. I Love you so sooooo much." He smiled at her underneath the mask and squeezed her hand gently, she fought back the tears. He couldn't see her cry. His eyelids were growing heavy she could just tell but he kept his gaze on her and all the love he had for her was apparent in his eyes. Then his eyes finally closed, the nurse nudged her on the arm. It was time for her to go but she didn't want to leave him, they had to pry her from his side and escort her to the sofas outside. Finally she let the tears flow, she couldn't pray not when she had a track record of unanswered prayers. So she cried instead and loved him with all her might.

The previous night their lovemaking had been slow, gentle, and passionate with an underlying desperation that had made it all magical. When she had closed her eyes as he began kissing her he had ordered her to open her eyes, "I want to see you all of you." As his hand had slid into her wet warmth her eyes had shrunk into tiny slits as the pleasure exploded within her instantly, he had chuckled at her quick orgasm and still looking into her eyes he had slid his finger even deeper. What was it about this man that he only had to touch her to send her to the abyss of pleasure, she thought distractedly as she felt her moans escalating. She wanted to close her eyes and get lost in the pleasure that his hands and lips were bringing to her but he wouldn't let her. Her hands were also busy travelling every inch of his body as if she wanted to remember the different textures of his skin and the changing contours of his body and commit it to her memory. Touching wasn't enough so she kissed him gently at first, tasting the cinnamon and cocoa in his lips a heady combination which made her want to taste even more of him. Then she playfully nipped at his lips, his response was an outlandish attack of her mouth with his tongue, he deepened the kiss and it became more frantic. Without breaking the kiss he had slide effortlessly into her from behind and Mpumi had swooned in his mouth. But he hadn't moved inside her he had just continued kissing her thoroughly while inside her till she felt as if she was on the edge of destruction. She had started moving her hips thrusting them provocatively towards him, even though he groaned he continued kissing her. They both wanted to prolong the act to remain one forever in the most intimate way possible. But they were simply delaying the inevitable, when he did move she pushed him over the edge and they were clinging to each other as wave after wave of pleasure ricocheted through them both at the same time. They were both sweaty but they clung to each other as if they were one. Mpumi had struggled to control her breathing and she could feel both their hearts beating in unison. After catching his breath Jarred had surprised her by asking, "Do you remember our goal plan back when we were at Harvard?" He could be so random at times but she remembered everything they had said and done when they were in Harvard hell she even remembered his Yankees jersey that she had stolen from him, it had been his favorite. "We promised each other that by the time we reached forty we would have started our own businesses." Actually he had made her promise him that in one of his serious moments. The younger Jarred had been carefree and reckless, the family business hadn't been his burden all he did was party and ride a motorcycle. It had been amazing how he had managed to pass. He was looking at her with that same serious glint as he said, "Yes we did and now we are just a year and a month from forty but we haven't even moved towards that goal."

"At least you have the hotels," she said soothingly.

"They don't count, that's my father's business passed on to him by his father. I want to start my own legacy to pass onto my children." He seemed to have given this a lot of thought as he continued speaking, "and what about you? I know you have investments and you enjoy your two jobs but you can't pass those down to our children. The Lelo I fell in love with wanted to change the world." A part of her felt defensive, criticism was
hard coming from someone close to your heart but part of her knew he was right. Yes she was highly successful at what she did but she had settled, she had been afraid to pursue her dreams because they were too risky. "My two passions are children and photography and I would want a business that encompasses both," she mused almost as if she were speaking to herself. But he heard her and squeezed her lightly and he said, "Well my passion is seeing you happy so why don't we combine our brains and come out with a business which encompasses children and photography." Mpumi had been dubious at that suggestion, "How will that work? I love you Jarred but at times you are too controlling I might end up strangling you." He had laughed at that remark but she had gone on, "When I was with Daniel I didn't want to start anything because it would be taken as some political move as the Minister's wife and I didn't want to live under his spotlight. With you, you're an international business mogul I wouldn't want to live under your spotlight too." He didn't like being compared to Daniel but he had conceded she had a point, "Ok I will be a sleeping partner then." Mpumi doubted that Jarred could manage the role of sleeping partner but she knew that with him supporting her she could take the risk. "What brought on this sudden walk down memory lane? Are you ticking off your bucket list?" she hated asking the questions but she had to know. He sighed

and kissed her lightly, "I might die tomorrow Lelo and I need to know that you're not settling or merely existing but that you are living to your full potential that you will turn your dreams into reality. That you laugh more, travel more and that our children will be taken care of." She felt anger well up but she wasn't sure who she was angry at but she directed her anger at him, "You don't get to re-arrange my life without you in it. Dammit Jarred you came back into my life and showed me what was lacking in it, you made me depend on you and you will not leave me. Do you hear me? You will not leave me alone to raise your children!" she was getting worked up but there were no tears. He tried holding her but she shrugged him away. She got up and put a robe around her which happened to be his robe and she stormed out of their bedroom. She heard him curse just as she banged the door and charged towards the furthest guest bedroom. She was thankful that her children were with Nomusa. Life had been so uncomplicated before Jarred had barged back into her life leaving a trail of turmoil behind him. She heard him shout her name as he opened other rooms but she shut him out. She couldn't put her arms around her legs any more so she put them around her big belly and she rocked herself slowly. She had begun rocking herself shortly after her father died when her uncles were busy shouting at her mother with her father's body in the next room. It had been her coping mechanism how she managed to shut the pain out and somehow it had stuck with her. She felt his warmth before she felt his arms snake around her. She continued rocking and he rocked with her, Mpumi tried shrugging him off but he didn't let go. They stayed that way for what seemed like the longest time. "I'm scared," just saying it aloud lifted a weight from her shoulders. He turned her around till she was sitting facing him and they were on the same eye level. "I'm scared too Lelo." The deep blue depths of his eyes told her that he was telling the truth.

"Promise me you will wake up from that operation."

"Babe I can't…"

"I said promise me Jarred!" she hadn't meant to raise her voice but she was feeling very emotional at that moment. He sighed and then he kissed her knuckles, "I promise that I will fight to come back to you. No matter what happens always know that I will come back to you." That had been enough for her. She let him help her up to her feet and lead her like a baby back to their bedroom. He had cradled her and watched over her till her eyes grew heavy and she fell asleep.

She must have fallen asleep there on the hospital chair because she was woken up by gentle nudging. Thinking it was the doctor with news about Jarred's operation she was instantly awake and wide eyed. She was surprised to see her mother standing next to her with a basket of food and a flask of Rooibos tea probably. "Nomusa told me about the operation," MaNtuli said but there was no judgment or recrimination in her voice. Mpumi felt embarrassed that she hadn't told her mother herself but her mother had been so disapproving of her current lifestyle. But she was glad to see MaNtuli there it calmed her down a bit. "What are the doctors saying Nompumelelo?"

"They haven't said anything mama, I think they are still in the Theatre." It was a relief to talk to someone. Her mother said they should pray, Mpumi held hands and bowed her head but it was her mother who was praying. She felt empty and devoid of any emotion. When she was done praying she turned to her daughter and asked, "Have they told you the sex of the child yet?"

"We're not sure maa but we do know that it's twins." Mpumi was surprised to see the happy look on her mother's face.

"Don't look so surprised Nompumelelo those are my grandchildren too." Her mother was always full of surprises, she clearly didn't like Jarred but she was there at the hospital. "You know Nompumelelo I could never be as brave as you." Mpumi was confused by the sudden serious tone her mother was using and she had no idea what she was referring to. "What do you mean maa?"

"I mean I wasn't brave enough to leave your father." Mpumi was shocked by this revelation.

"But Tata was a good man maa!"

"A good man and a good father yes but he was a terrible husband," her mother was so calm about this while she was turning Mpumi's world upside down. "There were other women, I always found notes in his pockets he thought I couldn't read but I could read enough to understand what was in those notes. He made sure you had everything but I had to pinch money from the grocery money to buy my toiletries. As for clothes I had to make my own clothes and I wore the same shoes till they had no more soles left. But he bought expensive clothes and shoes for himself and for you. He even had an affair with my cousin and bought her beautiful things, she would brag to me. He never once

appreciated anything I did, to him I was just there to do his laundry, cook his food and occasionally to release his seed." There was a slight bitterness in MaNtuli's voice and Mpumi saw her mother differently as a woman for the first time.

"Did he ever hit you?" She had to know.

"No he never laid his hands on me but he neglected me as his wife, he blamed me for not giving him more children or a son. I wanted to leave him so many times but he made it obvious that I was not leaving with you. So I stayed. And when he died I felt relieved." MaNtuli seemed ashamed by the last part of her revelation, Mpumi squeezed her hand warmly.

"How come you never dated anyone after Tata left us?" Mpumi had wondered about this.

"Nompumelelo." The way her mother said her name and looked at her put her back in her place though she had opened up to her they weren't in that level of confiding to each other yet.

"I'm glad you stayed for me mama but I'm sorry you had to go through that." They were having a bonding moment.

"I'm also sorry Nompumelelo that I pushed you to stay, I always thought that at least Daniel made sure that you wanted for nothing and he never showed you that he cheated."

CHAPTER

THIRTEEN

"It's all water under the bridge, but I'm going to need you maa when the twins are born. In case their father doesn't make it." Mpumi was surprised that her voice didn't break as she said the last bit.

"I will be there my daughter even when he makes it." Mpumi drew strength from her mother's reassurance. She didn't want anything to happen to Jarred but if it did she was comforted in the knowledge that she didn't have to carry the burden alone, she could depend on her mother and on Nomusa.

Her mother had forced her to go back home, she couldn't be sitting in the hospital the whole night in her current condition. Mpumi had been reluctant to leave but her mother assured her that she would remain in her place and if anything happened she would call her. The house seemed too big and empty without her man and her children. She gratefully ate the food that MaNtuli had packed for her, she hadn't realized how hungry she was. The twins kicked reminding her that she wasn't alone and she brushed her tummy and talked to them as she ate. She left the food containers on the kitchen counter and made her way slowly to their bedroom. Everything in that house reminded Mpumi of him. The pictures on the wall reminded her of how excited Jarred had been when he unwrapped the frames with the photos and how he had chosen each spot for each picture and placed them all along the corridor. There were pictures of her, of him with her, him with Lola, her with Oyama, her and Nomusa with Lola in Mozambique and
a family portrait of her, Jarred, Oyama and Lola. There was so much love and laughter shining through those pictures, her gaze lingered on the family portrait, they made a strange family but that they loved each other was obvious. She couldn't wait to take another family portrait when the twins arrived, she wondered how they would look like. She was finally in their bedroom and there Jarred's presence haunted her even more. They had chased each other in this room, they had fought in this room, they had laughed in this room and they had made love in

all corners of this room. The sheets still smelt like him all woody musk with a hint of his aftershave. She hugged his pillow to her chest and fell into an exhausted sleep. She dreamt that she was at her father's funeral. She was crying and leaning on her mother as the pastor was reading some verse. Her aunt was crying loudly and sniffing there was a slight rain. Then it was time for them to view the body, her mother walked up first and Mpumi was following behind her. Her mother stopped and looked shocked as she looked into the open cascade, Mpumi also looked at the open cascade and her blood went cold. Instead of her father there was Jarred in the cascade and on each of his side there was a baby, their babies they all looked dead. Mpumi let out a curdling scream and then she woke up she was crying and sweating. She quickly turned on the lights and checked the sheets. There was no blood she began to breathe and then she went to the bathroom still there was no blood, she exhaled deeply. That dream had seem so real and Mpumi was scared. She took out her phone and checked the time it was just after 5am yet it was still dark outside. She tried going back to sleep but she kept turning in the blankets. She finally took out her phone and dialed the number by heart, it was answered on the sixth ring. "Mpumi?" she sounded as if she had been woken from a very deep sleep.

"Nomusa I dreamt he was dead and my babies too. Jarred was dead!"

"Hey hey calm down, breathe chomma will you do that for me?" Mpumi tried breathing deeply and she felt a bit better, "Now tell me what happened."

"I was dreaming that I was at my father's funeral and when we went to view the body instead of my father there was Jarred and the twins." Her blood still went cold even as she was narrating her dream.

"It was just a dream sweetie Jarred is going to be fine and your babies too. You're just worried and stressed and your body is reacting to that." Hearing Nomusa's reasonable voice calmed her down and she felt a bit silly but the dream had seemed so real. "Are you at the hospital?" Nomusa wanted to know.

"No my mother forced me to come to the house and get some sleep."

"And that's what you should be doing, sleep some more you and the babies need the rest."

"I can't I just tried and I kept turning."

"Then go to the kitchen and drink some warm milk, it will help you sleep."

"Thank you Nono and sorry I woke you up."

"You can buy me that Prada bag I was showing you to make it up to me."

"You can just forget it, bye Nomusa I will call you if I hear anything." Mpumi felt much better after talking to Nomusa, one glass of warm milk later she fell into a deep dreamless sleep.

CHAPTER FOURTEEN

Nomusa smiled as she ended the call, she remembered how Mpumi had called her in the middle of the night sobbing about a dream. Yes 5am was still the middle of the night for Nomusa. Fortunately that control freak Amo had not been around he would have wanted to call her back to confirm that it really was Mpumi calling not one of Nomusa's 'side dishes'. His obsession with her was annoying. Nomusa had cheated in her previous relationships and she had never been caught, ever. The thing is women played their cards very close to their chests and they could be dating ten men and not show any difference in the way they treat the other nine men. But once a man tasted the forbidden fruit he became different and careless coming home smelling of perfume and women could easily pick up on the signs. For the first time Nomusa was fighting to be monogamous but the more Amo held her on a tight leash the more her inner bitch was driving her to give him what he wanted. Like the previous night they had gotten into a nasty fight. Nomusa had told Amo that she was going back with

the girls to wait for the arrival of the twins. He had accused her of neglecting their relationship by putting
Mpumi over him and that the only reason she wanted to go back to Jozi was so that she
could hook up with her exes. Nomusa had exploded, "Listen here Amogalang I am sick and I am tired of your whining, it's driving me crazy. You're worse than an insecure nagging wife, my godchildren are about to come into this world and all you are doing is nag me about your insecurities. No man votsek!" He had stared at her for the longest time with that hurt puppy look which made her want him and then he had this ugly expression on his face, "You're calling me a woman Nomusa? Me a woman?" Nomusa had fought the urge not to burst into laughter, seriously dude out of everything I said you're only touched by the fact that I called you a woman she thought to herself. Men are such sensitive creatures. "No I compared you to an insecure nagging wife," she had said to him her arms crossed against her chest. "Wow, ok go to your Gauteng men, we are done!" A part of her had panicked and wanted to apologize to him because she really did love him but the part of her which had always been a fighter hardened her heart. "This is me all of me Amo and if I'm too much for you then you're right we are done. Until you can learn to love me as I am and trust that I love you then don't call me or come to see me. Now please leave I have to pack." The look on his face had torn at her heartstrings so she had looked at the side willing herself not to cry. Without saying another word he had left and Nomusa had felt weak at the knees. What had she done? Maybe she really was destined to be alone for the rest of her life. Instead of feeling free to be herself again she felt empty and lonely. She pushed the pain of that argument away and she went to look for the girls, she found them giggling about something in their room. "I just got off the phone with your mother the jet is here, we have to go now." They got up excitedly, Nomusa would miss having them around especially now that she was newly single. "Aunt Nomusa will we be seeing uncle Amo we want to say goodbye to him," Oyama's innocently asked question made

Nomusa sad and she came up with some excuse. Lola looked at her like she didn't buy her story, that girl was too street smart but Nomusa didn't want to start explaining her failed relationship to two teenagers. She packed them into Jarred's Jeep and they were on their way to the airport.

Jarred came to get them from the airport looking like he hadn't been in any major surgery. Nomusa wondered if epilepsy had any effect down there like diabetes that would be a death penalty for Mpumi. He had that big smile of his ready for them as they got off the jet. Riding in the jet had been spectacular, the cream pure leather seats had made her bums tingle and they had been waited on hand and foot. Lola went running into Jarred's open arms and Oyama was only a step behind, Nomusa watched as he somehow managed to enfold them both into his arms and he was kissing them both. Her friend had scored herself a winner with this one, he had a heart as big as his chest. She heard Oyama refer to him as 'daddy' and that was a first for Nomusa but judging from Jarred's expression it was also a first for him to. Mpumi was overly worried about nothing that girl loved her more than life itself and she was also beginning to love her mlungu bae. Nomusa felt a pang, she wanted a man who would love her and give her a family. Every woman wants that feeling of being loved and being cherished and she didn't have anyone. After finally getting the girls off him, Jarred also gave Nomusa a
huge hug, "I hear we owe you a Prada handbag," he said mischievously and Nomusa laughed, "You better buy it before it becomes a whole wardrobe of Prada"

"Come on let's go before she comes down here to fetch us herself." Nomusa laughed Mpumi's hormones had clearly been terrorizing the poor man but she also knew that he couldn't stand to be away from her for any length of time. Lola was plying Jarred with tails from her 'internship' lol the little Mexican had been tagging along when Nomusa went to work and even her bosses had been impressed with her grasp and knowledge of IT. Oyama had been a hit with the design team and so both girls had tagged along to work every day. Oyama was more reserved but Jarred managed to draw her into their conversation and she opened up to him. Nomusa distractedly checked her phone, there were no notifications. Of course she had told Amo not to call her but she was still disappointed, he clearly didn't care for her as much as she cared for him. She couldn't bring herself to be the first one to contact him. He had taken down the picture of her on his profile and he had replaced it with a picture of his dog. It hurt. He had been last seen just a minute before she logged onto her account, at least he hadn't blocked her yet. But he had unfriended her on Facebook. Maybe she should be the first one to reach out but something held her back. Pride. If he wanted her, he still had her number. Purposely putting her phone back, Nomusa listened as Jarred told the girls news from his surgery. He said that the surgery had been successful and the doctor had assured them that he wouldn't have any more seizures. That was a relief, Jarred and Mpumi had been through so much shame at least things were beginning to look up for them. He said that Mpumi's surgery was scheduled for that night, she let out a silent prayer for the twins to come out alive and healthy. They drove into a winding driveway, Nomusa's breath caught in her throat. The house had a simple elegance that screamed Mpumi, it was painted a pale cream with big floor length windows. The inside was even more spectacular, seeing it in person was even better than the video chat tour Nomusa had been given by Mpumi. They found Mpumi sitting in the sun room with her mother, Nomusa noticed that Jarred immediately became scarce, shame MaNtuli could be very scary when she wanted to be. But the older woman seemed taken by Lola, the Mexican was hard to hate, she had that natural sparkle. Nomusa had never seen Mpumi look so ugly, she was huge and so was her nose. Her naturally clear skin had a few warts, it was freezing in July but she was sweating. Nomusa tried hugging her but her big belly came in between them. At least she wasn't going to carry full-term, she already looked like a hippo at 6 months imagine what she would have looked like at

9 months. "Wuuuuu chomma if that's what pregnancy does to one you can count me out shame." MaNtuli laughed but Mpumi looked like she wanted to jump on Nomusa. "Wait till that Tswana makes you pregnant you will become as dark as me," mention of Amo still hurt it was too soon. Mpumi was fast to catch up on something being wrong she asked her mother to go with the girls and show them the bags they had packed for the babies. Then she patted the armchair next to her, "Come and tell me what's wrong." Nomusa wanted to deny that anything was wrong but Mpumi had that 'don't bullshit me' expression on her face.

"We got into a fight with Amogalang yesterday and we ended things," Nomusa said.

"So what was the argument about?" Mpumi could tell she was holding back.

"He didn't want be to come this side he said I was coming to be with my Gauteng men and so I just blew up and told him that I had had enough of his insecurities." Mpumi's eye was speculative, "Ok I may have compared him to a nagging wife." Mpumi's eyes twinkled like she wanted to laugh.

"I'm sure that when he cools down and you apologize for emasculating him, you guys will be fine." Mpumi sounded so sure.

"I don't think so chomma, we've been fighting a lot lately, he was so controlling and I always held my tongue but I'm done shrinking myself for him. And I also told him not to call or to come and see me, I'm done apologizing." It hurt but Nomusa had put up with enough of the constant criticism and being put down, "I love him Mpumi but I love me more."

"I hear you love, I just hope you both patch things up because he did make you happier than all the other frogs you kissed." Nomusa was tired of talking about Amogalang so she changed the topic, "Are you ready to be a new mommy again?"

"I'm so excited I pee myself a little every time I think of seeing my babies," she was cute when she was talking about the babies she even glowed a little but that could also have been from her sweating.

"You still don't know their sex?"

"They hid each other on each scan we ended up giving up, but as long as they are born healthy we don't mind either sex." The way she was ugly though, Nomusa still thought it was going to be boys.

"You should start thinking about bleaching your skin, otherwise you're going to look like you stole your own children. Or someone will mistake you for the maid," Nomusa teased her friend and got rewarded by a cushion which caught her dead in the face. But Mpumi was so happy Nomusa could have called her poop and she still would have laughed happily.

"If you had asked me a year ago if I could ever be this happy I would have denied it totally. But look at me now." Nomusa agreed she couldn't remember the last time Mpumi had been this happy and content, no one deserved it more than Mpumi. Jarred was standing at the doorstep and he looked at Mpumi so lovingly as if she were the most beautiful woman in the world even in her current ugly state. Nomusa felt a pang hit her, she wanted someone to look at her that way too and that someone had been Amogalang maybe another person would come along again but she doubted that. "It's time to go babe." Jarred said as he brushed his lips on Mpumi's forehead. It was time. Nomusa squeezed Mpumi's hand to let her know that she wasn't going to be alone.

The twins came into the world just two minutes apart, Jarred told them he had been the only one in the theatre with Mpumi. When they went to see them, the little angels were in incubators and had drips attached to them as well as machines to help them breathe. They were the tiniest things Nomusa had ever seen and they were so red with heads full of curly black hair. It was a boy and a girl. The pride on Jarred's face was priceless. Imagine if the kids had been born black yuuuu Nomusa couldn't even begin to think of the horror. The girl twin was the feisty one, while her tiny face was scrunched she was kicking her tiny little feet and screaming her little lungs out as they watched them. That one was going to be a drama queen Nomusa could just tell. MaNtuli kept saying how beautiful they were and that the boy looked like Jarred while the girl looked like Mpumi. Nomusa couldn't tell them apart and she sure as hell wouldn't say they were beautiful. Maybe MaNtuli was operating on the maxim 'ugly on the cradle, beautiful at the table', Nomusa had heard that on some TV reality show. Newborn babies scared her, she concluded, at least they didn't have to hold them. Nomusa was sure she would have dropped them. The boy was the first to open his eyes and look at them solemnly like he could actually see them, which creeped Nomusa out. They had stormy grey eyes which Jarred assured them would change into the same electric blue as his. White babies were creepy, Nomusa thought to herself. With black babies you knew you had to look at the hands, feet and top of the ears, if those were dark you knew the babies were going to grow up and become darker. Mpumi had been wheeled to the nursery in a wheelchair, she must be in so much pain but at least her punani had remained intact. Nomusa had heard that having a head come out of one's vagina could cause permanent damage, let alone two heads. If she ever had a child Nomusa was definitely choosing C-section, she couldn't stand an oversized punani that made weird farting noises during sex. It was sad though that they couldn't touch the babies, they could only look at them through the glass. Lola and Oyama couldn't take enough pictures and MaNtuli was cooing happily. Ooh and the girls were the ones who had named the twins, Oyama had given them Xhosa names, the girl was Owethu (Ours) and the boy was Onathi (He who is with us) and Lola had given them Spanish names the girl was Aleja (Defender of mankind) and the boy was Anton (Praiseworthy). Nomusa had to admit that they were beautiful names, the twins would be the last to learn how to write their names imagine the Afrikaans teacher in one of those burgee schools were you had to register your child at birth for enrolment, trying to pronounce Owethu and Onathi. Aleja was going to defend them with her voice, the little diva had the strongest pair of lungs in the whole world, she was crying non-stop. Tshini! Mpumi started sobbing, not the pretty sobbing but the ugly crying with her face contorted as if she was in pain. Nomusa reached out to comfort her but Jarred was already cradling her in his embrace. Nomusa had to accept that Jarred had also taken the role of being Mpumi's best friend and constant comfort. It stung just a little but Nomusa was happy for her bestie.

Nomusa was about to upload the twins' first pictures on her Twitter when she saw it. They were back in Mpumi's room and Nomusa was relieved to see the big flat screen TV in the room. "Oyama quickly turn the TV on and go to SABC 3."

"What channel is SABC 3 aunty?" Jezus! Nomusa had forgotten that she was hanging around BEEs now.

"It's channel 193." Everyone was surprised that MaNtuli was the only one who knew the channel. Oyama quickly turned on the TV and there was Anele Mdoda in a killer formal black jumpsuit complemented by a thin silver belt. Those silver six inch heels Thixo! She was super sexy with her beautiful gapped smile and she was doing some introductory remarks, "Joining me on Real Talk today is our very own Minister of Mineral Resources Mr. Daniel Sisulu to discuss the speculation which has been going on about his private life and the plight of Miners everywhere following the Maricana Incident" Then the cameras turned to Daniel. Damn the man looked like the suit had been molded onto him, his Milan designer was on point, he looked like a sleek business executive and even though Nomusa hated him even she had to admit that he looked hot. He was lounging on that couch pretty much the same way he had been lounging the night before they went on that blessed safari. He still reminded Nomusa of a jaguar. He had his signature half-smile on and he seemed in control, "Thank you for having me Anele." His voice was cultured, Nomusa wondered if he ever got nervous.

"Minister Sisulu news of your pending divorce has

been breaking the Internet and trending on Social Media, so far you haven't made any comment. Would you like to shed some light for our interested viewers?" Anele had that thing nje which Nomusa loved but couldn't explain. Daniel laughed lightly as if he wasn't at all fazed.

"Oh yes my divorce which has been splashed on newspapers, actually let me correct you Anele, it's not impending but it has been finalized. I and my lovely wife of sixteen years are legally divorced." Yes because of your manipulative and cheating arse, Nomusa thought darkly.

"What is on everyone's minds Minister is why did your marriage end in divorce? I mean you and your wife seemed devoted to each other." Anele was like a dog with a bone. Nomusa held her breath, Daniel better not tarnish her friend's name because she knew where he lived and she was more than ready to re-arrange his face and decorate it with a scar or three and maybe a gold tooth.

"Well every marriage has its up and downs and when we realized that we were bringing each other down we came to an understanding that our marriage had run its tenure. It was a mutual decision, we decided to go our separate ways." Spoken like a true politician, he didn't really say why they had broken up but he sounded like he had put it all in a nutshell. There was no way Anele could continue prying. Then Nomusa went white, there on the screen was a picture of Mpumi with Jarred. It must have been taken on one of their many trips to this very hospital because Mpumi was wearing a loose jean shirt-dress which was above knee length with flip-flops and her baby bump was very visible. Jarred was also dressed casually in jean three-quarter shorts and a t-shirt written 'Baby Daddy' that showed off his buff physique. The picture had been taken in front of the hospital, Jarred had been leaning over Mpumi's bump, his hand was protectively holding her and Mpumi had a serene smile lighting up her face making her seem so young and pretty. There was no denying that those two were an item and that they
were madly in love. Daniel visibly flinched when he saw the picture but

he recovered quickly because he went back to being his stately in control self. Sensing a huge scoop Anele went in for the kill, "In this picture we see your wife with international business mogul, Billionaire Jarred Levine could that be the reason for the breakdown in your marriage?" The way she said billionaire made it sound as if it was Jarred's first name.

"As I have said we had our differences but if you are insinuating that my former wife cheated on me then I would have to correct you." Daniel sounded so cool and unbothered, Nomusa mentally gave him a high five.

"But clearly sir she has moved on and your divorce has only been brought to light recently you can't blame us for putting two and two together and coming out with five." Now this Anele bish was beginning to irritate Nomusa. MaNtuli let out an exclamation, she was probably thinking how the Reverend or Archbishop or whoever led her church would react. And maybe she was worried about her position and standing in the church being brought into disrepute.

"As you have said our impending divorce has only come to light recently because a greedy government worker decided to sell out confidential judiciary documents to the press. But I and my former wife had been legally separated before that and she was free to do with her life as she saw fit." The arrogance in his voice! Yeses Daniel could be savage, but it served those news mongers right. Anele wasn't one to back down easily though.

"You were together at the New Year's Gala just at the beginning of this year and now we are in July. Wouldn't you say your wife has moved on too quickly?" Nomusa felt like going over there and wiping that cute smile off Anele's face. Nx! why did all TV personas have to be so nosey. But Nomusa forgave her because she was only doing her job.

"I notice you keep referring to her as my wife, let me correct you once more. Nompumelelo is my former wife and the mother of our beautiful daughter, Oyama. Therefore she will always remain part of the Sisulu family. She agreed graciously that I must add

her to help me host the Miners Gala, because she feels deeply about the plight of our miners. But that does not mean we were still together. Even if we were, is there a prescribed period for one to move on from a failed marriage? It's not like I am dead so she doesn't have to abide by the customary one year mourning period. My former wife is a young, beautiful, kind and intelligent woman and of course any man would be lucky to have her and I am happy to see that she quickly found a man who is able to put that smile on her face. A happy ex-wife is better than a bitter ex-wife." There was laughter from the studio audience, Daniel had portrayed no bitterness whatsoever thus he had stripped everyone of any ammunition they might use against him and against Mpumi. There was a collective sigh of relief in the hospital room, maybe Daniel wasn't so bad after all. He could have easily tarnished Mpumi and Jarred's names but he had appeared more like a mature ex than a bitter jilted lover. Laughing that sexy laugh of hers, Anele turned to the cameras. "Well you heard it first on Real Talk with Anele. Our Minister of Mineral Resources has just moved back to bachelorhood and he has dispelled all rumors of bad blood between him and his former wife business executive
Nompumelelo Ndinisa. You can join our conversation on Twitter or send a voice note on WhatsApp with any questions you might have for him. We are going on a break and don't go away because we will be discussing the livelihood of miners after this short break." Oyama turned off the TV and no one wanted to discuss what they had just seen. "The twins are so adorable," Nomusa said to break the awkward silence and that worked. Soon they were all admiring the twins and fawning over their pictures and the interview was forgotten or stored away for later inspection.

People should really stop blurting things they were not sure about on social platforms. Nomusa was fuming at some of the Tweets that were circulating about Mpumi. They made her out to be a gold digger who was climbing the social ladder and had dumped the

Minister for a richer husband. One little girl had had the nerve to tweet **'How does Nompumelelo Ndinisa do it? I mean from the sleek and sexy Minister to the ridiculously rich hunky hotel owner and she ain't all that #JiltedMinister'**. Nomusa hadn't wasted any time putting that little skank in her place **'She went to school and got herself three degrees, she has class unlike you. You're busy lusting over men old enough to be your father. Oh and all of her is real unlike your complexion which is as fake arse as your Peruvian wannabe hair #IAmMyFriendsKeeper'**. Mpumi didn't seem bothered by all the comments people were making about her, she simply shrugged her elegant shoulders and said, "They don't know me and they are entitled to their opinions." WTF Nomusa was having none of that and she was willing to go on a one woman mission to protect her friend. What made Nomusa even angrier was that most of the people slinging mud at Mpumi were women. She was using her blood path on Twitter to take her mind off Amogalang. That Tswana man hadn't called or even texted her the whole week she had been in Jozi. Not even a single missed call. And she missed him but she realized that if she was the first one to contact him then she would turn into one of those women who were always groveling, kissing the ground their men walk on. And she didn't want that but dammit it was so hard. She missed his stalking, his midnight texts and his hour long phone calls. She did go out with a few of the guys she had hooked up with in the past. Don't judge there is only so much cooing over babies that one can take. Plus the babies and Mpumi were still in hospital and Nomusa hated hospitals. But the thing was being with those guys didn't feel as great anymore. She wondered what she had seen in them in the first place because it was clear all they wanted was to chow her pussy and go on with their lives. None of them cared about her life, they hadn't even noticed that she had relocated. One guy had thought she had had some sexually transmitted disease and that she had been curing it. Nomusa had been so mad she had sprayed his eyes with the paper spray she always kept in her purse. And to cool down his burning eyes she had poured her whole glass of Bloody Mary on him and she had strutted her arse out of that joint. She realized she had overgrown the night life when she was yawning just before midnight in the middle of someone's pool party. She just wanted to be home cuddling with Amogalang fighting over what to watch till they settled for a movie. Something was definitely wrong with her, she couldn't even enjoy riding this huge acquaintance of hers who was better endowed than Amo. Nx! That Tswana must have given her some love portion. She was seeing his face in very odd places. When she could get Mpumi to talk about something other than those blasted babies, aunty Nomusa still loves you though little angels, she told her about her dilemma. Mpumi listened attentively as Nomusa poured out her woes and that made Nomusa feel slightly better. Maybe she wasn't going crazy as she had feared.

"There's nothing wrong with you Nono, you just love Amogalang and you aren't over him." If that was the best advice Mpumi had for her then Nomusa was screwed.

"But he is always undermining me Mpumi, he is always belittling me and he doesn't trust me. I can't be with someone like that."

"Write down everything you love about Amo and everything you hate about him." Mpumi sounded dead serious. Nomusa was incredulous but she took a pen and paper and started writing. She had to think very hard to make sure that she had written everything. Then she handed the paper to Mpumi. "So you hate that he's controlling, overbearing, has trust issues, is too clingy and he is too traditional. But you love that he is financially capable to take care of you, caring, supportive, funny, attentive, and easy to be with, puts you first, makes you orgasm and… ok I think I've read enough." Nomusa laughed Mpumi had only gotten to half of what she loved about Amogalang. "My point is some of the things you hate about him are also the same things you love about him." Nomusa was about to protest but Mpumi held up her hand, "He comes across as controlling because he puts your welfare first and he is attentive to everything you say and do, he is too clingy because he cares about you. Now I'm not saying the things you hate about him don't matter but they are also things that you both can talk about and iron out before they get out of hand." Nomusa hadn't thought of it this way, but there was still the issue of who was going to contact the other first. "Men have huge egos Nono be the bigger person and reach out to him." Ok maybe Mpumi's happily ever after was messing with her mind. Everyone knew that the first person to reach out was the weaker. "I want to move back to Jozi, my family is driving me crazy." Mpumi laughed at Nomusa, "You're lying you want to run away from Amo." Nomusa sighed she was also trying to change the topic but this bish wouldn't let her. "Call him Nono." Nomusa agreed just to get Mpumi off her back. They went to see the twins again. At least now they looked less red, they were now pale pink and they little features were more defined and they looked perfect. For once Aleja was quiet and Anton was making cooing noises. Nomusa was glad that she had come to see them at birth and she was sad that she had to go back to her empty apartment. But she wasn't Mpumi who hadn't set foot to work since the previous year but she was still on their payroll and she was working at home. The older twins, Oyama and Lola, Nomusa called them that because those two were inseparable, were at school and Nomusa offered to go pick them up. The hours flew past and before she knew it, Nomusa was waving at Jarred and the girls as she boarded the Jet alone. She had thought she would take a commercial flight but Mpumi and Jarred had insisted that the Jet would take her back. One could get used to this kind of lavish lifestyle but Nomusa was the first to admit that for a billionaire Jarred was one of the most down to earth guys she knew. Her apartment felt empty without the girls. She switched on the lights and went through her mail. Mostly it was bills and junk mail,

then there were tickets to the Justin Bieber concert. Nomusa felt tears forming in her eyes, she had been bothering Amo for months about that concert and he had said she was too old to be drooling over a skinny white boy. She hadn't thought that he was going to buy the tickets to the concert. She put her bags away then she debated whether she should call him or text. He picked up on the second ring but he remained silent, this was harder than she had thought, "Hey, can we talk?" He remained silent and she thought he wasn't going to respond then he let out a frustrated breath, "I will be there in ten minutes." Then he hung up, that hadn't been a very promising conversation. He made it in eight minutes, she heard his car screeching to a halt. She wiped her sweaty on the back of her jeans before she went to open the door.

CHAPTER FIFTEEN

If she had to spend another day in that hospital Mpumi felt that she would go mad. She had lost most of the baby weight in the two months they had been in that hospital. Enduring test after test done on your babies was taxing both physically and emotionally. The twins had to undergo brain MRIs, they had to be scanned, they had to take X-rays and all she wanted to do was hold them. They had finally been allowed to hold them after a month and it had been the happiest moment of her life. Their skin was so soft and they smelt divine, Owethu had for once been quietly looking at her with those big blue eyes which made her look like a porcelain doll, then she had dimpled at her and Mpumi felt that smile tug at her heart. Jarred's mother had had dimples and she had passed them on to the grandchildren she wouldn't have wanted. Of the twins Onathi was the easy one to handle he wasn't as fussy as his sister, so Owethu got fed first and bathed first while Onathi waited his turn. The nurses did their bathing and feeding even when Mpumi protested, her twins were a hit with everyone in the children's wing. As much as they had been well taken care of, Mpumi wanted to go home. She had asked the doctor to remove her womb during the birth of the twins, Jarred had said he couldn't go through that again and Mpumi agreed with him. There was also the threat of cervical cancer as she advanced in years. Jarred wasn't even in the country, he had to attend to one of his new hotels in Dubai. Ever since she had given birth it felt as if he was avoiding her and the twins. He hadn't even been there when she and the girls got to hold the twins for the first time. Mpumi couldn't help feeling warning lights flash, she had been down this road before. MaNtuli was staying at their home and taking care of Oyama and Lola. They had protested that they were old enough to look after themselves but Mpumi felt better knowing that they had an adult with them, it wasn't safe for girls anymore to be alone. Mpumi was bored, the babies were sleeping and she was stuck in her hospital room. She decided to video call Nomusa, they hadn't had their girl talk in a while. "Chomma waka maan!" Mpumi laughed Nomusa was learning to speak in Setswana.

"Hey girlfriend, I see you already practicing to be a Tswana bride." Nomusa actually blushed.

"Hold your breaks we only just got back together."

"You never did tell me what happened when you got to Kapa." From Nomusa's smile, you could just tell she was in a happy place.

"So friend when I got back ne, I found tickets to the Justin Bieber show that Amo had bought for me. I was so touched I called him and he came. We talked like really talked, he said he felt insecure because I was way out of his league and I told him that the more he put boundaries for me he was suffocating me. We apologized and then he asked if I saw my Gauteng men and I pretended to be outraged that I would do such a thing. Then he was all over me. Tjo! Chomma I swear that Tswana man must have drunk some ZCC tea while I was away or imbiza because the way he drilled my punani, I couldn't walk properly the next day. I mean he made me bend at an angle I for the life of me do not know how he made me do that. The sounds he was making, I was afraid my neighbors would report us to the caretaker. And his face Chomma wuuuuu he looked like he was suffering from a minor heart attack. I gave it to him and I gave it to him good, he knows me now." Nomusa was gesturing and would have demonstrated the bend if she hadn't been at work. Mpumi couldn't help it she burst out laughing just imagining her friend turned into a gymnastic.

"At least one of us is getting some action, this hospital stay is cramping my style Nono." Nomusa made some sympathetic sounds and Mpumi rushed to change the subject, "So after patching things up how have things been? Besides your bend it like Beckham sex life."

"Things have been great love, we still ironing things out but now he is more aware of what he says to me and how he says it and I'm also more aware of his insecurities. I think we are going to be fine."

"You see I told you so."

"Nobody likes a know-it-all Mpumi. So where is your blue-eyed Adonis?" Mpumi sighed.

"He is in Dubai working on another hotel there, before that he was in Durban finalizing the one there."

"How come you don't sound too happy about that?" Nomusa was too perceptive.

"He's never around anymore lately, when he calls he sounds distant and he barely holds the babies. I keep thinking what if he's with some floozy there screwing her brains out. I mean it's not like we are married or anything I don't even know if we're dating or not. I don't even know if we are in an exclusive relationship." It was the first time Mpumi was voicing her fear.

"Hai Chomma come on. Jarred is not Daniel. I know there aren't a lot of good guys out there but Jarred is definitely one of the good guys."

"Yeah but even good guys fall into temptation Nono,

he's hot and rich. Women will be throwing themselves at him and beautiful women at that." Mpumi cringed even at the mental image of Jarred with another woman.

"That man is besotted by you Mpumi how can you not see it? If he was black his family would say you gave him a love portion that's how devoted he is to you and your children. Trust that the love he has for you will keep him in line."

"Maybe you're right babe, he hasn't given me a reason not to trust him. But I can't go through another cheating partner I just can't." opening up to Nomusa made her feel better.

"He won't and if he does I will re-arrange his face. I got to go love my boss just got here. Mncwaaaah" Mpumi also missed being at work. Owethu chose that moment to wake up and wail for attention also waking up Onathi who started crying as well. Mpumi pushed all thoughts of work out of her mind, she had her hands full with these two.

It felt so good to be going back home. The twins had been cleared on all their tests, they were not epileptic and they were perfectly healthy. Jarred had finally come back home the night before they had been cleared and discharged. Mpumi couldn't help it she was mad at him. He had promised that he would be with her all the way and the moment the twins had come into the world he had hightailed all over the world. She was cold towards him and he could feel it. He tried helping her dress the twins and she waved him off. "Its fine I can manage on my own. I've been managing alone for the past two months." He drew in a quick breath as if she had slapped him in the face. Mpumi didn't care, he couldn't just waltz back and act like the World's Best Daddy. "That's not fair Lelo I had to attend to the hotels and you know that." She ignored the hurt in his voice and continued dressing Onathi then she put them one by one into their double stroller in silence. Jarred opened the door for her and she struggled to get the stroller out of the door, when he made to help her she gave him one icy glare and he raised his arms in surrender. He was carrying all the baby bags and juggling their sleeper as well. The thing that irritated Mpumi the most was that she had missed him so much and he looked heavenly in cargo shots and a close fitting t-shirt. She wanted so much to tear his clothes yet she was also frustrated by his abandonment. Finally she managed to navigate the stroller through the door. The nurses there were sad to see them leave and she had to stop along the way for them to say goodbye to the twins. Owethu was preening from all the attention and she kept flashing that dimpled smile while Onathi looked at them all seriously without a smile. They got to the car and Jarred watched as she struggled to put them in their car seats, he didn't even offer to help this time around. He waited patiently for her to finish and get into the front seat. "I'm sorry Lelo if it felt like I abandoned you and our children but I just had to attend to the matters personally." She just looked at him then fastened her seat belt, he let out a sigh. "So you won't talk to me anymore? Very mature babe."

"You want to talk to me about maturity Jarred? Running away from your children while they are going through brain scans and they are breathing through machines is really mature." Mpumi hated that she sounded like a nagging wife but he had deeply hurt her. He didn't say another word, he just drove like a bat from hell not looking at her. The babies were sleeping peacefully unaware of the tension between their parents. When they got home, without waiting for her Jarred went to the back seat to get the sleeping babies out of their car seats. Feeling like the world's worst mother, Mpumi didn't offer to help him but she walked straight into the house. She found her mother watching some gospel channel in the lounge praying along to the people shouting in the TV. When she saw her daughter she quickly switched off the television and rose to give her a warm embrace. "Nompumelelo my child you're home, where are my grandchildren?" Mpumi was surprised and grateful for the warm embrace, she snuggled for a little while then she let go. "The twins are in the car, Jarred will come with them."

"Are you ok? You look a little pale." Feigning a headache Mpumi left her mother to get a bath and lie down. MaNtuli admonished her for not drinking enough water but she bought her story. On her way to the bedroom, Mpumi met Jarred at the door struggling to get the stroller in, it was too wide. She knew she was being mean but Mpumi didn't care she proceeded to their bedroom. She quickly took off her clothes and opted for a quick shower. When she was drying herself, Jarred came into the room. He stood just inside the door and stared at her for the longest time. She pretended to ignore him but her body was immediately aware of his presence. He just continued watching her as if he was unsure if he should proceed further into the room. Finally gathering some courage he sat on the bed and hung his head. "Lelo I'm sorry I know there isn't an excuse for what I did but please don't shut me out." Mpumi didn't dare look in his direction in case her resolve melted.

"Where are my babies?" He sighed.

"I put them in the nursery, they are fast asleep." She was still hurting but she couldn't continue shutting him out.

"Why did you leave? You only stayed for one MRI and you haven't been here since." The thing that hurt the most was that she hadn't expected him to leave her alone to deal with the twins.

"I felt helpless." He said it so softly she thought she hadn't heard him right but the shame on his face confirmed what she heard. She felt anger building up.

"So every time they are sick you're going to hightail to God-knows-where? For all I know you were with some skank in Hawaii."

"Lelo you know me better than that, I would never do that to you." His calm response was even more infuriating because it made her seem like an unreasonable woman.

"I don't know any more Jarred, I thought we were in this together and the moment we need you the most you left. All you did were those lame impersonal phone calls asking how the twins were doing. If you had really cared you would have been there with me in the hospital."

"I know and I'm sorry but some of those meetings really needed me in person, the negotiations were tricky and…"

"I already had one partner who put his career over me and his child, I am not going through that again with you!" She hadn't meant to shout.

"There it is, the real problem here is you are comparing me with Daniel and I am nothing like him."

"Well you haven't really given me a reason not to compare you to him."

"You know what, I can't talk to you when you're like this. I'm leaving before we both say and do things we're gonna regret." She wondered why he was getting angry, he was the one in the wrong this time.

"Leave isn't that what you're good at." He stopped by the door as if he wanted to say something then he wrenched open the door and banged it hard. Mpumi was shaking as she slid onto the thick carpet with her bare arse. She wanted to call him back and apologize but she was still angry at him. That headache she had been faking came at her in full force. She went into the bathroom and took the strongest painkillers she could find in the medicine cabinet. She got into the silk sheets and collapsed into a drugged sleep.

She woke up the next morning feeling like she had been riding a charging buffalo. Jarred woke her up with a tray of bacon, fish fingers, scrambled eggs, a slice of a tomato, a slice of toasted brown bread and freshly squeezed orange juice. She was feeling hungry and embarrassed by her outburst the previous day. She got up to go and freshen up, she had to ask "What time is it?"

"Just a little after 9am" Gosh she had slept flat through nineteen hours!

"What about the babies and the girls?"

"The babies are fed and bathed, your mother is playing with them. The girls wanted to see you last night and I told them you had a migraine. I took them to school on time. Don't stress." She felt ashamed, what kind of a mother was she.

"Where did you go yesterday?"

"I went to the nursery and I apologized to the twins for neglecting them and their mommy. I don't think Aleja forgave me, she screamed at me pretty much like you." Mpumi smiled without meaning to, she wasn't mad at him anymore. She got back into the blankets and he fussed over her and even fed her breakfast. She should throw tantrums more often, she thought to herself. Then Jarred turned serious, "You were right, you and the children should always take first priority. I shouldn't have left no matter how scared I was, you needed me. And you don't have to worry about me being with any other woman. I am all yours, exclusively for life, and I promise with the lives of our children." She kissed him on the lips, all was forgiven. She got up and dressed before her mother accused her of being a terrible mother. They found MaNtuli in the nursery holding both babies as she rocked in the swing-chair, Owethu that little diva cried the moment she saw them. Mpumi took her from the doting grandmother, she had missed her little babies. Their creamy almond skin looked squeaky clean and at least they weren't wearing any matching jumpers. Owethu had bigger eyes than Onathi and her chin was sharper, Onathi's lips were going to melt some poor girls' hearts in future and he rarely smiled but when he did he was the most beautiful little man in the world. Like any mother Mpumi believed that her babies could give Kim Kardashian's children a run for their money. After kissing both babies, Jarred retired to his office he was always scarce whenever her mother was around. Mpumi sat next to MaNtuli and she wasn't ready for what the elder said next. "Don't tell him I said this, but he is a good man, father and I have a feeling he will make a good husband too."

"Jarred?" Mpumi's voice sounded startled to her own ears.

CHAPTER

FIFTEEN

"Of course, last night he cooked us dinner, fed the babies and changed them for bed and made sure the girls had done their homework before he allowed them to watch TV. He did the same this morning even though I protested." MaNtuli sounded impressed and Mpumi was proud of her man.

"He raised Lola on his own from when she was born." She had to raise even more points for her baby-daddy.

"That explains how he is so comfortable around babies, your father only held you after you were six months old. He said he was afraid you would fall." Mpumi laughed, her father hadn't seemed like the coward type.

"I wish he had been around to see the twins."

"Me too, he would have loved them. And he would be so proud of you Nompumelelo, he always said you would succeed in everything. I am proud of you as well my daughter." Mpumi felt warm inside, it wasn't every day she got a compliment from her mother and she cherished the feeling. "I have to go back home now, you know those tenants I might find my house turned into a sheeben. I think the two of you can manage with the babies." Mpumi realized that she had actually enjoyed having her mother around and she would miss her. But it would be nice to have her little family to herself and for Jarred to be freer without MaNtuli's disproving eye. Jarred said she was punishing him when she asked him to drive her mother home. He was saved from an awkward drive by the girls volunteering to go with him and gogo.

A week after coming back from the hospital, while putting the babies down Mpumi heard what sounded like a screaming match in the kitchen. Making sure to close the nursery door and hooking the baby monitor on her sweat pants, she went to investigate. The loud voices were coming from Jarred's study. She found Lola with legs apart and hands on hips having a heated argument with her father in what Mpumi concluded was Spanish. Lola was a sweet girl with an easy and constant smile but get on her bad side and her Cuban roots came out in full force. She was as feisty as Latinos come and she was mad over whatever Jarred was saying. Jarred's Spanish was as good as hers and both of them didn't even notice that she had come into the room. All Mpumi could hear was Papi and the rest just jumped over her heard, she really had to learn Spanish but it sounded so complicated. Mpumi had to stand between them before they even acknowledged her presence and even when they did they continued exchanging a string of angry words. She had to stand to her full height and also shout, "Hey will you keep it down? I just put the babies down and they have been fussy today. Your shouting will wake them up." She managed to make them shut up but Lola was still throwing death glares at Jarred and she asked him something in an almost pleading tone and Jarred's tone remained stern in what was obviously a refusal. Mpumi didn't know Spanish but she had also raised a teenage daughter and she knew the universal "I hate you!" before the teen barged out of the room and banged the door with all her might. Jarred cursed and called after her but he was wasting his breath. Mpumi stared at him and folded her arms. He ran his hands through his silky hair in his signature frustrated look. "Will you tell me what that was all about?" he poured himself a glass of Scotch before he responded to her question. "It's Lola's birthday next month and I had promised her that I would throw her the Quinceanera celebrations." Mpumi was lost and it must have shown in her face because Jarred explained, "A Quinceanera is a traditional ceremony on a Latino girl's fifteenth birthday that marks the girl's passage to womanhood."

"So what's the problem?"

"The problem is she doesn't want me to throw her the ceremony here but she wants it in Havana, the capital of Cuba where her mother was originally from. And she wants me to help her track her mother's family. When I pointed out that we are already in September and it will be impossible to throw all that together by October and that the twins are too young to travel, she threw the tantrum that you just witnessed."

CHAPTER

FIFTEEN

"Jarred you own a private jet, unlimited funds and a fleet of employees who can make this thing happen. And my mother can babysit the twins, in fact I know she would love that."

"And spoil Lola even more than I already have? No Lelo we will hold the ceremony here and if she doesn't want then that's her problem." Mpumi sighed, Jarred's voice held a stubborn streak that she knew only too well.

"Do you know why it's so important for Lola to have her Quinceanera in Havana?"

"She's just being melodramatic and stubborn." She takes that from you, Mpumi thought but didn't dare voice her thoughts.

"No, do you know that her favorite picture of her mother is one of her on her fifteenth birthday?" he shook his head as she had suspected he had no idea. "She wants it in Havana so that she can feel close to her mother and relive the happy moments that her mother had. And we can't take that away from her."

"But I don't want to leave the babies babe," Jarred had mellowed considerably from when they started this conversation.

"It's only for a day or two. I don't want Lola to resent me and the twins because she feels like we have replaced her in your heart. I want all our children to feel loved and valued." He beckoned her and she went to sit on his lap and snuggled into him. "What have I been doing all along before you came along? I didn't realize how much Lola needed that mother figure in her life."

"And I don't want her to feel like I'm replacing her mother. Let me go and talk to her." He gave her a warm hug and let her go. When she knocked on Lola's bedroom door as she suspected she didn't get a response. She found her lying in a fetus position on her bed with tears on her cheeks and she had headphones on her ears while she looked at the framed picture of her mother at her Quinceanera. At that age Lola's mother had looked exactly like Lola without the dimples, she had lovely eyes which shined with laughter and she was wearing what looked like a white ball gown with puffed sleeves and a white thick chocker with a dangling stone on it. Mpumi sat on the bed and took Lola's I-pod she was listening to a song titled 'Despacito' and Mpumi turned it off. Lola looked up from the picture and angrily wiped off her tears and took off her headphones. "Your mother looks exactly like you in that picture." Lola didn't respond but at least she wasn't kicking her out of her bedroom so Mpumi forged on. "I know how much your fifteenth birthday means to you and I don't want to take that away from you. If I could I would bring both your parents back to life. But I can't, all I can do is try to raise you as best as I can, if you will let me."

"You're not the problem, it's daddy he doesn't understand." Mpumi leaned over and smoothed a lock of curly hair from Lola's face and looked her straight in the eye.

"I know pumpkin, we talked about it and he understands how important going to Havana is to you and also finding your mother's family. So you will have your Quinceanera in Havana." Lola laughed at her and Mpumi hadn't expected that.

"I'm laughing at the way you pronounce Quinceanera, you're supposed to say Ki-nsi-nyera." Mpumi was relieved.

"You have to teach me how to speak in Spanish." Lola looked at her like she didn't believe her but she agreed. Mpumi made to stand up when Lola gave her a sudden and intense hug. After the initial shock, Mpumi hugged her back. They stayed in the embrace for the longest time then Lola kissed both her cheeks and on the lips. "Thank you for coming into our lives Madre." Mpumi felt warmth in her heart, Lola had called her mother in Spanish for the first time. They were going to Havana.

CHAPTER
TWO

CHAPTER SIXTEEN

She was always the first to drop off to sleep and always the first to wake up. There was nothing she enjoyed more that waking up in their big bed and watching him sleep. He looked young and carefree in his sleep, with his golden mop of hair tousled, a stray lock falling over his eyes and the slight frown as if his dreams weren't pleasing him. His nose twitched slightly and it was the most adorable thing, Onathi did the same exact thing in his sleep too. He had slept late last night working over something. He must have been exhausted because he slept with his laptop on and it was next to him on the bed. Careful not to wake him up, she took the laptop and got out of the bed to put it in his study. His screensaver was the twins on their first photoshoot. Lola and Oyama were holding each twin in their arms and the photographer had captured them laughing while the twins were barring out their gums. Except for the blue eyes which had her golden highlights and the dimples and their coloring the twins looked more like her than their father. But again they had a lot of Jarred in them as she had predicted they were little pieces of them. Mpumi got into Jarred's study it was almost as organized as her but his showed signs that he spent most of his time here when he wasn't changing diapers and making formula. He had totally redeemed himself from the time when he had abandoned them at the hospital by being a very hands on daddy. As she was about to place the laptop on the desk an e-mail flashed on the screen. Mpumi wouldn't have paid attention to it but the picture of the sender caught her attention. There was no way those boobs were real, they made her self-conscious of her own boobs which were sagging just a bit. The owner of the perfect firm cleavage also had a flawless model looking face and looked to be in her late twenties or early thirties. Looking behind her to make sure that Jarred hadn't woken up and followed her, she read the e-mail. ***"Hey lover, you kinda left me hanging when you said you were going on some mission in Africa. Please reply my e-mails. See ya around mwaaahs xoxo"*** It even had cute emojis, it sounded as flippant and fun loving as the sender whose name was saved as April. Mpumi felt her hand go to her neck, she was tempted to open the e-mail and read all their conversations but then Jarred would really know that she had gone through his emails. Leaving the laptop on his desk, she quickly got out of his study. Mpumi had accepted that Jarred had had a life before they met again, it had been easy because there had seemed to have been no significant other in his life. But that perfect creature April seemed to think they still had a thing going on. Who was this April, how long had she and Jarred been an item, was she even a factor or threat. The questions darted through Mpumi's mind and she also struggled with what she was supposed to do now. Should she go back to bed and wait for him to wake up and ask him or take the laptop back and when he woke up he would see that she had seen or she could just go and make breakfast and pretend that she hadn't seen anything. Mpumi wasn't a very confrontational person so she headed to the kitchen in her pajamas and robe and started taking out bread, eggs, bacon and sausages. She didn't know where they stood in terms of privacy in this relationship. When they had dated when they were younger technology hadn't been as evolved and they hadn't gone through each other's phones. Now things were a bit different. From her experience with Daniel, his phone had been a no-go area and she had hated that. It made her suspicious of him and he thought she was too prying. She didn't want to ruin things with Jarred. Things had been going so well for them. They had gone to Havana in October. Google had been so helpful, Mpumi had managed to search what was required for the Quinceanera. She had taken Lola and Oyama with her to a local designer she had been introduced to by Nomusa who used to set up her table at Fox street just before Carlton Centre. They had samples of the gowns she had wanted, Lola had made it obvious that she wanted Mpumi to play the role of mother of the Quinceanera which was more like mother of the bride and she had to dress accordingly. According to Lola the highlights of a Latino's girl is her Quinceanera and her wedding day. So the two divas had their gowns custom made by Madeline Gardner, Quinceanera Collections called Vizcaya and Valencia. Jarred had almost collapsed when the bill was sent to him. Lola and Oyama were going to change their outfits five times. Yes five times! So they had ordered five gowns each. The first was the actual gowns, princess style gowns with embedded corsets and puffy skirts, Lola's was white with actual rhinestones it was breath-taking on her with her matching rhinestone earrings and a choker much like her mother, she was going to wear it with her mother's crown and some of her jewelry. But the crowning would be done by Mpumi as traditionally crowning was done by the mother of the Quinceanera. So Lola had also ordered another headpiece made of rhinestones talk about bling. Oyama had chosen a silver-grey ball gown and it was exquisite. For the photoshoot before the actual ceremony, they had ordered two gowns each in girly shades of pink and purple. Lola wanted Oyama with her in the photoshoot. Then they had ordered after-ceremony gowns which were more like cocktail dresses, Jarred hadn't been thrilled by the length or lack of length of the dresses but Mpumi had pointed out the no return policy. Then finally the girls had ordered dresses for their Salsa dance, it was a routine that they had practiced and it had been a highlight of their night. The cake had been ordered it had to be perfecto and the presents as well. Thank God for online shopping. In Havana they had stayed at the Iberostar Parque Central Hotel which was situated in the middle of Havana. Mpumi had fallen in love with the music and the dancers that had been at the foyer of the hotel and she had taken many pictures. There was a cultural vibrancy in Cuba that Mpumi envied. Jarred had kept his hand protectively around her all the time as if he was afraid that some tall Latino man would sweep her off her feet. The men were to die for but she had only eyes for her blue-eyed Adonis. Tracking down Lola's maternal family hadn't been easy. Most of them had either died like both her grandparents or emigrated to America or Europe. They had only found her aunt Jasmine who had been her mother's cousin. Jasmine had been very welcoming and warm and easy to love, it was easy to see that Lola had gotten those traits from her mother's family. Jasmine had wanted them to stay with her instead of the hotel as they were familia it wasn't right for Maria's daughter to be sleeping in a hotel but Jarred had gently refused. Jasmine had a whole brood of children with her husband Xavier and they had all formed part of Lola's court. Jasmine had been a mine of information about Quinces traditions because two of her daughters had also passed through the rites. She had insisted that it should officially start with a service at the Catedral de San Cristobal apparently the padre there was a close family friend who had also conducted Lola's mother, Maria's Quinceanera. Mpumi wasn't accustomed to Catholic services but the service was intimate and blessedly short. She hadn't expected to be touched but she had found herself tearing up when the priest had recognized whose daughter Lola was and that she was the splitting image of her mother. Jarred had squeezed her hand, all the money they had spent was worth that moment. The priest had given his blessing to Lola as she embarked on her journey into womanhood and then he had made the sign of the cross over her. Then they had been the walk on El Malecon, the walkway bordering the ocean. It was poignant and trapped in time, there were even small old boats dotting the ocean. People had been cheering and throwing rose petals it was sweet because they were strangers but they treated them like one of their own. Some people joined the dancers and it quickly became a huge procession like a carnival. Jarred's staff had outdone themselves at the venue. They had turned a large plain ball room into an enchanted winter forest wonder. There were large snowmen even complete with fake snowflakes, there was a real live deer and Mpumi had been so excited. Nomusa had died a little when they showed her the video. She hadn't been able to go with them because they had been rumors of lay-offs in her new company. The most precious moment was when Lola was lighting candles for the people in her life and making speeches. The first candle she had lit had been for her late mother, "Mamita thank you for fighting to bring me into this world even though you never got to hold me in your arms. I know you are always looking over me, and I hope that wherever you are you are proud of the woman I am becoming. I hope you aren't worrying about me because you left me in the best hands. All I have known in my life is love and comfort. I love you for eternity, I hope to finally meet you in the after-life." Mpumi had fought the tears, they would ruin her perfectly made-up face. Then she remembered that the mascara was water-proof and she had let the tears fall a little, that speech had been perfect. Then Lola had lit a candle for her late father then another for Jarred's mother, then she had lit a candle for Jarred, "the best father any girl could have ever been given. You are my rock, my first love, a friend and a constant comfort. I know I can be a handful at times but thank you for always loving me and cherishing me and making me feel like a princess." Mpumi had seen the tears that Jarred had discreetly wiped off, this candle lighting tradition was precious. Then she had been surprised when Lola had lit the next candle for her. "You took me under your wing when I was in a strange place and you made me feel at home. I had never known a mother's love till you came into my life. I strive every day to be more like you and to love as unconditionally as you. You might not be my biological madre but from this point onwards I know you will always been my Mamita and I love you." Mpumi had felt something lodge itself in her throat and she had to clear her throat a couple of times before she could breathe normally again. Then Lola had lit a candle for Oyama her "sister and partner in crime." For the first time in a long time, Mpumi had seen happy tears in her baby's eyes and she had sent a small prayer of thanks. Lola even lit candles for the twins, Nomusa lol and her aunt Jasmine with her family. Then it had been time for Jarred to change Lola into her first pair of stilettos, signifying that he was letting her go into womanhood and symbolizing her growth and the responsibility that was falling on her. They had then toasted Lola and Jarred's voice had broken a bit as he made a list of Lola's qualities. Mpumi had squeezed his hand. It was hard as a parent watching your baby turn into an adult, it was scary because then they need you less and less. Letting go was the hardest part but Lola would always be her daddy's little princess. The next time he would toast her would be her graduation and marriage hopefully but all a parent wanted was to halt time and keep their child shielded from the big bad world. The father-daughter dance was beautiful and Mpumi couldn't wipe the smile from her face. Then it had been her turn to crown Lola and hand her the scepter, she felt warmth and she hugged her warmly. Wow, the salsa dance routine had been explosive. Mpumi hadn't even been aware that Oyama could walk in heels let alone dance in them. The audience had been on its feet cheering and Jarred had wolf-whistled. That night had been perfect. But Jarred had had one surprise on his sleeve, he had hired Luis Fonsi and Daddy Yankee and flown them in to perform for Lola. The teenager had gone crazy and she couldn't stop hugging and kissing both of them. Just thinking of her girls singing along 'Basito Basito' to the song Despacito put a smile on Mpumi's face. "I hope thinking of me is what's responsible for that huge smile on your pretty face." Mpumi had been so lost in thought and pre-occupied by the food she was making that she hadn't heard Jarred come into the kitchen. He was standing behind her towering over her and his voice vibrated through his chest. She snuggled into him then she remembered the e-mail from

CHAPTER
SIXTEEN

Apriiil the woman with the perky boobs, in her mind she said the name with a drawn twang, and she shifted away from him slightly. "I was thinking of Lola's Quinceanera." Jarred faked a groan.

"Please don't remind me, my bank account is still trying to recover from that financial drain."

"Just think next you will be paying for her wedding," Mpumi teased him.

"Two weddings including Oyama's Lord help us!" Jarred could be so dramatic it was funny.

"Go away before I burn these eggs."

"You mean burn them more than you usually do… Ouch!" She had stepped on his bare foot hard, he jumped around the kitchen holding his foot and she laughed at him. This was the reason she didn't want to raise that email. They were in such a happy place. "Speaking of the Quinceanera, that photography studio just e-mailed me the pictures last night, they will send the framed pictures later this week. Wanna see them?" Oh No! Mpumi felt her heart stop, he would see that email and she wasn't sure she wanted to see it again.

"You'll show them to me later, let me finish making breakfast first." She was relieved that her voice had that normal timbre.

"No forget about breakfast the girls can finish up, come on babe." He was already pulling her towards the passage. He was headed towards the bedroom but she had to tell him that she moved the laptop to his study. He didn't seem to mind and he went into the study and made her sit on his lap. "Crap, I slept with the laptop on yesterday," she didn't offer any comment to this remark she just pasted a fake smile on her face. He barely looked at the email he just closed it and went to the email from the photo studio without even missing a bit. Ok maybe she was reading too much into the email and she was glad she hadn't confronted him with it but it still bothered her a little. Who was she kidding it bothered her a lot, she wanted to yank Apriiiil's perfect boobs off her chest. Maybe she had to deal with her trust issues but she was positive this was the standard female reaction in such situations. She

found herself wondering what Nomusa would do if she had found that email, that bish April would probably be dead by now. She chided herself and forced herself to concentrate on the pictures. They were all so beautiful and
she didn't know which one was her favorite and she wished they had gone with the twins. The girls had begged and begged but Jarred did not budge so they had left the babies with her mother in Soweto and she had been so happy. Mpumi had been afraid that they would find their babies eating porridge with peanut butter and finding them baptized in her mother's church. For the life of her she couldn't remember the name of that church. But they had found both grandchildren and grandmother healthy and happy, MaNtuli hadn't wanted them babies to go. But Mpumi had missed them too much and she hadn't been at all sympathetic with her mother.

Mpumi had still been undecided whether she should confront Jarred or not about Apriiil in the late afternoon. The problem with not asking when something is bothering you is that it grows into a big thing. It's like when a bee is trapped in your window, it will keep annoying you till you open the window and let it fly out or swat it down with a newspaper. And she had too much time on her hands since she had tendered her resignation. She had gone back to work but her mind was always at home with her babies and making investments just wasn't as appealing to her anymore. Her employers had been sad to see her go and they held her on a retainer at a rather alarming rate but her pocket was smiling at their expense. Jarred had reminded her that she should start her own business but right now she was just content to look after her babies at home. She would think hard and begin the new venture in the next year. She still wasn't sure how she could combine photography and children into a lucrative business but Jarred told her that for the business to be a real success she had to do something she was passionate about. Easy for him to say he had run a hotel chain into over billions before he reached 30. She was irritated with him because of that bloody email and she kept snapping at him. He kept asking if she was fine and she lied that she was great. Just as she was brooding a call came through and she smiled, a genuine smile this time. "MaMlaba" the caller said warmly.

"MaNgidi this is a wonderful surprise."

"You know I hate these telephone things but they are necessary. How are your babies doing?" MaNgidi had been the only one in Daniel's family that she had called and told about the twins, after all they had kicked for the first time when she hugged the elder woman.

"They're growing bigger each day, how is everyone at home?"

"The same my daughter we are just living on God's grace." Now that they had gotten the pleasantries out of the way, Mpumi waited for her to state the purpose for her call. "How is Oyama? Are we still holding the Intonjane ceremony for her in December? I ask because we need to prepare." Mpumi had totally forgotten about that. And it was November already. God! And she hadn't even spoken about it with Oyama.

"Let me call you back maa I hear someone at the door." Sometimes her lying abilities surprised even her. She couldn't commit without talking to Oyama first but that would seem as if she was pushed over by her own daughter. As usual when they got home from school Oyama had locked herself in her room. Mpumi had to knock a whole minute before the little madam opened her door and she stood in the doorway blocking Mpumi's entry. "May I come in?" she reluctantly let go of the door knob and walked to her bed where there were books strewn across it. She still couldn't get used to the gothic décor in the room but today wasn't the best time to suggest a remodeling of Oyama's bedroom. She came in peace and she needed to stay on her daughter's good side. Mpumi perched her arse on the corner of the bed, the atmosphere in the room wasn't exactly welcoming or one that allowed her to sit comfortably. "So I was thinking Yaya since you're turning 15 in December, how about we hold the Intonjane ceremony for you eQutubeni." The little diva wrinkled her pet nose delicately.

"You don't need to hold a ceremony for me just because you held the Quinceanera for Lola, I don't mind." When had it become so hard to talk to her own child?

"I actually discussed the issue with your great-aunt the last time I went to Transkei and now I want to hear what you think about the idea. I thought it was brilliant" she was overselling it, Mpumi could just feel it.

"Whatever I'm cool with whatever you decide." It wasn't exactly the enthusiastic response she had been hoping for, but Mpumi couldn't afford to be picky. How she missed the times when they talked about anything and everything. Oops she had thought out loud, Oyama was looking at her funny.

"I used to think we talked about everything and that we had no secrets but you lied to me mama about one of the most crucial things in my life and I just can't move along from that as if nothing happened." Oyama sounded so mature, when had her daughter grown up. Mpumi sighed.

"I know baby, I just want you to trust me again. I need you to know that you can talk to me about everything. That was the only thing I kept from you." Oyama didn't respond and Mpumi thought she was done talking then she said quietly, "I was afraid that when the twins came you would send me back to my father." Mpumi could feel her pain and even though she knew that Oyama wasn't into hugging anymore she pulled her daughter into her arms. Oyama was frigid at first but then she hugged her back. Mpumi spoke from her heart, "No one will ever take your place in my heart Oyama, you are my first born and I will fight anyone who tries to take you away from me. You can doubt everything else but never doubt the love I have for you. You're my heart beat, you, Lola, Onathi and Owethu always remember that." They stayed that way till Oyama got uncomfortable and started squirming, Mpumi let her go.

"So how's your crush Ryan?"

CHAPTER
SIXTEEN

"He was just that, a stupid crush. I got over him ages ago." Ok Mpumi knew when she was being kicked out, she pecked Oyama's high forehead and let herself out of the bedroom. She called back MaNgidi, "Sorry about that maa, you can start with the preparations is there anything I need to do?"

"No don't worry about it, I will see to everything. You don't know how excited I am. Maybe you can get her attire made that's all." Mpumi hoped that Oyama could get only half as excited as MaNgidi. But the ceremony was a big deal and Mpumi was glad that they were going to hold it. Her father had died and no one had held the Intonjane ceremony for her.

She loved Owethu with her whole heart but that little girl was exhausting. She hadn't wanted to fall asleep and Mpumi had tried all the tricks in the book from rocking her to walking her to singing her a lullaby. All Owethu wanted was to chat and gurgle about whatever it was that went around her little girl brain. Mpumi had tried laying her down then sneaking out of the nursery but the little diva had started screaming and had woken up Onathi in the process. Now her boy was usually a quiet and happy baby but he did not take kindly to being woken up from his sweet dreams. So she had had two screaming red babies to appease. Jarred had stepped in and he had taken Owethu first, he laid her on his chest and talked gently to her, the rumblings from his baritone must have done the trick because she had fallen asleep instantly. He did the same with Onathi like he was some kind of snake charmer and Mpumi had somehow been chaffed by how easily he had gotten the twins to sleep. They had tiptoed out of the nursery with the baby monitor and they had gone to their own bedroom. She was exhausted and she expected to fall instantly asleep but there was still the unresolved issue of the flirty email. Jarred was lying on his side and studying her quietly. "So aren't you going to ask me about that email from April?" Shit, she had forgotten he usually never bit around the bush and that he could see right through her so easily. Now she had two options pretend she didn't know what he was talking about or feign sleep. "I didn't know how to ask you," there went her mind colluding with her mouth against her. He turned her face to look at him. "I could tell that something was bothering you when you wanted to snap my neck the whole day. Then I concluded that you must have seen that bloody email."

"Who is she?"

"An ex who isn't aware she's an ex yet." She widened her brown eyes at that response, how does one become an ex without being aware that one is an ex?

"How long were you together?"

"On and off for five years." She almost sat up but what he had just said floored her, she didn't want to know anymore. He had been with April longer than they had been together even if she combined their time together in Harvard. She made to say something but it just wouldn't come out. "I know how it looks but we had broken up sort of before I even met you again. Then I met you and I forgot all about her." Why were all men so shady? No one 'forgets' about a woman with a perfect set of jugs like
Apriiil.

"Just days after meeting me you were already pressuring me to leave Daniel. Yet you didn't end things with your on and off girlfriend for ten freaking months Jarred. We even have children together now! Is April your escape route?" Mpumi was so angry she wished she could punch through something or someone. He couldn't maintain eye contact with her anymore.

"I'm sorry I thought if I ignored her long enough she would get the idea and leave me alone." Every word that was coming out of his mouth was making her angrier. She turned on her side and pulled the blanket over her shoulders. He hesitated for a beat then he gently touched her shoulders. "Hey I'm sorry I didn't mean for things to turn up this way." She didn't respond she just kept quiet. "Ok maybe I should email her back and tell her that I have moved on, permanently this time." You think, she fumed at him silently. "Please don't be mad at me Lelo." He was pleading now but she kept her back firmly to him. "I just said I'm going to break things off with April what more do you want from me?" it wasn't even about April anymore, but Jarred had been a hypocrite and that angered her. She had burnt all bridges to be with him but he had kept some bridges intact, she knew how it felt to be kept hanging.

"Maybe if I ignore you long enough you will get the idea and leave me alone," she burned him with his own match stick. He sighed and switched off the side lamp, he wasn't getting any that night not even a cuddle. Mpumi had learnt two things that day she could look through his things and he wouldn't make a big deal about it, that was a relief and no matter how smart or talented a man is, they were all idiots. She fell asleep easily after that and she left Jarred tossing and turning.

CHAPTER SEVENTEEN

Mpumi had packed her kids into her car, they needed some air before Jarred drove them all crazy. He was working on some deal and it wasn't going his way and he was barking at everyone in his sight. She headed to the Mall of Africa, the girls needed to have their hair done, they were leaving for the Eastern Cape the next day. She had sent Oyama's and Lola's measurements to the lady eNgcobo, MaNgidi had said it was fine they could bring Lola with them. Jarred wasn't exactly pleased with the whole trip, not because he didn't think it was a good idea but because Daniel would also be there and in his jealous mind images of Daniel wooing his precious Lelo in the hills of eQutubeni and the two of them kissing and making up were giving him an ulcer. Mpumi brushed his fears aside there was no way on this earth that she was going back to Daniel. Nomusa was coming along with them, there was no way she was missing the stir that her little Mexican was going to cause and the look on Rabhekha's face. Jarred was staying with the babies for the whole ten days and that was part of the reason why he was in such a sour mood. But he was better at this parenting thing than Mpumi, he was more patient. Besides he was the one who had strongly refused when she suggested that they send the kids to her mother in Soweto. He didn't mind staying with the babies but going ten days without sex irked him the most. Now to the task at hand after speaking with their usual stylist, there would be no white braids or any funny weaves, she took the twins on their stroller to Wimpy. She was sitting there enjoying the cool breeze and sipping on her extra-large strawberry milkshake which Owethu kept trying to reach for, when she heard a shrill voice she had dreaded ever hearing again. "Nompumelelo it is you! I thought I recognized you, it's been forever and you have gained so much weight. But I said to myself I know that person." Bitch, Mpumi thought to herself, she hadn't gained that much weight. But she pasted a fake smile and turned to the unwanted intruder. "Ronewa what a lovely surprise, fancy meeting you here."

"I know I was just coming from a meeting with a client. I am in line for Partnership at Steller and Borsch Associates." Must explain why her breath smelt like shit, it was from all the arse licking she had been doing. Mpumi hadn't even asked about where she worked and the chances of a female, a black one at that making partner in a white, male dominated firm where next to null but she would leave Ronewa to her dreams. The next thing she knew the crow had taken a seat at her table. Just great. "So let's catch up, I haven't seen you since graduation. I got a job at some law firm soon after that and I've been climbing my way up the legal ladder since then."

"That's so great hey, I went to Harvard and I've been working for an Investment group but I recently resigned."

"Oh so what are you doing now? Looking after other people's children? The economy is really rough now." Mpumi felt anger start but she had to take a couple of breaths before she could respond.

"No Ronewa these are my babies, Anton and Aleja." The shock on Ronewa's face was comical.

"Oh but I heard that you and Daniel just divorced."

CHAPTER
SEVENTEEN

Why was this bitch still here? Mpumi had had enough.

"Yes we did." She wasn't going to give an explanation.

"Anyways those are very cute babies. Where is their father? You remember Mulalo right? Yes we got married, he's an electrical engineer if you still remember." This woman was not giving up! At least her husband had finally graduated he had been repeating for the third year when they met him in tertiary. She was taking out an I-pad, Oyama had had the same model the previous year but she had been bought another newer model. Ronewa seemed to be looking for something then she found it and she was showing Mpumi, "These are my children the first born is turning twelve and the last born is ten years old." Mpumi made the appropriate sounds but it really was a pity that the girl looked so much like her dead beat father with the same flat nose which managed to be wide at the same time. Ronewa left after giving Mpumi her business card and Mpumi could finally roll her eyes. Ronewa had been one of those competitive know-it-alls in college. She hadn't liked Mpumi at all which wasn't surprising because Mpumi scooped all the awards. Apparently she had grown into one of the stand-offish lawyer types, pompous and ready to rub their 'successes' in your face. Those wives who flaunted how good their husbands were whilst they hadn't had sex since the birth of their last child. Those status climbers that made Mpumi's skin crawl. When she texted Nomusa and told her that one of her former classmates had thought she was the twin's nanny, her friend sent so many laughing faces ***"I told you to bleach, this wouldn't have happened if you had listened to Me."*** She was saved from replying that stupid text by the girls coming out. They had cornrows and braids on, they looked cute Mpumi took a picture of them. The next stop was Gold Reef City, she didn't need a ring and a job to be happy.

She told Jarred the same thing after telling him the story of bumping into Ronewa. Instead of laughing it off or making some silly remark about it, he didn't respond but looked as if he was thinking deeply about something. She let him be and she changed into her sexiest piece of night wear, a slinky little white number. She wanted to make their last night memorable. She was standing seductively in front of him when he looked at her and said, "Why don't we just do it?" Just do what? Was he now a Nike advert rep? She thought but she put on her serious face.

"Do what babe?"

"Get married. We already have children I don't see why not." Mpumi had dreamed of Jarred proposing but in all her wildest dreams she hadn't thought he would make it sound like a business proposition.

"I don't know, you just only broke up with Apriiil recently. Are you sure you're ready to move onto marriage."

"First of all I won't even ask why you are pronouncing her name like that. Secondly do you think I should wait another sixteen years before I'm ready to move onto marriage?"

"I don't appreciate your sarcasm."

"And I don't appreciate you rejecting me every time I propose! What exactly do you want us to be? Dating when we have grandchildren?" Mpumi realized that they had gotten into a fight.

"Oh was that a proposal? It sounded like you were suggesting we get the kids some tetanus shots."

"You will never agree to marry me will you?"

"Maybe if you asked as if it came from your heart not some half-hearted suggestion I would agree to marry you." Mpumi didn't know why she wasn't backing down but she felt like she deserved better.

"You know what, fuck it. I'm sorry I brought it up. Go and have fun with your husband's family and stay there if you want to."

"Jarred that's a low blow and you know it… where are you going?"

"To sleep in the guest bedroom I don't think I can even look at you right now." He was serious too because he banged the door and left her feeling shell shocked. A part of her wanted to go after him but a part of her knew that he needed his space. Besides she hadn't done anything wrong. She had already gotten one weak proposal in her life which was sensible. She also deserved to be swept off her feet and a proposal that spoke to her heart. The sparks between them were beginning to form veld fires.

When she woke up the next morning she found that Jarred wasn't next to her on the bed. It looked like he hadn't come to bed at all, she bit her lower lip in frustration. She had stomped on his ego the previous night but with Jarred she didn't want to settle, she wanted everything, the romance, the passion, the companionship, fidelity and the fireworks. She got up to go and look for him, she found him in the nursery he was changing Owethu's diaper. He barely looked her direction and he continued with his task. She went behind him and slid her arms around his waist and rested her hand on his upper back. He was too tall. "You should go and wake the girls up, you have a long journey ahead of you," at least he was talking to her but that wasn't what she wanted to talk about. "Jarred about last night..."

"We will talk when you get back. Go wake them up." He meant it and he wouldn't talk anymore, after kissing her babies and him softly on the lips, she went to wake up the girls. It was sad leaving her little munchkins and her love especially when she wasn't really sure where they stood. But she pushed what had happened into a box that she would open later and she concentrated on the journey. It was fun to be just the girls and even Oyama was a bit bubblier, they told stories about school and Oyama's Matric
dance and Mpumi laughed with them. The ride to Cape Town seemed too short and they were walking out of the airport with the girls hanging on to everything Nomusa said. It was going to be a proper road trip this time without her aunt breathing down her neck, her uncles' disapproval and her mother's judgement. There was music, gossip, selfies and so much laughter. Nomusa had a way about her that

brought them all together. She was crazy but she was also Mpumi's sanity at times. Before they knew it they were eNgcobo, their attires were so pretty, Nomusa was going to wear umbhaco and when Mpumi pointed out that she wasn't even married she did her carefree flip. "I am not going to subject myself to the prying questions of those mountain career wives. You know one of my aunts actually came to my apartment with amagqirha saying I need divine intervention." Mpumi laughed Nomusa's family were all over the top. The Jeep ate up the distance and in no time they found themselves in the Xhamela household. MaNgidi came out to welcome them with one of the junior wives MaMbanjwa, the other junior wife and Phindiwe stood looking at them from the veranda. When they saw Lola they started laughing and making snide gestures, Mpumi just ignored them and they went in to greet Tat' Xhamela. The elder smiled widely and they sat down on the chairs in the living room. "MaMlaba, welcome and thank you for letting us do this for Nokwindla," he always called Oyama by her clan name.

"Thank you Tata we are glad you invited us." Mpumi had a soft spot for the white headed man. Daniel had said he couldn't come for the whole ten days so he would come for umgidi which was the last stage of Intonjane. Phindiwe came in and sat next to Tat' Xhamela, Mpumi's heart sank that old witch was up to no good. "Uncle I understand that Nompumelelo and my brother are not together anymore but for her to bring that white girl with her here flaunting to us that she has moved on with a white man. I find that not only disrespectful but also unacceptable." Thankfully Lola couldn't hear what she was saying but it was still cruel, she was just a child.

"I am the one who invited her Phindiwe," MaNgidi came to her rescue.

"I see no harm in the child being here, I gave maMlaba my blessing." Tat' Xhamela said patiently. Phindiwe looked like a chicken drenched in cold water.

"Fine. But she can't be part of the Intonjane, she's not even Xhosa." Phindiwe sounded so triumphant, Mpumi had no idea what she had ever done to this woman to make her hate her so much. Oyama had been quiet all along but when Phindiwe dropped her last bomb she spoke up, "Then if that's the case aunty, we may as well leave now. If my sister isn't allowed to be part of the ceremony I want no part in that ceremony as well."

"You're my brother's daughter. How can you call that pig's child your sister?" Mpumi wished that she had strangled that witch to death in their apartment.

"Phindiwe! I will not allow such talk in my house. Do you hear me?!" Tat' Xhamela's voice shook a bit.

"But uncle I am right this is a sacred tradition we cannot have the Harvard wife make a mockery of our traditions." Phindiwe said sullenly.

"Grandfather, wasn't tradition started by our fore fathers? And can we not adapt it as we go? At the heart of our Xhosa culture is the spirit of Ubuntu, it takes a village to raise a child and your neighbor's child is your own. Does it matter then if your neighbor is not from the same lineage as you or of a different skin? Please don't exclude my sister because she wants to experience and embrace my culture which I am proud to be part of. Just recently at Mdeni, near Qumbu a Pakistan family performed the Intonjane for the daughter. Times are changing and as long as she wants to preserve our traditions, I think she should be given a chance to experience our culture." Mpumi wasn't sure what surprised her more that Oyama could say such a long and passionate speech in perfect Xhosa no less or that she knew so much. The respect and deference in that child's voice had been perfect. Oyama had seemed indifferent to the whole ceremony. The whole room became quiet. Underneath the surprise Tat' Xhamela seemed impressed by the depth of knowledge and wisdom that Oyama portrayed. Mpumi didn't know when her daughter had grown up so much but that was the proudest moment in her life. She had raised this human being. Tat' Xhamela scratched his beard and seemed to think deeply, "I hear you Nokwindla but this is an issue I will have to raise with the village elders first. Then I will get back to you when I hear what they have to say." There was nothing more to be said, so they were all shown to their rooms. Mpumi gave Oyama a big hug, "I'm so proud to be your mother nunu." Nomusa wanted to know, "How did you know about the Pakistan family in Qumbu. Even I didn't know that there is a village called Mdeni in Qumbu." Oyama laughed mischievously, "I read about it in some article on Goggle." Too bad Oyama was more inclined towards chemistry and physics, she would have made one hell of a defense attorney.

They were in the veld they had convened at some hill spot. Tat' Xhamela had spoken to the village heads and miraculously they had allowed Lola to be part of the ceremony. Both her girls were covered completely in blankets along with MaNgidi's youngest daughter Andiswa. Lola and Andiswa were Oyama's amakhankatha (orderlies or attendants). MaNgidi and two other elderly women in the family had been chosen to preside over Intonjane. There were other village women singing traditional songs and a group of girls the younger ones with their chests out and decorated in white clay, wearing only skirts in the traditional fabric of a bright yellow with designs in black. Their only adornments were short necklaces, a simple strip of head band and goat skin bands on their bare feet. The older girls had longer necklaces and their skirts were white but they were also adorned simply. The group of girls were dancing, the movement of their supple bodies was energetic and beautiful and it gave Mpumi chills and an idea for her business. When the sun set the elders led Oyama and her amakhankatha from the veld to the homestead. MaNgidi had outdone herself in the preparations she had even hired a professional crew to document the whole process. Mpumi was grateful but she still took some pictures to send to Jarred later. A hut farther from the rest in the homestead had been chosen to be the room in which the initiate was to be secluded with her orderlies. The elders went in with the initiate into the hut where she was being taught womanhood values and norms and also

CHAPTER
SEVENTEEN

being prepared for marriage. Oyama had
volunteered to interpret whatever was said for Lola. Since she hadn't had an Intonjane ceremony of her own, Mpumi had inquired from MaNgidi what happened inside the hut. She had been told that the initiate would sleep on amakhukho (grass mats), covered only by blankets naked apart from a black doek covering her head. She was also permitted to wear inkciyo which was traditional underwear but her breasts and buttocks remain exposed. Mpumi had painted Oyama's whole body with soft white clay which was supposed to make her glow. Lola had giggled when Nomusa was smearing the clay on her, she said she was ticklish. While they were in their seclusion, Mpumi and the rest of them had been around a huge fire while the dancing and singing continued. The teenage boys and girls would come to sing and dance every evening till the ten days was up. Mpumi missed Jarred she wished he and the twins were also there with them. But she was glad she was keeping them away from Phindiwe, the way her former sisterin-law hated her Mpumi did not doubt that she would have gone as far as poisoning her babies. They had to go asleep early, the next day there was ukushwama. A goat would be slaughtered known as umngena-ndlini it was a symbol that a maiden had entered seclusion. Knowing Tat' Xhamela he was also going to slaughter several sheep for his grand-niece. Mpumi wasn't even sure if Oyama was still a virgin or not that's how out of touch she had become with her child. But she comforted herself in that surely if something as momentous as losing her virginity happened, Oyama would tell her just as she had told her about her first period and her first crush. But she was also worried because the teen had grown into a sullen closed book.

The days trickled past, the sense of time wasn't as important in the rural areas. After doing their chores Mpumi and Nomusa mostly spent their days on the hills talking. When Mpumi told Nomusa about the fight that she and Jarred had had before they came to Cape Town, Nomusa hadn't taken her side. "How do you know that

his proposal didn't come from his heart? Because there wasn't a flashy romantic movie gesture? That man has been proposing to you since we bumped into him in Cape Town with his every action." Mpumi hadn't thought of it that way, she was stuck in her big romantic moment. Nomusa voiced her doubts of job security in her current employment, Mpumi told her of the business she wanted to start and offered her a place in the business. There was no one she trusted more than Nomusa. But Nomusa had her life and Amogalang in Cape Town now. They went to the hills to stay as far from Phindiwe as possible, that woman's bitterness was poisonous. She passed snide comments about Mpumi every chance she got and it was exhausting. On the seventh day of the seclusion an ox had been slaughtered for ukushatela intonjane. The real fun part had been at midday on that same day. As per custom Oyama had come out totally naked except for the inkciyo, she had hesitated at the door and looked around. One of the elder women spoke sharply to her and she had complied. Her model C daughter ran around the whole yard naked banging a pot as she ran as fast as she could. Nomusa's shoulders had been shaking with laughter but she had not dared laugh out loud. It had reminded Mpumi of that time when Oyama had been chased by a puppy around the yard. The previous day
Oyama, Lola and Andiswa had been dressed in imibhaco, Oyama had a black doek on
and they had looked so beautiful and grown up. The floor in the hut had been cleaned and smeared with cow dung while the grass mats they had been sleeping on had been burnt. Then the elders had taken her to the main house and they had given their report. Surprisingly Daniel hadn't missed the occasion but Mpumi knew that he was scared of his uncle. The ceremony had been a beautiful success but Mpumi was growing restless, she needed to be with her man and her babies. They went in to thank the Xhamelas for their hospitality and holding the initiation ceremony for them. MaNgidi was sad to see them leave and she suggested that they should stay on for another day but Mpumi pointed out that she had spent a lot of time apart from her babies. Daniel asked

to speak to her before they left. "You're looking well maMlaba I hear congratulations are in order."

"Thank you Daniel, you are not looking too bad yourself."

"I wanted to discuss how we are going to share the holidays. I won't be around for Christmas. So may I have Oyama for the New Year?"

"That won't be a problem just call when you get back and I will bring her over." He thanked her and was silent, she had been married to this man for almost sixteen years and she knew he still had something to say.

"How is she?" he was asking about Oyama.

"Some days she locks herself away and she is distant. But she is slowly coming out of that bad place. She's very attached to Lola and I think that's been helping her." Mpumi had worried about her Matric exams but her teachers had assured her that Oyama's academic progress was still advanced for her age and there was no doubt that she would pass with distinctions.

"I heard that she refused to participate in the ceremony if they didn't include her sister." Daniel sounded impressed, Mpumi laughed.

"She takes her stubborn streak from you, you should have heard the speech she gave. She is her father's daughter. But don't be surprised if you have to take them both for the holidays. They are inseparable now." They were both laughing now and then Daniel was looking at her with a serious expression.

"We haven't laughed like this in years," he stated. He was right.

"We really took each other down to hell," she agreed quietly.

"Thank you Mpumi for everything." She knew exactly what he meant and she nodded. It was time for them to leave. She had a big blue-eyed baby to appease and make up to in Johannesburg. It was just sad that Nomusa wasn't coming with them.

CHAPTER EIGHTEEN

"Your mother hates me!" he whined as she helped him with his bowtie. Jarred was a god in a tuxedo, she felt like locking him in the hotel room and not letting him out. It was New Year's Eve and they were at the opening of his Durban hotel. When they had gotten home from Transkei, Jarred had apologized and she had also apologized and then they had kissed and had the most mind blowing make up sex. But there hadn't been any further talk of proposals or marriage. They had planned to spend Christmas in Hawaii but then both the twins had a fever on Christmas Eve and they had had to cancel the trip. So they had spent Christmas at home. It had been fun they had been gifts, singing and Jarred had gotten her drunk on eggnog some concoction that apparently marked the holidays in America. She had danced so much and they had captured it all on video. As she had predicted she had to go with both Oyama and Lola to Daniel's place. They had left the twins with her mother on their way to Durban. Mpumi had blatantly refused when MaNtuli had suggested that she take the twins to an all-night prayer, they had their whole lives to be force-fed religion by her mother as she had been all her life. Her mother had already been hinting about their baptism. "Don't take it personally she hates all white people." She assured Jarred as she finished inspecting him. She was telling the truth as a maid, MaNtuli hadn't had happy experiences with whites in apartheid South Africa. So she wasn't a fan of any of the Caucasian race.

"That's very comforting, guess I also have to run back to America because your mother hates me."

"You wouldn't leave your babies and you would take them from me over my dead body." He kissed her lightly on the lips careful not to ruin her lipstick.

"You know you always turn me on when you're on feisty mode." she swatted his hand when it began to cup her buttock. They couldn't afford to be late to their own opening. She picked up her purse, the universal signature move of let's go. "Ladies first." He mock bowed, she laughed at his fake chivalry.

"Liar you just want to stare at my arse like the pervert that you are." She said softly and he had the grace to look guilty.

"Did I tell you how ravishing you look tonight my Aphrodite?" She felt warmth spread over her cheeks in the intimate way he was intoning his words and from the way he was looking at her from her red-bottom heels to her natural hair which her stylist had manipulated into a chic chiffon look. She had to admit to herself she was looking her best tonight. She was wearing a body-hugging simple silver-grey dress that shimmered at the bottom. It hugged her in all the right places, hid all that needed hiding, showed off her ample cleavage to perfection not in a tartly fashion and the slit was downright daring. She even had on daring red lipstick which made her pearly white teeth sparkle. She had hired a professional make-up artist pulling out all the guns.

"Mmmmmmh I don't think I heard you the first twenty times that you said that." She was in a flirty mood.

"You look stunning, breath-taking and if any man

even dares to look your direction tonight I am going to pluck out their eyes." He sounded like he actually meant it. They had reached the elevator and they got in luckily they were alone. "So when are you going to tell our children that they were conceived in an elevator? Because I think that story will be best coming from you." Mpumi laughed, at times it was hard to tell when he was joking and when he was serious. This hotel was similar in built with the one in Cape Town and it brought back many memories. "You mean tell them how you took advantage of my drunk state to ravish me in the elevator."

"I did not take advantage of you, you had been giving me the horny eyes the whole day even that morning at the beach. It took all my will power not to take you right there on that boulder by the ocean." It was a good thing that the material of that dress wasn't revealing because her nipples had become taut with need.

"I wanted you then so badly and I want you now even more." She admitted to him even her voice had dropped to a husky timbre. The way he was looking at her told her that he wanted her too.

"Keep those naughty thoughts for later tonight, I can't really concentrate on my guests with a hard-on." He was saved by the elevator stopping at the ground floor. He led her to the ball room with her hand tucked in his elbow. Heads turned the moment they reached the foyer. Every woman wanted Jarred she thought, they were looking at her with so much envy. The décor in the ball room was classy and everyone clapped as they got into the room. Jarred squeezed her hand warmly before letting it go and made his way up the mini podium. She barely heard a word of his speech because she was drinking on how magnificent her man was. His strong shoulders and chest looked like they wanted to burst out of his tux. She was so wrapped up in feasting her eyes on him that she was startled when someone tapped her lightly on the shoulders. "Mpumi, its funny how we keep bumping into each other." For the love of God not this again, she swore silently, then smiling she spoke to the intruder. "Wow Ronewa fancy meeting you here." What were the odds that she would meet her in Durban?

Ronewa cleaned up good, her slender model frame was in a flowing red gown which agreed with her light coffee complexion.

"My husband Mulalo was the electrical engineer heading the wiring of this entire hotel," the pride in her voice was evident, "He just left me to get us some drinks I will introduce you guys now. He is close to the owner of this hotel, maybe he can help you get a job here. What are you doing here? Alone?" Mpumi didn't even know what was more insulting but she was saved from replying by the arrival of Ronewa's husband. Mulalo was the nerdy chubby type, he was even wearing a tweed suit which made him look like some professor. He was even sweating a little and his wide nose was flared even wider than usual. Ronewa grabbed one of the drinks from him "What took you so long? Do you remember my college friend Mpumi?" Mpumi felt sorry for the man the way he was snapped at and she was surprised, she couldn't remember any time even in college when she and Ronewa were ever friends. Mulalo gave her a limp handshake, his hands were sweaty and she avoided the urge to wipe her hand. "Nice to meet you Mulalo."

"I was just telling Mpumi that you are good friends with the chairperson of this hotel chain. Maybe you can speak to him and get her a job?" Mulalo looked uncomfortable with what his wife was saying and Mpumi felt like slapping that condescending smile off Ronewa's face. She felt a presence behind her and a familiar hand go possessively around her waist and pull her towards a broad chest. She hadn't even heard the applause signifying the end Jarred's speech but she was grateful that he was back at her side. Ronewa was looking at them speculatively. Jarred was shaking hands with Mulalo with his free hand. "Mr. Mulaudzi tonight wouldn't have been possible, if you and your team hadn't worked so hard thank you." Mulalo was beaming at the praise and then he introduced Ronewa, "Mr. Levine this is my wife Ronewa, dear this is the chairperson of this hotel chain." That bitch was batting her eyelashes at her man! Mpumi felt like pulling her weave.

"And I see you have already met my partner, the mother of my children Lelo." Mpumi loved the sound of partner rather than wife. Jarred kissed her lightly on the lips as he finished the introductions. The shock and envy on Ronewa's face was comical.

"Actually babe my good friend Ronewa and I went to law school together and she was just asking her husband to hook me up with a job in this hotel." Sometimes one just has to put bitches in their places, one bitch at a time.

"No, Mpumi misunderstood me I was just making conversation." Ronewa's voice now held a soothing tone. She was back to booty licking. Jarred raised his eyebrow, Mpumi would explain later.

"Mr. Mulaudzi we might need to employ your services again. My partner is starting her own business and it's going to be even bigger than the hotels. I recommended your team to her but she will have the last say." This night just kept getting better and the look on Ronewa's face was priceless, Mpumi wished she could take a picture and send it to Nomusa.

"I would love to have another opportunity to work with you. And Mpumi you have lovely children." Shame Mulalo was so humble, Mpumi was definitely going to work with his team. But wait…

"Where did you meet my children?"

"Mr. Levine used to come with them to meetings and to the site when you were in Cape Town." Mr. Levine had a lot of explaining to do and he wasn't looking her in the eye. No wonder the twins had had a fever, he had taken them to a hotel site.

"Please excuse us, we need to move around the room, it was nice chatting with you." Jarred was such a coward. And shame Ronewa had been so quiet the whole time, Mpumi had almost forgotten that she was even there. She smiled at her and let Jarred lead her to the next elderly couple who from their accents were from Russia. Mpumi could barely make out what they were saying so she just smiled and nodded on cue. She hated networking but Jarred was a natural at it.

"What was that all about earlier on?" Jarred asked his voice close to her ear. They were dancing the waltz, at least they weren't talking to any more people. Mpumi's cheeks hurt from all that smiling.

"That's the lady I ran into at the mall the other day who thought I was the twins' nanny." Jarred laughed his low sexy laugh which sent tingles throughout her body, "It's not funny you should have heard her before you came to where we were standing. ' Dear, I was just telling Mpumi that you are good friends with the chairperson of this hotel chain. Maybe you can speak to him and get her a job?'" Mpumi did a good impression of Ronewa's shrill voice making Jarred laugh even harder, he threw his head back and laughed. People on the dance floor were staring at them and some enthusiastic journalist snapped a few pictures. They were going to make the news again tomorrow but Mpumi didn't care the night was perfect.

"Do you remember Havana when the girls had gone to sleep?" He asked her. How could she forget? They had sneaked out of their penthouse and gone to one of those open-air bazaars and they had danced to the Cuban drums the whole night. He had told her not to worry or think but just to feel the music and they had danced as if they were the only people in the world. She felt something poking her on her pelvis, she looked up at Jarred and he just widened his eyes innocently at her. Now it was her chance to laugh, Jarred had a hard-on in the middle of the dance floor with people all around them. "What happens if I move away from you right now?" She said softly with a challenge in her eyes.

"You wouldn't dare because all the thirsty women in this room will be lining up to get my services." He winked at her. The music was paused and the MC broke into their easy banter.

"Just a minute before we enter the New Year ladies and gentlemen. Please help us count down." They stopped dancing and stood facing the podium with Jarred behind her, his chin resting on top of her head. The countdown began and Mpumi also joined in "Ten… nine… eight… seven… six… five… four… three… two… one!" Jarred twirled her around and kissed her deeply as all around them people screamed "Happy New Year!!!" The sound of fireworks took Mpumi

back to that bedroom the previous year when she had locked herself in her and Daniel's bedroom and she was crying and rocking herself. It seemed like a lifetime away, before she knew that she would be laughing so hard and kissed so deeply. She hadn't thought that she would have Lola and the twins in her life. At that moment she had felt so alone and this man had come along and broke her out of
the prison she had locked herself into. She felt a deep wave of love choke her up and the tears began falling. But these were nothing like the flood of sorrow she had just thought of, these were little droplets of happiness. Jarred saw the tears and he was immediately concerned. "Hey, what's wrong Lelo?" he had to shout for her to hear what he was saying.

"I'm just so happy. I love you Jarred Levine!" she shouted back at him. He looked at her as if he was trying to figure out her strange mood. Then he must have thought what the heck because he just pulled her into his warm embrace and held on to her for dear life. She snuggled up to him and her joy was complete.

She woke up at midday her legs tangled under Jarred's legs. She couldn't remember the rest of what had happened but the night had been perfect up until they had left the opening and had taken shots, the rest was a blur. It was just like when they had been in college, never mind that they were nearing their forties with four children. She had a splitting headache reminding her that she was getting old. She tried dis-entangling her legs and Jarred was instantly awake and pinning her down. He didn't look like he had any effects from the previous night. She scowled at him and he grinned back kissing her lightly on the lips. "Happy New Year Lelo."

"What's happy about it? My throat feels like I've been dehydrated since the world began and my head feels like someone hit me with a sledge hammer." Jarred laughed at her and made some soothing noises. He let her go and she headed to the bathroom. Her hair looked like it had had a wild night of its own and she groaned. She looked like death. A cold shower, some pain killers and a coffee later

she felt a bit alive, she even braved combing her afro and plaited her signature cornrows. Jarred, damn him, had even gone for a jog and he looked not a day over 30. "You had your hair like that on the Safari," he noted. She had even forgotten that she had cornrows then but her man was like a walking encyclopedia. All Mpumi wanted was to get home and kiss her babies. They were all packed and ready to leave when they were stopped in the foyer. "I'm sorry sir but it's not safe for anyone to leave," the over friendly receptionist told Jarred. Mpumi let out a frustrated sigh, what was the matter now. They were told that the roads were barricaded with burning debris by angry mobs and that they were stoning any passing cars. It was all over the news, the violent uprising were caused by false reports that foreigners were responsible for a wave of false kidnappings. The attacks had started at KwaMashu Hostel in section A and had quickly escalated to the looting of foreign owned spazas and the killing of some foreigners. Mpumi's blood went cold as she watched a helpless woman lying on the ground as some big angry Zulu man ground her face to the tar mac road with his boot. Reports said even some police men had been shot and killed when they had tried intervening. How had they gotten here? To a state of lawlessness where violence had become law. They were at a place where mob justice reigned, where people assumed the roles of prosecutor and persecutor. Mpumi felt sad for the families who would get the news today that the father wouldn't be coming home anymore and Mpumi knew that in such instances the perpetrators were never arrested. Not because people didn't know who the ringleaders were but because of fear. Mpumi remembered how it had felt when her mother had sat her down and told her that her
father was gone that the heart attack had claimed him. It had been so sudden, he didn't even know he had a heart condition. That feeling had hurt and she could only imagine that it was even worse if you could see your father being killed with stones like a worthless animal. They had to stay in the hotel till the situation was under control. An Indian guy had posted on Twitter a video of the angry mob stoning his car at some

junction. It wasn't a pretty sight, they had broken his windows and some of the glass had cut him but he hadn't stopped, he had sped off with his life. When would all these senseless killings stop? She called her mother to tell her of what was happening and MaNtuli said they should pray. She promised to pray then she hung up and called Nomusa, the call went unanswered, and she assumed that Nomusa was still sleeping off a hangover. Then she called Oyama, her baby sounded panicked. "Mama we saw on social media the situation in Durban. Are you safe? Are you alright? Is daddy fine?" Mpumi waited for the wave of questions to pass before she assured her that they were fine and they were still at the hotel. She was touched by the concern not only for her but for Jarred as well. She also spoke to Lola and Lola started crying she had to calm her down assuring her that they were fine and safe. But she wasn't sure as well, what if the police failed to control the mob and they started throwing stones at the hotel. Jarred assured her that the hotel was a long way from all the violence but it still didn't comfort her or make any of that right. It was brutal and cold-blooded.

The police had eventually managed to put the situation under control by early evening and Mpumi wanted to be as far away from KZN as possible. As she had suspected no arrests had been made yet the police were still 'investigating'. The whole ordeal had drained her emotionally and Jarred sensed it. On the jet he cradled her like a baby, she was half-lying on his knees while her lower body was on the chair. They didn't talk much the whole journey. When they got to Joburg Mpumi wanted them to go straight to Soweto and get her babies. MaNtuli was surprised to see them at night but grateful that they had come in one piece. Looking at her babies sleeping so peacefully calmed her heart. How was she going to protect them from the world? They had grown so much you could barely tell they had been premature and they had been so tiny that they couldn't hold them. Mpumi suspected that MaNtuli had been feeding her babies mealiemeal porridge, they even felt heavy to carry as she and Jarred picked one twin

each and put them in their car seats. Her mother protested that it wasn't safe to travel at night with children but Mpumi just wanted to be in her own house. Mercifully they arrived at their place without any incident and when Mpumi was putting Onathi into his cot he opened his eyes sleepily and when he saw her he flashed her a huge toothless grin that reminded her so much of Jarred then he promptly returned to sleep. He was going to break his share of hearts as he grew up. He already had her heart twisted in knots. They went to bed and snuggled into the blankets. Then what had happened in the past twenty-four hours suddenly hit her and she started shivering. "Hey it's ok, I'm here I will never let anyone touch you," Jarred tried calming her and that only made her cry. He let her cry until she was empty of all the turmoil that had been building up within her. "I worry every day when I send my children to school, will they come back or will there be
a robbery at their school. What if they get rapped? And I realize I can't protect them all the time," she managed to say after she had exhausted her tears.

"I know I worry about the children and you too. I know we stay in a quiet neighborhood. But what if you get robbed while I'm away on business? Or if you get hijacked? What will I do if anything ever happened to any of you?" Mpumi had expected him to comfort her but his words only made the feeling worse.

"What should we do then?"

"We could relocate Lelo, move back to Washington. Oyama can go to Harvard and Lola finish her high school. And you can start your business there."

"I don't know the thought of moving away isn't appealing. And I doubt Daniel would allow me to take his daughter away from him." With all its turmoil and violence South Africa was still her home and she loved it, she didn't want to leave home.

"Then we should get a fire arm and you should also learn how to use it and enroll you and the girls into self-defense classes." Mpumi hated guns but they were now living in a world where it was becoming essential to own one. One couldn't always rely on the state to protect one. She liked the idea of self-defense classes. She also reluctantly agreed to take shooting classes with Jarred. They cuddled and she wondered how things would be when the twins were now teenagers. And when she and Jarred where no longer there to protect their children. She could only hope and pray for peace.

CHAPTER NINETEEN

Her business idea terrified her by its sheer magnitude. But Jarred assured her that if anyone could make this happen it was her. She had finally decided that she was going to build a child centre. It would host children's clothing shops, a day and night care centre, a dance studio which taught African dances, state-of-the-art learning centre, adoption offices, fertility clinic, a child photography centre and even a pediatrician's office. A child version of a mall with a small Disney-theme recreational centre. She was investing all her savings in this project and Jarred was making up the remainder as her sole investor and silent partner. Once the idea had begun taking shape in her mind her excitement had begun mounting. She was going to engage in local entrepreneurs like the woman from eNgcobo and the lady from Fox Street to be her suppliers. Child Line was already on board with her idea and she was thrilled. She had decided to name it The Child Centre, simple and elegant which was Mpumi personified. The main problem was going to be location, her connections as the Minister's wife were coming in handy. One female Minister in particular was very excited by the idea. Her name was Natalie Mkhwananzi, at first Mpumi had been reluctant to approach her because Natalie had had an affair with Daniel once upon a time. But Nomusa had rightly pointed out that she would be hard-put to find a female Cabinet member that her ex-husband had no canal knowledge of. Natalie was stylish with a robust approach to life that was refreshing and she was helpful, Mpumi managed to get allocated a piece of land in Braamfonteein, just after the Constitutional Hill. It was the best location as it was closer to the CBD but far enough from the hustle and bustle of Jozi. Mpumi had always marveled how two parts of town could be so close to each other yet so different. Wits University and generally Braamfonteein was quiet and peaceful and one could freely walk around texting on their phone. Then once you crossed the Mandela Bridge one came straight into Bree Taxi rank which was always punctuated by activity and noise. Once in Bree one does not dare bring out their phone but some still fell prey to pickpockets. Mpumi was shit scared of Bree. Back when she was in tertiary, she had once seen a man surrounded by muggers in broad daylight and people walking past as if it were an everyday occurrence no help proffered. She was still a lecturer at Wits so every now and again she drove past Bree and it always gave her the chills. It had grown worse from the times when she

would commute to Soweto from UJ. It was even more crowded, Mpumi often wondered why they didn't expand the taxi rank even further. Anyways Natalie had re-assured her that the tender for the space near the Constitutional Hill was as good as hers and Mpumi was keeping her fingers crossed. She was getting dressed for a function the law faculty had set up for the final year female students. It was supposed to equip them for life after tertiary. Mpumi wished they had had such functions during their times. And she also wished they had also included the male students. She was also nervous because she had been invited to be their guest speaker which put her on the spot. "Are you ready yet babe?" Jarred had a way of sneaking up on her which she had become accustomed to. She looked at his reflection on the vanity mirror. He looked smoking in a tailor made suit that fit him snuggly like a glove. He was her date for the night.

"I'm almost done, I just have to finish up on my make-up."

"Take your time we have the whole night." She threw a brush at him and he was already expecting it because he ducked expertly while chuckling. "I'm so nervous about giving this speech." She confided in him.

"Why are you nervous? You're the perfect person to talk to those girls." He kissed her cheek.

"It made me review my life, I don't feel accomplished enough." His eyes when they met hers in the mirror were incredulous.

"How much more accomplished can one person be? You got a scholarship to an Ivy League university, you have three degrees to your name, you are on the boards of many top businesses, you're a lecturer, and you're also becoming an entrepreneur all while raising my children." His praise warmed her, he really did keep tabs on her life. She was finally satisfied with the image in the mirror and she let him lead her out of their bedroom and they went to check on the kids. Oyama and Lola had protested when they had wanted to hire a babysitter and they had offered their services at a price. Mpumi had been reluctant but Jarred had said she should trust that they were old enough to take care of themselves and their siblings. She was still apprehensive. Oyama hadn't been herself lately and they assumed it was anxiety as the release day of Matric results grew closer. They found Lola and Oyama in the lounge with each twin on their lap. Owethu instantly reached out for Mpumi but Mpumi only kissed her and didn't take her from Oyama. The little madam began to fuss but Oyama calmed her. Onathi was taking their departure like a champ all gooey smiles. "Remember to feed them at 6pm on the dot, bath them before putting them to sleep at 8pm and don't let Aleja trick you into keeping them up later. Read from their bedtime stories, their favorite story right now is…"

"Mary had a little lamb, we know Mamita. We've got this. You lovebirds go and have a great time." Lola cut in and Jarred led her out of the room. They were taking the Cadillac since it was just the two of them. "They will be fine Lelo don't worry about them," Jarred said as they went out of the gate.

"And please put your hands together for our guest speaker Mrs. Nompumelelo Ndinisa-Sisulu." Amongst the applause Mpumi stood up and went to stand behind the podium. From her spot she could see every face looking up at her. Jarred smiled at her reassuringly. Some of the girls were looking up at her with hope in their eyes some with their notebooks open ready to jot down anything she would say. Oh the blind faith that the youth place on their elders, Mpumi suddenly felt old. Some were looking bored like they had better places to be. Close to two decades before she had been exactly were those young women were, armed with her education and a healthy dose of her own worth and she had been ready and raving to change the world. "Thank you Kimberly, its actually just plain Ms. Nompumelelo Ndinisa now," she corrected the MC and she saw the woman roll her eyes. "Hello ladies, it's such an honor to be standing in front of our future world leaders. I'm sure most of you are excited to finally be done with their tertiary education, I know I was." General laughter assured her that she hadn't blown her speech yet so she forged on looking at them, one girl at a time. "How many of you are in committed relationships?" her question provoked a ripple of murmured shock and half the room raised their hands confidently, she smiled. "And how many are in committed relationships with yourselves?" this question was met with silence and she looked around the room there were a handful of hands raised furtively. "I know I have taught some of you Corporate Law but today I stand before you not as your lecturer but woman to woman, one counterpart to another as a sister and maybe even a mother. I have two teenage daughters at home and like any mother I worry about them. Now I recently came across *'We should all be*

feminists' written by a woman that I think is one of the greatest writers of our time, Chimamanda Ngozi Adichie. And as I read I was struck by the truth in which she depicts our society. She said we raise our girls to shrink themselves, to aspire for marriage and that we teach our girls shame. Now I'm not sure whether I am the only one who has noticed that educated women have become some kind of conquest among men. A prize one tames and breaks from their pride. Forget what society has told you about marriage, that if you become too educated you intimidate man and grow into an old desperate maid. For one there is no such thing as "Too educated", learn as much as you can, dream as big as you can and always fight to be better than you are today. And secondly you have no business being with a man who is intimidated by you because he will try to dim your light every chance he gets. Do not lose yourself or shrink yourself for anyone or any ideology. I wish someone had told me when I was your age that I didn't need to marry the first guy who asked me to marry him or that being pregnant out of wedlock was not a shame I should hide behind marriage. Then maybe I wouldn't be here divorced with a sullen teen who has to be shuffled between two homes. I am not saying marriage is bad, contrary marriage to the right person can be a fulfilling and wholesome partnership. What I am saying to you is take your time and don't bow down to any social expectations." She paused to catch her breath, the room was silent and some of the girls looked like they were hanging on to her every word and some of the older women were looking at her with disapproval stamped on their faces. She soldiered on. "Unfortunately your generation does not have what our generation had, job security. The sad reality is not all of you will find jobs or internships after you finish your degree. Education is just a key but you get to choose and even hustle for the doors you want it to open for you. I know that your families and sponsors expect a lot from you. Trust me black tax is real and it's worse than SARS." There was laughter at that comment and she had to wait for it to subdue before continuing. "But don't let expectation pressure you into doing something you will regret later on. Be patient, Rome wasn't built in a day. Sleeping your way up is not only unethical but it is also degrading and it sets all women in general back. Speak up against any form of sexual harassment to someone you can trust to be discreet and fair. Discrimination against gender is still a reality in the workplace that unfortunately you have to fight against. I see the majority of you are black and you are likely to face twice the challenge of being black and a woman. Don't look so scared a lot of us have been fighting the system for years. You might not read of us in the media but we have had to stand up for our worth at every point and I believe your generation can fight even harder because now more laws are on your side." Wrapping up her speech Mpumi asked each student to look at the student sitting next to her. They looked confused by this request but they complied. "I want you to remember that face so that in future when your paths cross after tertiary you will be kind to her. In fact be kind to every woman you meet, you do not know what she has had to overcome at times in silence. The greatest obstacle to female empowerment I'm afraid is women. We hate on each other, we tear each other down and we do no support each other in the face of adversaries. That's why I urge you to be kind to each other because two voices carry more volume than one. Our greatest strength is empathy. At times you have to speak up for the next woman who may be subject to sexual harassment in the workplace or abuse of any kind because she may be too ashamed to speak out. Let your first instinct be to build another woman up rather than to shame and tear her down. The thing is being a woman is a circle, you come into this world as a daughter and at times a sister, and you become someone's girlfriend and at times a wife and a mother, then a motherin-law and if you are blessed a grandmother. Always remember where you come from and who you are. Being African is not only about your natural hair diary or about carrying out African traditions and looking natural. Being African is about showing Ubuntu to everyone who comes across your path. You are the daughters of Queens and warriors, never forget that." There was thunderous applause which Mpumi didn't know how to interpret. They were probably happy that the speeches were over and now they could get down to partying. She had also been a student once upon a time. Jarred squeezed her hand when she got back to their table. His silent way of saying you did good babe. And she squeezed back her silent way of saying thank you for coming along to support me.

Mpumi could not remember a time when she had been so busy in her life. She had back to back meetings with suppliers. Some brands had caught wind of her idea and wanted in on the cake but she had to stand her ground. She didn't want some big corporate swooping in and taking over. This was her baby and she wanted to nurture it herself and watch it grow. She had to talk to architects and to access catalogues for materials. She had to get her plan approved. Natalie had come through for her and she had gotten the land for her site. It was all moving so fast she barely had time to catch her breath. She talked to Nomusa less than she usually did and that bothered her. As she had feared Nomusa had been let go at work and she was having a hard time finding another job. She had had to let go of her apartment and she was now living with Amogalang. Mpumi wished Nomusa could come to Joburg but she had accepted that Amo was taking her place gradually. Being so busy with her project also meant she spent a lot of time away from her children. But she was grateful that Jarred wasn't building any new hotels and he worked mostly from home so he took care of the twins. Oyama was also at home waiting for the results to come out and she was also surprisingly good with the kids and she also tutored Lola. MaNtuli was whining that she had been neglecting her so Mpumi had made time and she was on her way to Soweto. She passed by the food stall and on a whim she stopped again to buy ikota. She found the same chirpy fellow and he smiled broadly when he saw her. "Ehh mamzo how are you?" he was so respectful even using his street twang.

"I'm good Sphola how are you?"

"I'm trying mamzo. I see today you didn't bring your beautiful daughters." Mpumi laughed his obvious crush on Oyama was adorable, not only was that one out of his league but her daughter would totally ice him over with just one sentence.

"I left them at home Sphola. How is business?"

"Business is starting to pick up mamzo, you know January disease nearly ran me out of business."

"So you own this food stall Sphola?"

"At first I used to work for the guy who owned it but I saved up my salary and I bought him out mamzo." Mpumi was impressed, she wasn't sure exactly how much he had made a month but she guessed it would have been around R1 200 and he would have had expenses such as rent and other necessities. How he managed to save up enough money to buy out the other guy was a miracle. He carried on chatting pleasantly with her as he made her food. Mpumi noted that he was very clean, even his food stand was spotless and he worked with precision. And she made an instant decision. "Sphola how would you like to come and work with me?" He looked surprised by her offer, "Work where mamzo?"

"I am building a centre at Braamfonteein and you can set up a food stall there, but you will have to widen your menu and make it healthier and more child friendly. Can you do that Sphola?" he seemed excited by the idea his whole face lit up and Mpumi had to admit he was a handsome kid. Then he seemed to think about something and his face fell. "Thanks for the offer mamzo but I couldn't afford the rates at your centre."

"Tell you what for the first year you will pay me the rent that you are currently paying here and by then your business should have a turnover then you will start paying me the standard rates." Instinctively Mpumi had known he would have refused any handouts and this was a way in which he could retain his pride. That cute smile was back on his face and he offered his hand for a handshake. Mpumi laughed this boy would grow into a real gentleman. They shook on it and she asked for his details and she gave him hers. "The centre isn't built yet Sphola so take that time to learn new recipes like hot dogs, burgers and you can even learn how to make ice-cream, children love that."

"No stress mamzo, Sphola here is a hustler. I won't disappoint you, I promise." She was happy with that assurance and she took her food. Sphola had revamped the place a bit and had placed two benches outside and had added a fresh batch of paint on the stall. Mpumi sat on one of the benches and indulged in her guilty pleasure. She said her goodbyes and proceeded to her mother's house. She found MaNtuli sitting on the verandah waiting for her. She hugged her and kissed her on the cheeks. Something about her mother made her awkward around her. "You're looking well maa."

"All thanks to God my child because my own child won't come to check on my health." Mpumi fought the urge to roll her eyes, her mother had to be the healthiest human being on earth she had never been admitted to a hospital Mpumi's entire life.

"I'm sorry mama I have been busy lately trying to get this centre off the ground."

"I hope you have time for that man of yours. It's not right that you leave him to take care of the children. And when is he marrying you? You can't live in sin forever and your uncles have been asking when he is going to pay lobolo for you." Coming home always gave Mpumi a migraine.

"He understands and supports my dreams maa. And we aren't getting married anytime soon. And you can tell those greedy men that hell will freeze over before I allow Jarred to give them even a penny."

"I can never understand you young people. Have you found a cleaning company for your centre yet?" Mpumi laughed silently, underneath all that matriarchy, her mother was as sly as a fox.

"No mother, no cleaning company has applied for the post yet." She wasn't going to make things easy for her.

"I see. Come inside and make us some tea." Mpumi stood up dutifully and followed her mother to hear what others had done wrong at church. She was also accosted about the twins' baptism how the Reverend had graciously offered to baptize them himself. The Reverend no less. Her mother always gave her headaches but she was happy she had come to see her. She figured that MaNtuli must get lonely all alone in this big house but she knew she would never come to live with them. She had brought her pictures of the twins for her mother and some pictures of the Quinceanera and the Intonjane and she put them on the wall along her graduation picture and her wedding picture. Why her mother kept her wedding picture on the wall was a mystery to Mpumi but she knew better than to take it down.

Later that week Mpumi had a chance to catch her breath from all the hustle of trying to be an entrepreneur in your late thirties. Oyama and Lola had gone out to God knows where. They had cooked up some story which Mpumi had pretended to buy. Teenagers often forgot that adults where once teenagers themselves and they knew all the tricks in the book. Although the wording might change here and there it was still the same book. Mpumi had known something was up because Lola had been the designated asker and she wasn't much of a liar. "Mamita, some of my friends are having a barbeque and they invited me. Can I go? Oyama can come with me to watch over me."

"Mmmmmmh which friends are hosting the barbeque?"

"Emily and Emma remember the twins in my class."

"Of course I do let me just call their mother and confirm with her."

"NO!!!" both girls had said in unison and Mpumi had raised her perfectly arched eyebrow. Oyama had been quick to recover. "That would make Lola seem like a baby to her friends, they are in matric mama and she is trying to fit in." Now her other daughter lied like a man but Mpumi had raised her literally from the cradle and she knew when she was being bullshitted.

"I see. Fine then I won't call their mother but I will

go and drop you off at their place." Both girls had looked at each other with panic but again Oyama bounced back.

"That won't be necessary maa, we will take an Uber and we promise to be safe and back before six p.m." Mpumi's maternal instincts had kicked in in high gear but then she had remembered the conversation she had had with Jarred that they shouldn't smother the kids but let them make a few mistakes along the way and trust that they had raised them well enough to have some sense of wrong and right. She had looked at them slowly and shrugged her shoulders in a non-bothered manner.

"Fine I won't cramp your style but be back by 5.30 or else I will come and pick you up myself." She had seen the relief in their faces and they had left soon after as if they had been afraid that she would change her mind. It was afternoon now and the lady who usually did their laundry had called in sick, instead of calling the agency and getting her in trouble Mpumi had decided to do the cleaning and laundry herself. Jarred had gone out to meet someone and the tasks were difficult with the twins. They had started crawling now and they were a handful. She had to run after them. Owethu threw Jarred's toothbrush into the toilet and Onathi almost pushed his sister into the toilet and they both ended up wet with toilet water. Mpumi had to bath them for the second time that day and she had finally managed to get them to take an afternoon nap. She went around the bedrooms collecting laundry and even emptying the bathrooms. She was about to pick up one of the girls' jersey from the floor when something white caught her eye. She was fuming, she would have to have a talk with the girls about just throwing their stuff on the floor when she had been distracted by the object. She had picked it up and had felt all the blood drain from her face. Her knees had actually gone weak at the joints and she had slid to the floor right there on the bathroom floor. The
tiles were cold on her thighs, she was wearing a bum-short but she felt numb. It was a pregnancy test. One of those advanced ones which showed how many months along you were. It had the plus sign and

it estimated the pregnancy to be about six weeks. Mpumi couldn't comprehend what her own eyes were showing her. One of the girls was pregnant. Amend that, one of her fifteen year-old daughters was pregnant. But which one of her daughters was pregnant? So it meant they were having sex and none of them had even confided in her. Her first bet was Oyama but Lola could also be a handful, she was more street smart and she was older than Oyama even if it were by mere months. Mpumi contemplated calling them. But no this wasn't a topic one raised over the phone. And she didn't want to alert them so that they could make up some cover story. Then she went into denial. It couldn't be one of her babies, it was probably the cleaning lady. Maybe that was why she had called in sick. Mpumi needed to have a talk with her and tell her not to leave such things lying around the floor, the twins could pick it up and put it into their mouths. Then reasoning slowly returned to her. Why would the maid take the pregnancy test in her house? As much as she hated to even think about it one of her girls was pregnant at 15. Then she remembered that she had no idea where they were and she felt a cold hand go up and down her spine. What if they had gone to have an abortion? No!!! Just the thought was enough to get her off the bathroom floor and she rushed to her bedroom. Where was her bloody phone? She found it underneath her pillow and she dialed their numbers. When both their phones went straight into voicemail she felt the hysteria rising. She dialed Jarred's number but then thought against it before it rang and she ended the call. She couldn't call Nomusa, her friend already had a lot on her plate and she couldn't add to that. Her mother would only lecture her and tell her to pray. She paced the length of their bedroom and tried their numbers again. Still straight to voicemail. Mpumi had never felt so powerless in her life. She was a bad mother, one of her daughters was probably lying in some illegal doctor's bed right now having an abortion. Alone. What if she died? She felt dread even thinking about either Lola or Oyama dead, it would kill her. They hadn't trusted her enough to come to her. Then she felt anger. How could those brats do this to them? One of the twins

CHAPTER
NINETEEN

was up, the baby monitor informed her. And from the sound of it, it was Owethu. She quickly went to the nursery before the diva's crying woke her brother and she would have to deal with two cranky babies on top of the sudden realization that one of her babies was having a baby or an abortion.

CHAPTER TWENTY

The year had begun badly for her, Nomusa thought glumly. As she had feared she had been amongst the first to be retrenched. It was harder to find a job when you were jobless than it had been for her to find a job when she was still employed. Her useless family hadn't been much help. They just told her to keep looking something would come up. She had gone back home first but her welcome had quickly dwindled with her last paycheck. She did not dare raise her savings or the rent the tenants at her Joburg house paid her. She lied and said she had sold the house. Then her brother had gotten arrested. No one ever knew what her brother Loyiso did for a living. Nomusa had figured that whatever he was doing was illegal but she hadn't wanted to ask any questions. They had been woken up by his brat of a wife early one morning. Nomusa couldn't remember if they had ever been any lobolo paid for Zukiswa, but everyone at her home regarded her as Loyiso's wife because they had been together for a decade and they had two boys who were such a nuisance Nomusa limited seeing them to twice a year.

Zukiswa had been hysterical she said that Loyiso had been burst on his last 'job' which they learned that day was bombing ATMs and robbing wholesale shops. Apparently someone had informed on them and their heist had been burst by the police. Zukiswa needed money to pay someone on the inside to make the whole matter 'disappear'. Nomusa had been irritated for being woken up in the middle of her dreams. She wondered why they had never made a provision for such a time since they knew that arrest was imminent in Loyiso's line of work. As usual everyone was looking at her for a solution. Never mind that she was unemployed now. But she couldn't let her brother rot in jail especially since Zukiswa told them they were expecting another brat. Nomusa had had to dip into her savings and bail her brother out. There ended up no case against Loyiso's gang because their docket had gone missing. Loyiso had promised to pay her back after his next job. Don't judge, no one chooses their family. But Nomusa had had enough. If it wasn't one of Noswazi's children needing something at school, it was her mother wanting to pay back someone who had loaned her R250 and the amount was always set at that amount or it was her father wanting some money to go and spend at the local sheeben. She loved her family but she was also trying to get by till she got her next job. And they were draining her dry. She wished she was back in Joburg close to Mpumi. They hadn't been talking much lately, Mpumi had tried reaching out to her but Nomusa was in a bad place. It stung at times how well her bestie's life was going while hers seemed to be going down the drain at a fast rate. So at times she had ignored Mpumi's calls when she couldn't pretend that she was feeling better than she really was. She didn't want to burden anyone with her problems most of all Mpumi because she knew her friend would drop everything to come and help her sort out her life. When she told Amo of her dilemma he offered her a solution. He suggested that they move in together. Nomusa had been reluctant she was used to her own space. But she was desperate she couldn't stand the demands at home anymore. So she had agreed and she had moved in with Amo. The first day had been so romantic.

CHAPTER
TWENTY

He had carried her into his house and there had been rose petals from the door step to the main bedroom. He had written on the bed with rose petals 'WELCOME HOME' and he had placed a balloon in the shape of a heart next to the petals. Nomusa had been touched, her man was so romantic. She had never dated a guy who was so thoughtful or who knew which shop sold rose petals. Amogalang had worked hard and was doing well for himself and it showed. His house was huge for a single person, it was a double-story with a swimming pool. The furniture was obviously expensive but it lacked a feminine touch. The sofas in the lounge where black so were the tiles then the curtains were white. The lounge no in fact the whole house looked like the pages of a furniture shop catalogue. The house was too clean for a man living alone and when Nomusa had suspiciously raised the point he had laughed at her and assured her that he had a cleaning lady who came in every day. Nomusa was secretly pleased, she didn't want to be cleaning the whole huge house. She didn't get to tour much of the house on the first day because Amo couldn't get enough of her. She was wearing the Victoria's Secret little number that Mpumi had bought for her and he was like a man possessed. His normally lazy eyes went all out and his hands shook slightly as he tentatively touched the pants which were held up by a suspender belt. His touch was warm and it sent a shock of electricity down her spine. Whoever said Tswana men were not well endowed had probably never been fucked by her Amo. He wasn't the biggest she had ever had but when he thrust into her he filled her up completely and she found herself shaking with need. The rose petals had spelt out romance and prolonged pleasure but Nomusa wanted him hard and fast from the back. She knelt on the centre of the bed, her face and the top half of her chest touching the bed while the rest of her back arched alluringly towards Amo. She knew from the way he was gulping that her punani was in full display in all its shaven glory. She felt like she was going crazy with his hand holding the nape of her neck while he rammed into her without restraint. She had to dig in her nails into the cover bed to avoid being toppled over. They fell on top of the rose petals exhausted and sweaty after their rigorous session, none of them had even the strength to get up and shower. When they had finally caught their breath and gone to shower they ended up shagging in the shower. Amogalang had never been so uninhibited in their lovemaking before, Nomusa was surprised by how amorous he had become. She thought to herself that moving in together had been the best thing she could have done as she screamed while he ravaged her punani and the shower water flowed over their joined bodies.

If Nomusa had kept a diary or been the writing type, she would have captioned the next entry 'Things began falling apart…". But Nomusa wasn't much or a reader or a writer and she didn't notice exactly when things started souring in her relationship. At first it was the little things. He wanted his clothes hand washed by her including his underwear, there was a freaking 30kg twin tub washing machine! And what grown arse man in his 40s couldn't wash his own underwear. But no, Nomusa was now his PHD (Permanent Home Defender) and she was expected to carry out her womanly chores. If maybe he only left the toilet seat up like most dudes then maybe she could have handled it. Amo was one of those confined bachelors who left everything in perfect order and he didn't want anything out of place. Then the cleaning lady magically disappeared and he said he wouldn't look for another one since she was at home all the time. Then there was the stalking. It had been cute when she was in Jozi and he had been in Cape Town but living under surveillance twenty four hours a day was not only exhausting but also frustrating. He wanted to know what she was doing every blasted minute of the day. If she wanted to go somewhere she had to tell him so that he would drop whatever he was doing and accompany her. She wasn't a teenager and she was capable of driving herself. One morning Amo had woken her up with a kiss and she had thought he was in a good mood. "Morning baby waka," she had smiled up at him. Then he had looked down at her as if he was thinking deeply about something. "I was thinking hun, isn't you said Mpumi lent you the Jeep?"

"Yes she did." Nomusa said slowly not sure where this conversation was headed.

"I think it's time you gave it back to her. I mean there are a lot of cars parked in the garage at your disposal."

"No its ok baby, she wants me to keep it so that whenever they come to Cape Town they get to use it." His face had suddenly changed and it shook her a bit.

"I don't want my woman driving other people's cars. It's insulting like I can't take care of my own woman."

"It's not like I even drive it anymore, you won't even let me go to the bloody mall alone. I can't even visit my own family on my own."

"I don't like your tone Nomusa." The words were softly spoken but they scared her.

"You are suffocating me Amo can't you see that?"

"I didn't know that loving my person constitutes suffocation or you're used to being treated like trash." The last bit had stung a lot and Nomusa had gotten off the bed and locked herself in the bathroom till he had left for work. Amo had a way of saying things that left her feeling small. The Jeep had stayed and as an appeasement he had bought her a metallic grey Audi Q7 with a Virtual Cockpit and air suspension. She was allowed to drive herself around in it, he promised to ease up on the stalking. And he had apologized for his hurtful comments. But their troubles didn't end there. The next issue was her phone. He went through it with a fine-tooth comb and he even went as far as to block most of her male acquaintances. Nomusa had no idea at first until she bumped into one old friend at the mall when she was coming from doing her hair. She and Simphiwe had learnt together in high school and they had kept in touch and every once in a while they kept tabs on each other. They had never had a romantic relationship but they did meet for drinks once or twice and he was fun to be around. She had been happy to see him and he had good-naturedly hugged her. "I shouldn't even be hugging you that's how mad I am with you." He never greeted like a normal person.

"What did I do now?" she had frowned up at him, he was so tall she had to tilt her head when she was talking to him.

"Hello! You sent me a message on Facebook like 'Don't ever talk to me again'. And you went further and blocked me on all social media. Honey that wasn't cool I thought we were tight." Nomusa was shocked and Simphiwe immediately read her expression. "Shit Nomusa don't tell me it's a new man."

"It is, he's the insecure type. I'm so sorry love I had no idea he would go this far."

"No I understand if I had a pretty woman like you, I would do the same. I'm kind of disappointed though because I always assumed that one day you would be my wife." Oh the Zulu charm, she laughed and told him that she had had enough trauma from one Zulu man to last her a lifetime. "Not all of us chase pebbles once we have a pearl in our arms. I know I could treat you better but somehow you were always out of my reach." He seemed serious now, Nomusa had had no idea that Simphiwe had a crush on her but it seemed like he had deep feelings for her. But it was too late, for all his faults she loved Amo deeply. She couldn't say anything that might encourage Simphiwe so she hugged him and kissed him lightly on the lips. Then she left to go and deal with her moron. The nerve of that Tswana infuriated her. When she angrily confronted him, he had been cool about it. "I don't want my woman talking to other men. Do you ever see me chatting to other women? I thought we were in a committed relationship here and we are exclusive so I don't understand why you should be talking to other men."

"They are my friends Amogalang and you had no right to cut them from my life. It was my call to make not yours!"

"If you want to be in this relationship and in this house, then be here with me and no one else. If you feel so strongly about this then you can pack your bags and go and stay with your male friends." He had said in that voice which told you case closed. She had silently fumed and had gone to prepare his meal while he watched the Discovery channel. He had a point, she had nowhere to go so she stuck it out.

She went home to pour out her problems to her mother. She narrated how his comments were often belittling and that she felt caged in the relationship. Her mother hadn't been very sympathetic especially about her washing his underwear and cooking his meals. "That's your job as his woman, you have to take care of him otherwise there are other women who are ready and more than willing to do that for him. You look pampered and you are driving the kind of car that we only see in the televisions. Stop your whining and take care of your man. You are not growing any younger Nomusa, we expected you to be married and settled down with children of your own right now." Nomusa was stung to the core. She was tired of always being labelled as some kind of failure because she did not have a ring on her finger or illegitimate children running around her parents' homes. "Maybe if you hadn't prostituted me out to any man who was willing to spend money on me mother I would be married right now. You didn't care who or what I slept with as long as I came with groceries and money for my school fees." Just talking about it brought back memories that made bile rise in her throat. She had been fourteen and walking alone because Mpumi as usual was in the library, when a man had pulled up for her in a car and had told her to ride and he would buy her something nice. She had refused and she had run home in tears. When her mother had asked her what was wrong when she finally managed to calm her down, Nomusa had narrated what had happened. She had expected her mother to soothe and calm her and tell her that she had been right to run away, that men in cars took advantage of young pretty girls like herself. What she had not expected was the slap her mother had given her and if it were not for the sting on her cheek, the light blood trickling from her nose and the ringing in her ear she would not have believed that her mother had just slapped her. "You stupid girl, would you have died if you got in that car and gone with the nice man? All he wanted was to buy you nice things."

"But maa Mpumi's mother said we shouldn't get into strangers' cars because they will hurt us." Nomusa had tried defending herself.

"What does that one know? Her daughter will never attract any man because she thinks she is too good just like her mother. Her own husband is sleeping with her cousin right under her nose and she still thinks she can raise her nose at us. Now listen to me I am your mother and next time a nice man stops his car for you get in. But don't ever go with a man without a car." She had been young and naïve, she trusted that her own mother would never tell her to do something that would bring harm to her. So the next time a car had stopped for her she had got in. The man had touched her in ways she hadn't understood. Her mother assured her that it was ok, that it had only hurt that first time and that it wouldn't hurt from now on. She had to bear it for her siblings. She had been fourteen. When the other children started talking about her getting into strangers' cars she had been labeled a whore. She hadn't understood then what it meant but her mother had assured her that it was alright. The only person who had never treated her

differently had been Mpumi, Mpumi always had her head stuck behind a book and she never listened to the other children's tales. Nomusa instinctively had known that she couldn't tell her best friend of her other life, that somehow it would mar their friendship. She looked at her mother now and the older woman looked bored. "Not that again Nomusa. You did what you had to do and don't act like you did not enjoy the nice things as well as the rest of us."

"Do you know how dirty I felt every time an old man grabbed my private parts with their dirty hands? I didn't want to get in any car but you told me it was fine, you made me wear makeup mama. And you let them sleep with me. I was only a child. What if I had gotten sick or pregnant?" The tears were flowing silently down her face yet her mother remained unfazed. In fact she seemed angry.

"Look around you Nomusa. This isn't the flashy apartments you have become used to. You didn't have the brains like your friend Mpumi to get you out of this dump. All you had were your pretty looks and the hood rat men would have gotten to you eventually. At least the rich men gave you money in return and you were able to go and do your little IT course. Now don't cry to me like you are some victim when you should be thanking me. Because of me you managed to get out of here. Do you think Amogalang would have noticed you if you were still in this dump with bastard children on your hip? Now stop being selfish and be grateful for the life you have now. I have no problems from your sister, I never had any with her. And she knows how to treat her man and now and again they remember us. But all you do is whine, I'm sick of it." Nomusa was done talking with this woman who claimed to be her mother. If she didn't look exactly like her she would have thought she was her step mother. She picked up her bag and keys for the Audi and she let herself out. She bumped into her father at the door. He was raving drunk. It was just after 1pm. He reeked of brandy and he smiled broadly when he saw her. "My beautiful daughter, is that car by the gate yours?" Nomusa wiped the tears from her eyes and braved a hug from her father. "My daughter, give something for your old man to quench his thirst." He couldn't even see that she was upset or if he did he preferred not getting involved. That had been the story of her life. She opened her purse and emptied all the money she had into his palm. He was happy and he asked her to drop him off at the local spot so that, "Those dogs will know that I am the man, my daughter drives a car that even the President doesn't drive. Tell that man to stop spoiling you and come and pay lobolo otherwise I will come down there and he will know me." Nomusa had no choice but to drive him there even though it was barely ten miles from their house.

She had nowhere to turn to Nomusa accepted that and she decide to make the best of her situation. It wasn't that she wanted for anything, Amo saw to it that she got everything that her heart desired. He took her out to posh places and he treated her like a Queen. The only thing is that whenever they were having a conversation he always seemed to be talking at her rather than to her. Nomusa couldn't explain it but she felt trapped in a beautiful gilded golden cage. Amo was everything she had ever thought she

wanted in a man but he made her see herself as a shallow person. When she raised the point that she really needed a job he brushed her off. "I don't even know why you would want to work I have more than enough to take care of you." She had argued that it wasn't the same that she needed to make money of her own. Then he had come up with a really stupid idea. "Fine I hear you then I will pay you a monthly allowance, twice the amount of your last salary." He had probably said it from a good place but she felt insulted like she was some expensive hooker. But she hadn't responded. She was becoming more and more withdrawn, she didn't talk as much as she had used to. She said things she thought he wanted to hear. She shrunk her voice to a pitch she thought he would approve. She did his laundry by hand and she cooked his meals. He seemed happy that she was finally turning into wifey material and he would reward her with jewelry and all the latest gadgets. But Nomusa had lost herself, she couldn't recognize herself. She barely took any pictures, she drank more and slept it off. She was careful not to show him how drunk she was. She finally thought there must really be something wrong with her. Here was a man who loved her, who made sure she wanted for nothing, who was interested in only her and treated her like an egg but she was still unhappy. Maybe her mother was right. She was ungrateful and she was used to sabotaging her own relationships. He didn't beat her. He didn't cheat on her and she should count her blessings. So she buried all the misgivings she had deep inside and laughed when he made fun of her and jokes that belittled her. He didn't mean it, it was just his way. A month passed and he was satisfied enough by her behavior to announce to her that he was ready to show her to his family. She was told to dress appropriately and not to embarrass him in front of his keen. She was told what to cook, what the family liked and she was told that she shouldn't laugh her loud ghetto laugh which made her sound like a sheeben queen. She took all of this staunchly, she could handle it. After all she had grown up in the mean streets of Khayelitsha and she had survived. It was a Saturday and the in-laws were supposed to come in the afternoon. Nomusa woke up and she cleaned the house top to bottom till it was spotless and she started preparing lunch. Amo started inspecting the house putting some things straight and telling her to wipe the surfaces again. Nomusa felt her teeth on edge but she didn't say a word and she quietly wiped the surfaces again. He kissed her forehead and said, "Don't worry I think you will do well." She finished cooking and went to bath. As she was dressing, in a high waist flaring long skirt with a matching doek, she heard a car pulling in the drive way. She quickly went on to apply makeup and when she was pleased with her reflection in the mirror, she slipped on her low heels. Amo came in just as she was finishing buckling up her shoes. "Let me look at you hun." She stood up for his inspection, he seemed impressed by her outfit. But as usual he wasn't totally satisfied, "Don't you think that makeup is a bit much? I mean you are meeting my family I don't want them to think that I picked up some high-class hooker." Nomusa felt the air catch in her throat but she counted to ten before she responded, "Of course baby, let me tone it down."

"Don't take too long, I'm going downstairs to keep them company." Nomusa wiped off the lipstick from her mouth then something stopped her and she looked at herself in the mirror. She felt something snap within her and she could see it in her eyes. She chose a deep ruby shade from her Kylie collection and she applied it on her full lips. She added

more bronze. It was heavier make-up than she was used to but she was past caring. High-class hooker would show him. She went downstairs smiling broadly. Amo's father gave her an appreciative look while his mother was looking at her with the same disapproval that Amo was giving her. Oh so that was where Amogalang had inherited his condescending attitude. She gave the mother a huge hug and kissed her on both cheeks even though the other lady looked like she wanted the floor to open up and suck her in. Nomusa laughed her loud laugh at the jokes that Amo's father was making and she could feel Amogalang's eyes drilling holes on her back. Finally when he couldn't stand it anymore, he called her aside. "What the hell do you think you are doing? Why did you change your clothes? What is that thing you are wearing that looks more like a t-shirt than a dress? And what is that makeup on your face?" he hissed at her.

"I am just being myself Amo, this is the woman you approached and this is the woman you said you loved."

"It's too late to change how you look but you will stop embarrassing me. Do you hear me?" Nomusa nodded meekly. They went back to the lounge and she called everyone to the dining room. The mother at least seemed impressed with the food and they all dug in. Nomusa asked them if they would like wine. Only Amo's father offered his glass. She filled his glass and filled her own ignoring Amo's sharp gaze. She drank more wine than she ate actual food and Amo's mother looked like she was watching a horror movie. Amo's parents left soon after that, his father looked like he hadn't wanted to leave but the mother made it clear that she wanted nothing more to do with Nomusa. Amogalang angrily turned on her the moment the car left. Nomusa ignored him and she went upstairs and she locked herself in the main bedroom and she slept. When she woke up it was dark. She went to the bathroom and showered. She changed into jeans and a sweater. She pulled her weave back into a ponytail and she began packing. When she was done, she went out, lugging her suitcase behind her. She found Amo waiting for her in the lounge. He was surprised to see her changed and the suitcase. "What's the meaning of this Nomusa?"

"I thought it was clear, I'm leaving Amo."

"But I love you Nomusa, is it about lunch? I'm sorry if I went too far. I just wanted my parents to love you. Give me another chance I can change baby." His pleading went straight to her heart.

"I can't do this anymore. I love you too but somewhere along the way I lost myself and I can't find myself and be with you. I'm sorry Amo, maybe I'm not the woman for you." She didn't allow the tears to fall but he was crying.

"I wanted to make you my wife Nomusa. No one else will want to marry you or respect and love you like I do."

"Maybe you're right. But I've lived almost forty years without marriage. I'm sure I will survive if no one else wants to marry me. Good bye Amogalang. I hope you find the woman you are looking for." He looked at her incredulously as she turned around and picked the keys to the Jeep.

"If you go out of that door there is no coming back." The finality in his voice halted her as her hands were on the door knob. Without looking back, she let herself out of the door and closed it gently behind her. She got into the Jeep after putting her suitcase in the boot. He had stood outside and watched her. She started the engine and drove away. It was only when she was a few miles from his house that she stopped the car and she let the tears flow.

CHAPTER
TWENTY ONE

Mpumi was surprised when the security guard at the gate called to say that there was a woman called Nomusa at the gate. The guard was new and he hadn't met Nomusa before. She told him to let her in and sure enough she saw Jarred's Jeep coming down the driveway. Something must be wrong, Nomusa hadn't called to say she was coming. But a part of her was also relieved. Nomusa would make sense of the mess she was in. Mpumi wished she could go back and maybe react differently. But the harm had been done. When she had failed to get hold of the girls she had called Jarred and he had come. He told her to calm down. If only she had listened. Lola and Oyama had come in at 5.30 on the dot and had found them seating on the lounge. Something had happened Mpumi could just tell because they failed to meet her eyes. "How was the barbeque?" she had asked softly, giving them a chance to come clean. But they had bold facedly lied to her face and they had quickly escaped to one of their bedrooms. Mpumi was scared and angry and Jarred had put a restraining hand on her arm and she had shrugged him off and gone after them. She found them in Lola's bedroom and they looked surprised because she hadn't knocked. She had folded her arms and looked at them, one at a time and she was relieved that none of them seemed in pain. "Now this is your last chance to come clean. Where have you been?"

"We already told you…"

"We were at a barbeque…" both Lola and Oyama had piped up at the same time. Mpumi had unfolded her arms and brandished the pregnancy test at them. Just the look on their faces were enough confirmation and they nailed the first nail on her coffin. "How… Where did you find that?" Oyama had been the first to recover but she was stuttering and stammering. Mpumi had felt weak at the knees but she couldn't show them how shaken she was. "Whose is it?" the calm and control in her voice was worthy of a SAFTAs award or whatever award was given to a good actress. Both girls had hung their heads, so they weren't even going to try to deny it. Oyama had slowly raised her eyes and Mpumi would never forget the look in her eyes. "It's mine." That had been too much for Mpumi and she had sat at the edge of the bed while Jarred had stood by the doorway. The bedroom had been a little crammed with all four of them in it. "No Oyama you don't have to cover for me. It's my pregnancy test." Mpumi had looked from Lola to Oyama in confusion. Both of them had the same fierce look on their faces. Her trip down memory lane was broken by Nomusa getting out of the Jeep. Mpumi had never seen her friend look so defeated. Nomusa looked like hell like she hadn't slept a wink in weeks. Mpumi rushed to her and hugged her, even though her hug wasn't returned. Nomusa looked weak. Mpumi shouted for Jarred and together they led her to the bedroom. Nomusa acted as if in a trance of some sort and Mpumi had to make her sit on the bed. "What happened Nono?" it took a while for her question to register because Nomusa looked at her blankly at first then she just broke down and started sobbing wretchedly. Jarred quickly left the room to go and get Nomusa's bags which he didn't return with. He was just running away. Mpumi held Nomusa as her body was shaking with sobs and she felt her own tears, which were never far, well up and trickle down her face. They stayed like that for a long time, one crying uncontrollably while the other tried to comfort the other while also crying silently. Finally when the tears were exhausted, Mpumi led Nomusa to the bathroom and helped her take off her clothes and sat her in the tub and bathed her like a child. When she was done, Nomusa stood up and Mpumi toweled her dry. She asked her to brush her teeth, helped her into a robe and led her to the bed helping her into the covers. She fluffed the pillows and went into their master bedroom. In the medicine cabinet she found some sleeping pills and she went back and held the glass as Nomusa drank the pills. She brushed her hair from her face and sat and watched her only friend till Nomusa fell into a drugged sleep. Mpumi wondered what had happened, she had never seen her friend fall apart like this before. Nomusa was the strong one, the funny one who never tolerated bullshit from anyone. Mpumi could count on one hand the number of times she had ever seen Nomusa cry. She left Nomusa's room and closed the door softly behind her.

"Amo called, he wanted to know if you were here and if you're ok," Mpumi told Nomusa. Just after 8pm Mpumi had put the twins to sleep and she had went to check on their guest. She found her just waking up. At least now color was back in her cheeks and Nomusa no longer looked like the walking dead. Mpumi had brought her the steak and fillet dinner that was Jarred's specialty. She also brought an unopened bottle of red wine, two flutes and a box of chocolates. Nomusa had sat up in the bed and devoured her meal like she hadn't eaten in ages. Mpumi let her eat and only in their third glass of wine did Nomusa finally open up and tell her about the fights they had had boiling down to the horrible family lunch, how she had left Amogalang in the middle of the night and that she had drove all the way from Cape Town to Johannesburg only stopping along the way to fill her tank. Mpumi felt that her friend hadn't told her everything but she didn't push for more information. What Nomusa told her was bad enough. Nomusa barely acknowledged what Mpumi had just said, she poured herself some more wine. The chocolate box was half empty. "I don't have anywhere to stay right now the tenant contract is good till December. Can I stay here till I find an apartment?" Nomusa asked.

"Nonsense, you don't have to find an apartment you can stay with us till December." Mpumi was quick to reassure her and Nomusa seemed relieved.

"What if he was the one Pum-pum and I just blew it? I mean he ticked all the right boxes. I don't want to die alone." Mpumi brushed the tear from her cheek, Nomusa wasn't one to cry.

"I think you're better alone than with him and hating him. I think you are the bravest person I know. You saw in a year what it took me sixteen years to see and you did in a couple of months what I'm not sure I would have had the courage to do if Jarred hadn't come back into my life. And if it means you have to be alone its ok hun, you're gonna be ok. It will hurt like hell but you will heal." Nomusa looked at her like she wanted to believe her but she still wasn't the Nomusa they all knew and loved. Mpumi had to get through to her. "You know out of everything Daniel did to me the worst was when he forced himself on me." Mpumi saw Nomusa's eyes widen, she had only ever told Jarred. "It wasn't even just the fact that it was painful it was the violation, I felt small and worthless and I doubted myself. I'm still trying to get to a place where I'm sure of myself. You've been hurt deeply Nono and you will love again but I would love it if you would love yourself again first." Nomusa hugged her and clung a bit to Mpumi and Mpumi let her.

"I'm done talking about him for now. What's been happening with you?" Mpumi sighed and she told Nomusa how she had found the pregnancy test and about when she had confronted the girls. She also told her how both girls had claimed the test was theirs. The old Nomusa would have put some money on whose the pregnancy test was but she was still a bit subdued and she just listened. "None of them were backing down Nono. But I know my children. I didn't back down until I broke them. It's Oyama, Oyama is pregnant." Just saying it out

loud made the pain start afresh. Mpumi had been so disappointed and she had looked at the child she had raised. "How Oyama? Who? But we had the sex talk! I even gave you those bloody pamphlets!" Mpumi's voice had sounded broken to her own ears and Jarred had tried holding her but she had shrugged him off. "Let me talk to my daughter. Oyama how could you do this to me? Haven't I
given you everything?" Oyama had looked at her stormily and her own child had said to her, "But that's just it mama. I am not your daughter. And just like my mother here I am pregnant at fifteen and there was nothing you could have done for me to turn out any different." Mpumi had felt hurt and it had transformed itself into anger, "I raised you better than this! I raised you since you were a baby and now you tell me of a woman you have known of for less than a year and whom you saw for less than twenty-four hours." Mpumi had screamed at Oyama and she did the thing that she had told herself she would never do. "I struck her Nomusa. I struck my own daughter. And I saw the blood come out of her nose and if it wasn't for Jarred carrying me out of that room I would have hit her again. But I will never forget the look in her eyes. She hates me Nono, Oyama hates me." Mpumi was getting emotional and Nomusa was now the one comforting her.

"She's a child Mpumi, she might be angry with you but we were all struck by our mothers at some point in our lives and we still love them. Hell if a child can forgive her mother for prostituting her at fourteen, Oyama will forgive you. She probably is scared right now and feeling like she disappointed you. You have to reach out to her." Mpumi didn't get the prostituting part but Nomusa was telling her exactly what Jarred had said to her. Only Jarred had shouted at her, he hated what he had seen her do and she had been ashamed too. Jarred made it clear that there would be no violence in his house.

"That's the thing Nono I have tried reaching out to her, apologizing but she has shut me out again. Completely."

"Who's the father?"

"She won't say. And Lola won't say either. All they

confessed to is that they went to some dodgy doctor to get an abortion."

"God Mpumi!" Mpumi had felt the same horror.

"Apparently the conditions in the doctor's ward were so bad that Oyama chickened out just as the doctor had been about to make an incision. She could have died Nomusa. No good hospital would have taken her without parental consent or a parent present so she had gone to some backroom doctor." Mpumi had been so relieved that she hadn't gone through with it. If Oyama wanted an abortion she wouldn't stop her but she wanted to be present and make sure she got the best medical attention. "I know you're going through a lot but can you please talk to her Nomusa? She listens to you and she usually opens up to you."

"You don't even need to ask Mpumi, it's my duty as her godmother." The wine bottle and the chocolate bottle were empty and it was past midnight. Mpumi was going to sleep in Nomusa's room, she hoped Jarred wouldn't mind. But today they needed each other and they talked till they fell asleep.

Nomusa woke up feeling lighter. The pain was still there. For a moment when she woke up she reached out for Amo but the bed was empty. And she hadn't cried or felt tears well up, that was progress. There was a note from Mpumi, 'Have back to back meetings, feel at home.' The bitch clearly didn't know her, she was home. Talking to Mpumi had freed her from some of the guilt she had felt and made her aware of her own strength. She loved Amo but she deserved to be loved and treated better. Probably in his own way Amo had been testing her and molding her into the sort of woman he thought encompassed the perfect wife. He had been in love with the idea of her not really with her. Yeah they had gotten really deep with Mpumi the previous night and she felt as if a burden had been lifted from her shoulders. She got up and made her bed and she remembered watching the movie 'A diary of a Mad Black Woman' Helen had said something like she was finding it hard to take one day at a time so she was just existing from one moment to the next. She hadn't understood then but now she felt as if she and Helen were one. The only difference was that she hadn't been dragged out of Amo's mansion kicking and screaming, she had let herself out of the door head held high and shoulders squared. The sad thing about breaking away from someone you are still in love with is that you remember only the good times and you romanticize about the idea of being with him and you find yourself back at his doorstep. And back to square one till he does the same thing and hurts you again and it becomes a circle, a pattern of heartache that you can't break away from. Mpumi had explained it to Nomusa so she was trying to remember the good and the bad times with Amo and that kept her from dialing his number. After showering and dressing up in jeans and a t-shirt, her suitcase had been brought in and her clothes neatly folded probably by Mpumi, she found the courage to go out of the room and brave the world. She found Jarred in the kitchen feeding the twins while they sat on their high chairs and made incoherent conversation with each other. Mpumi's babies had grown so much and they were so beautiful all chubby cheeks and gooey smiles, they pulled at Nomusa's heartstrings. She had thought she and Amo would have babies of their own. She forced herself to shut down that train of thought and she smiled at Jarred. He seemed relieved to see her smile, poor man she must have traumatized him with her tears. "Hey," she said as she headed to the coffee maker.

"Hey yourself. Feeling better?" for a brief moment their eyes met and she saw real concern in his eyes.

"I will live, I'm tougher than I look." She assured him and a brief awkward silence ensured which was broken by Onathi's cry, Jarred was late delivering his spoon of mashed butternut. Jarred and Nomusa laughed and Nomusa offered to feed one of the twins. Jarred told her to feed Onathi because he wasn't a fussy eater while he had to coax the little diva to even open her mouth. Owethu didn't like the butternut because even though Jarred managed to manipulate a spoonful she promptly spit it on his face and he was left a gooey mess.

Nomusa expected him to be frustrated but it seemed as if he knew the drill because he wiped his face with a napkin and coaxed another spoonful. This time he tilted the spoon in his daughter's mouth long enough for her to have no other option but to swallow. "You're really good at this," Nomusa commented as she
finished feeding Onathi who demanded more food by banging his tiny chubby hand on his chair and making gurgling sounds. "Just give him water, their pediatrician said we shouldn't overfeed them they will end up overweight." Jarred instructed her handing her a blue sippy-cup. Then he continued addressing her comment, "Well I had a lot of practice on Lola and it wasn't easy, I made a lot of mistakes and blunders. No one ever really prepares you for parenting not even all those parenting books. And worse off she was a fussy baby even fussier than this little miss here. But if I had to go back and do it all over again I would." Jarred was easy to talk to and she found herself laughing at tales from Lola's upbringing, she was pretty sure he made some of that up. There was no way Lola's hair had caught fire while he was trying to blow dry it. She wanted to make eggs for Oyama but Jarred warned her that eggs set off Oyama's morning sickness so she should rather make her some green tea and add lemon and honey and take some crackers to her. Nomusa knocked at Oyama's door and wasn't surprised when she didn't get any response. She opened the door and let herself in. She found Oyama sitted in the middle of her bed staring at the gothic wall. Nomusa would have to ask Mpumi about the décor in this room. Nomusa put the tray on the side table and sat on the bed. "Hey Kiddo." It was only at the sound of her voice that Oyama turned and looked at her, "Aunt Nomusa!" she cried and hugged her with such a fierce hug she knocked out the air in Nomusa's lungs. Nomusa stroked her back until her crying stopped murmuring "There now, it's going to be alright kid. Stop crying." When she was done being emotional Oyama took the tea and nibbled on the crackers and Nomusa sat quietly and watched, waiting for the kid to open up. "I messed up aunty. I messed up big time and now mama hates me."

CHAPTER
TWENTY ONE

"You did mess up baby, but the good thing is you haven't messed up much your entire life so that works in your favor. And Mpumi couldn't hate you even if you pulled a gun at her face." Oyama looked at her like she was lying. "Have I ever lied to you kid? You know Mpumi thinks that you hate her."

"Why?" Oyama was genuinely puzzled.

"Because she hit you and said things she regrets. But mostly because you didn't come to her. You didn't trust her to deal with your mess with you." Oyama sighed.

"I didn't want to see the look of disappointment in her face. I've already put her through so much."

"We all disappoint our parents Yaya, that's just what we do and they clean up after us that's kinda their job."

"But you don't understand aunty I'm turning into her! I'm turning into Candice and all I wanted was to grow into a woman like my mother. Poised, sophisticated. I wanted to wait to find a man like daddy…not tata but daddy" Oyama clarified as Nomusa had looked at her in confusion and she continued, "Now no good man will want me. That's what gog' MaNtuli always says." Nomusa cradled Oyama's hands.

"Now listen to me, you are not Candice. Yes you might have made a mistake and you might be the spitting image of her but you are not her. For one you have a brain, you're going to be some mean scientist and if a man cannot accept you because of one stupid mistake you made in your teenage years then he is not like your daddy and he is not good enough for you. Forget what your grandmother said. A good man will accept you for who you are. With all your flaws and all your mistakes. Trust me lala." Oyama didn't seem convinced. Her high forehead was beaded in worry.

"But aunty you don't understand. Like her I'm pregnant at fifteen. For a married man and he's also a Minister." Nomusa felt her blood grow hot and cold at the same time. No! She had thought that Oyama had gotten pregnant from a youthful romance.

"Who is it Oyama?" Oyama hung her head and she wouldn't look at her.

"I can't tell you aunty. He said he would kill me if I ever told anyone and he told me to get rid of it." Nomusa felt anger and bile rise up leaving her mouth with a bitter taste. What kind of a grown arse man slept with a girl young enough to be his daughter then threatens to kill her if she revealed his identity? But she had to play this out right, gain Oyama's trust and coax the bastard's name from her.

"I was fourteen when I lost my virginity," Oyama looked up at her in shock and Nomusa continued, "I never really talked about it not even with your mother, I only ever told my mother but she brushed it off. He was an older man, probably in his fifties and he took me to some cheap motel out of the way. Probably so that we wouldn't come across anyone who knew him. He was rich. When we got to the room I was uncomfortable and naïve, he had said we were going to get my present from his room. When we got there he locked the room and then he started kissing me and fondling my vagina. I tried pushing him off but he was too strong so I bit his tongue. He slapped me and I fell on the bed. I will never forget the look in his eye. The rage and loathing, he looked at me like I was a piece of trash. Next thing I felt my panties tearing and he was on top of me pushing my thighs apart. Without any warning he penetrated. He was huge and I was so tiny, still only just a child. The pain… The pain was so excruciating. I screamed and he put his hand over my mouth and he just kept going till I stopped fighting and felt numb. Then when he was done he got off me and told me to get dressed he would take me home. At least he used a condom. I got up, I could barely walk and there was blood on the bed. He said I should leave it, he said he hadn't tasted a virgin in a long time. He took me home and handed me a wad of cash. I got off and went crying to my mother. I expected her to comfort me but she only took me to the bathroom and told me to wash myself thoroughly. She said I should stop being such a cry baby, that it would only hurt the first time that every woman went through it. That I was a woman now and that I shouldn't tell the other girls because they wouldn't understand they weren't women. And she took the money and she left. I hated myself and I was in so much pain." Just thinking about it opened so many old wounds but Nomusa didn't cry, she had exhausted all her tears. Oyama was the one crying and Nomusa let her cry. At least someone seemed to share her pain. When Oyama stopped crying she started talking. She rubbed the scars on her wrists as she talked.

"It happened on New Year's eve. We were bored at Tata's function so I suggested that I and Lola sneak out. We had money we took an Uber and went to The Royal Hotel in Hilbrow. When we got there the bouncers wanted to see our IDs and when we couldn't produce any he had wanted to throw us out. Then he… the other man he showed up he was with his friends and he recognized me. I knew him too I had seen him a lot of times before at family functions and Parliament functions. He told the bouncers that it was fine we were with them and the bouncer let us in. We went in with his party and they bought us alcohol. We drank and started dancing with Lola, they were cool and I trusted him. Then… then I left Lola on the dancefloor and I went to find the toilets. I got lost then I bumped into him in the corridor he asked me what I was looking for then I told him that I wanted the bathroom then he led me to the VIP bathroom. I got in and left him outside when I got out of the toilet stall I found him inside the bathroom. I was drunk I asked him what he was doing in the ladies bathroom and he said that he wanted to see my face in the bright light. He said I had grown into a pretty little thing. Then he started kissing me and I let him. I had made out with Ryan a couple of times but this was different. He didn't fumble with anything and he knew what he was doing. I knew that it was wrong but a part of me wanted him to continue. It got heated and then I wanted him to stop but he already had my panties thrust aside and his pants around his knees. The first thrust was painful and when he noticed he seemed to halt and said 'Shit!' Then he continued and he was done in under two minutes. That's when he told me that if I ever told anyone about what happened he would kill me and if there were any accidents I should get rid of it. Then he left me there in the ladies room. The alcohol was wearing off and I realized what I had done I sunk to the toilet floor and sat there with my bare butt and that's where Lola found me. I told her everything and she comforted me then she helped me clean up then we took an Uber back to Tata's function and swore to never talk about what had happened." Nomusa had felt the anger mounting as Oyama had gone through her narration. What kind of a pervert took advantage of a drunk girl in the toilet and then threatened her? And how could Daniel let them out of his sight for such a long time?

"Who is it Oyama you can trust me with your secret." Oyama had still looked uncertain then she had looked at Nomusa and gave her the name. Nomusa could not believe her ears. The Minister of Finance! No wonder their economy was taking a nose dive, their nation was run by perverts. It didn't matter if they were called 'Honorable' in public, they were all dogs, all of them. To think he flaunted how much of a family man he was! That man had been present at Oyama's christening, at her fifth birthday party and his daughter had gone to the same school as Oyama but the daughter was older. Nomusa wished she could get her hands around his neck and squeeze till his eyes bulged in the throes of death and he crapped his pants. Now for the difficult part. "You have to tell your mother baby."

"No! She can never know aunty promise me you won't tell her..."

"No listen to me Oyama. You have to tell her. I won't tell her but you have to tell her. She and Jarred will protect you, I will protect you and I know Daniel will deal with him.
What that man did is wrong, he took advantage of you and he must pay. He won't hurt you I promise."

"I'm scared what if he hurts them just so that we don't cause a scandal for him?"

"He won't touch them Oyama, he belongs in jail. Now I didn't have people in my corner but you do lala. Trust them to protect you, let them be there for you. You don't have to fight this alone pumpkin." It took the whole afternoon to persuade her but Oyama finally agreed to confide in her mother. When Mpumi came back from her meetings she looked drained shame and Nomusa felt bad for her but she had to know. Nomusa first sat Mpumi down and told her not to do anything rash, Nomusa knew that when it came to her family Mpumi could kill anyone who hurt her family. She had seen it when she had given Phindiwe a thrashing. Mpumi agreed and Nomusa led her to Oyama's room. They found Lola there as well and she was squeezing Oyama's shoulders in support. Mpumi sat next to Oyama and she apologized for striking her and Oyama broke down. Mpumi kept saying "I'm sorry. I'm sorry" while holding Oyama and Nomusa and Lola watched. Then when she stopped crying, Oyama looked at Mpumi and said quietly, "The person who got me pregnant is Mhlanguli Lubisi." There was deathly silence after her announcement. Then mayhem.

CHAPTER TWENTY TWO

"Where is that little slut? Where is she?!" Telling Daniel hadn't been easy, Mpumi hadn't wanted to tell him but Jarred had insisted. Daniel was Oyama's father and he deserved to know. Mpumi had called him to set up a meeting but Daniel hadn't been cooperative. "What's the meeting about Mpumi?" he had asked on the phone, Mpumi had forced herself to calm down. She blamed Daniel for everything. "It's about Oyama Daniel, we can't talk about this through the phone." He had sounded impatient even on the phone,
"I don't think you have a choice, my time is too precious to come over there and discuss whatever my brat of a daughter has done this time."

"You know what I shouldn't even have bothered. Congratulations Daniel, you're going to be a grandfather." Mpumi had said then she had hung up. The phone call had taken place less than an hour ago and she hadn't been surprised to see Daniel's car pulling up in the driveway. He had come barging in and hadn't even greeted them. Mpumi looked at him, "You will not call her that Daniel,

Oyama is not a slut."

"She's my daughter and I will call her whatever I want to call her. Where is she?" Daniel was barking at her, he looked ready to pounce on someone.

"I will not allow you to use that tone with my woman in my house," Jarred's words were quietly uttered but they held a menacing threat.

"Or what white boy? You think I'm scared of you? Now where the bloody hell is Oyama?" Daniel was shouting now.

"If you can't calm yourself down I will have you chucked out of here and arrested for trespassing." Jarred was now towering over Daniel but Daniel wasn't one to be easily intimidated or to bow down.

"This isn't America, I own the entire police force so don't fuck with me. I want my daughter." Mpumi had to step between them before things got ugly.

"Daniel sit down and hear us out first." Daniel looked at her then at Jarred and he knew he was outnumbered so he sat down on the edge of the couch. Mpumi and Jarred sat on the opposite couch facing Daniel. "Oyama was taken advantage of by an older man," Mpumi began.

"So you are saying she was raped? Then why didn't you call the police?" Daniel interrupted and he was already taking out his phone. "Let me finish!" Mpumi hissed at him and he immediately put his phone back. "As I was saying, Oyama was taken advantage of. Apparently during your New Year's Gala event, she and Lola snuck out to some club called The Royal Hotel. When the bouncers were about to kick them out one of your friends recognized her and went into the club with them. Where he proceeded not only to buy them alcohol but also to take your daughter's virginity and impregnate her in the ladies' room. He also threatened to kill her if she ever told anyone and told her to get rid of any accidents." Daniel looked shell shocked.

"So you think all of this is my fault? I can hear the

accusation in your voice."

"Of course it's your fault! She was in your care and you were too busy licking butts to keep an eye on her. And you are the one who introduced your pervert friends to my daughter! She almost died while trying to get an abortion at some backstreet doctor's surgery!"

"Bloody hell Mpumi, you should have raised her better. And what example have you set for her shagging up with your lover in front of her and you are the one who drinks alcohol. So don't you dare put this on me."

"Oh shut up! How can you even bring Jarred into this? It's yo…"

"Enough!" Jarred's voice cut into their squabble. Both Mpumi and Daniel had stood up as their argument had gotten more heated and Jarred pointed them to their respective couches and he remained standing. "I have a fifteen year old girl who is scared out of her brain right now and you pointing fingers at each other will not solve anything. Now I want you to talk like civil adults and come up with a bloody solution." He looked from Mpumi to Daniel and back at Mpumi again. Mpumi cleared her throat uncomfortably but didn't say anything.

"Who is he? The scumbag who violated my daughter, who is he?" There was a mad gleam in Daniel's eyes that Mpumi had only seen when he had taken a gun and put it next to her. He would kill him and Mpumi wanted the bastard dead.

"It's Mhlanguli Lubisi." Just as she finished talking, Daniel was already up and about to walk out but Jarred put a restraining hand on his arm. Daniel looked at Jarred's hand, "If you still value your hand take it off my arm." Jarred wasn't scared of Daniel either so he kept his tight grip on Daniel's arm. "Where do you think you are going?" Jarred asked Daniel. Daniel looked at him for a while then he responded, "To kill the bastard who defiled my daughter." There was something menacing about Daniel right now. "Then I'm coming with you to finish him off." Jarred said. Mpumi couldn't comprehend what was happening but for the first time the two men seemed in agreement and it chilled her to the bones. Jarred let go of Daniel's arm and followed him out. Mpumi ran after them, there was no way she was letting them go out alone baying for blood.

In Daniel's car, Daniel was busy on the phone. He called someone and asked for the location of Mhlanguli and dropped the call. The person called back ten minutes later with a location Mpumi presumed. Then Daniel told the Driver were to take them and then settled into the seat to make more calls. Mpumi looked at Jarred he was sitting with his legs sprawled out and there was no denying his physical strength. Coupled with Daniel's maniac rage Mhlanguli would be lucky to escape from these two with his life. As much as she wanted him dead, she didn't want to end up with a dead body so Mpumi was going to be the voice of reason. They were heading to Pretoria, Mpumi assumed that is where the bastard was. There was quiet tension in the car, only Daniel talked on his phone. Mpumi held Jarred's hand and he squeezed her fingers. It was weird being in the same space as both of these men and they barely said a word to each other. Mpumi had travelled this road a lot of times before as Daniel's wife so she was familiar with where they were going. They should have taken the Jet but their trip hadn't really been planned or agreed upon. As they turned into Nassau Street, Mpumi felt tension mounting. They were going to the Bryntition Estate the official residence of the President and some of the Cabinet. She and Daniel had had a property in that Estate and
Mhlanguli's mansion was close to theirs. Mpumi felt a chill as they were let into the electrified detection fence. First they passed the Mahlamba Ndlopfu house, where the President resided there was barely any movement in the impressive gardens, the house looked deserted even though Mpumi knew there was security there 24/7. Mpumi was so apprehensive that she didn't marvel as usual at the beautiful manicured gardens which included rose gardens and water features in the Oliver Tambo house. They passed a few more properties including Daniel's mansion until they turned into a huge black gated driveway.

CHAPTER

TWENTY TWO

The security at the gate knew Daniel and let them in without so much as an inquiry. There was only one car parked in the driveway. Good it meant that bastard didn't have any company. Strangely there wasn't much staff swarming around the place which implied that Mhlanguli was there in his unofficial capacity. Daniel didn't even wait for the driver to come around and open the door for him and Mpumi and Jarred followed him closely behind. The door was open so they let themselves in. Daniel went room by room opening doors and they followed him closely behind. There was no one in the bedrooms. They continued their search and while Mpumi was looking in one of the other rooms she heard a female scream. She rushed to what turned out to be a study and was met by a naked woman clutching her clothes to her chest. Recognition dawned. It was…no! Was there no one who wasn't fucking around in the Cabinet? Worse off this female MP was married to a very unassuming man, Mpumi looked at her in disgust. She couldn't look Mpumi in the eye and then Daniel's voice sounded, "Get her the fuck out of here Mpumi!" Mpumi did as she was told leading the lady in her walk of shame and handing her to Daniel's driver, Mpumi rushed back into the house and as she got to the landing, Mhlanguli came crushing out of the study naked, as if he was propelled by some kind of rocket. He tried getting up but Daniel was already on top of him punching and kicking. When Daniel stood up to catch some breath Jarred took over and punched the living daylights out of Mhlanguli. Mpumi just stood quietly on the side and watched. The man looked pathetic there on the floor cowering and trying to block the blows but they just kept on coming. When he lost consciousness Mpumi had to intervene and both Jarred and Daniel stepped away from him while Mpumi felt for his pulse. Yes they had beaten him to a pulpy mess but he was still alive and if no broken rib punctured his lungs he would survive. Daniel went to the kitchen and brought a pitcher filled with cold water and unceremoniously dumped the water on Mhlanguli. The battered man woke up splattering and seemingly unaware of where he was and then he winced as pain and recollection came rushing back. He tried sitting up and Daniel helped him up. Then Daniel was holding him by the scruff of his neck, his face menacingly close to Mhlanguli. "So you decided to screw around with my daughter?" the words were quietly uttered but they could all hear them clearly. Mhlanguli seemed to labor hard to be able to speak and his voice came out in a croak.

"I was dr…drunk D…Daniel I di…didn't mean for it to happen." He got a stinging slap across his face for his efforts.

"Don't freaking lie to me. You deflower my daughter in the toilet like some cheap hooker! Then you threaten her! You Mhlanguli." Daniel was right up his face but he was shouting at him. Mhlanguli seemed to shrink even more as if he wanted the floor to open up and swallow him.

"I'm so…sorry. Pl…plea…se don't ki…kill me," his voice came out in a hiss and blood oozed out of the corner of his mouth.

"Death would be too kind for you. And since you have begged so pathetically I will let you live." Mhlanguli seemed relieved but Daniel wasn't done yet. "You will fax in your letter of resignation and you will take your family out of this country, I know you have money stacked in your Swiss bank account. I don't care where you relocate but if you even think of setting foot back in this country or anywhere near my daughter or my family… then you're dead. Do you hear me?"

"D…Daniel Pl…please man, do…don't exile me. You know how th…these things just ha…happen." Mpumi felt disgusted by Mhlanguli's plea and Daniel's eyes narrowed to tiny slits.

"No one fucks around with my family and lives to tell it. I am being lenient here." Daniel stood up and kicked him in the crotch and Mhlanguli doubled up in pain. "Twenty-four hours. I give you twenty-four hours to do as I say or you and your whole family is dead." Mpumi felt a slight shiver go down her spine. She knew that Daniel wasn't bluffing, there was murder in his eyes. Mhlanguli must have seen it too because he nodded painfully. "Let's go." Daniel said to them and just before they left Mpumi spit on Mhlanguli's swollen face and she took Jarred's hand and they walked out.

CHAPTER

TWENTY TWO

When they got home, Lola and Nomusa were back and they looked in shock at Jarred's bloody t-shirt. They should have seen the other guy. Mpumi would explain later. First she had to tend to her man and give him his accolades. She led him into the bathroom and when he made to take off his t-shirt she refrained him by putting a hand over his hand. "Let me." She said looking into his gorgeous blue eyes. She took off his clothes and led him into the shower. His hands were bruised around the knuckles. She soaped him from his toes to the ends of his golden hair and then rinsed him off. She felt his erection poking her belly. She had to admit that she had also been turned on by watching him beat the crap out of that pervert. Fuck civilization every woman got turned on by the animal in their man and she proceeded to show him just how much she was turned on. He was grunting and holding on to her for dear life. When they were done, she dried both of them and then applied antiseptic on his bruises and slowly bandaged his knuckles. She kissed his bandaged hands one at a time and then kissed him on the lips and said, "Thank you."

"For what?" he asked looking at her quizzically.

"For going all John Cena on that bastard. For being there for Oyama and me."

"I would do anything to protect you and the children. You're my world." He said it so simply but it touched a chord in her heart.

"When you're being all macho it really turns me on." She said looking into his eyes with longing and he grinned at her. Then they were kissing and there was no more room for talking. Only their bodies were communicating in a language as old as time.

The question of what they were going to do with Oyama's pregnancy had arisen on the ride back. Daniel was of the notion that she should have an abortion and Mpumi had stated that Oyama should be the one to decide. It was her pregnancy and they would support whatever decision she made. Mpumi made her way to Oyama's bedroom, knocked once and let herself in. She found Oyama sitting on her bed and staring at the wall. Oyama had gone back to that dark place where she shut everyone out but Mpumi wasn't having it anymore, life had to go on. She sat next to Oyama and slipped her hand into her daughter's hand. Oyama's fingers were icy cold and a bit stiff. Oyama looked down at their entwined hands. "You're not alone Yaya, please let me in baby. Let me be you mother. Let me help you through this." Mpumi spoke softly like she was afraid she was going to chase Oyama away. Oyama was quiet for a while, "I'm sorry mama…"

"You don't have to keep apologizing to me…"

"No mama let me finish. I'm sorry I should have never gone to that club in the first place. Lola didn't really want to come but she wouldn't let me go alone. I put us both in danger. You don't know how much I wish I could turn the clock back. I'm sorry I tried to commit suicide I didn't mean to hurt you. All you have ever been to me is a godsend. You've always been my best friend. I'm sorry that I didn't come to you sooner, I'm sorry that I constantly shut you out. I'm scared mama." That was the longest speech Oyama had said to Mpumi in a long time and her voice had dropped to just above a whisper on the last part. But Mpumi heard everything and she squeezed her hand.

"I forgave you the first time you said you were sorry." This was really cozy and Mpumi felt the void that had grown between her and Oyama ease up. They were going to be alright. Now for the hard questions. "Have you decided what you are going to do with the pregnancy?"

"Can't you decide for me?" Oyama asked with a sad little smile on her face.

"No I'm sorry darling but no one can make that choice for you. This is your first adult decision. Whatever you decide now will change your life forever." For the first time Mpumi was addressing Oyama as an adult. That was what she was now, a young adult. It was a hard pill to swallow.

CHAPTER
TWENTY TWO

"That's all I've been thinking about. A part of me wants to get rid of this baby, so that I can totally erase this experience. But then I have morning sickness and I realize that a life is growing in me. I'm torn." Oyama already sounded mature. "But if I keep it, how will I pursue my dreams?"

"Jarred and I talked about that. If the only reason you don't want to keep the pregnancy is because of pursuing your dreams we might be able to help. We are willing to raise the baby while you go to Harvard as planned. You will just have to delay your plans for a year which shouldn't hurt you much…" Mpumi hadn't even finished talking before Oyama jumped on her with a huge hug and she clung on to her daughter. "But it's not a permanent situation. We are giving you six years after the birth to get your life in order and to be financially independent to take care of yourself and your child." Mpumi managed to say after the hug had ended. Oyama looked like she was trying to hide her tears.

"It's more than I deserve mama, thank you." Mpumi was relieved, she had been afraid that Oyama would have wanted to go through with an abortion. So she was going to be a grandmother at forty, Mpumi felt an overwhelming love for Oyama's unborn child.

"I'm going to need your help mama."

"You don't have to ask Yaya, I will walk you through it." This baby was bringing them closer together before it even arrived. Mpumi saw the first gleam of excitement in Oyama's eyes then her eyes became a bit clouded.

"What about its father?"

"Don't worry about him he is out of your… our lives for good." Oyama seemed uncertain and Mpumi squeezed her hand in assurance. "Trust me baby, no one will hurt you or my grandkid. They will have to go through me first."

The Newspapers brought them good news the next morning. The first was right there on the front page in bold letters

"FINANCE MINISTER'S MYSTERIOUS RESIGNATION." The reporter was not sure what had led to Mhlanguli Lubisi's change of heart but it was speculated that he might have embezzled some State funds. Embezzled state funds sounded a good reason as any and there was a general outrage throughout the country even the nyaope boys were baying for his blood for the Tax payers' money. Fearing for his life and that of his family and looking pretty beat up, it was reported later that day that Mhlanguli Lubisi had fled the country. Served him right, Mpumi thought without even an ounce of remorse. Daniel called to inform Mpumi that he was keeping a close eye on Mhlanguli in case the idiot was licking his wounds and bidding his time till he could affect his own revenge. Daniel wasn't happy that Oyama wanted to keep the child, if the scandal came out it would ruin him. "This has nothing to do with you Daniel, for once in your miserable life will you think of someone else's needs before your bloody career. We have all had to sacrifice something for your precious name and that's enough. Oyama is having this baby with or without your support." She had snapped at him and hung up on him. Daniel easily got on her nerves. Then even greater news in the middle of the newspaper were the Matric results. Not only had Oyama been the best student in her school she was the third best in the entire country. Mpumi was screaming and running to her bedroom in a suit, she had been getting ready to go to a meeting. Oyama wasn't in bed and she came out of the bathroom looking green. Oyama hadn't started showing yet but her lean features had begun filling out. Mpumi excitedly handed
her the newspaper and when Oyama looked at her blankly, Mpumi had impatiently opened the centre page. Oyama stared at the newspaper for the longest time and then she had started laughing and crying at the same time. And Mpumi had screamed with her and they jumped up and down and hugged. Nomusa came out of her room looking peeved, "What's all the noise about? Some of us are trying to get some sleep, hau." Mpumi handed her the results. They caused such a racket that the twins had woken up. Mpumi was strutting around like a rooster but

CHAPTER
TWENTY TWO

she had to change her suit it now smelt of Oyama's morning sickness. She called Nomusa aside, "Can you arrange a secret small party for Oyama? You can get Lola to help but it has to be secret." Then she did something she was probably going to regret. She handed Nomusa one of her credit cards. Some spark was back in Nomusa's eyes, "Don't worry chomma leave everything to me."

"Don't go crazy Nomusa," Mpumi's pleas were falling on deaf ears, Nomusa just smiled mischievously at her and reminded Mpumi that she was getting late for her meeting. Her bank account was about to suffer, at least that card had a swiping limit. Mpumi had to rush to her meeting but she felt so happy that she felt like kissing everyone she came across.

CHAPTER TWENTY THREE

Time did heal. As the months had gone by Nomusa had dreamt less of Amo and thought of him less each day. Even though she still missed him terribly, she was finally getting to that happy place in her life. She kept herself insanely busy. She had accepted Mpumi's offer to work together and she had also put all her savings into their project and she was so excited. Her role was creating a digital footprint for the Centre. She was heading the web design team and they were also chiefly responsible for the marketing of the Centre. Social networks were her specialty and Nomusa was enjoying herself. This was the most she had challenged herself professionally in a long time. Then Oyama and Lola had come up with a brilliant idea. They proposed that Nomusa and her team should develop a learning app that not only had all the subjects but that also one that could identify the users' strengths and weaknesses and highlight possible career choices. Nomusa was excited about the app and she worked with Oyama and Lola to build the app. Oyama had all the intellectual brains and Lola was an IT whiz, she knew more about programming than Nomusa. Oyama was glowing, she had gotten over the morning sickness and she was carrying the pregnancy well. She looked so beautiful, Nomusa immediately knew that the baby was going to be a girl. Black biology, you wouldn't understand unless you were black and an African. Like most teen pregnancies there were no complications with her pregnancy. Nomusa noted how it was bringing Oyama and Mpumi close again, they went together for doctor's appointments, the first sonogram it was just precious watching them get all excited. Jarred was excited too, he was responsible for remodeling the new nursery and he seemed to be going overseas less and less, he preferred spending most of his time with the Terrible Two. That was what Nomusa called the twins. Those babies could have you fooled by their angelic faces but they were trouble personified. They could walk now and say a few words, their first word had been Yaya. Those little midgets loved Oyama to destruction and both of them wanted her to carry them at the same time. Which was getting harder as her tummy ballooned. For the twins' first birthday Mpumi and Jarred had taken them all, including MaNtuli to Disney Land. Nomusa had had more fun than the twins. She had especially loved the rides and the Water World, Nomusa got to flaunt her perfect pear shaped figure and her flat belly. She had posted so many pictures on Instagram and they were all pretty if she could say so herself. The cutest ones had been of the twins, for their birthday they had been dressed up as Princess Jasmine and Aladdin. They were precious in blue. The party had been going well until Aladdin had taken Jasmine's cake and tossed it on the floor and Jasmine had burst into tears. That was Onathi for you, he wasn't as dramatic as his diva twin but all the drama seemed to emanate from him. Then he would stand and look at you innocently and solemnly with those big bluegolden eyes and if you were weak you would melt into a poodle in the floor. But Mpumi was a tough cookie, to restore peace she had promptly given Jasmine Aladdin's cake. Even MaNtuli seemed taken with Jarred now but shame mlungu bae was still scared of MaNtuli, it was even funny how scarce he became when she was around. Nomusa

hadn't wanted to leave Disney land. She often wondered how Jarred and Lola had left America for South Africa. That was one hell of a downgrade if you asked Nomusa. But
she couldn't blame them, they were smitten with Mpumi and her friend was smitten with South Africa. Oh and Phindiwe blamed Mpumi for Oyama's pregnancy. Big surprise there. The old witch had called one day and Mpumi had put the phone on loud speaker, it had been just her and Nomusa in the room. "So it was not enough that you left my brother penniless, you had to get his daughter pregnant too mfazi ndini we Harvard." The way she was talking you would swear Mpumi had grown a penis and done a hit and run stunt on Phindiwe's niece. Nomusa had almost burst into laughter but Mpumi had given her a warning look and so she had shaken with silent laughter instead. "Molo we Phindiwe." Mpumi had greeted her non-bothered.

"Cing'ba I would waste my airtime to call and greet you?" Phindiwe sounded irritated by the flippancy in Mpumi's voice.

"No I don't think so but do you also think I won't hang up on you?" Yaaas Mpumi wasn't cowering to that old cow anymore.

"Tshini! You're evil wena Nompumelelo, I curse the day you came into my brother's life."

"Curse, go to ogqirha, do whatever you want Phindiwe, I don't care anymore. You tried all you could to bring me down but you are just mad because I kept flying higher. Now if you know what's good for you, you won't call me again unless it's to tell me you are dead." Mpumi had ended the call and then they had continued discussing ideas on the Centre's website. Mpumi's idea was to keep the project as indigenous as possible. Now the problem was a lot of the small black businesses they wanted to come on board didn't have any digital footprints some were virtually nonexistent on the internet. So Nomusa had been faced with the task of meeting with them, sampling their supplies and creating digital images for them. Most of their clothes were beautiful and the kids' clothes were so cute. Nomusa was travelling a lot to meet with these businesses and she loved her new job because she got to fly in the company jet which really Jarred had loaned to them. On the road she met a lot of men who were yummy and promising but Nomusa was off men for the time being. She was taking Mpumi's advice and focusing on herself and she felt great. She had lost some weight which she was slowly gaining back. She was coming back from meeting with Mpumi's traditional designer eNgcobo when Jarred asked to talk to her. They stepped into Jarred's study and Nomusa wondered what all this hush-hush was about, she had never been in Jarred's study before. He first checked that no one was in the corridor then he closed the door and came to sit in front of her. "I need your help Nomusa." He seemed so serious, Nomusa immediately started to panic.

"Anything Jarred, what's up?" he looked down like he was ashamed of what he was about to ask.

"It's Mpumi's birthday next week and I want it to be perfect for her. Last year what with the twins in the ICU and me being overseas I didn't even give her as much as a present. And this year I want to sweep her off her feet. But I can't plan anything without her catching on to me. So can you plan the whole thing for me?" Nomusa had laughed in
relief, she had immediately assumed it was something bad like he cheated or something.

"That won't be a problem. I'm going to have to start charging y'all for all this secret party planning." Jarred had looked thoughtful for a moment.

"You know that's not a bad idea, you should study a bit of event planning and turn it into your own side project and then when people want to hire the Centre to throw their events, you would be their designated event planner and that could be a lucrative business for you."

"Do you really think I could be a good event planner or organizer?" Nomusa had been hopeful and skeptical.

"Of course, that party you threw for Oyama and the twins' birthday were all wellorganized. All you have to do now is to learn to do that in a grand scale like maybe volunteer to organize the opening of the Centre." He was after all an international business mogul so Nomusa trusted that he knew what he was talking about. She had taken his black card and left him deep in thought. He was right, Nomusa had a knack for throwing parties that suited people's personalities because she was more of a people's person. She googled Event Planning courses and sure enough there were also online courses that she immediately signed up for. She was done looking to be an employee. Then she got down to planning the perfect 40th birthday for her lifelong friend. Who knows maybe Jarred would propose and it would turn into an engagement party, Nomusa thought as she took out her notepad.

Planning a surprise party for Mpumi had been more challenging than Nomusa had anticipated. She had sent the invites to her friend's close associates and the boards she was in, stressing the need for privacy and that it was a surprise party. Forty people had RSVP'd and assuming they would all bring plus ones, Nomusa had to plan for a hundred people just to be on the safe side. She had managed to trick Mpumi into thinking they were going for a late meeting with one of their troublesome clients. Her friend seemed peeved about something. "What's the matter? That scowl on your face is going to scare away Mr. Molefe."

"It's a bit silly really but its Jarred. He forgot about my birthday again this year, he didn't even send me a single rose." Nomusa had smiled secretly, Jarred had played his part well. But she had put a concerned act on for her friend.

"You know men don't like to fuss like us women, he probably bought you a gift and you will get it after our meeting." Mpumi had bitten her lower lip which meant that she was frustrated.

"I expected him to make a big fuss. I turned the big forty, is that asking for too much to get a romantic dinner away from the kids or even some roses with a box of chocolates at least?"

"Eish chomma what can I say, men just don't get us." They got to The Hilton hotel and they went to their reserved table. It was one of the most posh hotels in all of South Africa and Mpumi complained that they would have to foot the bill yet the client was the one who had called the meeting here and where the fuck was he they had been waiting for ten minutes. She was in a cranky mood which was perfect for Nomusa's plan. The waiter came in with a note for Mpumi, Nomusa watched as her friend transformed from being cranky to a blushing love-struck teen. "I think Jarred is up to something. He sent me a note to go to room 187." Mpumi gushed and Nomusa thought if only she knew. "Then what are you waiting for chomma, go I can handle Mr. Molefe."

"Are you sure?" Mpumi looked doubtful but Nomusa shooed her away. She waited till Mpumi got in the elevator and as soon as the elevator closed she got up and she was busy on her phone. She knew exactly what Mpumi would find in room 187. She had been the one who sprinkled the white rose petals in the room creating a trail to the big four poster bed. And there was a single red rose next to a package wrapped in silver foil with a note from Jarred on top. Nomusa had gotten the Fox Street lady to make a figure hugging floor length white evening gown which had a halter neck simple and elegant on the front. But the back would be open just to above Mpumi's generous behind and it was lined with silver sequins. The gown was breath taking and Nomusa had no doubt it would go well with the silver shoes she had picked out and the silver chandelier earrings. The bracelet that Jarred had bought for her with an engraved message would also be a nice finishing touch for the whole outfit. Nomusa had manipulated Mpumi to go to the saloon and her naturally wild hair had been tamed into an elaborate up-do. The make-up she had on will have to do anyways Mpumi looked beautiful even with the barest make-up. Nomusa had planned everything even buying her signature scent J'adore. She imagined the look on Mpumi's face as she took another elevator to the rooftop of the hotel. She found the guests already seated.

CHAPTER
TWENTY THREE

The décor team had excelled themselves, silver and white chairs lined up the aisle and there was even a red carpet. It looked like a rooftop wedding though the black balloons written 40 in silver gave away that it was a birthday. The stars looked so close as if one could reach up and touch them, Nomusa knew that Mpumi had a thing for stars. Nomusa walked straight to her family and they looked perfect. Jarred was a dare-devil in a black and silver tux and the girls were goddesses in their silver gowns. The rest of the guest had been told to dress in black, at least they had all followed instructions Nomusa didn't want anyone upstaging her friend. She was relieved to see bra Hugh had made it, he was Mpumi's favorite all time singer and he would be their main performance. Even MaNtuli looked elegant in her black gown and she was holding Owethu who was in a beautiful white frock, her eyes all out even though it was almost their bed-time. Onathi was a mini Jarred in his own custom-made tux it was just so adorable. After checking that the sound system was perfect, the photographer and his crew were set up and that the food was ready, Nomusa took her gown and shoes from Lola and quickly went to the bathroom to change. She barely made it in time in her silver gown as well, when Jarred got a text. Mpumi was on her way up. Jarred went to his position next to the elevator door and the rest of them waited quietly. There was his African goddess coming out of the elevator, from where she was standing Nomusa could see Mpumi's smile it shone brighter than

the night stars. Mpumi hadn't noticed them yet, it seemed as if all she could see was Jarred, and she flung herself at him and kissed him passionately. Oh no, they were going to be subjected to live porn if Nomusa didn't intervene she signaled to bra Hugh to start singing. The passionate embrace was broken up at the first sounds of the music then Mpumi seemed to take in her surroundings. When she saw everyone looking at her she went from lily white to a scarlet black. Nomusa would be embarrassed to if she had been jumping her man in front of most of Joburg's elite. Then Mpumi started laughing and crying as Jarred took her down the aisle. Bra Hugh's deep throaty voice was leading in singing 'Happy Birthday' to Mpumi. Her friend was so happy she was literally glowing and Nomusa felt complete. She had pulled it off. Owethu got off from MaNtuli and rancrawled to her mother. Trust the little diva to try and steal the spotlight but the moment was still perfect. Nomusa moved around making sure the toasts were said on time and the food was eaten early enough. MaNtuli left with the twins soon after the cake had been cut, Oyama and Lola point blankly refused to go with her. The party was just starting and Nomusa made sure that their guests glasses were always filled with wine, champagne, whisky and juice for Oyama and Lola. She also made sure that the guests who were getting a bit rowdy or drunk were escorted discreetly out. When she noticed that the couple couldn't keep their hands off each other, she told them to go to their hotel room while she and their guests danced the night away under the stars. There hadn't been a proposal but the night had been a mighty success.

After Mpumi's wonder birthday, Nomusa had gotten calls from guests and others who had heard about the party to plan their parties, events some even weddings. Mpumi's party had made headlines and everyone wanted a piece of Nomusa's magic. Jarred had been right at the rate she was going she was going to make a lot of money. She had no idea though how to start a business and that is where Mpumi and Jarred came in. they taught her a lot and she registered her business. She had ten clients in her first week. It was all happening so fast and she still had to work on the Centre. Nomusa could barely catch her breath she was often so tired that when she got home, she went straight to bed and dropped straight to a dreamless sleep. But she had never felt more alive. Her life had purpose, she hadn't ever thought in her wildest dreams that she would be leading a web design team and planning bourgeoisie events. Her, the simple girl from Khayelitsha whose own mother thought that all she had was looks. She hadn't been in touch much with her family. Mostly she talked to her little sister and she sent the monthly check. Deep down she still thought of Amo, she didn't talk about him much but she still missed him. She had deleted all his contacts but she knew his phone number by heart even the number plates on his favorite car. She missed him so much that when he had called her out of the blue one day, in a moment of weakness she had picked up. She hadn't said anything she just answered the call and kept quiet. "Nunu waka please don't hang up," Amo's voice had sounded desperate and just hearing his voice shame melted her heart. She hadn't known what to say but she hadn't hung up. "Nomusa are you still there?"

"Y…Yes I'm still here…" She stammered.

"Can we meet up? I need to talk to you and I can't do it over the phone." Nomusa had been torn she didn't think it was a good idea meeting up with him but she wanted to see him so badly and hear what he had to say.

"I'm sorry but I'm very busy these days." She had decided to hide behind work.

"I know, I read about your Event planning business. I'm so proud of you. But please just give me an hour of your time, I promise you won't regret it." He was following her work, she was touched. How could she say no to a man she was still deeply in love with? She had agreed to meet up with him and so a week later here she was sitting across him at Michael Angelo's and she couldn't stop staring at him. He was still so fine she could just gobble him up instead of the Greek salad she had ordered. He was wearing a soft blue suit with a white shirt which wasn't buttoned the last two buttons. He had grown a Maps Maponye beard since she had last seen him and it made him look like sin. He seemed nervous because he hadn't said much, he kept twirling his watch and he also barely touched his food. "You look beautiful," he said randomly. "You look well," she responded. He was going to waste his hour on small talk and she was going to let him but when the hour was up she was going to shake her Chanel clad tosh out of that hotel. She hadn't told Mpumi about Amo's call or that he had come to Joburg to meet up with her and talk, she would tell her after their meeting.

"Nomusa I'm deeply sorry that I treated you badly. It's just that I have never loved anyone the way that I love you and I didn't know how to love you right. And so I messed up. Big time. But I still love you, I can't get you out of my mind. Remembering your crazy laugh is driving me insane. I need you baby." Nomusa looked into his big brown eyes and that was her mistake. His eyes were deep and they pulled her in. They told her he meant what he said and that he was willing to do anything to make things right. Damn those eyes were doing something to her, drawing her in like a magnet. She couldn't even hear her own response and as if in a trance she watched him put some bills on the table and when he took her hand she let him. She let him lead her to the elevator and her excitement rose as they got into his hotel room. The moment he closed the door he was on her, kissing her so thoroughly that she swooned and felt light headed. She felt every sense in her body awaken, it was a heady feeling like she had drank a whole bottle of red wine. She thought of nothing else except of him in that very moment. He was tossing away her cream jacket and her brown silk blouse, unzipping her skirt till she was left standing in her brown heels and pearl necklace only. He simply looked at her like he was imprinting her body to his memory. She began to feel shy and a husky voice she was not sure belonged to her said, "You seem a bit overdressed, here let me help you with that." She quickly unbuckled his belt and helped him out of his trousers, his jacket, shirt and his boxers. She needed to touch his skin and feel it to actually believe that this was real that she wasn't dreaming. His skin felt warm to touch and smooth even though his muscles were chiseled to perfection. As she kissed him, his lips tasted of the wine they had barely drank and she sunk her teeth playfully into his full lower lip. Amogalang had the most gorgeous lips and he moaned as she explored them again. She found herself pinned to the wall, he was straddling her while he carried her. He cupped her buttocks as he brought her to his pulsing manhood and when he thrust deeply into her she cried out. She had missed this, missed him how he managed to fill her up completely. He looked at her in concern his eyes small lilts. She rocked slightly to encourage him not to stop and to show him that she was ok. He proceeded to rock the daylight out of her. With every thrust she felt as if they were connected. Then he claimed her lips again and she lost all coherent thought. She was literally drowning in his lips and as he quickened his tempo she felt the tide carrying her higher till she felt her orgasm juices shout out of her in an orgasm so high that she felt herself shudder as spasm after spasm rippled her body. For the first time they had come together and it was the most overpowering feeling she had ever felt. Still inside her, Amogalang carried her to the bed and laid her gently down. He wiped the weave strands which were plastered on her face away and then he held her so closely as if he were afraid if he loosened his hold she would slip away from him. His erratic heartbeat matched hers in perfect synchrony. None of them said anything for a while then she felt his cork harden again.

Two hours later, Nomusa felt satiated and her body seemed to be floating in bliss. Amogalang kissed her gently on the lips. "I missed you nunu," he said softly and she smiled at him. "I missed you too."

"So are we back together again?"

"I guess so," she said shyly and he was smiling broadly.

"Great I can't wait to get back home with you, my mother can't wait to see you she wants to apologize and we can start the lobola negotiations."

"Whoa Amo, we only just got back together."

"I know baby it's just that we've spent so much time apart and I want to make up for every minute we were apart." He kissed her forehead.

"Besides I can't just up and leave with you. I have an obligation to Mpumi and the Centre and I just started my own business it's only just taking off."

"Mpumi will understand baby and you can move your

company to Cape Town there are also top clients in Kappa."

"Wow. Just like that? So you have already re-arranged my life?"

"Nunu don't be like that, I want this, us to work out and we can't when we are thousands of miles apart."

"Then move to Joburg."

"Nomusa don't be unreasonable, we talked about this. I can't uproot my company."

"But I can uproot mine because it's small and just starting?" Nomusa sat up and faced Amo.

"Exactly baby, I knew you would get me."

"This Amo, this is why I left you. I'm the one who always has to compromise, to bend over backwards. I can't do that anymore. I can't lose myself to you again."

"What are you saying Nomusa?" He was looking at her in frustration.

"I'm saying we are too different and we want different things in life and I can't fit into the box you have crafted for me." Nomusa didn't wait for him to respond, she got up and started dressing. He also got up and tried holding her, "Poncho please don't do this to me again. I love you Nomusa, I want you to be my wife."

"I want that too but I also want to see myself when I look in the mirror. I just started something great and I want to know that my husband supports me and I want to see where it leads me. I'm sorry Amo but I can't go down this road with you again, it only leads me to pain." She finished dressing up while he was still pleading with her. But Nomusa knew in her heart of hearts she was making the right decision for her. She kissed him deeply and then looked into his hurt eyes, "I love you Amo, I always will. But right now I choose to love Nomusa." She let herself out of the hotel room and out of his life again without any tears this time.

CHAPTER
TWENTY THREE

CHAPTER TWENTY FOUR

Tat' Xhamela passed away in his sleep one peaceful September night. Mpumi was crushed when she heard the news, the elder had been like a father to her and his death brought back memories of her own father's death. Death was never easy to accept. She could only imagine what MaNgidi was going through. She hated that she had to break the news to Oyama, Oyama was now eight months pregnant and Mpumi feared that the news would put a strain on her. Mpumi knocked tentatively on Oyama's door and she found Oyama sitting in bed going through her laptop. "Hey baby, can I talk to you for a minute?"

"Sure mama what's up?" Oyama said while smiling and putting her laptop away. This pregnancy had really been a blessing. Even though Oyama wasn't the bubbly girl she had been once upon the time, now she smiled more and laughed more and she was easy to be around, she even cried a lot when the hormones hit her hard. Mpumi sat on the bed and held her hands while she stroked them re-assuringly. "I just heard some terrible news, your Great-uncle is no longer with us.

He passed on in his sleep." Oyama broke down at the news, she had had a very soft spot for Tat' Xhamela and it had been a mutual affair. Mpumi held her and let her cry, just grateful that she wasn't bottling in the pain. After crying and washing her face, Oyama came back and cuddled with her mother and they drew comfort from each other.

"Mama?"

"Yes princess."

"Can we go to his funeral?"

"Of course honey, we can go. But are you sure you are up to it?"

"I will be alright, I just want to say goodbye."

"Ok sweetheart, we will check with your doctor first." The doctor did clear her to leave when they assured her that they were going by private jet and that they would hire a private mid-wife to go with them. But the whole arrangement didn't sit well with Jarred. He didn't want Mpumi going to Transkei. "He was like a father to me Jarred, I can't miss his funeral." They were in their bedroom that night while Mpumi sat in bed and Jarred was pacing the room.

"Mpumi you have back to back meetings, your project is at a critical stage. You have
babies that you need to take care of and Oyama is in her last trimester. Yet you want to drop everything and go hightailing to Cape Town."

"Nomusa can take care of my meetings. Plus I'm only going to the burial, I will only be away for a day." Mpumi tried to reason with him.

"We all know it's never just a day when you go there. Next thing you will be calling saying you have to sleep over. Why is this so important to you?"

"Because he was family baby."

"What about us? Ain't we your family too? Do we even matter to you? Because I'm beginning to think that we come second after Daniel's family."

"God not this again," Mpumi muttered under her

breath but Jarred heard her. His eyes narrowed into tiny slits and he looked pissed.

"So we are 'this' to you Lelo?"

"Jarred that's not what I meant and you know it. Just that every time I have to go anywhere where Daniel is going to be, you become insecure."

"This has nothing to do with Daniel, but now that you mention it have you ever given me a reason not to be insecure?"

"Excuse me?" Mpumi couldn't believe what he had just said.

"You were so reluctant to leave him in the first place and you kept the fact that he killed our unborn baby to protect him and you jump at any chance to go to his home. You do not want to commit to me. What Lelo? Do you still want to go back to him?" Jarred wasn't joking either his eyes had changed to a stormy grey.

"I can't believe that after all this time you still doubt that I'm in this with you till the end. Just because I refused to settle for your lukewarm proposal, you are going to throw that in my face every time? And we share a child and a history with Daniel we are bound to meet every now and then but I have never put him before you or loved him more than I love you and you know it Jarred Levine. I am just sick of having this fight with you!"

"Or maybe you just sick of being with me!" Jarred's words hit Mpumi straight in the heart and she could only look at him with pain filled eyes. She got out of bed and put on her robe and as she was about to pass him but he held her arm. "Where are you going, we are not done here." Mpumi winced his grip was too tight and he immediately relaxed his grip a bit.

"I'm going to sleep in the guest bedroom, I can't talk to you when you are like this."

"Get back in bed," he said softly looking at her through narrowed eyes. She tried freeing herself from his grip but he tightened it hurting her again. "I said get back into the freaking bed

Lelo!" Jarred had never shouted at her so menacingly or manhandled her like this before and she got scared. He must have seen the fear in her face because he let go of her arm and she went back to bed quickly while he stared at her. He stared at her for a while as if he wanted to say something then he cursed and left their bedroom banging the door so hard that Mpumi feared it would come off its hinges. This was a side of Jarred that she didn't know and she hated what she had just witnessed. She didn't dare follow him in the state he was in.

When Mpumi woke up the next morning she wasn't surprised to see that she had slept alone. Whenever they had a huge fight Jarred would sleep in one of the other bedrooms. She got out of bed and freshened up then she went in search of him hoping to settle their differences. She looked for him first in the nursery and only the twins were there sleeping peacefully in their cribs. She tiptoed out of the nursery and went to look for him in the guest bedrooms, he wasn't there and there was no sign that he had slept in any of them. Then she searched his study still no sign of him, in fact there was no sign of him in the whole house. Mpumi began to panic the last time he had left the house in such a blind fury she had ended up being called to a Nigerian club where she had found him in the throes of an epileptic seizure. She tried his phone at first it rang till it went to voicemail and when she tried again his number had been disconnected. Mpumi felt hurt. Jarred's reaction was uncalled for, it wasn't like she was going there for pleasure. To distract herself she started preparing breakfast. Nomusa came in as she was banging the pan on the kitchen counter. "Whoa there soldier I know those pots have a life warranty but I doubt they can survive such force." Mpumi let out a frustrated cry and Nomusa immediately saw that something was wrong and she stopped teasing her. Nomusa made Mpumi sit down and made her water and sugar. After drinking Mpumi felt a bit calmer, Nomusa was looking at her with that expression which said bitch you better start talking. "It's Jarred. We had a fight last night and he left in a fit, I have no idea where he slept or where he is and he isn't taking my calls." It was embarrassing saying it out loud but she trusted Nomusa with her life.

"That's unlike him, what was the fight about?" Nomusa asked.

"He doesn't want me going to Transkei, he feels like I'm putting Daniel and his family before him and our children."

"Yoh chomma that's deep. So are you still going to go?"

"I have to Nono, he was like a father to me and Oyama needs my support."

"I hear you and I love you for being so caring but Jarred has a point," Nomusa held her hand up to stop Mpumi's protest. "If the shoe was on the other foot and he was the one who was still close to his former wife's family how would you feel?"

"But it's a funeral Nomusa!"

"It is and I know that you doing what's expected of you, but honestly Mpumi ever since you left Daniel you have been to his home more times than when you were actually married to him. Just take Jarred's feelings into consideration." That stung but Nomusa was probably right. Mpumi was caught in between a rock and a hard place. Oyama and Lola came into the kitchen already bathed and dressed and that took the decision from Mpumi's hands. "Give me thirty minutes girls I will be ready and we can leave."

"Where is daddy Mamita?" Eish that question.

"He had to go to a meeting, we will see him when we get back." Nomusa looked at her while shaking her head in disapproval, Mpumi felt bad enough as it was so she fled to her bedroom. With Jarred MIA, Mpumi had no other option but to ask Nomusa to go and drop the twins in Soweto with her mom. She had to bathe them first and put them in their car seats before they could leave. They had to hurry otherwise they were going to miss the burial. Mpumi tried Jarred's phone again and it went straight to voicemail. She was getting frustrated but she had to make sure that Oyama and Lola didn't catch on to her. She hoped that she hadn't driven her man away.

Nomusa was bone tired, it had been a hectic day. She had had a hectic day covering Mpumi's meetings as well as her own. She looked at her Gucci watch it was just after 6pm, she wouldn't be able to go collect the twins so she called MaNtuli to tell her and the older woman sounded very pleased. Nomusa wondered why Mpumi's mother had never re-married and committed herself to a life of loneliness. But part of her understood, she didn't think she would ever want to be with anyone other than Amo. Before she settled into gloominess, Nomusa packed her briefcase and made her way home. She found the house in darkness, so Jarred hadn't come back yet. Luckily for her she had been craving hot wings and she had passed by Chicken Licken. She punched in the alarm code and went room by room switching on the lights then she warmed her food, dished up and took out a bottle of Jarred's expensive wine collection. She was settling into the couch when her phone rang, it was Mpumi. "Chomma," she answered chirpily.

"Hey hun," Mpumi sounded drained and Nomusa felt sorry for her.

"How did it go?"

"As well as a funeral can go, it was dignified but it dragged on forever. MaNgidi is a mess, she's so broken Nono."

"Death is never easy…" Nomusa could tell that Mpumi had another question but she waited for her to come out and ask it.

"Is… Is Jarred home yet? I ca…can't get hold of his phone." This was hard on her Nomusa could just tell and her reply was probably going to kill Mpumi.

"No babe, he's not home yet but it's still early I'm sure he will come home tonight." She heard Mpumi let out a pain filled breath.

"This is killing me Nomusa, I keep thinking he is somewhere with his hands around some bimbo and what if he has finally given up on me? I swear if Jarred ever cheated on me it's going to kill me…" Mpumi sounded like she was crying and it hurt Nomusa hearing her friend sound so crushed.

"Hey don't even think like that. Jarred needed to blow off some steam but he is going to come back to you. You the only woman in his heart and in his life boo." It took some persuading but Mpumi stopped crying and Nomusa promised to call her the moment Jarred came back home. Nomusa continued with her solo wine spree. When TV became boring she went online and she was checking her timeline on Facebook. Most posts were boring so she scrolled on then a picture caught her eye. It was Amo, he was tagged in a picture of him and a beautiful dark skinned woman who looked to be in her twenties. Nomusa wished she had a big mole or some other disfigurement but she didn't. The girl was fucken flawless and the look on Amogalang's face as he looked down at the girl stabbed Nomusa straight through the heart. Yes they had broken up but dammit Amo was hers. She still loved him. And he seemed happy with another woman. She would always love him. She wanted him to be happy but it still hurt like hell. She went down strong on the wine and it didn't seem to numb her pain, she opened another bottle of whisky this time. She was on her second glass of whisky when she heard the door open, she wanted to stand up and go and investigate but her legs wouldn't allow her. It was Jarred, he came into the lounge looking like a tornado had gone through him. He looked like he hadn't bathed in days and he was drunk, he wasn't steady on his feet. He came and sat next to her. Nomusa watched in silence as he took her glass and filled it up to the brim and gulped down the whisky. "I'm no different from Daniel I hurt her Nomusa and she looked at me in fear." His words were a bit slurred but Jarred was making perfect sense. "Amo has moved on with a girl who looks like a cross between an angel and a model," Nomusa confided in him. He poured a glass for her and she also gulped it down but the whisky burnt her throat and she started choking. Jarred had to rub her back before she stopped choking and spluttering. Even her eyes were watering.

Jarred gently wiped the tears from her eyes and his hands lingered on her face. She looked into his eyes and they had an eye lock moment. Nomusa saw him lowering his head and a part of her wanted to break the moment. But she didn't and she felt his breath on her face, he smelt of whisky. Then his soft lips were on hers and she tilted her head ever so slightly allowing him to deepen the kiss. It was a drunk kiss but it felt darn good, she felt warmth spread down her nether region. Nomusa found her hands wrapped around his neck and she was kissing him back passionately. She felt his hands move up her thighs and a female voice moaning as the kiss intensified.

After the call with Nomusa, Mpumi had felt very restless. She hadn't gone this long without talking to Jarred ever since they had started living together and it was killing her. She missed him and she couldn't shake the feeling that something was terribly wrong. But she had to have faith that he wasn't lying alone somewhere in a ditch. The funeral had been beautiful a lot of the speakers had heartwarming things to say about the deceased and they were all true. Daniel seemed to be taking Tat' Xhamela's death harder than Mpumi had expected. Of course he didn't cry but his face looked withdrawn and his eyes were bloodshot. The burial had ended late and Mpumi was reluctant to drive with Oyama in her state in the dark but she really needed to be back home. She had been with MaNgidi at the burial although they hadn't talked much, the elder woman had been crying and Mpumi had been comforting her. She could only imagine if she lost Jarred how she would react. Jarred was her life just the thought of him leaving her for another woman brought tears to her eyes what more his death. It wasn't healthy
being this dependent on another human being but she couldn't help it, he was her happiness. She was so deep in thought that she didn't see Daniel approaching her till he was sitting next to her. He had to hold her hand gently to get her attention. "Mpumi are you ok?"

"I'm at a funeral of course I'm not fine." He held up

his hands in mock surrender.

"I was just trying to be caring, no need to bite my head off." Mpumi let out a slow breath, her reaction had been uncalled for.

"I'm sorry, I'm just under a lot of stress. It's been a long day."

"I know his passing hasn't been easy on all of us. Thank you for coming and bringing Oyama."

"No need to thank me, he was like a father to me."

"He thought very highly of you too. You know that time when we were going to pay lobolo for you, he said you were worth all the cows your uncles demanded and that I should treat you like the diamond that you are." It sounded like something Tat' Xhamela would say and Mpumi felt the tears sliding silently down her face. "I wish I had listened to him. That white boy rubs me off the wrong way but at least he is smart enough to recognize the diamond that you are. " Daniel's voice sounded wistful. Mention of Jarred just made Mpumi break down even more and Daniel was slightly alarmed. "Did I say something wrong?" he sounded concerned and Mpumi shook her head no, she was even having hiccups. He let her calm down and then she started talking.

"I think I pushed him away Daniel, he thinks I put you and your family over him and our children."

"He probably said that out of anger but I know that man would do anything for you Mpumi." Hearing Daniel say that was a bit comforting.

"I just want to be with him home right now."

"Then let's go I will drive you to the airport." Mpumi's eyes widened, Daniel looked like he meant it because he got up and pulled her up. Mpumi was so relieved she hugged him gratefully. Mpumi went and said her goodbyes, Oyama and Lola would follow the next morning with Daniel. Mpumi got into the car and they headed to the airport. The first few minutes were awkwardly silent then Mpumi decided to break the silence. "How are you holding up? I know he meant a lot to you."

"I'm pretty shaken up. Tat' Xhamela made me into the man I am today. He was more of a father to me than that drunk that my mother married." There was bitterness in Daniel's voice, he and his father hadn't had much of a relationship from the little that he had ever told Mpumi about his late father.

"Your father's death must have come as a shock too, I mean the way he died was sudden too." Daniel was silent for a while then he sighed.

"It wasn't much of a shock Mpumi. I am the one who pushed him and he was so drunk he didn't have any balance so he fell and hit his head on the stone. And I just looked at him. I didn't even touch him to feel for his pulse. I thought I would feel some remorse or pain for his death or at least some relief. But I felt nothing." Mpumi was shocked by Daniel's confession. He wasn't even looking at her, he was concentrating on the road.

"Why are you telling me all this?"

"Because it's been in my chest for a long time now. And I know you are loyal you would never repeat it to anyone." Mpumi had always suspected a certain darkness around Daniel but she hadn't known just how twisted and damaged he really was. Mpumi shivered, she wondered how many people Daniel had killed but she was too chicken to ask him. She was glad that Jarred had come back into her life, they had their shares of ups and downs but Jarred wasn't anything like Daniel.

CHAPTER
TWENTY FIVE

Mpumi was staring at the portrait they had taken at her fortieth birthday party. She had been in the middle with her white gown, Jarred had been next to her holding Aleja, MaNtuli had been on her other side holding Anton and the girls were next to Jarred while Nomusa was next to her mother. It had been a magical night indeed and Mpumi had felt loved and cherished. Just looking at her mother in the picture reminded Mpumi of their conversation when she had come back from Transkei and she had gone to take the twins in Soweto. After asking how the funeral had gone MaNtuli had asked her an awkward question, "Nompumelelo how are things between you and your man?" Mpumi hadn't wanted to lie to her mother and she told her of their fallout over the whole burial saga. MaNtuli had been sympathetic then she had said something which had surprised Mpumi even more, "When is your friend moving out? You shouldn't bring people into your union my child, if my own cousin could have an affair with your father, how can you trust a friend with your man?" Yeah Mpumi's father had did a number on her mother but Mpumi assured MaNtuli that she had nothing to worry about maybe if they were talking about Daniel and Nomusa would never betray her like that. The older woman had clicked her tongue suspiciously, "I'm just saying be careful who you bring into your home. If they can plan a surprise party behind your back, God knows what else they can do behind your back. Worse you left them alone in the house, these things happen especially with Nomusa's history."

"Which history is that mama?"

"When you were teenagers Nomusa started sleeping with rich married men who gave her money. That's why I tried to discourage your friendship, I didn't want you going down the same road." Mpumi had been shocked by that revelation, she had had no idea. Then she had remembered Nomusa's comment about a mother prostituting her child and her heart had gone out to the young Nomusa. It hurt a little that her best friend hadn't confided in her but Mpumi wasn't going to confront her and she didn't feel threatened by Nomusa staying or being close to Jarred. She wasn't about to turn into that woman, the paranoid spouse who couldn't trust her friend around her man. Things had been rocky between her and Jarred since she had come from the funeral. She had found him smelling like a whisky distillery passed out in their bed. He had apologized the next morning which had taken her aback a bit but that was Jarred, he was always sensitive and never slow to admit when he was in the wrong. But Mpumi just felt that things were awkward between them, it had been a month but they were slowly getting over that fight. Usually when they fought, their fights blew over quickly but there was always a first time for everything. Their sex life was taking a strain too and

it was breaking her down. Mpumi was so deep in her thoughts that she didn't see Jarred come into the passage till she felt him drawing her into his arms. He kissed her neck and she felt the electricity going down her spine, "I didn't expect you to look so glum while looking at memories from your fortieth." He was speaking against her neck, his warm breath sending ripples down all the way to her vagina. She was finding it hard to think straight or talk. Jarred hadn't been like this with her in a while now and it felt good. "I miss you." She spoke without thinking but it was true, at times it felt like there was a wall between them. He turned her around to face him and he lifted her chin holding it in between his thumb and fore finger. "I'm right here Lelo and I am never leaving your side." His eyes said he meant every word.

"I know but you've been distance lately, like you are here but you not really with me." Mpumi felt the tear slide down her face and Jarred gently wiped it from her face with his other thumb.

"I'm sorry baby, I never meant to hurt you like this. Please don't cry, you're paining me." Mpumi didn't respond she just buried her face in his chest, he smelt of sweat and woody masculinity. He was coming from his morning jog. "Let's go to the bedroom before the evil two walk in on us." He was referring to the twins, they had somehow learnt how to get down from their cribs on their own and wreak havoc. Mpumi wasn't prepared for Jarred scooping her up in his arms and walking with her in his arms into their bedroom. Whatever concerns she had had about their sex life were dispelled by the way he loved her thoroughly not once but twice before they had to wake up and face their responsibilities. Jarred even bathed her, Mpumi felt pampered and blessed. She was blushing as they made their way to the kitchen where they found the whole family already eating breakfast. Everyone looked up as they entered and there seemed to be collective relief when they saw Mpumi smiling and blushing. "It's about time you guys kissed and made up, you are about to be grandparents." Oyama's pregnancy had made her very cheeky, she said whatever she wanted.

"Hey I don't care that you are pregnant I'm still your mother I will box those ears little miss," Mpumi tickled her lightly as she sat down and started dishing up. Oyama was late, her due date had passed by two weeks and today they were going to the hospital to induce her labor. "Yaya kiss!" Onathi had to bang his chubby hand on the high chair to show that he meant business. Amidst the laughter

Oyama leaned over and kissed his little pink lips causing Owethu to scream for a kiss of her own from 'Lolo'. Lola also leaned over and kissed the little minx. Mpumi felt at peace for the first time in a long time only Nomusa seemed a little out of it. "Nono are you ok?" There was awkward silence and all eyes turned on Nomusa, she looked a bit pale.

"I'm ok I just have been feeling very sick lately." Nomusa did look sick.

"Sorry love, tell you what when we take Oyama to the hospital I will take you to my doctor." Mpumi offered soothingly.

"I said I'm ok Mpumi!" Nomusa said standing up and leaving the kitchen. Ok that was weird and everyone was left in uncomfortable silence. Mpumi made to get up and follow her but Jarred restrained her and they continued with their breakfast. Something was going on with Nomusa but Mpumi had been so consumed with her problems with Jarred that she hadn't taken much notice of her friend and she felt bad. Amogalang had moved on and it clearly had shaken Nomusa more than she had let on at first. After they finished eating Lola did the dishes while Jarred attended the twins and Mpumi made her way to Nomusa's room. She knocked cautiously and when she didn't get a response she let herself in. there was no one in the room and Mpumi was about to get out when Nomusa came in from the bathroom looking green. "I'm sorry about my reaction in the kitchen," Nomusa said while looking down. Mpumi felt that there was something that Nomusa was holding back from her.

"What's happening Nono?"

"I'm scared to go to the doctor."

"Why?"

"Because I might be pregnant." Mpumi was beyond shocked by this revelation.

"When? How? I mean whose?"

"Amo, he was in Joburg about two months back and he wanted us to meet up and talk. We met up and one thing led to another we had sex but I felt like our relationship wasn't salvageable so I left." This was a lot to take in for Mpumi, Nomusa hadn't even told her that she had hooked up with Amo. It seemed like there was a lot that her friend had kept from her. Pregnancy would explain why she had been acting so weird lately.

"You have to know for sure, I'll take you to my doctor."

"What if I really am pregnant Mpumi?"

"Then you will have to tell Amo, he has to know about his child."

"He's moved on, this is all such a mess!" Nomusa buried her face in her hands and Mpumi rubbed her shoulders soothingly.

"It will be alright love, let's just take the doctor's visit first then we'll take it from there, ok?" Nomusa nodded her head glumly. Mpumi left her to go and help Oyama get ready for labor. They had packed the baby bag weeks ago and the nursery was also ready for the arrival of the next generation. Mpumi texted Daniel to let him know that they were going to the hospital for the birth but he didn't respond. He had made it clear that he wanted nothing to do with his grandchild. Mpumi let him be, everyone was ready to go even the twins were going with them and they were all excited.

Amandla Natalie Sisulu came into the world kicking and screaming. She was a whopping 3,3kgs even the doctor was surprised how Oyama with her slender frame was able to push her out naturally with only just two stitches. Mpumi was the one to name her Amandla because she had strengthened their bond as a family. The nurses thought it was because her granddaughter kicked and screamed like a little warrior. Mpumi was biased but she thought her granddaughter was the most perfect baby, she was a little replica of Oyama. Oyama was exhausted, her face was glistening with sweat but she held her baby and they looked so cute together. It felt like only yesterday Mpumi had been holding Oyama with the same dotting love and today her baby was holding her own baby. Mpumi was proud of Oyama, she had been brave even though she had cursed them a lot and had almost torn off Lola's hair but she had braved through child birth. Jarred had been with MaNtuli and the twins in the hospital lobby while Mpumi, Nomusa and Lola had been with Oyama in her private delivery room. After being cleaned up Amandla was taken to the nursery and that's where the twins got to see their niece for the first time. They just went crazy pointing their chubby fingers at Amandla. "Mamita baby! Baby! Baby!" Owethu wanted to hold the baby and she was now screaming for her, Mpumi had to hold her tight and assure her that they would get to touch the baby just not now. Jarred joked that he and Onathi were outnumbered by females but he was also in love with Amandla. Daniel didn't come but Jarred more than made up for his absence. After cooing and oohing over the baby, Mpumi took Nomusa to Dr. Babalwa. Luckily he was available and after they told him the symptoms he made her pee in a cup. Nomusa was clutching Mpumi's hand a bit painfully but Mpumi let her be. As they had suspected the tests came back positive, Nomusa was pregnant. After leaving the doctor's office, Mpumi and Nomusa went to the bench outside the hospital. "Call him Nomusa." Mpumi had to be firm with her best friend. Reluctantly Nomusa took out her phone and dialed Amo's number by heart and she put him on loudspeaker. It rang forever and just as it was about to go to voicemail he picked up. "Hello," his voice didn't sound very welcome Mpumi squeezed Nomusa's hand and she responded.

"He…Hello Amo, it's me Nomusa."

"I know who it is what do you want?" Ouch that stung, Mpumi squeezed Nomusa's hand again.

"Umm… I wanted to tell you something…"

"Baby are you coming or not?" they heard a husky voice saying in the background and Mpumi saw Nomusa's face flinch in pain. Amo said something to the person and then he returned to the call, "Nomusa are you still there?"

CHAPTER

TWENTY FIVE

"Yes I'm still here, I can call you later if you are busy."

"No it's fine you were saying you need to tell me something?" this was hard for Nomusa, Mpumi could just feel her friend's struggle and she squeezed her hand in assurance. Nomusa had to clear her throat and take a deep breath before she uttered the words.

"I'm pregnant Amo." There was silence on the other end of the line for the longest minute that Mpumi even feared that the call had been cut off.

"So you called to tell me you are pregnant?" he sounded pissed.

"Yes."

"Well congratulations then." Now he sounded sarcastic.

"No Amo you don't understand. It's yours. The baby I'm carrying is yours." There was another prolonged silence on the other side of the line.

"Is this your idea of a joke?" Yerrr Mpumi had never heard the soft-spoken Tswana sound so menacing.

"No Bab…Amo I'm telling you the truth. I just came from the doctor."

"So let me get this straight, one minute you want nothing to do with me then after a month you call me out of the blue to tell me you carrying my child Nomusa?" Amogalang laughed a nasty mirthless laugh. Dang this was harder than Mpumi had thought it would be. He didn't sound happy at all.

"I'm not over the moon about it either but you did screw me when you were here." Nomusa was done being timid, shit was about to hit the fan.

"Yeah but how do I know that one of your Gauteng men didn't knock you up and now you setting me up. Entlek what's this about Nomusa, is it you sick twisted way of getting back at me because I've moved on?"

"Fuck you Amogalang, I just thought you wanted to

know that we are going to have a baby not that I want you back. You know what I'm sorry I even bothered calling you. Me and my baby will do just fine without you so go to hell." Nomusa didn't wait for him to respond she hung up. Mpumi didn't know what to say, that phone call had not gone well at all. He called back and she declined his call and blocked his number. Mpumi looked at Nomusa she seemed angry but calm, if it had been Mpumi she probably would have been a mess. "So what are you going to do?"

"Work my butt off, I have a baby on the way and I am all that he or she has."

"That's not true, that little munchkin also has a godmother and a bunch of crazy godsiblings and a niece." For the first time that day, Mpumi saw a genuine smile cross Nomusa's face.

"Thank you Pum-pum, for always being here for me and for taking me into your home, I don't deserve you."

"Nonsense you my only friend and sister remember? Now let's go back before Owethu pokes Amandla's eye out." They made their way back to Oyama's room.

Jarred couldn't believe it when Mpumi told him later that night that Nomusa was pregnant. "God save us from another hormonal woman," he said in mock prayer and Mpumi through a pillow at him which he ducked. "Does she know the father?" Jarred asked and Mpumi found that question weird.

"Of course she does, it's Amo her ex."

"Ooh I thought they broke things off ages ago."

"They did but apparently they met up and hooked up about a month ago."

"So does that mean she's going back to Cape Town?" he sounded hopeful. He was beginning to sound like Daniel, he hadn't liked Nomusa.

"No. If I didn't know better I would think that you want her out of here. Things didn't go well when she told him about the baby, he claimed it could be another man's child."

"It's not that I want her out but it would be nice to just be alone with my family. And I don't blame Amo I would have reacted the same." Wow were was all this coming from? Mpumi looked at Jarred and he shrugged his shoulders.

"I thought you liked Nomusa."

"I do babe but she has been a house guest for ages."

"She will be out of our hair by December when she moves back into her own house."

"Yes milady." Jarred was acting weird but Mpumi shrugged it off, she didn't want to get into another fight with him.

"I can't wait for Oyama and Amandla to be discharged and come home." She changed the topic.

"Look at you all excited to be a grandmother." Mpumi laughed it was still weird to think of herself as a grandmother.

"I will have you know that I still have some tricks up my sleeve even as a grandmother."

"You are one sexy grandmother. Come here Mima. I want to make my way into you granny knickers." Jarred was crazy but she made her way to him and he spanked her generous butt then squeezed it and she wanted him so badly, she never thought that grandparents ever got horny for each other. She loved this side of Jarred and he hadn't showed her this side in a long time.

Everything was good with Amandla and Oyama and after just two days in the hospital they came back home. It was fun teaching Oyama how to be a mom, from teaching her how to breastfeed with her complaining that it was painful to teaching her how to bathe the baby and how to change her diaper. MaNtuli came to help out on the first week. You would swear Lola was the new mother, from the moment she got home from school she kept fussing over Amandla and she was the one who wanted to bathe her and change her diapers. Mpumi was blessed to have such a close knit family and she loved every moment she spent with them. The twins could walk on their own and being with them was exhausting at times. There had been a few delays in the building of her centre but everything was coming together just fine. She had decided to include a dance studio where traditional dance was going to be taught and she was excited about it. She was still getting offers from Foschini, Truworths, Woolworths and other big franchises but

she stuck to her original dream of having local designers and local brands. Jarred kept his word, he was a silent partner he advised her and helped her with her ideas but he kept in the background. Mpumi had commissioned Nomusa to organize the opening launch of the Centre. She was proud of her friend, Nomusa's event planning company was growing she even had it registered and she was going to open her offices in the Centre. MaNtuli had gotten the cleaning gig and her company would be responsible for cleaning the mall. Life was good, Mpumi spent most of the day on her feet but she wouldn't trade it for her old life for anything. She hadn't told anyone of Daniel's confession to her, it had been disturbing but she didn't want to get involved in anymore of the Sisulu drama. She was just going to focus on her centre, on Jarred and on her children and her granddaughter.

CHAPTER TWENTY SIX

You know that feeling you get when everything is falling in place? The contentment that comes after rough patches and you feel like you on cloud nine. That's exactly how Mpumi felt the day before the official opening of The Child Centre. She had come out to stand next to the pool and gaze at the stars and she felt at peace and at one with the stars. She should have been nervous but she wasn't, she had worked hard and nothing and no one was going to steal this moment from her. Mpumi had come a long way from being Mrs. Sisulu-Ndinisa, she had grown so much in a space of two years. When she had been married to Daniel, her image had meant everything to her she had worked hard to build up the image of being a happy and devoted wife but she had been far from happy. The things they wrote about her in the press now would have broken the old Mpumi but they barely fazed Jarred's Lelo. They said she was a horrible mother that's why her daughter had a baby at fifteen. Others may look at Amandla and see shame but Mpumi saw a blessing, sure they could have made Oyama have an abortion and forget that anything ever happened but then her daughter would have gone down the bitter self-destruction road. Seeing the look of love on Oyama's face every time she held Amandla filled Mpumi with so much warmth and if that made her a horrible mother then so be it. Oyama had put a picture of Jarred holding Amandla as her profile picture on WhatsApp and that must have struck a chord with Daniel. Before Amandla's birth he had made it obvious that he wanted nothing to do with Oyama's 'shame'. He didn't even come to the hospital to see her when she was born. But after seeing that picture, Daniel had rocked up at their house with a miniature replica of a Lamborghini in Pink custom made and written Amandla on the number plates for his grand-daughter. Never mind that Amandla was only six weeks old and she couldn't even sit yet. Owethu true to form, had gone crazy over the toy car and she thought it was hers. Oyama and Lola had dressed her up in a cool biker's jacket, leggings and cute mini sunglasses and they had a photoshoot with 'Owethu's car'.

"Penny for your thoughts?" Jarred's voice cut through Mpumi's thoughts. Mpumi smiled up at him, he always had a way of sneaking up behind her and hugging her from behind, she didn't get startled anymore.

"I'm thinking how did I get here?" Jarred frowned at her and she had to explain, "I had resigned myself to being the perfect wife who turned a blind eye to her husband's infidelities and I had accepted that I would never have kids of my own. I was stuck in my job which didn't excite me anymore but it was safe, it was a life others envied. But here I am today about to open my own centre and it's scary all my investments are tied with it, if anything goes wrong I will be bankrupted. It's funny though because I'm not nervous
I'm not even scared because I have the love of my life with me, I have my babies and my grand-baby. My life isn't as perfect as it used to be well at least from the media's point of view but this is it for me. I'm perfectly happy." She didn't know if she was making any sense but his arms tightened around her and he kissed the top of her head. He

understood. "I know I've fucked up in the past, even more than you know…" she tried turning her head to look at him but he imprisoned her in his arms. "But I want you to know that I will spend the rest of my days making it up to you. The only tears I want to cause you are tears of joy and anger because I've said something stupid but I never want you to cry in pain because of me. I promise to make you happy Lelo." His deep voice sounded huskier than usual, if she didn't know better she would think he was crying but she guessed he was just emotional. She was getting emotional too from his words, this man right here completed her. He didn't have to buy her anything to make her happy, every gesture from him big and small made her heart smile. She remembered that day in Cape Town when she had woken up in his arms. She hadn't known that it was him but she had felt safe, protected and even though he was a stranger she had felt instinctively that he hadn't violated her or that he ever would. Theirs was a connection so deep that she felt as if she wasn't complete if he was beside her or near her line of vision. Nomusa had been right, Jarred had been proposing to her since that day in Cape Town. The table set for breakfast next to the ocean. The ridiculously expensive bottle of wine at the wine tasting. The night of seduction at the tree house in Sabi Sands and even that night when they had their naked shouting match on the beach in Mozambique and he had broken down and cried because he didn't want to let her go back to Daniel. And the way he had been there for her when she was pregnant and how he had been there for her children that had been his declaration of undying love. And her surprise birthday party had been icing on the cake. Of course as he said he had fucked up a lot of times along the way like his stupid lame arse proposal and his disappearing acts but he was in this for the long run. Mpumi knew now that she didn't need a big romantic moment with her blue-eyed fool because even random moments like the one they were having now filled her heart with so much love. "Let's elope." Her mind had colluded with her mouth against her again. He turned her around slowly to face him.

"Wait are you proposing to me or are you messing

with me?" she could clearly see his surprise in the moonlight.

"I mean it Jarred let's get away after the launch and get married. I don't want a big eloquent wedding, I just want to be part of you, completely in every way possible. What I mean to say is if you still want me to be your wife, I would be more than honored to be your wife."

"What happened to not settling this time around?" he sounded suspicious now, Mpumi sighed.

"I realize that with you settling was never an option and that everything you say and do is heartfelt and I want to be your wife, your life partner and your constant support." He flashed his smile at her in the dark and she melted but she knew he was about to say something stupid.

"I have to think about it. I mean all of this is so sudden." She punched him lightly in the chest, "Ouch! No need to physically coarse me Miss Ndinisa, there is nothing I want more than to be your husband."

"So is that a yes?"

"It depends. Were you serious about elopement? Because I'm saving all my money for my daughters' weddings." There was only one way to shut him up when he was being this idiotic. She pulled his head down slightly and she had to stand on her toes then she proceeded to kiss him till both of them were literally breathless. "Well since you have such skills of persuasion, my answer is hell yes!" he said before swooping in for another kiss.

Nomusa had outdone herself. There was a red carpet and a mini stage on the entrance of the Centre. All the speeches were to be made before the cutting of the ribbon and the official opening of the centre took place. Then after the opening people would sample the merchandise and party the night away. The turnout was spectacular, the who's who in the Jozi scene had come out in full force. Mpumi's designer hadn't disappointed she had whipped up a simple dress with

CHAPTER
TWENTY SIX

a drop neckline and sleeves it had a synched waistline and a full flared skirt. It was black, the belt was made of African print material as was the neckline and the sleeves, and she had shoes made from the same material. Colorful bead bangles graced her arm and she had a Zulu choker on her neck. Her natural hair had been manipulated into a funky upbeat style and she represented the style that the Centre sought to promote. Jarred was wearing a black suit but his tie was made from the same material that her belt and shoes were made from and they looked beautiful as they took pictures on the red carpet. Nomusa's bump was shown off beautifully in her black frock and her weave as always was on point but she looked more nervous than Mpumi. Mpumi didn't know why she was nervous she had managed to get Somizi to be the MC, the night was a guaranteed success. Natalie Mkhwananzi made her way to the stage, she was the first speaker. "When Nompumelelo Ndinisa approached me with the idea of The Child Centre, I fell in love with the concept. It held so many opportunities for our local entrepreneurs…" Mpumi didn't really concentrate after the opening lines of the speech. There was Daniel making his grand entrance, he had his new beau on his arm. Apparently she was somehow related to Steve Biko. She was willowy with beautiful legs and a gorgeous face, they seemed to be going strong they had been featured together in the media on numerous events. Mpumi wondered how Candice was taking all of this, she hadn't seen Candice since she had rushed her to the hospital to give birth. The new beau was called Mandisa and she was the perfect candidate for the Minister of Finance's wife. Yes Daniel had taken over Mhlanguli Lubisi's position after his 'untimely resignation', Daniel was now the Minister of Finance. It was funny how the world operated. Mpumi felt a gentle nudge on her arm. Ooh it was time for her speech, Jarred squeezed her arm in comfort and she made her way to the stage. "Thank you so much for making time to come out and support The Child Centre. This project has been very close to my heart. A child represents purity and the present as well as the future. Africa at heart is a child, there is the purity of our culture and our craft that no matter how much other continents may exploit and abuse our resources, that part of us remains untouched and pure. We have been told for so long that our ways are backwards and barbaric and we are only now slowly waking up from that exploitatively induced sleep. It begins with closing doors to international franchises who already have more money than they need and opening doors to our local designers growing them into franchises. Only then can we begin to secure our future. I hope that more and more initiatives such as this will be taken across the country and across the continent. Please continue supporting our local content." Amidst the applause Mpumi made her was back to Jarred and her kissed her lightly on the cheek, there was a flash from a journalist's camera Mpumi hated the media but the Centre needed the exposure. Oh no, Daniel was making his way towards them with his date. Mpumi crossed her fingers that Daniel wouldn't make some jab at Jarred and blow up the entire launch. He was smiling broadly while Mandisa's smile seemed more fixed and painful. Mpumi could totally relate to her discomfort. Mandisa was even prettier up close. "Great turnout Mpumi," Daniel said as he kissed both her cheeks, another flash and Mpumi cringed inside. Jarred remained calm but Mpumi knew he was pissed.

"Thank you Daniel." She said sardonically.

"Levine my man how are you?" Since when was Jarred Daniel's man? Mpumi wondered what her ex-husband was up to.

"I'm fine Daniel and how are you?" Jarred's tone was bland.

"Never been better. Where are my manners, this is my lady Mandisa Biko." "It's nice meeting you Mandisa," Mpumi flashed her a smile.

"Same here," something told Mpumi that Mandisa wasn't a fan of hers.

"Mpumi you need to come and cut the ribbon," Mpumi was saved by Nomusa from that awkward situation and she excused herself. She took Jarred with her even though that hadn't been the original plan but she couldn't just feed him to the wolves. Suddenly she was nervous as she held the clippers in her hands. Jarred must have sensed that she was nervous because he stood behind her and held her hands, "You've got this Lelo." He whispered to her and she felt her nerves calming down a bit. She cut the ribbon and Nomusa popped open champagne and there was thunderous applause. This was it. Her legacy had been born. Mpumi was the first to step in followed closely by Jarred and they were holding hands.

The next morning when they woke up they found the children waiting for them. They wanted to know how the launch went. The launch had been more successful than Mpumi had even dreamed it would be. Lola and Oyama had been grumpy that they couldn't attend the launch. But Mpumi had left them behind to protect them from the glare of the media. Especially Oyama, the media was always on her case and Mpumi
didn't want her daughter to sink back into depression. She had been doing so well lately. Mpumi listened with one ear as Nomusa was telling them about the launch and she poured cereal on her bowl. Jarred was showing them pictures and they were all going crazy over them. Around this table was Mpumi's whole world and she looked at them as they laughed and her heart was at peace. "So your mom and I have an announcement of our own," Jarred said as he held Mpumi's hand. Mpumi looked into his eyes and it felt like the ocean was tugging at her soul, she had never been more certain of anything else in her life. "Hello we still her!" Lola broke into their eye lock moment and Mpumi laughed slightly.

"We decided to elope. We're getting married." There were screams and hugs, only the twins were confused what all the commotion was about.

"Wait, when you say you eloping what does that mean?" Nomusa asked after they had all calmed down. Mpumi looked at Jarred, they really hadn't gone into details.

"Just go away somewhere and get married maybe go to Las Vegas." The response to Mpumi's suggestion was unanimous 'No!', 'Hell no!' and the most insulting 'You're too old for a Vegas wedding.' Ouch.

"I understand if you want a small intimate wedding but you have waited too long for this wedding for it to be some hush-hush unmemorable thing."

"We don't want to waste more time planning for an elaborate wedding. She has to be my wife today." When he said things like that Mpumi wanted to take him on top of the breakfast table lol.

"Just give me one week and I will give you the wedding of a life time." Nomusa wasn't going to let this one go.

"Fine. Just one rule, no guests it's just going to be us." They weren't happy about that either but Mpumi didn't care it was her wedding, they could invite whomever they wanted to their own weddings. It was really happening, after sixteen years they had met again and now two years later they were going to get married.

"You have only one week to pull this off Nomusa, if you don't I'm taking her to the court and we will get married there." Lola rolled her eyes, she knew how her father could be when he had set his mind on something.

"Then there's no time to wait, come on girls we have a wedding to plan." Just like that they left Jarred and Mpumi to clear away the breakfast things and they went to plan for their wedding without them. Mpumi had a feeling she wasn't going to be allowed to put any input forget that it was her wedding.

Mpumi had been right, she wasn't allowed to have any input and they kept all the details of the wedding away from her. She didn't mind though, she had wanted to elope because she had wanted to avoid planning for a wedding. The only other request she had was for them to include Dzie. Dzie whose full name was Dzikamani was an upcoming poet and Mpumi loved her work, she had recited some of her poems at the launch and they had been spectacular. Dzie was petite, peaceful with a killer cleavage. Mpumi asked her to make a poem specifically for her and Jarred, she told Dzie how they had met in Harvard and took her through the course of their relationship. Mpumi also had to go to Soweto to tell her mother about her upcoming wedding. MaNtuli was happy till Mpumi raised the issue that there would be no lobolo paid, that the wedding was in a week's time and no her family was not invited neither were MaNtuli's church members invited. "Tyhini! What witchcraft is this Nompumelelo?"

"It's what I want ma. My last marriage was about people, pleasing my family and pleasing you but this marriage is all about me and all I want there is people who I hold close to my heart."

"But my child, we can't exclude everyone like that it's just not right."

"It may not be right but it's what's best for me." When MaNtuli saw that Mpumi's heart was set on having no one at her wedding she conceded defeat but begged for them to be officiated by Reverend Mphahlele at least. Mpumi almost laughed when she remembered that this was the same reverend that her mother had called upon to intervene in her marriage with Daniel but Mpumi had refused. Mpumi agreed to have the pastor officiate because she wouldn't have heard the last of it if she had refused. But Mpumi had also come for something else.

"Maa I want to go and visit Tata's grave and get his blessing too," her mother was silent for a few seconds.

"Of course it's the right thing to do." They left for Mdeni the next morning, Mpumi hadn't been there after her father's burial because of the manner in which her uncles and aunt had treated them, Mpumi and her mother. They found overgrown grass around his grave and Mpumi started clearing the grass even though it was hot and she was sweating. MaNtuli swept around the grave and at least it was more presentable.

"Ndinisa, Mzomba, Mlaba, mbhobho kabikwayo,

Mzomba, Thuliswayo, Masibekela, wenowasibekela inkosi ngothuli, amazomba ayekhathana maseyebandla, kwasuka dludlu kwahlala unkalakatha, intuthwanencane ngokubhala amadoda, ibhejelibomvu labothul'swako. I'm sorry we have neglected your grave and we haven't come to see you since we laid you to rest. Not a day goes by that we don't think of you. I came here with Nompumelelo, you were right Mzomba she has grown into a successful, strong woman and I know that you are looking over her and you are as proud of her as I am," her mother was talking in a low voice and Mpumi felt the tears well up in her eyes. MaNtuli gestured for her to start talking. This was harder than Mpumi had anticipated.

"Tata. I wish you were still here. I wish you had spent more time with us. I have four children now Tata and they are beautiful, I know you would have loved them. And I found him Tata, the man you told me about. The man willing to lay down his life for mine. He loves and respects me as deeply as you did and I can depend on him just like I always depended on you. We are getting married next week and I hope you bless our union and I know you will be watching over us. I promise to bring your grandchildren to see you next time. Ooh and you have a great-granddaughter now. We love you Tata, we always will." It was hard talking to him like this and not seeing him. Mpumi had always been her father's princess and she hadn't gotten over his death. Suddenly she felt a sense of peace like he was surrounding her and she was safe in his embrace. It was a feeling that she couldn't explain or describe in words but it was a good feeling.

"We have to put a headstone over his tomb," Mpumi suggested to her mother.

"We have to talk to your uncles about that first and do it the proper way." Yeah at times culture was such a bitch, Mpumi didn't want anything to do with her uncles but her mother was right they couldn't do anything without them. After putting the flowers around his grave and staring at it for a while in silence they had to leave. Mpumi was glad they had taken this trip. Now there was nothing holding her back from marrying the man of her dreams and living her own happily ever after.

CHAPTER
TWENTY SEVEN

Jarred had expected to get cold feet but he had never been more sure of wanting anything in his life. Lelo was and had always been the one for him. No one ever even came close. Seeing her sitted alone in the cafeteria a lifetime away his heart had literally stopped and had started pumping after what seemed like hours later. When he had made his way to her, he had been nervous and that had been a first for him. Even his palms had been sweaty. He had turned back about two times before he had gained the strength to actually walk straight up to her and she hadn't even noticed him. She had gone on eating her sandwich like he didn't even exist. Then he had heard the sound of her voice and it sounded like the trickling of a spring. Her laugh stirred things in him that he hadn't even known existed. He had told his brother about her and he hadn't been able to shut up about her. The more they had hung out together, the deeper he had fallen for her intellect, her wit, her feistiness and her gentleness. She was the first girl who hadn't been fascinated by his family's wealth, she had contrary opinions and their arguments had always been heated and lively. Then she had given herself to him. Call him sexist but there was something awe-inspiring about being the first to bring her the pleasures of love making, the first to unleash the passion in her. At that moment he had known that he wanted her to be his and only his, he couldn't bear the thought of her making the same sounds with any other guy. Then when she had left without any explanation not even a goodbye have a nice life note, he had been devastated. At first he had been bewildered, then he had been hurt and when the pain became too unbearable he had let it turn into anger. Anger he was used to not pain. He had only ever experienced such pain when Joseph had died. Just thinking of Joseph clouded his happiness, he wished his brother could have been his best man as he had been Joseph's best man at his wedding. He had asked Hakim, his lawyer to be his best man. Jarred didn't have friends but Hakim was the closest thing to a friend that Jarred had. Nomusa had pulled off the best wedding by the look of things. They had agreed never to talk about what had happened that drunken night. It had been stupid and meaningless and it would hurt Lelo if it ever came out. They both cared about Lelo too much to hurt her like that. Nomusa had chosen a lodge at Sir Lowry Pass in Cape wine lands called Lalapanzi, it was small and intimate just perfect for what his woman had demanded. The lodge actually looked like a mansion in the middle of the hoods, it was surrounded by mountains and tall trees the kind of place that Lelo loved. It was whimsical and romantic perfect for their 'elopement'. The colors for the wedding were white and gold but Jarred had flatly refused to wear a white tux so instead he was wearing one of those Indian style suits and even though it had little buttons from the collar to below his crotch, the embroidery was exquisite. He had been skeptical at first to wear it but the material actually felt light and he found that it suited him. "You can still make a run for it," Hakim said as he passed him a glass of champagne. Jarred laughed, Hakim had been there through his string of women and had even had to pay off some of the women to keep away. He hadn't believed Jarred had turned down his bachelor card when he had come to

South Africa till he had come to the opening of the Durban hotel and he had seen for himself Jarred with Lelo. "No man, this is it. No more running for me." Jarred meant it, there was no turning back.

"She's one phenomenal woman to have you so whipped."

"And I'm one lucky bastard to even have her in my life."

"You really love her don't you?" Hakim sounded skeptical.

"I love her more than I love myself. I mean what's not to love, she's the total package."

"I'm still paying alimony to my two 'loves of my life' I ain't catching no more feelings man." Hakim had wanted to draw up a pre-nup but Jarred had rejected that proposal.

"Maybe you had to meet them to truly appreciate your soulmate when she finally comes. With me I never thought of marriage with anyone else besides Lelo."

"Good luck then," Jarred didn't need luck. He and Lelo had the till death do us apart kind of love. A kind of love that had defied, time, distance and race. Before Jarred could respond there was a knock on the door. It was Nomusa looking beautiful in gold.

"Are you guys ready? It's time." They were having a sunset wedding because "that's when the pictures look prettiest." Jarred didn't care as long as by the end of the day Lelo was his in every possible way.

"We're ready to go. And my bride? Is she ready?"

"She looks like a dream, you can go outside and wait for her there." Nomusa was satisfied that they looked 'presentable' enough and she left to do whatever it is she was taking care of. Hakim was looking at Nomusa like he had spent forty days and forty nights in the desert without any water.

"Damn, now that is one damsel I would like to ride on my mount. Too bad someone already knocked her up."

"Don't even go there my wife would skin me alive when you break her heart." They made their way outside and there was a pavilion set up, a gold carpet and about ten chairs on either side of the carpet. Lelo's mother was already sitted near the front holding Amandla. Jarred hesitated before he went over to greet her. He always felt this vibe around her like she didn't like him much. "Hello my son, are you nervous?" Ok, so he had graduated to son. It was a great feeling but she was still scary. After threatening to hunt him down if he ever hurt her child she let him go to stand next to Hakim and the pastor. Lelo had told him that her mother had insisted on the priest and they laughed about it, she still pestered them about the twins' baptism. There were also two guys with microphones, those must be the singers they were going to be accompanied by a
pianist. What had Oyama said their names were again? Oh yeah Nathi and Vusi Nova. Apparently his wife to be thought that Vusi Nova 'was dreamy and a sight for sore eyes.' So they had gotten him to come and sing as a surprise for Lelo. Another surprise was that Jarred was going to say his vows in Xhosa. Oyama had been teaching him and it had been difficult to pronounce the cliques, it had taken him a whole year but the look on his Aphrodite when she heard his vows would be worth it. There was also the lady who was going to do the poems, she seemed so tiny and she seemed a bit reserved. They were next to a water body and it was beautiful how the calm blue of the water contrasted with the lush green of the grass. Jarred couldn't wait for his goddess to come down the small aisle. There was some commotion from the lodge. It was the terrible two, those twins would be the death of him one of these days. They were a tag team from hell and Jarred held his breath as they came down the aisle. His little princess looked like a real life princess in her white ball gown with gold wings. She had demanded the wings and the wand because she wanted to be 'Thumbelina' they were still working on differentiating between tiny people and fairies. Her unruly curls had been manipulated into a neat bun on top of her tiny head and she had her own little tiara. Instead of flowers she was throwing around 'pixie

dust' which was some gold dust that Jarred did not want to know where it came from. His little man was walking next to her solemnly holding on to the rings. He was wearing a Jarred's miniature suit but his was all white and he had those gold Aladdin slippers. Anton was finding it hard to keep up with his hyperactive sister. Just looking at them a lump formed in Jarred's throat. But the lump quickly dissolved when Aleja ran out of pixie dust and she threw her little basket down in disgust. Then she headed straight to Anton and tried to snatch the ring pillow from him but Anton held on for dear life. And so the tug world war 3 commenced. The little diva was now screaming and scratching Anton who promptly retaliated by pushing her hard and she tumbled to the carpet. Nomusa had to rush over and separate them before more harm was done. Jarred was only able to breathe when they were both sitted quietly on either side of their grandmother who made it clear that she wouldn't tolerate any nonsense. Nomusa signaled the singers to start singing afresh, they had stopped when the tug war had started.

"Noma kanjani Dali wam
Ngeke ng'kshiye
Sofa silahlane
Noma kanjani Dali wam
Ngeke ng'kshiye
Sofa silahlane"

Jarred thanks to his lessons with Oyama could understand what they were singing their melody was beautiful and perfectly harmonized. Then the dreamy one was singing in a deep timbre, except for the fact that Lelo had a crush on him Jarred had to admit that Vusi's voice was musically perfect.

"Whe dali wam
Yintoni na ondenza yona mh
Mh xa ndivuka ekuseni, ndincumile
Oh, kungenxa yothando lwakho
Yeah
Mna ndiyoyika ukubuza nesiduko sakho

Mhlawumbe siyazalana
Oh, mntwan' omuntu
Indlela obundiphethe ngayo izolo
Ndisithathil' isigqibo
Nakanjani, noma kanjani..."

There were his girls, they looked like beautiful young ladies, and the lump lodged itself back in his throat. They were wearing gold figure hugging gowns which had only one sleeve but they were beautiful, their hair had been braided with white flowers in the hair. He wished Joseph were here to see his little baby now almost a woman. Oyama had gone back to being her slender self and later that year both of his princesses were going to Harvard. Dammit he had promised himself that he wouldn't cry but the tears were sneaking in on him. He was about to be that groom who teared up. He couldn't help himself Nomusa had been right his Lelo looked like a dream. Hakim handed him a tissue and he knocked his hand away. Lelo was in a flowing white gown but it also seemed to mold her body in all the right curves... ummmh places. But more than that was the glow she had, Lelo was glowing and she literally took his breath away. She was carrying a single white rose and she looked perfect. His cry baby already had tears in her eyes Jarred could see them all the way from where he was standing and he was pleased with himself because they were tears of joy that he had promised her. The singers were now humming and the poet cleared her throat, when she started talking Jarred was taken aback by how big and strong her voice was.

"Intrinsically different but perfectly matched
The resemblance is striking, they are ideally suited in temperament Yet the disparity is apparent, but each completely understands the other Soul mates they are.

Like pieces of a jigsaw, they fit perfectly

CHAPTER

TWENTY SEVEN

All the seemingly rough edges merge into one beautiful picture There is no telling where one ends and the other begins A perfect symmetry they are.

By a force bigger than them they are bound
Perhaps it's written somewhere in the stars
Their meeting certainly wasn't chance nor has luck kept them together But perhaps because fate wills it, have they stood the test of time.

Theirs is a joinder of souls, two lives entwined, interwoven
Each sees through the other, between them things unsaid have meaning
For one to look into the other's eyes and see into their soul To see the yearning, of one soul pleading for the other.

Around each other they are at their most vulnerable
Around each other their guard is down, they risk all and for a moment lose themselves
Around each other they are their truest selves
They let each other see into the deepest and darkest parts of them And there is no fear and there is no shame.

They know they cannot have what they have outside of each other
Though they be together or apart, they do not forget for both of them, Home is with each other.
SOUL MATES THEY ARE."

She was now standing in front of him, looking up at him and all her love was written clearly in her eyes pulling him in and the tear he had been fighting slid down the corner of his eye. She wiped it away with her thumb. What had he done in this life time to deserve such a strong and enduring love? He felt his chest burning literally with the love he had for this woman standing right in front of him. Their eyes were locked and in that moment no one else mattered. No one else existed besides them in their own little world. The pastor had to clear his throat a few times to catch their attention, he said some words and read from the Bible but Jarred wasn't following what he was saying. He was still trying to take in Lelo's beauty. She was blushing and trying to hide the fact that she was blushing and that made her even more adorable in his eyes. The gold eyeshadows made her eyes pop out and they were big he could even see the gold highlights in her iris. Jarred was focusing on her face because he knew that if he even glimpsed her boobs he was going to lose it and he wasn't about to subject his motherin-law to his boner. Huh, why was she looking at him like that? Oh it was time for him to say his vows. The nerves hit him full force and even when he opened his mouth nothing came out. He had to clear his throat twice, he caught Lola's smirk he would make her pay later. This was it, his moment. "Nthliziyo yam'," he saw her eyes widening in surprise then she was blushing again and blinking back the tears. Yes he had crushed the first part. "Ungowami ndingowakho, no one has ever completed me like you. I wasted so much time apart from you but somehow I found myself in your arms and I knew I had come back home. I love the way you laugh, the way your face lights up and whenever you feel pain I wish I could take the pain and feel it in your place. Ulunolwabo lwami my happiness is only complete when you are by my side. You have seen me at my lowest and loved me as much as you have loved me at my highest. You never lose sight of what's important in life and you always hold me accountable for my actions. You're my conscious, my weakness and my strength. Thank you for giving me a family and for raising our children with me. I promise to always honor, love and protect you till my dying breath." She was in tears when he finished his vows and now it was his turn to wipe away her tears. Even before the priest had given his blessing, Jarred was crushing Lelo's lips under his. This kiss felt different like heaven itself was watching them and cheering them on. He wasn't letting her go ever, this time he would on to her forever.

EPILOGUE

FIVE YEARS LATER...

"Wake up babe, you're gonna miss your flight," she could hear the voice but it was irritating her, she wanted to sleep some more. She tried pulling the pillow over her head but he was stronger than her and she had no choice but to wake up. Crap! Was that the time? No, no, noo!!! "Why didn't you wake me up earlier?" she snapped at him as she sprinted to the bathroom and left him shrugging. After taking the world's shortest shower, she squeezed into her tiny shorts, a crop top then she wore a long red checkered shirt which reached just under her shorts and she put on her Timberland wedge boots. Luckily she had cut her hair recently and she slightly combed through her mini-fro, the cut emphasized her high fore-head and it suited her to perfection. Zach had been a darling and had already put all of her luggage into the boot of his mini cooper. She rushed out of his Manhattan apartment knowing that she probably wouldn't see it again. She did her make-up in the car, at least there wasn't the usual traffic jam yet. "So when am I going to see you again Onyx," probably never but she couldn't tell him that. When they couldn't pronounce her name they had nicknamed her Onyx. "I don't know Zach but we will keep in touch," she had no intentions of keeping in touch with him but she was a smooth liar. Zach had been a friend with benefits who mistakenly thought they had a real thing going on. This was it. She was going home for good this time. She looked at the passing landscapes, Manhattan was sunny and beautiful in July. They had been celebrating the Fourth of July last night and it had been so lit she couldn't remember how they had gotten back to Zach's apartment. She had to wear sunglasses to curb her hangover. They were at the airport now and Zach was taking out her luggage. Make no mistake about it Zach was fine, he had the looks and the brains but he just didn't have that thing nje. She was still into bad boys, she had even dated Crips and Bloods members at some point. The airport was a hubbub of activity, she hated it. She couldn't remember the last time she had flown commercial. It had been her sister's clever idea that she 'surprise' the parents, they thought she was coming the following week. Thus she couldn't take the jet and she found herself being frisked by airport security. Lola would pay for her dumb idea. She had to go through the metal detector machine and it made that irritating beeping sound. She was asked to step aside. She had to remove her bloody belly ring. She went through the machine again and set it off for the second time. That machine must be broken… then she remembered the bet she had lost to Lola. She wished she could strangle her right now. The official who was sent to accompany her to the ladies room had a very judgmental look on her face. It had just been a silly bet that had ended with her getting a piercing in her… well ummmh down there. The lady was watching her like a hawk as she lowered her shorts and looked even more disapproving when she saw that she had no underwear on. Oyama rolled her eyes and took out the other intimate earring then dressed up. This time around the machine didn't make a sound and she found herself past Immigration. Then she was kissing Zach goodbye, she really hoped he wouldn't do something stupid like pine after her or worse try to follow her home. She was sitting in first class but that wasn't comforting because she still had to come in contact with other human beings. Their supervisor had always said she had militant precision when it came to administering procedures but her "bedside manner was disappointing to say the least." But that hadn't stopped her from graduating valedictorian in her Medicine class and her Quantum Physics class as well as a first class Pharmaceuticals degree. She was sitted next to a man who seemed very fascinated by the tattoos on her belly. "That is some cool ink you have there," it always started like that and next thing he will start making conversation and hitting on her and she wasn't in the mood. "Thanks," she said it as blandly as she could but he still persisted.

"If I may ask what do they say?" Here we go again.

"Onathi, Owethu, Amandla and that one there says Atlegang."

"Fascinating, what do they mean?"

"It's the names of my children. Wait let me show you their picture, yes here are my little munchkins," she was showing him her screensaver. It was the last picture of the fantastic four that she had taken on her last break. Suddenly the man had lost all interest on her tattoos or on her and he was now totally focused on his I-pad. Mission completed. The kids' card always worked like a charm. After texting Lola that she had boarded the plane she settled back to enjoy not being bothered, she even put her headphones on in case her trick didn't hold up for long.

Oyama had not thought this through. It had been sunny and warm in America but it was windy and drizzling when she got to OR Tambo airport. And she couldn't even take a jacket because she wasn't sure which suitcase she had thrown it in. To make matters worse her internet wasn't working so she couldn't use her Uber App. She tried calling Lola but that bitch's phone went straight to voicemail. Great, just great. So there she was standing alone with her luggage and she was shivering from the cold in her shorts and she couldn't really button her shirt because then she would look totally naked. Then she did something she hadn't ever done before, she got into a meter taxi. She prayed that she wouldn't be abducted but she texted Lola the number plate just in case she didn't turn up. "Where to ma'am?" she could go straight home but what if there was nobody there? She had lost her key again. Her mother was probably at the Centre so she directed the driver to go there. She tried fixing her internet but that was Lola's area of expertise. She tried calling her again and it still went straight to voicemail. She was going to kill Lola. The minx had gotten her into this mess and now she was unavailable. Nx! And now she couldn't even call her mother because it would ruin the 'surprise'. Finally she was at the Centre and she took out her Platinum card. The driver who had grey hair told her that he didn't have a speed point. Bloody hell! Who in this day and age still operated any business without a speed point? Oyama was getting more frustrated by the minute. And he wouldn't let her go to a bank to withdraw the money because she might run away and she didn't want to leave her luggage with him what if he ran away. She tried giving him her Rolex watch but he refused, he probably didn't know that if he sold it he could buy another taxi. Lola's phone was still unavailable, Oyama had no other option but to call the next best thing. "Lala what are you doing back so soon? Weren't you supposed to be back next week?" trust aunt Nomusa to start barricading you with questions as if she was the one who had called Oyama, not the other way round.

"It's a long story aunty but can you come down to the entrance with some cash." "Which entrance?"

"The first one at The Child Centre."

"Sorry lala I'm out of the office meeting a client at Morningside." This day just kept getting better and better. And the driver looked a bit aggressive now, he had taken out his knobkerrie. Not that Oyama blamed him, Jozi was full of chancers. She heard someone clearing their throat next to her, she was standing next to the taxi door. She turned around in irritation and looked up at the intruder. He had the most piercing eyes. That was the first thing she noticed. He was so tall and handsome as hell… ok maybe she was just stealing from Taylor Swift's 'Wildest dreams'. But dang, the nigga was fine. Well that is except for the UZZI brand that he was wearing which screamed ghetto thug. Oyama like everyone else had witnessed the heist which had taken place a couple of years back.

"Ousie wee I don't have the whole day!" the driver's angry tone dragged her from her daydream. She was still in hot soup.

"Sorry to interrupt Ntate but what seems to be the problem?" Mr. Handsome here had a very deep but lazy voice.

"She doesn't want to pay her taxi fare and I've been waiting here for ages. I have to make a living I have children to feed." Oyama fought very hard not to roll her eyes at an elder.

"It's not my fault that you don't have a speed point Ntate and you refused for me to go and withdraw some cash."

"How much does she owe you?" Ok, just who did this

guy think he was? A black Bill Gates in the making?

"R1 156 and 50c," WTF?!! "The meter is still running." Damn this driver was conniving. Oyama was boiling in anger and she watched in disbelief as the stranger took out his wallet and extracted six R200 bills and handed them to the driver.

"You can keep the change sir and sorry for any inconvenience." Oyama just clicked her tongue, what was it piss the fuck off Oyama day? She hadn't asked for this stranger's help and here he was taking out her luggage as if he knew her.

"Wait, where are you taking my luggage?" she had to rush to catch up with him. He stopped and looked at her like she was crazy.

"I don't know about you but I will not stand outside in the drizzling rain." He said and continued on his way into the Centre. The nerve of the guy! Oyama fumed silently as she tried keeping pace with his long strides. She was shivering and even her teeth were chattering. He didn't seem to notice and he led her straight to a cozy restaurant that she hadn't been in before. The décor was warm and child friendly like every other shop in that Centre. He dumped her luggage unceremoniously next to a table next to the counter and he went behind into the kitchen. Oh so he worked here at The Piper's Dream, maybe he was the manager which meant he was a bit well of but still R1 200 would put a dent on his budget. Oyama would have to pay him back. At least the place had an air con and it was warm but she was still shivering. He came back with a steaming mug of hot chocolate, he had even added tiny marshmallows just how she liked it. Wait she had come to this place once with her mother and she had ordered hot chocolate extra creamy with marshmallows but she wasn't sure anymore, the memory was hazy. She was very forgetful if you hadn't already established that. He looked at her from her sodden boots to her damp shirt. But it wasn't a lustful look, if she read him correctly he seemed angry. She had no idea what his problem was. "Why are you dressed like that in this cold?" she didn't think he was going to understand her explanation that where she came from it was summer so she didn't bother responding. Anyhow, who had died and made him her daddy. "Take that off." Excuse you? Ooh he meant the shirt, she took it off while he went to the back again. This time he came back with a huge fluffy towel and he began to rub her down roughly. Luckily the shop was empty but the cashier was giving them speculative looks. His touch wasn't sexual in any way but she found herself becoming aware of him. His masculine scent, he smelled like Hugo Boss the body spray but suddenly she found it the sexiest smell in the world. Ok Oyama get a grip, she admonished herself. When he was done rubbing her dry he took off his jacket and made her wear it. By then she had stopped shivering and she felt warm and cozy in his jacket it was an oversize for her. She was beginning to feel weird about this whole set up, she didn't even know this guy's name but she was wearing a jacket which smelled exactly like him. The anger had abated in his face and he looked less scary and as handsome as when she first saw him which was less than an hour ago. She wanted to go home now. As if he read her mind he said, "If you're done I will take you home." Alarm bells started going off in Oyama's head. Why was he being so kind? She didn't trust people, the last time she had trusted a guy she actually knew she had ended up pregnant at 15. He must have read her unease because he was speaking gently now, "I would never hurt you Nokwindla." What the hell was going on here? How did he know her clan name? Only her great-uncle had called her that. Who was this guy? "If you don't trust me you can call sis Nomusa and confirm." Oyama looked into his eyes and they told her that he didn't mean her any harm. But the way he seemed to know everything and everyone in her life still creeped her out and she still didn't even know his name. Aunt Nomusa answered her call on the fifth ring, "Yaya." Oyama hated that name but it had stuck with her even her daughter called her Yaya.

"Aunty sorry to disturb you but do you know ummmh…" she looked at him for some help and he smiled rakishly at her and she felt a different warmth down there. He mouthed the word

EPILOGUE

Sphola, what kinda dumb arse name was that? "…do you know Sphola?"

"Yeah, he's pretty close with Mpumi. Why?"

"No reason, he offered me a ride home."

"Ok sweetie you can trust him, I've got to go now love you." The only problem now was Oyama didn't trust herself around this guy. He was just too intense. But when he smiled she felt weak in the knees. He took her luggage again like it didn't weigh a ton and they left. She was now engulfed in his jacket and she tried keeping up with him as he made his way to the garage. She expected him to be driving a GTI, it went well with his UZZI brand. But no he was driving a Ford Ranger, now she felt really bad for that taxi fare he was probably still paying off the installments on this car. He put her bags in the back seat and opened the front door for her. He was a gentleman wasn't he? Well Oyama didn't trust gentlemen they are the ones who fucked you over. He also had some bad boy vibes that she was catching on, but that could just be wishful thinking on her side. He reversed and drove out of the car park in silence. He only stopped to greet the security guards on the exit. It seemed they knew him well. He didn't try to chat her up which was strange, he didn't even glance at her thighs. He's definitely gay, Oyama thought glumly and she didn't even want to question why the thought of him being gay hurt her so much. He took out a disk from the glove compartment and put it on. Oyama braved herself from some awful house mix, he was just the type. The song began.

"Been sitting eyes wide open behind these four walls
(Hoping you'd call)
It's just a cruel existence like there's no point hoping at all…"

Wait! She knew this song!

"Baby, baby, I feel crazy, up all night, all night and every day Give me something, oh, but you say nothing What is happening to me?

I don't wanna live forever, 'cause I know I'll be living in vain
And I don't wanna fit wherever
I just wanna keep calling your name until you come back home

I just wanna keep calling your name until you come back home
I just wanna keep calling your name until you come back home!"

She found herself singing along to the chorus. She couldn't help it she was a Taylor Swift fan. And the song took her back to when she and Lola had sneaked out to go and watch Fifty Shades Darker. She missed her almost twin, Lola had come back two weeks back to start working on her very own IT company and Oyama was excited for her. She had been singing along and she had even forgotten that she was a passenger in a stranger's car. She caught him staring at her and he had that little side smile, she found herself looking down. Oh my God I'm blushing what is happening to me, she thought to herself and she looked out at the window. "You have a beautiful voice," that was the first personal thing he had said to her and she bit her tongue before she said something as lame as "Thank you?" this guy really got to her and she felt uncomfortable around him yet she didn't want him to go. It was Ludacris! She cleared her throat, she had to say something otherwise he would think she was a slow teenager.

"So is your name really Sphola?"

"You make it sound like you hate my name," he was frowning at her slightly. Dammit she hadn't meant for it to come out that way. "Its fine you can call me Sipho." Now Sipho she could live with not Sphola.

"I like Sipho, I think it suits you," why did she say that? He just looked at her and smiled. She had to stop making him smile because his smile would be the death of her. They were turning at their gate that had been quick. Too quick in fact. The guards at the gate let them in without questioning him, it meant that he had been here before. But when? She was sure she would have remembered him if she had ever met him before. He parked close to the door and took out her bags carrying them to the door. At least the door was open but he didn't get in. he put her bags down and he came up to her. He cupped her face up by placing his forefinger and thumb under her chin. Her breath caught in her chest. She was already anticipating how those full strangely pinkish lips would taste. But he didn't kiss her, he just stared deep into her eyes. Then he let her go with an, "I'll see you around nana." Just like that he left her standing there like a drowned rat and he got into his car and he left. Who was that guy? He hadn't even asked for her phone number and too late she remembered that she was still wearing his jacket. There was only one conclusion she came to. He was gay. She stopped being disappointed and went in with her bags. After putting them in her bedroom, the gothic décor she had definitely outgrown, she went out to look for her family around the house. The house seemed empty which was strange. She went into the living room, it was also deserted then she looked through the floor length glasses and saw her parents in the pool. Their living room was like an Aquarium and it was so cool. She could see them swimming but it seemed like they were playing tag or some sort of underwater game. Her mother looked like she wasn't a day over 30 but Oyama knew her 45th birthday was coming up in August. Not that he mother was skinny like her, her mother was curvy but she still looked youthful. From the looks of it her daddy had been forcing her mother to hit the gym and his efforts had paid off. They started kissing underwater and they looked so cute. Then her dad was untying her mother's bikini top. Now that was gross. On top of her horrible day she didn't want to be subjected to her parents' live underwater porn. She left the living room and went back to her bedroom. Before taking off Sipho's jacket she smelled it and it was like he was wrapped around her. She took off the rest of her clothes and went to the bathroom all the while thinking about the tall stranger who had left her puzzled and wanting more of him.

After taking a long bath and dressing up in warm sweat pants and her favorite sweater she made her way to the kitchen. She had put Sipho's jacket in her closet, she wasn't going to wash it, ever. She wanted to keep smelling him, which was weird she would be the first to admit. After the day she had, she was starving and she decided to make herself an omelet. Her parents came in as she was finishing up her meal. Her mother lost it when she saw her. She was screaming and laughing and crying and squeezing the breath out of Oyama's chest. Then she was also wrapped in her dad's bear hug and it was crazy. Seeing her parents' joy made her forgive Lola her 'surprise' suggestion had paid off.

"When did you get back?"-her mother asked.

"Earlier today."

"Why didn't you call us to come and pick you up?"-her dad asked.

"Because I wanted to surprise you guys but then I found you in the pool…" at least Mpumi had the decency to blush while Jarred was grinning like a Cheshire cat that had swallowed a big fat rat. "Next time you should call princess," her goofy dad was impossible.

"Where's the fantastic four?" that was her name for her twin siblings, her daughter and her god-sister.

"They are at a friend's birthday in Gold Reef city, we were preparing to go and collect them."

"No its fine, you old people can relax and I will go and pick them up."

"Are you sure you not tired?"

"I'm fine mama, I want to surprise them too and I miss them." Even though Oyama skyped with them often it wasn't the same. She left her parents looking all cozy to go and get her phone and her car keys. She decide to take the Mercedes Benz, it was more child friendly. Her biological father Daniel, had bought her a Lamborghini Aventador for her 18th birthday. He thought he could buy her love and forgiveness. Their relationship was still rocky but at least she could talk to him now without cringing. She was about to start the car when she got a text. "It's about time that cunt responded to my texts," she said thinking the text was from Lola. It wasn't. She didn't know the number. The text read, **"It's good to see you back home Princess. But know that I'm coming for you. I told you what would happen if you opened that big trap of yours.**

Ooh and kiss my daughter when she comes from Gold Reef City."
Oyama felt her blood going cold. No it couldn't be! How did he know she was back? Most importantly how did he know where Amandla was? Oyama felt the panic rising. She tried breathing as she had been taught during therapy but it didn't help. She was hyperventilating and sweating even though it was cold. She felt the pressure in her chest as if she was having a heart attack. Her medical training taught her that what she was having was actually a panic attack but it
could be as painful as a real heart attack. She tried controlling her breathing but the attack only seemed to worsen. She tried calling the number back but it said the number she had dialed did not exist. That only worsened her anxiety and she had to clutch her chest as wave after wave of the panic attack shook her. This couldn't be happening. Not today. But it seemed like Mhlanguli Lubisi was back in her life and he was baying for her blood.

THE END